"Don't Move Yet,"
He Said.

"I want you to understand this pose you're doing. . . . Have you any idea what it's supposed to express? You're waiting for your lover, Domini. And that's what I want to feel in your face. The invitation in the lips, the tremulous expectancy.

"I want you to pretend you're watching him undress, waiting for him to come across the room. The feeling should be languorous, expectant, the ardor smoldering just below the surface . . . do I have to tell you more? You're not an innocent. You must know what it's like, that breathless moment just before the lovemaking begins."

". . . a moving, emotion-packed story that grips you at the very beginning and doesn't let you go until the last page."

—*Brooke Hastings*

HOLD BACK THE NIGHT

Abra Taylor

PUBLISHED BY POCKET BOOKS NEW YORK

Distributed in Canada by PaperJacks Ltd., a Licensee
of the trademarks of Simon & Schuster, a division of
Gulf+Western Corporation

This novel is a work of fiction. Names, characters, places and incidents are either the product of the author's imagination or are used fictitiously. Any resemblance to actual events or locales or persons, living or dead, is entirely coincidental.

Another *Original* publication of POCKET BOOKS

 POCKET BOOKS, a Simon & Schuster division of
GULF & WESTERN CORPORATION
1230 Avenue of the Americas, New York, N.Y 10020
In Canada distributed by PaperJacks Ltd.
330 Steelcase Road, Markham, Ontario

ISBN: 0-671-45863-9

First Pocket Books printing May, 1983

10 9 8 7 6 5 4 3 2 1

Chapter One

*I*t was in the window of a tiny art gallery, not ten blocks from the loft where she lived, that Domini saw the yellow unicorn.

She came to a sudden dead halt, impeding the flow of pedestrians and causing a small collision with a fellow New Yorker, a middle-aged woman who had been hurrying along behind Domini, head bent against the fresh-falling December snow. Several seconds and a hasty apology later, Domini was standing in front of the gallery window, heart pounding erratically and palms clammy inside her wool-lined gloves.

The unicorn was a marvelous creation, not just a piece of wooden sculpture, but a rocking horse meant for a little girl. Its flanks were the flanks of a horse, its tail was the tail of a lion, its legs were the legs of a buck, and its proud pink horn was tossed high in an attitude of pure joy—almost as though the mythical creature had been modeled on a living, breathing animal. For a magical moment time stood still as Domini closed her snow-frosted lashes and felt her eyelids warming with the honeyed sunlight of a stone-walled courtyard in summer, smelled the clean mountain smells of her childhood in the Pyrenees, heard the murmurous splash of a fountain and the husky gentleness of a woman's voice crooning a sweet, oddly sad song in the Basque tongue of the region.

When Domini opened her eyes again, she saw at once that the unicorn was only a copy. The paint hadn't been worn away where small fingers had once triumphantly clutched the creature's horn, there were no nicks in the wood where small heels had dug in, and the pommel was far less intricately carved than the pommel in Domini's memory. Moreover there were no bold, rounded letters on the saddle where the artist's distinctive signature had been. There were other differences, too, differences of shape and size; in some ways this was almost better than the original. If there were any lingering doubts in Domini's mind,—the past, after all, had been firmly put behind her—they were laid to rest by the tiny sign nested next to the unicorn's curved base, on a Christmassy bed of crumpled pink foil. A COPY it said in small print, without giving credit to the artist who had conceived the famous original.

In glitter-dusted letters affixed to the glass of the gallery window were several much more legible words: SANTA'S WORKSHOP SHOW—TOYS BY ARTISTS. Domini's eyes returned to the unicorn, homesickness and nostalgia like a great ache of emptiness in her breast. Suddenly she knew she had to have that unicorn—or rather, Tasey had to have the unicorn, no matter what the cost, no matter if the overlarge toy took up every last spare inch of a loft already crammed to overflowing with Domini's papier-mâché constructions. A little girl who had never known a father's love deserved some moments of magic, and before long Tasey would be in kindergarten, too old for toys like that. Besides, Domini wanted this to be a very special Christmas: now that Tasey was in day care where other children talked, it might be the last year her daughter believed in Santa Claus.

"Every little girl needs a unicorn once in her life," Domini muttered to no one in particular. The decision made, she reached resolutely for the handle of the gallery door, reminding herself firmly that a unicorn, *that* unicorn, was far more important than the winter coat she'd been eyeing, hoping its price would come down to a manageable level in next month's January sales. Lucky thing she'd been saving for it, though—even without asking, Domini knew the toy would cost a pretty penny.

Inside the gallery she looked around. This southern part of New York's SoHo district lacked the fluted cast-iron pillars and ornamentation of the converted warehouse where Domini lived; all the same the old building had its charm. On this street it was not old warehouses but narrow old homes that had been restored for use as restaurants, charcuteries, bakeries, and boutiques, all now busy with the traffic of pre-Christmas shoppers. The little gallery was less busy than most.

"I'll be with you in a minute," said the dark-haired woman minding the gallery. She was tall, too thin, and in her early thirties, about ten years older than Domini. She had tired gray eyes and a quite pretty profile. Her impeccable black wool dress was saleslady chic personified.

While the woman finished with another customer, Domini glanced around the interior, deciding that it wasn't much of a gallery if the art toys on show were any sampling. There wasn't a worthwhile piece in the lot, and most of them were too precious for words. It was easy to see why there were so few "sold" stickers, and also why the yellow unicorn had earned its place of honor in the window. Domini reflected that it was little wonder she'd always hurried by, scarcely noticing the narrow shopfront although she must have passed it dozens of times over the last few years.

"Isn't that a charming doll?" The saleswoman fixed an overeager smile on Domini the moment the other customer departed without making a purchase. "It's by one of our very best young artists. Would you believe it's made out of an empty Chianti bottle? Clever, isn't it, the way he's painted it to—"

"That isn't exactly what I had in mind," Domini interjected hastily, forestalling the necessity of passing judgment on the indifferent and impractical objet d'art she had been eyeing during the wait. "My daughter isn't interested in dolls. She's far too active for that. The yellow unicorn is more her kind of thing."

Suddenly the saleswoman grinned, endearing her to Domini. "It was a bit idiotic to make a toy out of glass, wasn't it," she admitted with wry honesty. "But over there there's an even sillier toy—push a button and it self-destructs. Can you feature giving that to your kid?"

"No." Domini laughed, her amethyst eyes dancing with a sunniness that seemed to reflect some of the highlights in her hair. The hair was dark gold, no longer the flyaway cap of trapped sunshine it had once been, but long and worn smoothly twisted into a French knot, partly because Domini thought it changed her appearance and partly for practical purposes: it kept her hair out of things like paste pots and paint and plaster of Paris.

"My daughter can destruct perfectly well without help." She smiled. "Why waste money on a button?"

The other woman chuckled and then sobered, as if she had just remembered that her mission in life was to make a sale, not a sally. Her eyes flicked briefly over Domini's boots, slacks, and coat, perhaps assessing her ability to pay. Pride sent Domini's chin a millimeter higher, because she knew perfectly well that the cuffs of the wheat-colored corduroy coat, badly nap-worn after four winters, had not escaped inspection.

"How much for the unicorn?" she asked, casually unbuttoning her coat so that its toasty nutria lining

4

could be seen. Linings like that didn't wear out, and if the saleswoman had any eye for the niceties of fashion she would know that the featherweight luxury fur was enough to justify not putting the garment in the ragbag.

"Six hundred and fifty."

"Oh," said Domini, disappointment rising like a hard ball into her throat.

The woman looked genuinely regretful. "I'm sorry, but a lot of work went into that copy—well more than a hundred hours in all. I read in *Time* that the original went for three hundred thousand at an auction a while ago, so you see it's not really out of line."

"What?" asked Domini faintly.

"Wild, isn't it? But it's the only piece of sculpture Le Basque ever made, and he's far too old now for that sort of thing, so I doubt he'll ever make another."

"I didn't . . . even know it had been . . . sold," Domini managed, her voice choked with a knot of painful feelings that the saleslady had misinterpreted as astonishment over the price. How could Papa have sold the unicorn? Did he still hate her so much?

"Three hundred thousand is a bit outrageous, isn't it?" agreed the woman dryly. "But if you're at all familiar with the price of a genuine Le Basque nowadays . . . and then, of course, the unicorn was the subject of his most famous painting. Surely you're familiar with *Didi and Unicorn?*"

The woman crossed to a sales desk and extracted a flimsy book-sized reproduction from a neat pile of papers and magazines. Even before it was thrust in front of Domini's eyes, she knew what she would see.

"The original's hanging in the Louvre," the woman chatted on, not remarking Domini's sudden extreme paleness because her eyes were turned to the picture in her hands. It was of a small girl in a flagged courtyard, laughter lighting her amethyst eyes and wind tossing a short halo of hair the color of spun sunlight. She was triumphantly astride the unicorn, one hand clutching the single horn and one raised victoriously in the air like a small fearless conquerer, a joyous young creature as magical as the yellow unicorn whose back she rode.

"Isn't she wonderful?" the woman remarked, fortunately expecting no answer. She returned the picture to her desk. "Of course, you must have seen it before—copies, I mean. You can hardly pick up a book on contemporary art without finding a reproduction."

"I . . . yes," Domini returned with some difficulty.

"I expect that's why a private collector paid so much for the unicorn, even though it's actually only a toy Le Basque made for his daughter." She turned toward the unicorn in the window. "Ours isn't an exact copy but it's close enough. It's wonderful, isn't it? Whimsical yet totally practical. If I had a daughter, I'd want her to have a toy like that. How old is your little girl?"

"Tasey's three," Domini said, her voice still strangled with hurt. How could Papa have sold the unicorn? *Her* unicorn? Had he so thoroughly written her out of his heart?

"Tasey?" the saleswoman queried.

"Short for Stasy," Domini responded automatically, although Tasey's real name was Anastasia. To hide her distraction, she turned away from the saleslady and stared at the unicorn. Despite everything that had happened four years before, she had always clung to the belief that her father must still care for her somewhere deep in his innermost self. He might have disowned her, scourged her with his tongue, and heaped her with his scorn, but love that had once been strong shouldn't evaporate as if it had never existed. And if he loved her at all he would not have sold the unicorn.

"They say I am a man of change," he had said once in an interview, "because I change my palette or my style, because I experiment with cubism or surrealism, because I change my subject matter or my mood. But in my heart I never change. I am a simple man. The truth is in my heart, and the truth never changes."

And yet he had sold the unicorn.

The saleswoman sighed imperceptibly, interpreting Domini's strained expression as a negative sign. She turned away from the window, still hopeful of a sale. "There's something a little more reasonable over here —did you see the abacus? It's quite sturdy, and it's only seventy-five dollars. That may sound expensive for an abacus but it *is* a work of art."

Domini shook her head in a negative motion, remembrance of things past still too strong to permit easy words.

"I can let you have it for sixty-five," offered the saleswoman. "I can't change the artist's price, but I can cut the gallery commission. It's really quite a decent piece. One of my favorites, in fact."

Domini swallowed the lump in her throat and turned to face the woman, putting painful thoughts aside for the moment. There was Tasey's Christmas to think about, and all the hurt of all the happenings that had been could not change the fact that for Domini the unicorn symbolized a father's love, the one thing she could never give her daughter, not if she had all the money in the world. Domini was no longer the impulsive young girl she had once been, but she knew with every fiber of her being that she had to have the rocking horse for Tasey. Not any rocking horse, but *that* rocking horse. The cost wasn't important.

"I hate to ask, but would you consider cutting your commission on the unicorn? Six fifty is a bit much." Domini didn't add that she had nothing even close to that amount; there was no point prejudicing the woman against striking a bargain of some kind.

The woman pulled a regretful face. "No, I can't, because I'm not taking a commission on that piece at all. It's all going to the artist, every penny, and he needs the money very badly. I'm sorry."

"Couldn't you . . . ask him? It's only three days before Christmas. Surely you're unlikely to sell the piece now? He might decide that half a loaf is better than none."

"Well . . . perhaps if it's still here on Christmas Eve," the woman agreed kindly. "But until then I don't even want to ask him. That piece has brought a lot of inquiries."

"I see." The words were filled with disappointment. Briefly Domini wondered if she might be able to construct a similar creature—she could, after all, work wonders with papier-mâché. At once she discarded the notion, partly because there wasn't time before Christmas Day, especially with several big display props still to be constructed, but mostly because papier-mâché, even built over an extra-heavy armature, simply wouldn't stand up to the kind of punishment a rocking horse had to take. There was no use making a toy that couldn't be played with. Domini trained a determined glance in the direction of the yellow unicorn. Its secret smile seemed to hold a message for her alone.

"I'll take it," she said with a rashness she had not shown for four years.

The woman was surprised too. "I . . . that's wonderful," she said, breaking into a nice smile. "Will that be cash or charge?"

"I'll give you a deposit," Domini hedged, her long sooty lashes falling to conceal the worry in her eyes. Where on earth was the money going to come from? Oh, to have a charge card now! But that was one modern convenience Domini had abjured since coming to New York, realizing that it would merely seduce her to spend beyond her means. She fished into her wallet, extracted most of its contents, and handed the bills over with a forcedly bright smile. "I'll give you the rest when I get it," she said. "I can't take it today because I'll be Christmas shopping until I pick my daughter up from day care."

"You can't take it at all. It's far too heavy to carry," the woman reminded her dryly as she moved behind the sales desk, unlocked a cash drawer, and placed Domini's hard-earned dollars inside. She relocked the drawer and picked up a pen, poising it over a sales bill and looking at Domini expectantly. "If you give me your address I'll have it delivered."

"Of course," said Domini. "How silly of me." That was something that hadn't occurred to her, possibly because she was accustomed to carrying unwieldy display props through the New York streets. Free-lancing, she saved money wherever she could, and wherever she could meant on delivery charges if the objects were at all portable. As most of Domini's customers were in the SoHo district, within a few blocks of the loft that doubled as her studio, it didn't entail an extraordinary amount of effort—although one tended to earn a few amused glances while transporting an armless mannequin or an enormous pot of six-foot-high petunias or an oversize ostrich complete with tail feathers. Such things drew attention even in the artist-ridden district of New York's SoHo, where the curious was commonplace.

Domini gave her address with a request that the delivery be made to the dry goods store beneath her studio, where the owner was agreeable to accepting packages on her behalf.

"I'll need your name," the woman reminded her.

"Greey, with two e's. Domini Greey. And please don't deliver until Christmas Eve," she added hastily, thinking that would give her at least two days to come up with the rest of the money. Perhaps one of her clients would give her an advance on next year's work? Or perhaps the bank manager could be cajoled this time. . . .

"Now about the balance," the woman said.

"You can sent it C.O.D.," suggested Domini.

"I'm afraid not. You see, we don't have that kind of arrangement with the delivery service we use. They won't handle cash. But you can give me a check."

When Domini remained still a little too long, not reaching into her purse for a checkbook, the woman finally looked up anxiously. "You can postdate it to Christmas Eve if you wish, Mrs. Greey. Normally I

wouldn't allow that, but . . . well, I can see you want
that unicorn very badly. I think you can be trusted."

"Miss Greey," Domini corrected in a low, level
voice. "I'm not married. And no, you shouldn't trust
me. If I write you a check it might bounce."

"But if you could promise to pay on a C.O.D., surely
you must have—"

"If I hadn't managed to find the money by then, the
delivery man simply wouldn't have left the parcel,"
Domini pointed out, her face set and pale. "It wasn't
dishonest. Yes, you might have missed an opportunity
to sell the unicorn to some other customer, but surely
the hundred dollars I just gave you would have paid the
artist for his disappointment. It was quite a gamble for
me. I can't afford to lose a hundred dollars."

The woman's face changed from accusatory to sympathetic. "I'm sorry," she said quietly.

Domini laughed ruefully. "No, I am," she said.
"I shouldn't have tried it. It was an impulse. Would
it be too much if I asked for my hundred dollars
back?"

"You really want that unicorn badly," observed the
woman softly.

Domini nodded, not trusting her tongue. How could
she explain to anyone that the unicorn in the window
had become not just a desire but a compulsion? That
she had to have it for Tasey? To understand, a person
would have to know all the joy and pain of Domini's
personal history—the warmth and love of her cosseted
and unorthodox childhood, the agony caused by her
father's rejection, the terrible circumstances that had
attended Tasey's conception by a man Domini had once
been infatuated with but had grown to hate.

The woman started to insert a key in the cash drawer
and then paused. "I have an admission to make, now
that we're being honest," she said. "I put the paint on
that unicorn myself. The man who did the carving is
blind, you see. I didn't tell you before because I didn't
want to influence your thinking."

Domini closed her eyes as another wave of memory washed over her, the force of it this time like a tidal bore. But therein lay too much pain to contemplate, and she willed the memory back into the recesses of her mind. This was no time to think of the man who had fathered Tasey.

"By the way," the woman went on, "my name is Miranda, Miranda Evans, and I'm a sucker for a trustworthy face. Would it help if I allowed you to pay the balance in January? Mind you, I'd have to have it by the end of the month for sure. The cost of credit nowadays, you know."

Domini shook her head, a small shivering shake because she wanted so much to say yes and in all honesty couldn't. Finances weren't likely to be easier for some time to come. And once Tasey had the unicorn there would be no going back. The gift once given could not be snatched away, to be returned to the gallery in lieu of payment.

As the cash drawer came open Domini made one last desperate bid. "I could work it off," she suggested. "I do window displays. I'm freelance, and I'm good, really I am. Perhaps you've seen some of my work?" She mentioned several shops in the neighborhood, earning an admiring nod from the other woman. "I'll do all your displays for a year, props and everything, and you'll be getting a terrific bargain."

"I don't need a display person." Miranda's words sounded like an apology. "I hang pictures in the window."

"Part-time sales help, then."

"No, I'm sorry. I live directly upstairs, and if I need to go out I simply close up the gallery for an hour. I find I can get along without hiring anyone. There isn't—"

"In that case I could pay you in installments," Domini interrupted quickly. "A hundred dollars a month. Plus interest, of course."

Domini could practically see the wheels turning in the other woman's head as Miranda fingered the cash, torn between accepting the sale on Domini's terms and waiting for a better offer, which might not materialize in the short time remaining before Christmas. "I'll have to speak to the artist," she said slowly. "He may not like to wait for the money. And he'd have to wait, because since my husband died the gallery hasn't been doing too well. This has been a particularly slow year."

"A slow sale is better than no sale," urged Domini, sensing an impending victory. "Couldn't you phone him and speak to him right away?"

"Even better." Miranda smiled, reaching a decision and rising to her feet. She started toward the back of the shop where a stairway was half concealed by a movable shelving unit displaying plain wooden toys quite unlike the other items in the Santa's Workshop show. "To tell the truth he's my brother, and he lives right upstairs. Can you mind the gallery for a second? I'll bring him down and let you speak to him yourself. When he hears how anxious you are, he won't say no!"

Domini turned to gaze at the unicorn again while she waited to meet the artist who had carved it. Not that any man could really be called an artist, reflected Domini, under those tragic circumstances. Any more than Sander could have continued to be a sculptor, especially in a medium as unyielding as stone, if the operation had not restored his sight.

With Miranda gone, Domini allowed herself to think about Sander, about the months in Paris, because at this moment there was no other person present to witness the expression on her face. How ironic that it was a blind man who had carved this creature, a creature she longed to buy because for her it symbolized the father's love Tasey would never get from Sander. Not that Sander had been blind at the time of Tasey's conception. Then his dark eyes had been silvered with anger, a terrible consuming anger such as Domini had not seen in any other person's eyes in her life, not even in Papa's. . . .

* * *

The man on the second floor had listened to his sister in silence, his resentment building with every word she spoke. Did she really think him such a fool? Miranda was perfectly capable of making decisions of this sort; there was no need for him to go downstairs.

Too annoyed to answer at once, he continued the task she had interrupted, first unscrewing the lid of the instant coffee. In the kitchen drawer he fumbled for a spoon and then dipped in for a measure of the granules he could not see. By the sound as he scraped the excess off against the jar's rim, he wondered if a large-size spoon had been placed improperly in the drawer. He tested with his left hand, found it was so, and started to return some coffee to the jar. Annoyance at Miranda's transparency caused his hand to tremble. The spoon collided with glass and the granules spilled, causing his fury to turn inward, where there was no more room for rage. Like a festering boil, his temper burst.

"*Miss* Greey! Unattached, of course!" he lashed out. "Did you think I wouldn't understand your motives?"

"She might not be unattached," Miranda replied defensively. "She has a child." She moved to the counter and with a curved palm started to sweep the coffee into a small neat pile. The soft sounds grated on her brother's nerves.

"I'll do it," he snapped, seething at his inability to function in a world designed exclusively for the sighted.

Chastened, Miranda backed away and watched. Moments later the spilled granules went into a mug, along with a scattering of crumbs left from the breakfast toast. For once she held her tongue, saving it for more important matters.

"You'll never meet anyone up here. Was it so awful the last time I introduced you to a woman? It turned out to be quite—"

"A novelty for her! And why not? She had slept with everything else, in every country of the world. A blind man must have amused her."

A terrible bitterness had entered his voice, and his movements were far jerkier than usual as he felt for the lever that turned off the gas jet on the outmoded stove. He reached too rashly for the singing kettle, fingers springing away from hot steam and then moving more carefully to locate the insulated handle. He felt for the readied coffee mug, found it, and eased his thumb down over the rim. He lowered the kettle's spout until he heard the faint clink of it against china, and then slowly, to avoid another accident, he poured. The little shock of pain in his thumb told him when the boiling water had reached the right mark. He gritted his teeth, replaced the kettle on the hob, and remained at the counter with his shoulders hunched against Miranda, hating her concern, hating his dependency, hating the awful black abyss in which he existed.

"Well, are you coming downstairs?"

He controlled his voice. "You know the answer as well as I do. If she's willing to pay, take what you can get."

"No," Miranda said fiercely. "I won't. Either you come and meet her, or there's no sale at all. Make up your mind!"

He lifted the mug and took a swallow that burned his tongue. Damning himself because he had known full well it was still too hot, he dashed the coffee toward the sink, his inaccurate aim splashing the counter and his own shirt. The soggy toast crumbs in his mouth tasted like gall, a fitting bitterness to feed the wormwood that was his soul.

"Will you never leave me in peace?" he raged in a cry that encompassed the whole world. Miranda turned and left the kitchen without a word.

After a few minutes he followed because he knew he must. His pride stuck in his craw, but normally Miranda didn't make threats; she might mean what she said.

On this familiar floor he could move with the outward surety of a sighted person, although in his long night no step could be taken in full, true confidence of its outcome. The internal mechanisms, refined by necessity, told him what path to follow, how many steps to take, when to lift his hand to ascertain the position of the door frame. Against it a white cane rested. He passed it by, bitterly conscious that it was there but not touching it. Only when he neared the top of the bannisters did he slow, testing with one outstretched hand to feel what hazards might lie in wait in the sinister void that loomed ahead.

There was only Miranda, waiting to lead him down.

Domini was still immersed in her own wrenching thoughts, eyes turned to the window and the unicorn, when she heard the squeaking noises of descent. "Well, here we are," came Miranda's voice, sounding artificially bright, from the direction of the stairs. Then, to the person whose measured footfall Domini could now hear: "Now mind, there's one more step. And watch for those shelves—"

"I know," came the rejoinder that sounded very like a curse. "Now let go of my arm, will you? I'll manage."

"Stop scolding," Miranda sighed as the footsteps started to cross the room. "I'm only trying to help."

Domini schooled her face in preparation for the introduction. When the footsteps neared she turned, still smiling, and took in Miranda's face on a level with her own. Then her gaze slid upward to find hooded, sightless eyes of a silvered darkness that was graven in Domini's memory. The room started to swirl around those eyes, making it impossible for her to see the rest of the face. . . .

But it couldn't be. It couldn't. It must be a trick of the light, a function of the sudden terrible dizziness that had assailed her, robbing her brain of blood and her knees of strength. Clutching for sanity, she tried to tell herself that her imagination had been working too hard since her first sight of the unicorn, that it had been overstimulated by the return of too many bitter memories all at once. Sander was in Europe. Sander was not in New York. Sander had regained his sight. Those sightless silvered eyes couldn't be Sander's because *Sander was not blind.*

"Domini Greey," said Miranda, "I'd like you to meet my brother, Sander Williams."

And then the silver changed to black, all black. For the first time in her life Domini fainted.

She opened her eyes to an unfamiliar sloped ceiling directly above her, where a small gable window was frosted by the curve of a white snowdrift. For a moment of confusion she remembered nothing of what had happened and could not imagine where she was. But then she heard the sound of breathing near her, steady and almost inaudible, and smelled a clean tang that was purely male, and saw the long outline of a man's body at the edges of her vision. And she knew.

She remained perfectly still, only shifting her eyes to see the man who stood tall beside the bed where she lay. Her pulse stopped and then started again, beating faster than before. The sight of him confirmed what she had known in her innermost heart at first sight of those dark eyes, even before his name had been spoken aloud.

It was Sander.

He was standing above her, his head bent toward her, frowning directly at her face in such a way that she could see him well although the scant light in the room came only from the small window. It took an effort of will to remind herself that he could not see her too.

Sander blind. Why had he lied, that time she had phoned? Why had he led her to believe the operation had been a success? Oh, God. He was blind, and all the old guilt came flooding back to Domini, displacing the hatred she had felt for him during the intervening years.

Instinctively she knew they were alone in the room. Her subconscious mind formed an impression of the strange surroundings, an impression composed of or-

derly space and gloom and dingy wallpaper, but for
Domini the enormity of being face-to-face with the man
who had fathered her child prevented her from assimi-
lating more.

He was the same and yet not the same. The virile
physique was still there, a little leaner perhaps, but
unchanged in other ways. There was still that powerful
structure of chest and shoulder created by the demands
of working in stone, the constant pitting of muscle
against marble. The rough textures of him were the
same—the hard-hewn jaw, the granite cheekbones, the
strong bridge of his nose. The impact of him was
the same, the intense sexuality that had once caused
Domini to respond with such ardent abandon, like the
unbridled child of nature she had been brought up to
be.

And the eyes, they too were the same but for their
sightlessness: the brows and the thick lashes so utterly
black, the pupils so dark they were almost black too.
And yet in other moments those eyes would seem
totally silver, like a black fabric shot with metallic
thread that caught the light only at certain times, or like
the mercury in a thermometer, elusive unless turned in
exactly the right way.

All those things were unchanged, and yet he was
different. His brow was cruelly creased and there were
harsh new lines chiseled alongside the edges of his
nose. In his mouth, the mouth that had once crushed
hers in passion and rage, there was a hardness and
bitterness, an inward-turning anger that had not been
there before. It was the face of a man who had suffered
and was still suffering, a man who had not come to
terms with his blindness and perhaps never would.

Did he still hate her for what she had done to him,
just as she had spent years hating him for what he had
done to her? Oh, God, to think he was still blind. . . .

He moved his head now, a fractional move that sent
splinters of that uncapturable silver shooting through
the darkness for one brief moment. "You've come to,"

he said with the perspicacity of a sightless person whose other senses had been honed to a knife-edge sharpness. And when she didn't answer at once for the clamor of her senses, he added in a dry voice, "I may be blind but I'm not deaf. You've been holding your breath, and you just let it go."

"You're blind," choked Domini. "*Blind*. Oh, God, I didn't know . . . I swear, I didn't know . . ."

Sander's expression closed in upon itself, shutting out pity. "That shouldn't matter to you one way or another," he clipped discouragingly. "It's not contagious."

Then, as if remembering with effort that Domini had just recovered from a fainting spell, he added brusquely but politely, in the voice of a total stranger, "How are you feeling now?"

Why did his voice sound different? Why were his words so impersonal? Why had he not called her by name? Then, with a flood of realization followed by an even greater flood of relief, Domini understood that he could not possibly know who she was.

Of course he sounded different, and so did she. In Paris, four years before, they had spoken nothing but French—Sander as fluent as she after the many years he had lived and worked on the Left Bank.

And her name, the name his sister had used in the introduction, would mean nothing to him. Of course! There was no earthly reason why Sander would connect Domini Greey, a New Yorker with no trace of a French accent, with the headstrong young girl he had known in Paris. When her father had disowned her, he had told her angrily never to use his name again, and she had not.

Domini was her true name, and so was Greey. Didi had merely been her father's fond childhood nickname for her, one she had not been able to shrug off for much of her life because of the many famous likenesses her father had painted during Domini's growing years, that happy period the art critics still referred to as the Didi

Years. And although Domini had grown up as a member of her father's household, loved and accepted and using the name Le Basque, she had never had a real right to it. Her father had not married her mother.

Sander could not possibly know who she was, and moreover Domini needed no introspection to decide that she didn't want him to know. There had been too much hate between them; too many hurtful things had been said. And if Sander was still blind, he must very surely blame her to some extent for his condition, just as she had blamed herself at the time.

"Surely you haven't fainted again," Sander said with a heavy touch of sarcasm, and Domini realized that she was taking an inordinately long time to answer the question he had put about the state of her health.

"I'm . . . fine," she said, pulling herself to a sitting position so that the blanket fell away to her waist. With a small sense of unease she noted that someone had removed her heavy sweater and replaced it with a man's shirt. Domini never wore a brassiere.

As if he had seen, Sander said, "Your clothes are on a chair. Perhaps you'll want the sweater; it's cooler up here than in the gallery. You were bundled up like an Eskimo—cable-stitch sweater and a fur lining in your coat. My sister says you look young and healthy, so we thought perhaps it might be a case of overheating."

Which didn't tell Domini who had removed her sweater, although she had a good guess. Not that it mattered. He had mapped the territory long ago, mapped it and claimed it with a vehemence the mere memory of which sent a tingle running through her core, caused her skin to grow heated and her heart to grow chilled. How could she ever have been naive enough to think she could handle a man like Sander?

But maturity had given her some poise and common sense after all. Sander's sightlessness, tragedy though it was, made it easier for Domini to prevaricate, although her voice was still jerky in the aftermath of traumatic shock. "Overheated . . . yes, I suppose that's it." She paused, fighting to control her words and her over-wrought emotions. "I didn't feel too hot, but I must have been. I . . . I can't think of another thing that might have caused it. I've never fainted before in my life."

"You're not pregnant?"

Because that brought back memories, her voice was shaky. "No," she said.

"Or anemic?"

"No."

"Well, we'll soon find out. Several women share a loft nearby, and one of them is a nurse. When you fainted, Miranda closed the shop and ran down the street to see if she happened to be off duty. They should be back very soon."

Domini licked her lips and was glad that Sander could not see the uncharacteristic sign of stress. "If your sister ran off, how did I . . . get up here?"

"I carried you to my bedroom," he said coolly. "Is that what you're so nervous about—being in a blind man's bed? Then relax, I'm not as dangerous as you seem to think. I've never forced a woman in my life."

Suddenly it was too much for Domini. Hit by the bitter irony of it all, she started to laugh and laugh and laugh. And she didn't stop until Sander reached down to the bed, seized her arms forcefully, and slapped her full on the face.

Chapter Two

Domini lay tremulous as a leaf in Sander's bed, face still stinging from the sharp impact of his hand, arms still hurting where his fingers had dug so deeply into the flesh. But those physical things were not the cause of her present distress. This time she knew his rough behavior had been necessary; she knew she had been hysterical.

Nor was she even conscious of her physical state, beyond a sensation of weakness so extreme that she felt she could not move a muscle. Moments after the slap that had restored Domini to some kind of rationality, Sander's sister, Miranda, had materialized in the door-way, bringing with her an attractive young off-duty nurse. Miranda had clicked on the light and started to lecture Sander at once.

"Sander, how *could* you!"

Miranda's teeth had been practically chattering with anxiety and anger, all of it directed toward Sander.

"You should never have brought her upstairs! I nearly died of fright when I realized what you'd done! What if you'd fallen on the way? Think of that torn stair carpet! What if you'd missed the broken floorboard in the hall? It's practically rotting through! I ask you, Sander, *what if?*"

"Then there'd be two patients." Sander's voice had been clipped, irritable. He had swerved on his heel and left the room at once, moving with a certainty that suggested Miranda should not be quite so anxious for his safety in these familiar surroundings.

The nurse had done little more than look Domini over to ascertain that her state was not critical. Domini had been given an injunction to see her doctor, and over her objections Miranda had procured the number and promised to make a phone call, setting up an appointment for the following day if possible. The nurse had administered a tranquilizer and a stern order that Domini was to stay exactly where she was for the next few hours.

"But my Christmas shopping," Domini had protested feebly.

"You'll stay there for the afternoon," the nurse had said with professional firmness. "At least until you have to pick your daughter up. Didn't someone say she's in day care?"

"I'll wake you up later," Miranda had offered. Domini had acceded because to object would have taken more strength than she was capable of; shock had taken its toll. And then Miranda and the nurse had departed, clicking off the light and closing the door softly behind them.

With all now silent, Domini at last began to think over the improbable chain of circumstances that had culminated in the day's events. It was all so incredible —or was it? "There is no coincidence as great as that of life itself," someone had once said. Her father perhaps?

The day's happenings, Domini realized, were not the result of pure coincidence. Sander was a New Yorker by birth, and it was natural enough that upon returning to this country he would move in with his widowed sister. In any case, it would not have been extraordinary for him to gravitate to SoHo, just as Domini herself had done.

SoHo was among other things an artists' colony, as was its more famous namesake in London. In the nineteenth century it had been built as a manufacturing and warehousing district, with stunning cast-iron architecture to be found in such abundance and variety nowhere else in the world. The innovative cast-iron construction permitted huge fluted pillars, marvelous exterior ornamentation, immense windows that admitted floods of sunlight, and enormously high ceilings. When Greenwich Village attics had become too expensive and the area too much of a tourist trap, artists, photographers, and artisans had begun to discover the huge lofts and low rents of SoHo—the name not a copy of its British counterpart, but an acronym meaning simply South of Houston Street. Galleries and good restaurants had followed, and the revitalized district was now an exciting, energetic melange of art and industry, where twine factories and fantastic food emporiums existed side by side with jazz lofts and theater workshops. Loft rents were no longer so low, as Domini well knew. But there were still pockets of poverty and low rental in SoHo, and the district continued to draw artists as honey draws flies.

No, there was no particular astonishment to be found in Sander's presence in the SoHo art colony. Had he been living there all along, only a few blocks away from Domini and the daughter he did not know he had fathered?

Even the carving of the unicorn—that, too, Domini realized, had been no farfetched accident of random chance. Sander had seen the famous painting in the

Louvre; she knew that for a fact because he had told her so. At the time something in his words had conveyed the impression that he might have studied it with care. Perhaps he had memorized it with some subconscious part of his mind. He must have done, if he could remember the unicorn well enough to carve a fair copy four years later, even in the dark void of his sightless world. Perhaps he could see it in his mind, as she could see it in hers, just by closing her eyes.

She closed them now, shutting out the gloomy wallpaper and the dingy panes of the attic window. Was it really only such a few years since she had been a forthright, fearless eighteen-year-old ready to conquer life? In terms of maturity, it might have been a decade ago. Sander had called her unreal at the time, and with hindsight Domini now knew it had been an apt description. What an odd mixture she must have been then, so knowledgeable in many ways and so naive in others. How much she had known of the world, and yet how little! Still, with the unconventional and extraordinary childhood she had had, how could it have been otherwise?

Usually Domini tried not to dwell on the past, because to do so was to feel a great sadness for the lost simplicity of her childhood, the essence of joy that life and Sander had destroyed. But drifting in a strange bed, in a strange house, with a strange weakness assailing her limbs, the past seemed very close, very real. In her mind she could see old scenes like pages turning in a memory book. . . .

The unicorn had been given to her for her third birthday. At that age Domini had not been aware that she was the daughter of a famous man. To her, Le Basque was simply Papa, the center of a small universe bounded by great stone walls, with the soaring strength of the Pyrenees towering in the purple distance. Her world extended no farther than the huge flagged courtyard where Papa kept his special stone and where sun glittered on a spilling fountain.

Papa's stone was a central fact of his existence. But even now, with her third birthday nearly twenty years and many tears past, Domini was not sure why it was so important to him. It was a large piece of rough stone, crudely hewn out of bedrock, far heavier than a person could lift but not so heavy that it could not be moved by one powerful man with the help of chains and crowbars. From her earliest youth Domini knew that Papa had quarried it himself, high near a mountaintop, and somehow brought it down, singlehanded, to the great walled farmhouse he had bought shortly after Domini's birth—a great bastion of a place on a high rocky pasture in the mountainous Basque-speaking district of the Pyrenees. And he was not a young man then: he had been in his fifties at the time.

Domini was the child of Le Basque's later years and he gloried in her, lavishing her with a love that shone through every brushstroke in every canvas she graced. She found nothing odd in having no mother, because she knew no better. Papa's models, a succession of placid dark-eyed Basque women during those years, accepted without question that they should also fulfill the double role of mistress to the great man and mother to his child. And perhaps he did not ask too much of them after all; it was a small price to pay for immortality.

Domini's mother, Anastasia Greey, had died in childbirth. She too had been one of Le Basque's models and mistresses, but an American, chosen during the period when he had lived and worked in the United States, that long, tormented period of his life that the critics referred to as the Bitter Years. She had not been one of his more famous models; he had painted very few portraits of her. From three likenesses—two at the farmhouse and one she had since seen in the Museum of Modern Art—Domini knew her mother as a graceful woman with an aureole of golden hair, somewhat shallow she guessed, according to the studies. Anastasia had been painted with cynicism, not with love. Le Basque had never considered marrying her; nevertheless Domini knew her death had for some reason moved him deeply.

As a child, Domini sometimes asked about her mother. "She was like light and air," Le Basque had answered one time with a deep rue aging his eyes. "But I had forgotten that a man needs air to breathe and light to see."

His cynicism of the Bitter Years, which had lasted until the time of Anastasia's death, was generally believed to have been caused by his one and only church-sanctioned union, a marriage to an American woman who had borne Le Basque's three legal children —Domini's much older half-brothers, whom she did not know. The marriage had broken up some years prior to Domini's birth; the woman had subsequently died; the grown sons had scattered. The Bitter Years had come to a close when Le Basque, with the tiny bundle that was Domini, had left America and returned to the country of his birth.

"Oh, God," whispered Domini, hurting, wondering if she would ever see her father again. There were times, especially in the beginning when Tasey was tiny and money had been very scarce, when she had been sorely tried not to turn to him for help. Pride had prevented it then, although Domini had always known she would contact her father in time. But now that she knew he had sold the unicorn . . .

The child Domini, known as Didi, grew up a golden and happy creature. Hers was a free-hearted existence, her boundaries the waterfalls and rugged amphitheaters of the mountains. Her father's great rambling house was far more than a simple farmhouse: it had once been owned by a wealthy man who had extended it for use as a hunting lodge. Nevertheless it was remote from any spa or ski resort. Certainly it was a far cry from that craggy coastline, the Côte d'Argent, where silver breakers from the Atlantic marked the western boundaries of a Basque domain that stretched like a tiny kingdom from the picturesque fishing villages beloved by tourists, to the high and lonely domes of the mountains, true heartland of the Basque heritage.

In the remote fastnesses where Domini grew up the flocks were not of tourists but of sheep. Against the sharp green of summer grasses, Basque sheepherders, accustomed to the solitude of the mountains, grazed their tangle-haired *lacha* sheep, prized not for wool but for milk. Rugged rimrock rose from the pasturelands, and there the craggy heights were ruled by the majestic horned *isard*, the agile goatlike chamois of the Pyrenees.

Other than the *isard*, neighbors were scarce. The nearest village, a hamlet of tidy whitewashed houses decorated with the hearts and birds beloved by Basque peasants, was ten miles distant, too far for easy walking. Somewhat nearer lay a mountain pass that breeched the lofty Pyrenees to give access to the Spanish border; it was used by the peasants for the netting of pigeons during the annual migrations. The household servants, the simple villagers, the Basque sheepherders, peopled Domini's earliest memories; natural caves and tumbled Roman ruins were the closest sights to be seen.

But Domini traveled beyond the wild, rocky domain of the Pyrenees in the pages of books, and later there were real travels too. Her upbringing was far from that of a simple, uneducated farm girl. There were long, memorable visits to places where great art and architecture could be seen—Venice, Rome, Siena, Paris, New York, Florence, London, Vienna, Prague, Greece. Even in the farmhouse it was not a wholly isolated existence. At times, when Le Basque failed to seek the world, the world sought him. Often Domini met great and famous men at her father's table and heard them talk.

Nor was she raised to be naive; in fact, the opposite was true. Her questions, from an early age, were answered freely and fully and without inhibition, especially in matters of sex, for her father had little use for social taboos.

She thought she knew a good deal about the world, and certainly she knew many facts. She had tutors, all of them American at her father's behest, because he said she must grow up speaking all the languages of her roots. And so she grew fluent in three tongues—English, French, and the archaic language of the Basque people, a language related to no other in the world, a language so old that its origins remain shrouded in the dim mists of prehistory; a difficult language in which counting is done by twenties, in the strange manner of the ancient Mayas. To Domini the obscure and enigmatic tongue, spoken only by Basques, became as natural to the ear as the sound of wind soughing through the mountain passes, or the bleating of ewes at lambing time, or the murmurous cooing of pigeons in a quiet dawn.

During Domini's early years her papa was playmate as well as father. Often he deserted his easel to join in her childhood pastimes, which seemed to delight him as much as if he himself were discovering the joys of growing up all over again. Roaring with delight, he would romp in games of tag and hide-and-seek; he would roll up his trousers and wade in frigid mountain brooks; he would skip stones in still pools and watch as fascinated as any child at the interlocking ripples they created. As if rejuvenated by Domini's high young spirits, at the age of sixty he once spent half a day rolling exuberant somersaults in the pastureland beyond the farmhouse. On another occasion he lay for long minutes in the courtyard alongside his small daughter, chin like hers solemnly propped on his hands, watching with awe the progress of one single ant trying to move one overlarge crumb across a flagstone.

He loved to dance, as all Basques do, almost more than he loved to eat. Sometimes he would don traditional peasant costume and in the courtyard fling himself into teaching Domini the vivacious and demanding *jota* or *mascarade* dances of the Basque people, his rope-sandaled feet flashing and stamping and kicking high, his powerful arms raised high above the Basque beret he wore, his scarlet sash swirling around a sturdy body clad in a white so brilliant it hurt the eye.

Sometimes he would take her to the nearby village, where beside the quaint three-spired church the men of the mountains played *pelote* or jai alai, that most strenuous of games, invented by the Basques and so beloved that it was virtually a national sport. When he saw the players sweating and the hard goatskin ball slamming against the wall of the court, he would become as excited as a small boy. "Ho!" he would cry. "Ha! Ha, ha!" And then his feet would become restless, and perhaps if he had had one of the wicker baskets used as a racket strapped to his own arm, he would have rushed to join in the game himself. But instead he would contain his excitement and hoist Domini to his powerful shoulder to give her a better view.

When she grew older, he taught her to drink wine from a goatskin *bota* such as the sheepherders used, sending a ruby stream from the leather pouch unerringly to his mouth. He would miss no drop himself and would chuckle with glee when Domini's less practiced arm sent red liquid splashing over her cheek or her chin. And then, seizing the *bota* again and deliberately misdirecting its neck, he would send wine squirting over his own chin to dribble down on a clean shirt while Domini clapped her hands in merriment.

He taught her also to play *mus*, a high-spirited variation of poker, which Le Basque insisted on playing with pebbles as the only stakes, because except for a

mistress or a visitor who sometimes joined in, the other
players were generally Basque peasants or perhaps an
itinerant sheepherder who had no spare sous to lose. Le
Basque would trounce everyone unmercifully, and
when Domini groaned in exaggerated disappointment,
he would cry:

"I give you the world's riches, Didi, and all in
exchange for one single smile!"

When Domini rewarded him as she always did with
her sunniest expression, he would rumble with laughter. And while the peasants or sheepherders watched,
grinning but not understanding, he would pour all his
pebbles into her lap as if offering the most precious of
jewels.

To others, his behavior might have sometimes
seemed odd for a man in his declining years; but to
Domini, who somersaulted or waded or danced the *jota*
or played *mus* with an eagerness and enthusiasm equal-
ing her father's, he was just Papa, her papa, friend as
well as father. When she grew old enough to understand such things, she came to know that he was a man
whose artist's vision made the whole world seem constantly new.

And sometimes she saw another side of him as well.
When the peasants spread their nets to trap migrating
pigeons, his furrowed eyes would sometimes turn sad.
He said nothing, because the Basques did such things
not for sport but for food; but when Domini managed
to save an occasional netted pigeon and carry it back to
the farmhouse, he would allow her to keep it in the
courtyard until its broken wing was mended, and he
took as much interest in its progress as did his warm-
hearted daughter.

She had learned compassion from Le Basque himself, and some harder lessons too. One year during her
youth, when there were sheep grazing near the farmhouse and the sheepherder was busy with lambing, Le
Basque had taken little Domini to witness the phenom-

enon of birth. Early in the day they had seen a newborn
lamb lying dead alongside its mother. With no hesitation Le Basque had borrowed a sharp knife from the
sheepherder, rolled up his sleeves, and started at once
to skin the small lifeless creature. When Domini cried
out in horror to see the blood on her father's hands, he
had paused long enough to explain.

"It is to save another lamb, Didi," he had said with
great gravity and gentleness. "In the lambing, some
ewe will die, and then there will be a newborn with no
mother at all. This ewe will suckle only a lamb she
believes to be her own, and she knows her own by its
scent. And so I make a little wool coat for some other
lamb to wear. There is no cruelty in what I do. It is not
death that matters, but life."

And after that Domini had watched with no revul-
sion, her confidence in the order of the universe
restored, until the moment when her father laid an
orphaned lamb clad in its strange vest alongside the
bereaved mother, who allowed it to feed and so stilled
its piteous bleating.

Once, when she was about eight, her father took her
beyond Basque country and into the town of Lourdes in
Béarn. Although he was not a religious man himself, he
thought she should know of the nearby shrine of
Bernadette and of the pilgrimages that were made by
more than two million visitors each year. "Are there
miracles, Papa?" she had asked after watching a torch-
light procession that had caused her young eyes to turn
troubled.

"Oh, yes," Le Basque had said simply, dropping to
his knees to hold her close. "There are miracles in the
heart. The world is a miracle. Life is a miracle. I know
it is so, because it gave me you."

It was several years after the advent of the unicorn,
when Domini was nine, that her father had taken the
mistress who remained with him to this day. Like the

women who had nurtured Domini from babyhood, Berenice à Soule was a Basque with a calm country beauty and fine dark eyes. But she was a woman of more education than her predecessors, a separated woman undivorced because of church law.

"How many lovers have you had?" Domini had asked shortly after Berenice's arrival in the Pyrenees, her question prompted by an open curiosity she had never been taught to suppress.

Berenice had looked a little surprised, but she hadn't taken offense. "My husband and your father," she had said.

Domini's nine-year-old eyes had widened. Papa's women were usually more experienced, and it was not the answer she had expected. "Really? You mean Papa is your first affair?"

"Really. I've never done this sort of thing before."

"Not even before you married?"

Berenice had taken one deep breath, steadied herself, and then smiled with admirable calmness. In fact, she had begun to look quietly amused. "Not even then. In fact, I was a very innocent bride. I had some ideas, but they were nearly all wrong, for the nuns didn't tell me a thing. Nor did my mother. I had to marry in order to find out."

In her teens Domini had grown to love Berenice second only to her father. And gradually over the course of the years, because Domini was not shy with her questions nor Berenice with her answers, she learned a good deal about the older woman's background. What Berenice did not tell, Domini learned from Le Basque.

In her youth Berenice had been carefully shielded from the world's changing ways. Daughter of a wealthy and prominent landowner with strictly orthodox views, she had been convent-bred in Bayonne and married off in the Old World way, by family arrangement, before she was mature enough or sophisticated enough to rebel against a loveless match. Her chosen husband was a man she hardly knew, the scion of a landowner whose vast holdings abutted on her father's.

During the fifteen years of her marriage she had lived in Paris, where her worldlier husband, a flagrant and incurable womanizer, had become a lawyer of consequence. The marriage had been bitterly unhappy for Berenice. Her husband's insatiable thirst for conquest left a great emptiness that was not filled by children, although specialists assured Berenice the fault was not hers. Her husband refused to consider fertility tests, adoption, or the prospect of a working wife. Berenice had found herself relegated to a meaningless role as hostess in a social milieu for which she had no taste. Eventually she had walked out. The parting had been amicable enough, with the husband—perhaps out of guilt for his peccadilloes, and perhaps out of genuine fondness for his wife—offering an extremely handsome settlement at the time of separation. His generosity had made Berenice a rich woman.

She had met Le Basque shortly thereafter while buying one of his sketches at the opening of a show. He had been at once intrigued by her classic bone structure and extraordinarily fine eyes, as well as by her Basque background. Berenice's features were not perfect to the casual eye, and because of her close acquaintance with heartache the little lines of living had already marked her, but there was about her a serene and ageless beauty that transcended minor flaws. She had the kind of face Le Basque most liked to paint: a face with character.

And with character, Berenice had almost immediately become involved in the open liaison with Le Basque, although her rich and deeply religious family had been shocked and furious at her public flaunting of convention, especially as she was also serving as an artist's model for Le Basque, a measure sure to advertise her equivocal position to the world. Independent because of her husband's generous settlement, Berenice had refused to listen to their entreaties, even at the risk of losing the very large inheritance her father threatened to withhold. For the first time in her life she was in love, with a man many years her senior.

Despite her considerable private means and the polish acquired during her Paris years, Berenice had simple tastes, and she was endowed with an earthy wisdom that allowed her to hold the interest of a man who had become one of the truly influential artists of the twentieth century. She was wise enough, too, to interfere little in the strong relationship between father and daughter. Like Picasso's Jacqueline, Berenice was to be the companion of a great man's twilight years, although, unlike Jacqueline, Berenice was unable to seal the relationship in marriage. Domini's father was well into his seventies now; he would not take another mistress.

All through her youth Domini painted a good deal. Her father allowed her to use his paints and a corner of his huge studio. Her efforts produced bright, joyous paintings, and Le Basque seemed to take delight in them, roaring with laughter, chucking her under the chin, rewarding her with huge bear hugs before he went back to his own easel. But he taught her nothing and voiced no comment and gave her no encouragement to continue.

Nevertheless, she thought she could paint. On the brink of adulthood she had a childlike faith in her own invincibility, and she had not yet learned that it was difficult to be the famous child of a famous father. She was headstrong and proud at that age—fearless because she had known no fear, impetuous because she had known a minimum of restriction, demanding because she had known no deprivation, overly confident because she was unaware of the extent of her own ignorance, tactless because she had never known reason to tell anything but the truth.

But because she had known much love, she was also joyful, warm, trusting, loyal, courageous, passionate,

generous to a fault, and capable of loving very deeply—
too deeply—herself.

The first of the clashes with her father came when she
was seventeen and wanted to go to Paris to study at the
École des Beaux-Arts. Of course she was going to be a
great artist! Didn't she have her father's genes?

"Great art is here in the heart!" he had shouted in
return, slapping the barrel of his chest. Papa still had
the build of a bull and a great peasant strength, for all
that he was past seventy at that time. "Naive little girl!
What do you think you can learn in Paris?"

"*You* lived in Paris when you were younger than me!
What did *you* learn?"

"I learned what it is to starve! To steal! To lie! To
hate! To love! To live!"

"And to paint!"

Yet, because it was the most he had ever told her
about his early years, years even the art historians had
not been able to reconstruct after the most arduous
investigations, his objections silenced Domini for the
time being. Later she wondered about his words—they
were not the words of a man who had been born and
bred to think the whole world a miracle. Yet in his
earliest youth no unhappy marriage had existed to sour
his views. Had Papa not been happy before the Bitter
Years, as Domini had always assumed?

But when she pressed him to tell her about his
childhood, he merely chuckled and muttered, "I am a
child still!" just as he had always said in answer to her
questions about such things.

Though momentarily routed in her quest to go to
Paris, Domini had not conceded the battle. Berenice,
who usually confined herself to listening sympathetical-
ly instead of interfering, became a strong ally in
Domini's fight, pointing out to Le Basque that it was
ill-advised to launch Domini into adulthood with as
little experience of the outside world as she herself,
with her strict convent education, had had.

"I would never have agreed to marry, if I had known

anything of the real world!" she overheard Berenice arguing one day. "You must let her become an adult, Pierre. Are you going to protect her forever?"

While Domini couldn't agree that her own upbringing had been as cloistered as Berenice's—nuns didn't teach the kind of things *she* knew, and she didn't believe she had been protected from life's harsher facts in any way—she was grateful for the help. And perhaps it was the extra pressure exerted by Berenice, in addition to Domini's own stormy persuasions, that finally changed Le Basque's mind. One year and several hundred confrontations later, her father capitulated suddenly and completely, taking her by surprise. Thrilled, she threw her arms about his neck.

"Perhaps the lessons will be harder than you think," he muttered, hugging her.

"Oh, no, Papa! I can do it, I know! You'll be so proud of me!"

He sighed heavily and detached himself from her embrace and said, "Oh, my little Didi. Can I bear to see you grow up?"

"I've already done that!" she cried, dancing away from him in an impromptu whirl of delight. Her father merely smiled sorrowfully.

He made arrangements for her to move into a pension on the Left Bank, a well-run establishment that housed a colony of art students and artists. It was owned by an acquaintance of Le Basque's Paris dealer, Monsieur D'Allard, who personally attested to its cleanliness and offered to keep an eye on Domini's progress. She was registered in classes, circumventing the usual admission requirements with an ease she failed to recognize, and was given a generous allowance that she accepted as her due. Berenice à Soule accompanied her to Paris to help in the selection of a suitable new wardrobe, choosing good but casual clothes that to this day, after more than four years had passed, still formed the nucleus of Domini's closet.

During her first few days in the pension she made a

brief attempt to rid herself of the childhood sobriquet of Didi and gave it up as virtually impossible. The other boarders, fellow students most of them, knew who she was. They treated her in friendly fashion but with guarded awe, giving rise to a sensation that Domini found vaguely uncomfortable. In those days she bore a more striking resemblance to the famous portrait in the Louvre: her hair was still sun-kissed and feathered in a windblown pixie cut that emphasized her youth and her large dark-lashed amethyst eyes.

The pension was clean, comfortable, and cheerful, a friendly place where everybody seemed to know everybody's business but minded his or her own. The food was good and the widowed landlady pleasant, but for a tendency to complain about the electricity bill and replace bright light bulbs with lamps of lower wattage. Domini, never averse to new experiences, swiftly passed through a brief stage of homesickness. She reported to Monsieur D'Allard, when he dropped by the pension to inquire, that she was going to be very happy.

More than a week passed before she met Sander Williams, and by then she knew a few things about him, most but not all learned at the communal dinner table shared by the boarders. She knew he lived in the loft, in a separate apartment that took up the entire top floor and had its own kitchen. Although he used the stairs shared by everyone, stairs that passed right by Domini's door, it happened they hadn't connected. She knew his bedsprings creaked badly; the floorboards were thin and his bedroom was directly above hers. She knew he was a sculptor and an American from New York. She knew he had been living in Paris for eight years, working not studying. She knew he had only recently acquired a reputable dealer on the fashionable Right Bank, and although the others spoke of that with some respect, as though it were a feat in itself, she wondered if he lacked talent. Eight years to find a good dealer—surely he was second-rate at best!

She knew he worked in stone, a circumstance that aroused her curiosity because so few contemporary sculptors did, preferring more malleable materials such as plaster, plastic, and even bronze, which although unyielding itself usually resulted from the casting of clay models. She knew his art was characterized by realism, another anachronism that caused her to wonder about his capabilities—even her father experimented with a variety of techniques, as Picasso had done. She decided he must lack imagination. She also knew he did his sculpture in a huge shed at the rear of the house because stone was too heavy to be transported up the stairs.

And she knew he had a mistress.

She had even seen the mistress on occasion, a sloe-eyed creature with long black hair, a vague smile, and a stunning figure. One glimpse and Domini understood the frequency of the creaking springs. The relationship was also passionate in other ways—the mistress had a temper. Her name was Nicole, according to reports, and she served as Sander's model too. It was an arrangement that seemed perfectly natural to Domini, whose unconventional childhood had not been filled with examples of wedded bliss.

It was curiosity one morning that impelled Domini to investigate the shed. By habit an early riser, she had been up with the sun. Throwing open her curtains to greet the new day, she had seen Nicole sauntering off down the street, yawning, with an empty string bag over one arm. It was a sure sign of a trip to the market, which had to be visited not long after dawn if one wanted the best produce.

A follower of impulse then, Domini hesitated only fractionally. Surely, after the sounds that had finally caused her to put a pillow over her head the previous night, the sculptor would be sleeping late? Anyway, what could he do without a model? She scrambled out of her thigh-length lawn nightdress and into a thin cotton smock that was scarcely longer, not one of her new dresses but a garment she wore while painting. She took no time to brush the morning tousle out of her hair or to apply eye makeup, something she had taken to using—with glee—since her arrival in Paris. Lipstick she never wore; she felt it didn't become her.

In the communal bathroom down the hall she splashed the sleep from her eyes and was out the back door within minutes. She paused long enough to assure herself that no fury of hammer and chisel sounds, such as she had heard on other occasions during the past week, emanated from the shed. And then, without knocking, she flung open the door.

"Nom de Dieu!" exploded a man's voice at once.

Domini came to a startled halt, staring at the source of the words. At first she saw only a huge block of uncut marble, an irregularly shaped piece still rough from the quarry. Above it, a block and tackle suspended from the ceiling was still swinging gently. There was also a space heater, not in use, standing close to a mattress-sized platform of the type a model might pose upon.

And then, on the floor behind the marble, she spotted bare feet attached to a pair of long supine legs covered in faded blue denim, knees braced because of the uncomfortable angle at which the man was lying. Gradually he came to a sitting position, bringing all of him into view. His top half was naked, already drenched in sweat although the sun had not been up long enough to heat the air, and it was quite cool in the shed.

He had the build of a man whose main work was physical: the deep chest, the flat corded stomach, the well-developed biceps, the powerful shoulders and forearms. The ripple of tendons and sweat-sheened muscles, the sheer virile beauty of his torso, caused one part of Domini, the artistic part, to soar with admiration and open pleasure; at the same moment she was tongue-tied for the first time in her life.

His fingers were tightened murderously over the sculptor's chisel and hammer he still held in his hands. "Do you have any idea what you nearly *did?*" he demanded, glaring at her.

"I'm sorry," said Domini, finding her voice. Why should she be disturbed at the sight of a half-naked man? In Florence she had seen statues that showed far more; some of them hadn't even had fig leaves. And Papa often worked stripped to the waist.

"I really am sorry." She spoke French as a matter of course because that was what he had spoken. Standing in the doorway, hair haloed by the sunlight behind her, she smiled, expecting instant forgiveness because most of her life she had had it. "I suppose I caught you at a crucial moment."

He was far from appeased, reminding Domini that some passing comment at the meal table had suggested that he was a proud man, quick to anger and unafraid of speaking his mind. "You're damn right you did! I was about to whack off a great chunk where there happens to be a fault. One fraction off and I'd have cut into the wrong part. This piece is a commission, and I'll be out bread and butter if I ruin it. Do you know how much this Carrara stuff costs?"

Domini bristled. People didn't glower at her like that! "You don't need to get so angry! I'd have paid for it, if the worst had happened. It's not as though you've put any work into the thing."

"Oh, haven't I," he said grimly. "I've been studying this piece of rock on and off for months. If you knew a damn thing about this kind of sculpture, you'd understand why. Marble isn't exactly plasticine! You don't rule it, it rules you."

"Then you can't be very good at your work," Domini retorted, although she knew perfectly well the remark was unjustified. Before lifting a chisel to his famous "David" Michelangelo had spent a long time thinking about the raw material, a fine but strangely shaped piece of marble known as the Duccio block; its irregularities had challenged the artist's genius and governed the final design.

This ill-mannered sculptor might be right about the marble, but he probably deserved the criticism anyway. His angry assumption that she knew nothing about art had pricked her pride, and besides, didn't she already know he must be second-rate? Tact, in those days, was not one of Domini's strong points.

"If you were any good I'd have heard of you," she said.

"Frankly," he snapped, "I'm not interested in your good opinion. Now will you get the hell out of here? And *stay* out?"

"Gladly," she retorted with a haughty toss of her bright head. She resisted the human temptation to tell him exactly who she was and started to pull the wooden door closed. But then she saw the sculptures in a shadowed part of the shed and stopped stock-still. All were small, much smaller than the huge piece he was working on, but there was no denying their impact. "Why, you're good," she said, surprised. "You're really quite good."

He put down the tools of his trade and got to his feet slowly, unfolding to an imposing height. "Are you always so condescending?" he said coldly.

Changeable in her mood, Domini was excited now, too excited to heed the warning note in his voice. "But I never condescend, and I wouldn't lie. I *like* your work. May I come in and see it properly?" Impatient, she waited for no answer before taking several impetuous steps into the shed. "I do know something about art, more than you'd guess. I've had a lot of—"

"I know perfectly well who you are," Sander sliced in. "You'd be surprised how fast it got around that Le Basque's little lovebrat was living in the house."

Domini gasped. In all her life no one had talked to her like that! Instantly her chin lifted, challenging him.

"I'm proud of my ancestry," she flashed, trembling. "Can you say the same of yours?"

For a brief moment his dark eyes silvered with building anger, Domini's first sight of the phenomenon. And then to her astonishment he threw his fine dark head back and laughed, long and uproariously. She made fists of her fingers, raging inside. People didn't laugh at her like that!

Sobering, but with his dark sardonic eyes still mocking her, he said, "You're perfectly right, we are from different sides of the track. I grew up in genteel poverty—which is a polite way of saying a slum."

From what she had heard about slums, Domini could believe that he had. He was hot-tempered, mercurial, and aggressive, and she didn't like him at all. Injured by his mockery, she was still glaring at him angrily when he made a sweeping gesture at his sculptures. "Be my guest," he said. "I'm afraid most of my work is at the dealer's. Not selling yet, I'm sorry to say—he sets too stiff a price on the stuff. That's why I'm anxious to get at this commission."

"I think I just changed my mind," Domini replied tautly. "I don't want to see after all."

She rounded on her heel to go, but Sander was too fast for her. He moved like a panther on his bare feet, and his arm shot out to bar her way. "Oh, no you don't," he ordered coolly. "Now that you're in the door you can damn well stay."

"I don't want to see your work!"

"Ah, but I want to see you."

His hands closed over her unclad upper arms, the grip light but firm. Domini started to pull back and then stopped, her eyes widening, her anger evaporating as swiftly as it had appeared. His palms were callused, his fingers rough with incessant exposure to hammer and chisel. They were the hands of a day laborer and yet they were not, for the fingers were long and strong and sensitive, the hold of the palms light but persuasive on her flesh, like fine sandpaper grazing over satin. His touch was a new experience, and not an unpleasant one. Little tingles started to travel along her bare arms.

He pulled her to the best-lit part of the shed, the place occupied by the big marble block. Without hurting her he held her against it, pinning her there with those powerful hands. She didn't try to protest. The male scent of him filled her nostrils, causing an intense exhilaration Domini did not at once understand; the closest sensation she could remember had been caused by a particularly wild storm in the mountains, terrifying and thrilling all at once.

"I couldn't see you too well in the doorway, with the sun behind you. I'm curious to know if the famous Didi lives up to her father's vision."

No instinct told her to resist now, any more than she had resisted the excitement of that long-ago storm in the Pyrenees, which she had watched from her window with dancing eyes. When his hand came up to twine lightly in her hair, she didn't cry out. When he tilted her head to the light, resting it against the marble block, she permitted it although the bend of her throat was sacrificial. Fearless, she gazed up into his probing eyes, filled with a wonder beyond telling.

For now she understood. She had read enough and heard enough and seen enough, and it only surprised her that she had not understood at once. In her youth her father had never tried to protect her from the knowledge of why he kept a mistress to warm his bed, nor from the sight of mating animals, common enough in the open, mountainous countryside where walls hid no secrets. It was perfectly right, perfectly natural that she should thrill to the touch and the smell and the heat of a man. In body Domini was an innocent, but in her heart she was a pagan.

"Extraordinary," he breathed.

He was hardly making bodily contact at all, only that hand twisted in her hair and one palm against her shoulder, resting against the thin cotton. And yet she could feel the male textures of him as if they touched her—the stretch of tendons, the roughness of chest hair dampened by exertion, the firmness of flesh, the scratch of denim that didn't quite connect with her thinly clad thighs. She quivered to close the gap.

"Why, you're still a child," he murmured half in wonder, as if speaking to himself.

She tensed slightly for the first time but made no move to struggle, and the directness of her gaze shifted only in that it returned to his eyes. She had been feasting on the shape of his mouth, exulting in its firmness and virility, dwelling on a particular curve of lip that she imagined would be hard and soft and sensuous all at once. She wondered what he tasted like. "I'm eighteen," she said levelly. "I'm not a girl, I'm a woman." Her blood sang with triumph because it was so.

He smiled and freed her shoulder, but his right hand remained very lightly laced in her hair because he was not through with his inspection yet. She wished his fingers were stroking her scalp or her temples or her eyelids.

"I was speaking relatively," he returned in a dry voice. "When you reach the ancient age of thirty, as I have, you'll know what I mean. Anyway, I wasn't speaking of age, I was speaking of something else. Call it purity. Innocence. Lack of worldliness. Lack of fear. That total trust—although God knows why you trust a perfect stranger like me. You shouldn't trust men at all. Do you know, I believe I could free your hair and you wouldn't even move away?"

But his hand remained where it was, as though he were reluctant to end the light contact, while his gaze dropped to her mouth. Intuitive in her reactions, Domini knew instinctively that he was wondering about the texture and taste of it, just as she had wondered about his. Her head and her back and her bare arms still rested against the unyielding marble and that was part of the excitement rising in her, because her skin had grown very heated despite its pervasive chill. She had wondered sometimes if she was going to have a passionate nature; now she knew. She moistened her lips.

"Please make love to me," she whispered simply, certain that he must want such a thing as surely as she did.

He reacted as if she had slapped him, jerking away swiftly and forcefully. He stared at her disbelievingly and swore softly in English, some raw, explicit words he probably thought she couldn't understand. She had heard them before and wasn't shocked. Then he returned to French. "My mind must be playing tricks," he muttered. "You can't mean that."

"But I do," she smiled. "Please make—"

"Don't bother repeating yourself!" he thundered. He was truly angry, even angrier than he had been at first, his brows drawn together in rage and his eyes glittering with an unholy light that seemed out of all proportion to Domini. What she had asked for was very simple, wasn't it? *He* did it all the time.

"I don't know why you're so angry," she said, honestly puzzled. Papa had always been very direct about such things with his mistresses, even in Domini's presence. "Come, we make love," he would say to his companion of the moment, and Domini would be left to play alone for a time. Making love was as natural as breathing, as laughing, as running in the rain. "You should feel complimented," she added. "I wouldn't want to have sex with just anybody."

"Good God." With a short harsh laugh that held no amusement, Sander cast his eyes skyward toward the block and tackle and rubbed a hand around the back of his neck. Then he looked back at Domini, less enraged than before but no more encouraging in his mien. "You're a virgin," he said tightly. "And don't bother denying it, because I'm as sure of that as if I'd tested the evidence with my own hand. When I said you were a child, that is the precise thing I had in mind—your virginity. You are a *child*."

"Is that all that's stopping you?" she said, her expression somber. She was a little hurt by his rejection, but she could still see no reason to be ashamed of her directness. "I can't be a virgin forever," she pointed out with great reasonableness. Even Papa had told her that.

"You can as far as I'm concerned," he gritted through his teeth, the words barely audible.

"Or is it just because you made love to Nicole last night?" she asked seriously. "I heard you, you know. I always hear you."

He looked shaken by that, so she added, "Well, not the words or anything, just the bed. I can't help it, I have the bedroom directly below."

"Mother of God," he muttered, staring.

"You haven't promised to marry her, have you?" Domini asked anxiously. "If I thought so, I'd never have made the suggestion. The other boarders told me you were just having an affair, and the landlady mentioned you'd had several mistresses before Nicole. It made me think you must be very good at making love."

Sander groaned to his depths and swiveled on his heel, putting his back to her and moving another step away in one single fluid movement. Then he flexed his shoulder muscles deeply as if to ease stress, a slow, effortless motion that only accentuated their power and male grace and made Domini feel sure he wasn't quite as immune as he pretended. Nor did she think there were any promises between Sander and Nicole, who often flirted with other boarders in the house.

"I'd like to be taught by you," Domini said. With that she stepped forward and touched him lightly on the shoulder, a contact that caused a cataclysmic chain reaction. He started violently, shoulder blades springing backward as if she had scalded him, and rounded on her like lightning. Enraged, he swept her toward the door.

"Out!" he roared. "Out! And don't come back, or I'll spank your backside till it burns!"

The next day, when they happened to meet in the hall outside her bedroom, he stopped long enough to exchange a brief, reserved greeting. "I'm not always so angry when people walk in on my work," he said. "But the first cut is the worst. Another time, I might not even have noticed you."

Encouraged, Domini smiled, the engaging, eager smile that her father's paintings had captured so often. "Does that mean you're not angry at me now?"

"No, I'm not angry. I've been thinking about it. I realize you meant no harm." His expression eased marginally, returning some of the warmth in Domini's. "In fact, if you want, you can come out to the shed this morning and have a look at those sculptures. It's a little messier today—chips and marble dust all over the place. But you're welcome, if you want to see."

"I've been thinking about it too," sighed Domini. "I realize I made a bad mistake yesterday."

Sander looked definitely relieved. "We all make mistakes." He shrugged.

"Can you come into my room for a minute? I want to show you something."

He looked briefly taken aback but then smiled in quite friendly fashion. "I'll give you one minute," he agreed, stepping in at Domini's invitation. "That's all I can spare. Nicole is waiting for me in the shed."

Sander walked into the room. Evidently assuming that she was about to show him some of her work, he strolled over toward an easel where one of Domini's watercolors rested. Domini closed the door, leaning on it so he could not leave until his minute was up. At once she started to unbutton the shirt that topped her casual jeans, hurrying because she had so little time. She had been taught no false modesty, but all the same her fingers trembled a little and she was biting her lower lip with nervousness as she looked down to negotiate the fastenings. Would he like what he saw?

"What in God's name are you doing!" Sander exploded. He had turned, and his eyes were riveted by the sight of Domini's young breasts. She had thrown the top aside and was starting to unzip her jeans.

"I'm showing myself to you," she said, her hands pausing in their task. Troubled, she gazed at the black fury blazing out of those eyes, the silver pinpoints of anger fastened on the soft curves she had revealed. What had made his mouth turn so grim this time?

"I realized I should have shown you before," she said hesitantly. Her heart was palpitating in extraordinary fashion. She had not expected to be embarrassed by a man's eyes sweeping her like that, but she was, and embarrassment was a new sensation for her. But she didn't try to cover herself, because Papa had often told her she should never be ashamed of her body. "I knew I'd made a terrible mistake yesterday," she went on helplessly. "I should have let you see, before I asked. That's why I'm undressing now."

"The hell you are," he snapped. He reached to the floor, snatched up Domini's garment, and flung it at her. "Now put that top back on, and thank your stars that I'm not whaling the daylights out of you. And don't go around displaying yourself in front of other men either!"

"I wouldn't," she said, dismayed and hurt. Nervous now, she held the shirt against her young breasts, sure they had not met with his favor. "But I thought . . . well, Papa always used to choose new women by looking at them first. His models have been undressing for him as long as I can remember, even Berenice. I thought you might change your mind if—"

"I'm not in the market," Sander interrupted, his voice brutal. "I make love when *I* choose, and I don't choose to make love to a muddle-headed teenager who doesn't even know the meaning of the word no! Hasn't anyone ever told you it's the *man* who does the asking?"

"I thought . . ." Domini swallowed, bewildered. "Well, I've read about women's lib. Nobody told me it was wrong. In fact, I thought it was the thing to do nowadays."

Sander muttered under his breath, hooked his thumbs into his hip pockets in a gesture of resignation, and said wearily, "Will you please move aside? And don't bother coming to see my work. Obviously you're not safe to have around!"

After that Domini stayed away from the shed, and Sander stayed away from her. Every time she saw him, his face turned grim. At first she tried smiling, until she realized that only deepened his frown. If he chanced upon her in the street, he looked through her as though she weren't there. If their paths seemed likely to cross in the house, he would turn and retrace his steps, slamming some door pointedly behind him. If he was with Nicole he would immediately drape his arm around his mistress's hip, spreading his long fingers in an intentionally possessive way. The sound of the bedsprings became aggressive.

Before too long Domini got the message. As a matter of course, she took to bedding down with a pillow pressed to her ear, just in case. She learned to pretend that Sander was invisible, just as he pretended with her. She threw herself into her classes and started to paint with a fury and dedication she had never shown before. She dated some of her fellow boarders and even let one of them kiss her, a disappointing and repugnant experience because he tried to deepen the kiss right at the outset, something she was too naive to expect at all. No one had ever described kissing to her and she had never read a contemporary romance. Startled by the affront, she bit his tongue.

It wasn't until later, lying in her bed and thinking of Sander, that she realized she wouldn't have done that to him. But then, he mightn't have done that to *her*. She made a mental note to ask Berenice or her father if that kind of kissing was natural. They always answered such questions without reserve and had once given her a remarkably explicit text on the subject of sex, complete with line drawings. The drawings hadn't covered mouths. She knew more about the act of love than she did about kissing.

She thought about Sander all the time. She wanted not to but couldn't help herself. She visited his Right Bank dealer several times, thinking that if she could not touch him, she could at least touch his sculptures. Their beauty and power enthralled her, but she touched only those sculptures that were not of Nicole. Those Domini hated even looking at. They made her feel as if she herself was only half ripe.

Much of the time she was dizzy with wanting, imagining the feel of him from the few fleeting contacts she had had. She was sure she was in love with him; she had read the great classics of literature and had formed the opinion that love, true love, involved quite a lot of heartbreak and pain. And if this was not love, what was it? Racked with the agonies of unrequited adolescent desire, with no past experience to guide her and no close friends to consult, she imagined it must be love.

A frank conversation with Berenice, during a weekend visit home, provided a lot of specific information about kissing. Berenice's gently amused smile held no censure. Domini decided she had been too hasty with her teeth and resolved, as a cure for her preoccupation with Sander, to let the next importunate student have his way. But there was no next. Domini's teeth had inflicted a good deal of damage; the story had spread like wildfire. No one tried to kiss her again.

And so she suffered. Her flesh was on fire, but she also had her pride. Never in her life had she been rejected, and Sander's rejection was a revelation to her, just as the physical impact of him had been a revelation. She made up her mind that she would never speak to him again in her life, not if he went down on bended knee and begged, a vision that occupied many of her young erotic dreams. Oh, if only he would!

Chapter Three

The next few weeks made Domini a little wiser about the world, and she began to understand that one could not be as frank and forward in Paris as her father had taught her to be. Forthrightness might be fine in the environment where she had been raised, but in this setting it only raised brows and set tongues to buzzing. She became somewhat more guarded in her ways, but even so there were times when some innocent remark would set a roomful of fellow students to roaring while Domini looked around her in bewilderment. At such times her natural resilience stood her in good stead.

Gradually she came to realize that her upbringing had been unique, not merely because her father was a great and famous artist but because he was a thoroughly unconventional man. She had been brought up as a child of nature because Papa was a child of nature; for all his genius, a man as rustic and unsophisticated as the great crude stone he kept in his courtyard.

During those weeks she filled several portfolios with

charcoal sketches, still life studies, vivid watercolors. She painted a few canvases in oils and acrylics and stored them carefully on their stretchers, sure they would someday be important. Great artists always suffered with some great love, and she was suffering, wasn't she?

She also made friends, attended classes, and discovered Paris—not just the Paris her father had shown her, the city of the Louvre and the Arc de Triomphe, of the Palais-Royal and Notre Dame, of the Place de l'Opéra and Napoleon's Tomb. New smells and sounds and sights had always intrigued her, and so alone or with her new friends she explored Montmartre, stood on worn cobblestones on impoverished streets where Piaf had once starved and sung, found out-of-the way parks, shared cheese and wine in humble bistros, spent a whole day riding the métro, splashed her fingers in quaint fountains unlisted in any guidebook, discovered what it was to see a movie. She was enthralled and sometimes even forgot Sander.

It was at the Eiffel Tower, on a chilly morning in late November, that she spoke to him again. With no classes that particular morning, as other students in the pension had, she had gone on a sketching trip alone, but she had become dissatisfied with the angle from which she was rendering the lacework of the famous metal structure. She left the Champ-de-Mars and paid her admission to the tower itself, thinking to look over the surrounding streets from on high and choose a new vantage point for her work.

She was moving toward the rail on the top level when she happened to see him at some distance, brooding over the view. His eyes flicked in her direction, caught by the bright beacon of her hair. He swerved away from the rail at once, his goal the elevator that was about to make the long descent, but its doorgate closed before he could reach it. Domini hugged her new nutria-lined corduroy coat close to her chin and pretended that all her attention was directed toward the

view, but for once she took no pleasure in the panorama of Paris laid before her in such spectacular detail.
Of course she wouldn't approach him! Did he think she
had no pride?

Two minutes later she risked another quick look
around, only to see that Sander was nowhere in sight.
Perhaps he had moved around to the other side in order
to avoid her? It seemed a natural conclusion. She
turned on her heel, looking neither left nor right, and
aimed for the only instant escape route she could think
of.

They practically collided at the top of the stairs.
Sander stared and she stared, and then suddenly, in
unison, they burst into laughter.

"It's a long way down to the next level," said Domini
when she was able. "Am I that bad?"

"Worse," said Sander, but with laughter in his eyes.
Domini's legs turned to liquid; it was the first time he
had smiled at her in weeks. In hip-hugging suede
trousers and a heavy white cable-stitch turtleneck, with
his dark hair curving over its high collar, he looked
immensely virile and vital, a man who enjoyed life, a
man who would be good at teaching a woman what it
was to be a woman.

"I'd run all the way to the ground if I had to," Sander
went on, his eyes still fixed on her in friendly fashion,
"just as they did in *The Lavender Hill Mob*."

"What's that?"

"An old movie, a good one. Too bad you're too
young to have seen it."

"Until a few weeks ago I'd never seen a movie in my
life," Domini said, tilting her head to one side with an
artless and age-old coquetry the knowledge of which
had been born in her bones. She was breathless with his
nearness and wanted to prolong it. "I'd never seen
television either. Papa won't have one around, even in
a hotel suite."

Sander laughed again, delightedly, as if he had just

opened a Christmas present. "What an astonishment you are," he said.

Domini knew it was a compliment of sorts. She glanced down the dizzy descent of the airy spiral staircase, with solid earth nearly a thousand feet below. She felt lightheaded, and not just from the view. "Have you ever tried the stairs before?"

"Once." He smiled. "But not all the way down, heaven forbid. What about you?"

"Never," she replied, excitement leaping in her eyes and in her veins. "I'd like to go all the way!"

Sander frowned, perhaps uncertain of her meaning. "Not with that sketch pad, you wouldn't," he cautioned dryly, but Domini laughed with the *joie de vivre* of a child. Abandoned to the happiness of the moment, she ripped the day's efforts off their heavy backing and flung them to the air. The pages fluttered, caught by a high breeze, soaring like her spirits.

"Dare you! We'll catch them at the bottom!" she cried and took off with a flying leap before he had even agreed to the challenge. At ten revolutions of the stairs she was giddy; at twenty she was reeling; by the time she had gained the halfway mark all Paris was reeling. When she reached the bottom, her head was spinning like a top, her chest aching with laughter, her inner ears ringing at the wild distortion of balance.

Sander was close behind. Still reeling himself, he caught her before she had staggered very far. The sketchbook pages, some still fluttering down at a distance, were forgotten. They clung together, Domini laughing to the point of tears, conscious of Sander's deep amusement, too, too far gone to be aware of the curious glances of others.

And then suddenly their mouths were also clinging. To Domini it seemed the most natural thing in the world—his mouth was there and she met it. She did not need Berenice's advice to know what to do, because her body had known all along and needed only the right instructor. She responded out of pure instinct, and her lips parted as eagerly, as unselfconsciously, as a rose responding to the natural rhythm of the seasons, unfolding when its particular moment of maturity has come. This time, if the kiss had not deepened of itself, she would have invited it. But Sander's lips had opened against hers with no holding back, and it seemed to Domini that his need was as deep, as urgent as hers. His mouth was hungry, his tongue searching, his hands commanding. She closed her eyes and drank in the taste she had so thirsted for, the taste of a man. It was all she had imagined and more—as exhilarating in its own way as the crazy descent from the tower, an experience that would for Domini be forever linked with the bittersweet memory of her first kiss.

Sander broke away long before Domini had any thought of doing so. He gripped her arms to steady her and looked down into her face, his eyes now dark, devoid of laughter. "I think we'd better go at once," he said huskily and unsteadily.

For the first time Domini became conscious of curious spectators. She held Sander's gaze and quivered with expectation, because she was sure no man could kiss so passionately without demanding more. "This isn't the right place to make love," she agreed happily, with all the directness of her nature.

Sander's face tightened. "Is there a right place?" he muttered grimly and somewhat obscurely, bundling her toward one of the omnipresent taxicabs of Paris. Throughout the trip to the pension he remained silent, his head thrust back against the seat and his eyes resolutely closed. He didn't touch Domini. His expression was not prepossessing; he appeared to be in a black and brooding mood. Wary because of his previous rejections, Domini sat well away from him, her throat in a knot, wondering what his enigmatic pronouncement had meant. Did he intend to make love to her or not?

He escorted her up the squeaking stairs of the

pension and came to a standstill on the second-floor landing near the door of her room. Domini avoided his eyes, wanting any advances to come from him. "Thank you for bringing me home," she said, and because she wasn't accustomed to hiding her feelings, her voice betrayed her lovesickness and her longing.

Sander nodded in acknowledgment and remained silent for a moment. Then he said unexpectedly, with far more warmth than usual, "I went to the Louvre yesterday. Did you know they'd moved your portrait to a more prominent place?"

It had been in a prominent place before. "Papa will be pleased," Domini said, feeling a stiffness in her lips because she had not yet grown accustomed to this kind of polite, meaningless talk. If he wanted to come into her room, why didn't he simply say so? And if he didn't want to come in, why didn't he simply leave?

"The yellows look good in the new location," Sander said quite gently. Domini knew he was trying to set her at ease but it didn't help; her fists were clenched in misery. Sander sighed and added, more abruptly, "Did you know that unicorns are never yellow?"

She shook her head, still not looking at him, still unsure of his intentions. She opened her door, not enough that it looked like an invitation, but enough to suggest that she was ready to let the encounter come to an end.

"White is the right color, according to legend. Yesterday, after the Louvre, I also went to the library to look up unicorns."

"You were that . . . interested?" Domini said, her pulses fluttering as she darted one swift glance at him. Might he be leading up to something after all?

"You intrigue me," Sander said somberly. "I can't understand what makes you tick. I had the crazy notion that the unicorn might provide a key, perhaps because it's only a myth, as unreal as . . . as you are."

"I'm made of flesh and blood," she said, trembling, hurt.

"Of course you are." He smiled, his eyes warming. "And feelings too. But there's a quality about you that's very rare, and your father captured it in his painting. Since the first time I saw you, I haven't been able to get it out of my mind." He spoke swiftly, not allowing Domini a chance to comment. "I was interested in one quote I read at the library, and I wish I had read it weeks ago. It came from a book written in the thirteenth century, when men were mystics and really believed in mythical animals. Perhaps you should hear it; it might help you understand my feelings toward you and what I'm about to ask of you."

"Tell me," she said, still holding her breath.

"Here it is then, not exact but as near as I can remember. It's to do with hunting the unicorn. According to legend, it can be caught in only one way—by placing a young virgin in the area where it roams."

Domini really looked at him now, her eyes widening and her heart racing. She was sure he could only mean one thing. His eyes were unreadable but his mouth was encouraging, more encouraging than she had ever seen it before. Hope leaped in her blood, like champagne bubbles bursting into life when the bottle is opened. She gazed at him and thought she understood, and gladness rose inside her like a freed bird. Sander wanted her; he wanted her!

"No sooner does the unicorn see the virgin," Sander went on with a dark enigma in his eyes, "than he runs toward her and lies down at her feet, and so suffers himself to be caught. I wish that—"

"Sander, is that you?" called a woman's voice. Bringing his recitation to an abrupt halt, Sander turned to the source of the interruption, and so did Domini. It was Nicole, craning over the bannister, clad in a striped jersey minishift as skimpy as it was flattering. When she saw she had been correct in her guess, she came down the stairs, yawning. Clearly she hadn't been up for long; her hair was still tousled, and although her eyes were made up she had not yet donned her usual dark red lipstick for the day.

"Did you remember the croissants?" she asked Sander.

"No." The word was somewhat curt. He made no apology and gave no explanation, and to Domini it seemed that he too was annoyed at the interruption, a matter that tended to confirm her conclusions. Oh, why had Nicole turned up just at the critical moment? Sander had been about to state his desire for her; Domini knew it with every yearning fiber of her infatuated heart.

"But you promised, *chéri.*" Nicole pouted. She draped manicured hands over Sander's arm in a posses- sive gesture that caused Domini an agitation of emotion she didn't recognize, because she had never before experienced intense jealousy. "Will you take me to a cafe, then? I'm famished."

Sander nodded his assent. "Go on upstairs, Nicole," he said crisply. "I'll be with you in a moment. I want to have a word with Didi."

Nicole flicked a glance at Domini, her almond eyes thoughtful. Well aware of Sander's quarrel with the younger girl, she was instantly curious. "Are you two making friends?" she asked lightly, smiling.

"So it would seem," Sander replied dryly. "Now go, Nicole, this is a private matter."

Nicole's eyes narrowed briefly, but she took one step toward the stairs. "Don't be long, *chéri.* It won't take me a minute to put on my lipstick." She gestured toward Domini with a watchful half-smile that seemed too patronizing. "I don't suppose you have anything to say to your new little friend that can't be said in one minute."

"Nicole," Sander warned, his voice low but steely, and his tone gave Domini heart.

"He might take longer," she said, lifting her chin to the challenge. Green poison was flowing through her veins, infecting her reason. "He told me I intrigue him."

Sander muttered something beneath his breath, something Domini could not hear. For a moment Nicole looked as though she would like to scratch Domini's eyes out. Then her expression glazed and she laughed a light, sophisticated laugh. "Does the child amuse you, Sander? I remember how amused you were when I told you the story about—"

"That's enough, Nicole!" thundered Sander, truly angry now at the catty undertone of the conversation.

Domini turned cold, knowing in that moment that Sander had been kept well informed of every gaffe she had committed during these past weeks. The biting episode was not the only one; there had been other incidents that had betrayed her naiveté. Domini knew that others in the boardinghouse gossiped, but she hadn't imagined that Sander did, and she hated the thought of him laughing about her with Nicole behind closed doors.

Nicole didn't heed the warning note in Sander's voice. Her gaze dropped to Domini's mouth, cool and scornful. "Such pretty little teeth," she murmured mockingly. "And so sharp."

Something inside Domini snapped. "I don't always bite when I'm kissed," she flashed back, caution thrown to the winds. "Ask Sander!"

Sander's face froze into instant stone, but Nicole reacted with a fiery fury that did Domini's vengeful heart good. She rounded on Sander, screaming. "So that's what you've been doing with the little bitch! Here in the hall, practically beneath my eyes! Man of a thousand lies! So I was right, you have been fancying the child! Obsessed by her! Cheat! Pig! *Bâtard!*"

Domini's adrenaline was high, and Nicole's words only added fuel to the fires of her vivid imagination. "He wasn't kissing me just now," she said succinctly and steadily. "He was in the middle of telling me he wanted to make love to me."

"Mon Dieu," Sander muttered.

"Oh—oh—oh!" Nicole gasped. She directed one more aggrieved look at Sander and fled up the stairs, holding her skirts high.

"Nicole, *wait!"*

Domini's fleeting sense of triumph evaporated as she realized that Sander was bounding up the stairs, two at a time, in pursuit of his mistress. "Listen, for God's sake! It isn't quite that simple—"

The rest of the words were lost as he vanished out of view to the crash of breaking crockery. Domini stared with troubled eyes at the empty staircase, totally unsettled. She knew she had said the wrong thing; these past weeks had taught her that the truth was seldom appreciated. It occurred to her that Sander was going to be very angry with her for being so frank with Nicole, but it couldn't be helped; what was done was done. And as for Nicole . . . well, she had been unkind and deserved some payment for her innuendos.

Besides, Sander would forgive, wouldn't he? He wanted her—even Nicole had confirmed that conclusion. Oddly, at the moment the thought gave Domini little consolation.

The noise of battle seeped down the stairwell all day long. There was no mistaking the sounds of female fury, and from her room Domini was aware that occasionally other boarders converged in the hall to listen and to whisper, but not to interfere. Too miserable to join the others for meals, she remained in her room all day, her uncertainty and anguish growing with every shrieked imprecation, every muffled curse, every explosion of shattering china. She hoped Nicole's aim was as wild as her temper.

The sounds from the third floor ceased near bedtime, to be replaced by the insistent toot of a car horn down on the dark street. Domini hurried to her window in time to see Nicole fling herself into a taxicab and slam the door behind her. The taxicab pulled away at once.

A new kind of apprehension seized Domini as her

eyes turned to the ceiling above her. Would Sander come down to see her now? Ought she to go up and apologize? Exactly how angry was he going to be? He had, she knew, every right to be furious. Domini had long since repented her lack of tact; in fact, she was writhing with inward agony because of it.

There were no further sounds from upstairs, and no one appeared at her door. At length, long after midnight, with the house all in silence, Domini donned her light lawn nightgown and crawled into bed to nurse her misery in the dark. Two sleepless, remorseful hours passed before an alarming new thought occurred to her. Might Nicole have done real damage with the crockery just before her departure? Might Sander be lying unconscious upstairs, slowly bleeding to death?

Instantly she was out of bed, translating impulse into action. Fear was a powerful propellant, and at that moment she was more afraid for Sander than of him. She flew up the stairs on silent bare feet, taking the steps almost as swiftly as he had done, slowing only when she reached the third-floor landing and had to start picking her way past a broken flowerpot in order to reach the door to the living room.

The scene was a shambles and Sander was nowhere in sight. She found him, finally, in the bedroom, sprawled face-down on the bed with an empty brandy bottle in one hand, still clad in the heavy white turtleneck and brown suede trousers he had been wearing at the Tour Eiffel. Open drawers and spilled lingerie attested to Nicole's hasty and hot-tempered departure.

Holding her breath with apprehension, Domini wrestled Sander's considerable weight over in order to assure herself that alcohol, not crockery, was responsible for his condition. There were no major contusions on his forehead, although the long scratch marks down one cheek testified to the ferocity of Nicole's fingernails. Relieved, she sat back to think.

It occurred to her that Sander's anger might be somewhat tempered if he woke to less of a madhouse. In the litter of the bedroom she found a quilted satin robe and a pair of fur-trimmed satin mules that belonged to Nicole, and put them on to keep her warm and protect her feet. Slowly, and with no great hope of appeasing Sander's righteous rage, she started to tidy up, first in the bedroom, then in the living room. An hour had passed by the time she was ready to begin on the kitchen, where most of the breakage had occurred.

She was on her knees over a dustpan when she heard the voice behind her. "You," groaned a thick male voice, and she turned to see him looming in the doorway, his face rough with the beginnings of stubble.

She came to her feet and said simply, "I'm sorry."

"You're *sorry!*" He laughed harshly, without mirth, and cast his eyes heavenward. Although Domini could smell the odor of brandy hanging heavily in the air, he didn't appear to be drunk, and for that she gave silent thanks. But the raked cheekbone gave him the look of a ruffian, and there was no mistaking the intense hostility in every muscle of his tall, powerful frame.

His eyes came back to rest on her, hot with unconcealed antagonism. "You spoiled little bitch," he grated. "Won't you stop at anything to get what you want?"

Domini had expected criticism, but this was unfair. She drew herself to her proudest height, still many inches short of Sander's despite the slight heels on Nicole's slippers. "I only told the truth," she retorted levelly.

"The truth? You little idiot!" His lips drew back into a snarl, briefly baring strong white teeth. His hands were flexing at his sides, as though he would like nothing more than to wring Domini's neck. "Are you so damn sure the world revolves around you? One impetuous kiss and you think a man has thrown himself at your feet!"

"But that's exactly what you were doing," Domini

replied; with justice, she thought. "When Nicole interrupted, you were telling me that—"

"That I wish you would realize a man is not a unicorn! That he can't be seduced into bed just because you offer yourself at every turn! That when I ask you to stay clear of me, I mean it! In my book virginity is no prize—in fact it's a damn impediment!"

"But you kissed me," she said, eyes uncertain.

"Only because your mouth got in my way—and because your lips were damn aggressive! I wasn't in my right mind after all those stairs, and it took a moment to collect my wits. Besides, one impulse isn't an invitation to go to bed, as you assumed on the spot. I'd never have been unfaithful to Nicole—good God, we've been together for nearly three years."

Insecurely Domini said, "But you haven't married her. People marry when they want to be faithful. I thought—"

Acidly Sander broke through her words. "Married or not, I wasn't about to have an affair with anyone—least of all you! There simply seems no nice way to tell you that you are *not wanted!*"

There was real fury glittering in his eyes, and Domini's face drained. Had she misunderstood so much? She stared at him, eyes huge, sick at her own naiveté, sick with realization. What she had interpreted as desire had been only impulse; what she had interpreted as a proposition had been only kindness, an easy letting-down of a young girl who had been too forward.

"I didn't understand," she said, her face white.

"Even if you misunderstood, you had no right to do as you did," he gritted. He had moved several paces toward Domini, and there was menace in the brandy smell of his breath. His hand closed over her shoulder, the work-roughened fingers rasping against the silky surface of the cloth. "Did it never occur to you that I might actually love Nicole? That she might actually love *me?*"

Domini shook her head in denial, a little fear touching her eyes. It was her first experience of real fear and she could no longer speak. Sander's harshness had caused the words to clog in her throat. She was alarmingly aware of her utter helplessness and of his superior physical strength, of the muscles made strong by the manual demands of his calling. But through it all, like the theme of a composition, ran another refrain—the sexual excitement evoked by his nearness and his touch. For once she wanted not to feel such sensations, wanted not to respond to Sander's powerful physique, but she had not yet learned the lesson of curbing her body's impulses.

His gaze dropped from her face and moved scornfully over the length of her, as if the contact with her shoulder had caused him, too, to become conscious of her physical vulnerability. What he saw seemed to anger him anew.

"Nicole's robe," he uttered in a hissing whisper. "Were you so anxious to fill her role? Let's see if you like it when you do!"

With that his mouth clamped over hers, tongue and teeth grinding mercilessly to pry her lips apart. With alarm she realized his self-control was far more impaired by alcohol than she had at first suspected; that despite the lack of slur and unsteadiness, he was still suffering the effects of the brandy he had downed not so very long ago. Uttering little strangling sounds deep in her throat, Domini clenched her teeth and fought desperately against the unwanted invasion. Her fists pounded against his broad chest but it might have been rock, immutable and unfeeling. Within moments her hands were manacled roughly in one of his and wrenched swiftly behind her back. With his other hand he gripped her jaw, trying to force her submission.

When she gasped for air, mouth already bruised and swollen by his savagery, he at last intruded deeply, ravishing the inner softness with such thoroughness and lack of mercy that she thought she would surely faint. On his tongue were the pungent tastes of alcohol and tobacco, mingling with the pervasive and powerful flavor of masculinity. Against all reason and against her will, the violent and loveless probing overpowered her senses and set them to swirling. The delirium of the earlier kiss returned, dizzying her and sending flushes of anticipation over skin that felt chilled and heated all at once. His anger notwithstanding, she began to respond—and in that moment he jerked himself abruptly away.

But already Domini was past protesting or resisting. Hurting all over, and with her defenses in total disorder, she could only lean her head weakly against his shoulder, drinking deep gulps of air and hating herself because she wanted him so.

She clung to him sobbing, trembling with a desire induced by too many erotic imaginings, tears streaming over cheeks raw from the stubble of his jaw. Unmoved, Sander gripped her shoulders and held her a little away so that he could look full into her face. If her anguish moved him in any way, it didn't show in the bitter hardness of his mouth.

"Have you changed your mind, now that you've had a taste of what I feel for you? If so, get out of my apartment and out of my life! Or perhaps you need a stronger lesson, and perhaps I shall enjoy teaching it after all. . . . Is that what you want?"

She longed to leave but could not, and so she stood helplessly swaying in his grasp, desperation fighting a losing battle with desire. As if Sander sensed this, his mouth curled into a deeper contempt.

"What, no answer?" he mocked. "Well, I shall find the answer for myself."

Steadying her with one hand, he jerked away the sash of the satin robe. It parted in front, revealing the almost childlike simplicity of the cotton garment beneath. For a moment his eyes smoldered over the soft swell of Domini's breasts and the crests of them, visible as faint shadows behind the fine thin fabric.

"Aroused, I see," he taunted.

Instructed in such things, Domini knew what bodily changes he must have detected in her breasts. She hung her head, shamed. "No," she murmured. "no . . ."

"Yes," contradicted Sander, lifting her chin so that she could see the cruel derision hardening his mouth. "Yes."

With deliberation, watching her face as he did so, he grazed the tip of one nipple lightly through the lawn and then molded it between thumb and forefinger. Hard already, it hardened yet more, springing erect beneath his ungentle seizure. Sick with mortification and yet shaking with strange uncontrollable new feelings, Domini closed her eyes and moaned, swaying forward with parted lips.

"Oh, God," exploded Sander as if in pain, "is there nothing you won't allow?"

She opened her eyes and saw the naked hunger in his eyes, the wanting that had twisted his mouth into a slash of anguish. Primitive in her reactions, she listened not to his words but to her own instincts. They told her that his blood was pounding, too; that he hungered for the conquest as much as she ached to be conquered; that the anger in him was in large part the anger of frustrated desire. Wouldn't the anger pass if she allowed what he wanted? And didn't she want it too?

She knew that with a few words she could make all the erotic fantasies of the past few weeks come true. "I love you," she whispered with no second thoughts.

In the next instant Domini felt herself swept into strong arms. With rage and passion warring in his face, Sander strode for his living room, gaining it in moments and kicking the door to the landing closed behind him. He deposited Domini on a couch and then crossed to the bedroom, closing that door, too, with one violent sweep of his hand. It said more clearly than words that she was not being invited to take Nicole's place in his life. A chill of doubt touched Domini's skin. But wouldn't his rage soon end?

"Undress," he rasped, turning to face her from across the room. His stance was vengeful, his jaw grim. When she failed to obey at once, he demanded, "At least get Nicole's robe off or I'll tear it from your back!"

Shivering, she slid the satin garment from her shoulders and sat watching him with apprehensive eyes. Nothing in her life had prepared her for the perplexity of sensations she felt—the clamor of heart, the clamminess of skin, the wild trembling of her limbs.

With no ceremony Sander peeled the sweater from his back, revealing his wide shoulders and broad chest. At his lean waist the chest hair arrowed, drawing the eye downward even as it disappeared. The lithe, aggressive thighs hypnotized Domini as a flame hypnotizes a moth. Unconcealed by the close cut of the suede trousers, the powerful contours of his body were taut with readiness. Even knowing what to expect, she found herself shaken at such visible proof that the textbooks had not exaggerated about male anatomy.

He advanced across the room, closing in until he came to a stop at the side of the couch. Domini realized she must have been staring openly when Sander paused with his hands at his zipper and said angrily, "A man's body can't help itself any more than yours can. Didn't you know what to expect, you foolish child?"

She nodded, too heartsick at his tone to respond in words, unable to tell him that it was his anger, not his desire, that alarmed her. But the anger would pass, wouldn't it, when the lovemaking began? She smiled up at him uncertainly and tensed her fingers over a cushion, a gesture that betrayed her nervousness.

It seemed only to infuriate Sander further. "This is your doing, not mine! Turn your eyes away, then, if you don't dare to look at what you've done to me!"

"Sander, please," she whispered in agony, her eyes enormous, bearing a silent supplication that he cease his cruelties.

"Saints preserve us," he groaned, and for a moment he stood there with head thrown back, eyes closed as if in extreme pain, teeth clenched with effort and agony. Domini saw beads of sweat form on his forehead and slide unchecked over the dangerously clenched jaw. At length his entire frame shuddered and he muttered shakily: "Go, then. But for the sake of my sanity do it at once! If you're still there when I open my eyes, I won't be responsible for my actions!"

Domini caught her breath and held it, the desire to flee evaporating with the opportunity to do so. For too many weeks, too many erotic fantasies had filled her head, and Sander's strong sexual urge excited her, just as his last-minute forbearance reassured her. Wasn't this what she had wanted all along?

When there were no sounds of departure, Sander opened his eyes. He took in her tousled hair, her expectant eyes, her mouth reddened and swollen by his earlier onslaught. His dark pupils silvered not with compassion but with contempt. Nervously Domini wetted her lips, unaware that the mannerism appeared thoroughly provocative.

"So ready to submit to a man, even one who doesn't love you?" The cruelty had returned to his voice, replacing the anguish of moments before. Angrily he lowered his zipper. His flanks came free, the virile hips hard, marble-smooth, untouched by sun, the maleness of him overpowering now that the trappings of civilization had been discarded.

"You little fool," he muttered savagely as he came down beside her, his voice thickened with dangerous emotion. "You seductive little fool . . . don't you know I'll never forgive you for what you've done?"

But Domini thought he would. She met his fiercely intrusive kiss ardently, offering openly and fully the softness, the vulnerability of herself. Her hands were pressed against his naked chest, and the first feel of its textures sent a shock of electricity running through her fingertips. Reckless in her abandon, she moved her palms to explore what only her eye had known; to mold the unyielding muscles of his upper arms, to feel the sculpture of his powerful shoulders, the straining tendons of his nape. Each part of him felt hard, warm, wonderful. And then she wound her passionate arms around his neck and clung, willing away thoughts of the unkind things he had said, optimistic in thinking that he would surely forgive and forget once he had taken her in the act of love.

Impatient, he took no time to strip her of her nightdress. His palms blazed over the flimsy cotton, caressing the young breasts to peaks of desire, moving restlessly downward to push the fabric to her waist, baring the golden goal he intended to brand as his. Clinging to his kiss and as hot-blooded as he, Domini clutched his shoulders and gave herself up to all the passion of her nature. Delirious with pure sensation, she arched and moaned as his searching hand roughly sought her vulnerable thighs, lingering only long enough to test her readiness. Finding the answer, he pushed her legs apart to receive him and mounted her at once, mastering her easily and deeply without once freeing her mouth. The thrust that cost Domini her innocence came before Sander lifted his head away from that long, reckless, impassioned kiss.

"Oh, God," he groaned, as if from the very depths of his being, as he sank his face into the softness of her throat. A deep spasm shook his shoulders. *"Oh, God,* it's done."

Domini moved her fingertips to the base of his hair, digging into the vital crispness while she gasped through a rigid moment of deep-driving discomfort. But nothing could stop what nature had started, nor restore what Sander had taken. Moments later his dark head lifted, his eyes smoldering with black, embittered passions too strong to be long denied.

"That's what you wanted. Are you so sure you like it, now that it's too late?"

For Domini, the stirrings of desire were already rising to blot out the pain of first possession. Quivering at the fullness of his need for her, proud of her new womanhood and longing to discover the moment she had read of but never known, she ran her fingers into his hair to bring his face close to hers. "Teach me to make love," she whispered eagerly.

"This isn't love," he shot back at her, a terrible silver fire leaping in his eyes. "It's lust. Lust and rage and nothing more! Love is what I had with Nicole!"

Suddenly more frightened than she could tell, Domini shook her head in a soundless denial, willing him to stop when the stopping point had long been passed. Her whole body tensed and arched, willing his away, but the joining had already been done, and the movement seemed only to incite him to a frenzy of passion. His hands cupped her head to hold it still, and his mouth descended again, forcing her lips apart with a ferocity that should not have been required, had he given any heed to Domini's needs. The cry of protest she might have voiced was driven into silence by the depth of that kiss. His lips were cruel, barbaric in their assault. Stifled and shocked, Domini was too well pinioned by his virile limbs to think of struggling free. But she no longer thrilled to the masculine texture of his hair-roughened chest, no longer responded to the hands that moved over her with such bruising urgency, no longer wanted this thrusting possession that seemed to have become an act of brutality, not of love.

Her rigidity seemed only to enflame whatever terrible demons drove him, as though he wished to take by storm what she now refused to give. As if possessed with fury at her sudden lack of response, he tried to wrest it from her with burning caresses, with fiery kisses, with the domination of his male sexuality. But the battering of her defenses only caused every part of her to tighten, rejecting his hurtful and unwanted invasion. And when at the finish she started to rake his shoulders in a belated effort to fight him away, he imprisoned her hands above her head.

That was the end; it was over in the next moment. He finished with a soul-deep groan, his hard-muscled body cleaving her with a final vehemence that left Domini limp, shaking, and gasping when he was through. He lay utterly spent for a time, still a part of her, the weight of him heavy over her vanquished body, the labored sound of his breathing harsh in her ears.

"I hate you," Domini sobbed. "I hate you."

"Shouldn't you have thought of that before?" he gritted as he rolled away. And then, with not one backward glance at her shivering frame, he flung away and banged into the bedroom he had shared with Nicole.

And out of that brutal union, Tasey had been born. Domini pressed taut fingers against the pain in her eyes, remembering, hurting as if it had all happened yesterday. . . .

Sander had vanished at noon the following day. From her bedroom, where she had been huddled in misery with the shattered remains of her adolescent dreams, Domini heard his footsteps descending the stairs. There was a short rap at her door, unrepeated, and Domini did not answer. She thought she had learned the meaning of true hatred in the happenings of the previous night. Violated in mind even more than in body, she burned for vengeance, wanting to hurt Sander as much as he had hurt her.

At the dinner hour, not having eaten for more than twenty-four hours, she rallied enough to brave the trip downstairs. And then came the news of the accident.

"He was in a rented car," the landlady explained to the unnaturally hushed group at the supper table after announcing that Sander had been taken to a hospital. "It happened on the road to Rouen."

"Rouen?" puzzled someone. "Then he must have been on his way to Nicole. Isn't that where her family is from?"

It seemed that the brakes of a school bus had failed at the intersection of a crossroad. To avoid collision, Sander had swerved off the highway, braking hard but still traveling at considerable speed. The rented car had telescoped against a tree. Miraculously, when Sander's unconscious body was finally extracted from the wreckage, no bones had been found broken. But there were severe contusions about his scalp and some damage from shattering glass. A brain operation had been performed to halt internal bleeding. It appeared to have been a success, but he was bandaged and still under heavy sedation. Although groggy, he had been asking for Nicole; the landlady had been able to provide the hospital with her home address in Rouen.

Numb with shock, Domini felt as if the heavens had opened to wreak their vengeance. And she felt that it was her doing, not only because Sander had been seeking out Nicole and perhaps driving recklessly fast in his despair, but because she knew in her heart that she had wished upon him fates a thousand times worse.

"Isn't it the way," sighed one of the boarders. "And so soon after he started his first important commission. It's going to be good, too, that big sculpture of Nicole in the shed. Such talent!"

"And half finished already," said another. "How he flies at the marble!"

"Not half as hard as Nicole flew at him," someone sniggered. "I wonder what caused the fight?"

"Who knows?" shrugged someone. "He was working too hard, probably—I heard Nicole complain about that. Or perhaps it was her extravagance."

"Maybe it's another woman. Yesterday I heard Nicole scream at him that he wasn't the only one whose eyes had strayed. When he was out of town for two days last month, she said, she had done some kissing too. When he got angry at that, she claimed she had gone no further and attacked him about something else."

That caused a renewal of gossip about Nicole's various flirtations and whether or not kissing had been the full extent of her straying. At least one young man at the table remained unnaturally silent. So did Domini, who also knew something about the subject. At last someone said, "Odd that the American was on his way to fetch her back. I would have thought him too proud to put up with that kind of shrewishness from anyone."

"I wonder who his other woman was?"

"I don't believe he's been unfaithful to Nicole. He's besotted with her," came a disgusted comment from the landlady, who had little love for Nicole. As the only continuing inhabitant of the house, she also knew more about Sander than the transient boarders did. "For nearly three years she's managed to enchant him, when before that . . . well, he was not always so patient with others."

She sighed, having left the impression that Sander's previous amours had been of short span and no particular consequence. "Oh, I grant you, Nicole has wiles to make a strong man weak. No doubt he decided he couldn't do without her . . . ah, Didi, leaving the table so soon? And you have not yet tasted my raspberry flan!"

After what had happened, there was no question of visiting Sander in the hospital; Domini knew he would not be pleased to see her. Her emotions confused her. Hate and hurt were all mixed up, and to add to that there was guilt. Sander had wronged her, she was sure—but hadn't she wronged him? He had been cruel, brutal even; but surely he deserved no punishment as dire as a car accident!

The following morning her sense of personal guilt was multiplied a thousandfold. She learned the rest of the news about Sander, the worst of the news, in the worst possible way. She had skipped classes and was lying agonizing on her bed, trying to sort out the tangle of her emotions, when a sharp knock came at her door.

It was Nicole, her eyes full of poison and her arms full of personal possessions. Behind her in the hall was a pile of suitcases, and when Domini appeared at the door Nicole flung her armload of clothes on top of them in a gesture of pure spite. "Well, are you satisfied with what you've done?" she said.

"Nicole, I—"

"I could kill you," Nicole interrupted, walking into the bedroom without invitation. Not wanting to be overheard by anyone who happened to be in the house, Domini closed the door behind her unwelcome visitor. Nicole rounded on her furiously. "He was the only man I ever truly loved. You destroyed him! You destroyed us!"

Domini learned a swift lesson in lying, although the lies were larded with truth. "Nothing's happened between me and Sander, Nicole. He's never even looked at me. Why, he asked me to stay away from him the first time we met. There was no truth to the things I said, not a bit. And he . . . he despises me for saying them, for coming between the two of you."

Nicole's eyes snapped. "Liar," she said. "He made love to you after I left. I know he did, for yesterday at the hospital I accused him of it, and he didn't deny a thing. Besides, do you think there are no signs of you upstairs, signs I have just seen with my own eyes? Or are you too naive to know that a little virgin always leaves her traces?"

Domini swallowed deeply, remembering how she had fled down to her own room without giving thought to telltale evidence. There was no point trying to continue the lies. "What happened was all my fault. He tried to resist, but I seduced him. He . . . he really loves you, Nicole. He told me so."

Nicole's angry gaze narrowed on Domini's earnest

face. "I don't need you to tell me that," she hissed. "He's told me often enough himself! But when a man lusts elsewhere, what use are his words of love? I want to hear them no more."

"But surely, now that I've told you he never encouraged me in any way . . ."

"Pah! Let him rot in his hospital bed! The faithless snake! I never want to see the man again in my life!"

Domini stared, hardly believing her ears. "Have you always been faithful to him? I don't believe you have. Last month when Sander was away, I heard the bedsprings creak."

Nicole shrugged, a little sulkily. "What a man does not know, does not hurt," she said at last. Nicole's double standard, evidently, did not include faithfulness on her own part.

"Nicole! He loves you. He needs you, especially now."

"Needs me? I suppose he does. But even if I could forgive him, do you think I intend to support a blind man for the rest of his life?"

"Blind," choked Domini, clutching at her bedpost for support. The world whirled. *"Blind . . ."*

"Didn't you know?" Nicole retorted, her eyes bright with malice. "I was told yesterday, when they called me to the hospital. Well, are you pleased with yourself? You took from me the man I loved, and then you took from him his sight! If he hadn't been driving so fast, it would not have happened."

Domini shook her head numbly, as if by denying the facts she could change them. "It can't be," she whispered.

"It can't be, but it is. And for that, blame yourself!"

"But surely . . . there are operations . . ."

"Operations, yes, if he is lucky enough to be helped by such things! But who knows if they will be successful? Even with operations, it will be months without work, months of pain, months of poverty! Half finished in the shed, the big sculpture earns not a single sou. Sander has only the money he makes with his own hands, with his own eyes! And where do you think the money will come from to pay the doctors, the nurses, the hospital bills? To pay the rent and put food in his stomach? Not from me. I will have trouble enough to keep food in my own! I am through—finished! And I hate you for what you have done to me!"

Domini stared wild-eyed. "But Sander . . . you can't walk out on him. Not just like that. Not now!"

"Watch me," said Nicole, nostrils flaring. She walked to the door and opened it, but stopped long enough to look back at Domini with poisonous eyes. "Oh, I almost forgot. I have a message for you from the hospital. Sander asks that you stay away. Perhaps you should listen this time!"

Domini grew up in many ways during the days that followed. She writhed with remorse. Face-to-face with the terrible consequences of her infatuation and her thoughtless words, she ceased almost overnight to be the joyful, carefree, impetuous person she had been on coming to Paris. Her feelings for Sander were in a state of suspension: it was hard to hate a man for whose blindness she felt responsible.

More news came through the landlady, and none of it was particularly good. Sander would be in the hospital for some time. Though the accident had not disfigured him, severe inflammation from his injuries made it difficult as yet to determine the precise cause of his blindness. The doctors were watching and hoping that it might be a temporary condition, due to traumatic shock. And if not, new techniques of laser and micro-surgery held out considerable hope; but no thought of performing any operation could be entertained until the exact cause had been pinpointed.

After an inspection of the third floor, the landlady had more to report. Nicole had indeed cleared out all of her possessions, and some of Sander's too.

"Money grubber," she muttered. "Would she have left so fast if there were still money under the mattress? She is a sharp one, that one, and make no mistake!"

As time went on, the subject of Sander's mounting financial problems came up for discussion at the pension table. There were bills to be paid, too few checks from his dealer, even a request that the advance on the commission of the unfinished sculpture be returned, as he could no longer meet the deadline. As for the eye operation, a necessity as it grew apparent that the loss of vision was not going to cure itself, how would Sander pay for that? The doctors had advised a clinic in Germany, and such things cost money. Moreover his rent was overdue, and although the landlady was sympathetic, she was in need of the income and could not hold his rooms empty forever. . . .

On her next visit to the now wintry Pyrenees, over the Christmas holidays, Domini asked her father for a large sum of money, so large that he stared at her in disbelief. When she tried to explain, he interrupted, "Do you love him?"

Guilt had caused her to be unsure exactly what her feelings were, but she was sure of one thing. "No, Papa," she said honestly.

"Has he been your lover?"

Domini's eyes were cast downward. She had expected to be truthful about such things, and perhaps if the man had been anyone but Sander Williams she would have been. But she found herself saying; "No, Papa, he hasn't. But it's very important. I couldn't bear to stand by if there's something that can be done to help."

Le Basque heaved a great weary sigh. "Yes, it is hard sometimes to stand by and let people help themselves. But it must be done. Why do you think I let you go to Paris? Not because I wanted to, but because I knew you must start finding your own way in the world."

"But, Papa, he could be a great sculptor. If you could only see his work, you'd understand. Besides, I feel . . ." She had been going to say responsible, but because that entailed many explanations she did not want to make, she changed it to something else. "I feel sorry for him," she said.

"Then I want to hear no more of this! You are past the age of taking in stray cats and birds with wounded wings, as you used to do when you were little. You asked to learn life, and life is hard. The world is hard! Perhaps I made a mistake by not letting you learn of it sooner."

"I've learned of life now," said Domini steadily, and her father looked at her sadly. For the first time she became conscious of how much he had aged, a slow, natural process that had not been so apparent to her while she was living at home.

"Have you?" he muttered. "I wonder."

"Please, Papa."

Once, her pleading might have softened her father, but now his expression only became more stern. "Berenice is right, it's time I let you grow up. You have chosen to be an artist, and art is a hard master. Artists suffer! Will you help every painter, every sculptor, who tells you a sad story? It you want to help them, first learn to help yourself!"

"I promise I'll pay you back when I start selling paintings. I'll be doing that soon. I know I will!"

Le Basque took a deep breath as if about to say a good deal on the subject, but instead closed his mouth firmly over the single word, "No." He turned his back on Domini to return to the painting he was executing, dismissing her with a curtness he had never shown before. And because Domini was not quite the same person she had been a few months before, she pleaded no more. Help herself? Indeed she would!

Back in Paris, on the same day that she learned of her pregnancy, she gathered together a portfolio of the work she had done since her arrival at the pension and called for a taxi to take her to the Right Bank. She wasn't sure her paintings were quite ready to be shown to the world, but she was strongly motivated by her determination to solve Sander's problems and assuage her own guilt. And if Sander was too proud to accept—well, that was simply cured. The money would go to him through his dealer, and Sander would believe it came from the sale of his own sculptures.

Monsieur D'Allard, Papa's dealer, had continued to take a benign interest in Domini over the months. There had been no problem arranging for a personal appointment: Le Basque was not the only well-known artist in D'Allard's stable, but he was by far the most important. On the telephone Domini had not explained the reason for her request.

His gallery was discreet and exclusive, the kind of establishment where the clientele seldom asked the price until after the decision to purchase had been made. Domini was ushered into an inner office with no waiting. D'Allard, a bald, beaming man who had made himself prosperous by knowing exactly what wealthy people would pay for, gave her the warmest of receptions. His eyes narrowed fractionally when Domini explained her purpose, but he made no objection when she began to lay out her offerings for his inspection. He regarded them intently, pursing his lips and stroking his chin, giving them serious thought.

"Mmm," he said at last. "Yes, I think these would be of interest to some collectors. You'd have to sign them, of course. You can do that right here. And then we shall see . . ."

When she started to scrawl a signature over the first painting, he instructed her suavely: "No, no. Print it, please, as your father does, nice round printing so people can read with ease. What collector will buy if he cannot see the name? A simple D. Le Basque, I think, will do. Or Didi might be better—it is more memorable, hmm? For who is not familiar with your portrait in the Louvre?"

Domini had been too naive in those days to know of the importance of trivia to collectors. Delighted with her instant success, and not realizing that D'Allard would have willingly accepted Le Basque's palette or Picasso's old paintbrushes, she signed as she was told. And then, with buoyed confidence, she asked for a large advance and got it, mostly because she was her father's daughter and D'Allard knew better than to say no; he would more than make it up on the sale of his next real Le Basque. The transfer of money to Sander's dealer was also smoothly arranged. D'Allard agreed to negotiate with the man, a friendly rival among the exclusive galleries of the Right Bank, and if he raised his brows slightly at the oddity of the request he was too polite, or too urbane, to probe.

A short time later she heard that Sander was soon to be transferred to the clinic in Germany. "Such a nice man," the landlady beamed to the supper table at large. "It will be good when he comes back, with his sight restored."

"What luck he made those sales," someone commented.

"Yes," said the landlady. "And just in time. Today a man came to take out his telephone, and I was able to send him away. Monsieur Williams sent me enough money to pay all his bills. And three months' rent in advance!"

"In that case I shouldn't wonder to see Nicole back too," laughed one of the boarders. "When she hears of his new success, there'll be no keeping her away!"

The landlady sniffed. "Well, I for one would not be glad to see her. Scum of scum! And why would he take her back? In two months she has not been to the hospital."

"Excuse me, I'm not feeling too well," Domini said and left the table although the meal had barely begun. She needed desperately to be alone with her thoughts. Too driven by self-recrimination since Sander's accident, she had not been able to examine her own situation or her feelings with any degree of rationality.

But now, with the relief of knowing that she could start putting guilt behind her, it was time to come to grips with herself. In her room she sat down at her dressing table and stared into her mirror, suddenly realizing how pinched and pale her face had become. It was not the first time she had had to leave the meal table recently, although usually the excuses were made at breakfast.

Pregnant. The suspicion that there was a life growing inside herself, and then the confirmation of it, had shaken her more than she had allowed herself to acknowledge until this moment. But through all the worry about Sander, there had been that undercurrent of concern, a river running deep through her days.

Pregnant! And by a man who didn't love her! But what did she feel for him? Clearing guilt away had helped clear her eyes in other ways, and she began to explore her feelings for Sander, starting from the first moment they had met. First there had been sexual attraction; that had been real enough. Then infatuation, not so real and probably induced in large part by his rejection. Had it ever been love? No, she decided; she had grown up enough to know that.

And hate. That had been very real, an emotion that had choked her with its strength. He had hurt her, humiliated her, taken her without compassion for her youth and inexperience. He had destroyed a part of her—a trusting, special part that Domini knew would never exist again, except on the sunlit canvas of a painting in the Louvre.

She was mature enough now to recognize that his cruelties had not been rape; she had encouraged him too much for that harsh word to be applied. Considering his feelings for Nicole and her own forwardness, perhaps there were even excuses for his behavior. But then, when she remembered that awful moment when she had whispered with her heart and he had answered with his hate, it was very hard to excuse. . . .

Even thinking about that moment, with remorse no

longer chilling her to the bone, she felt waves of hatred flowing through her. Domini closed her eyes, faint with returning remembrance of the fear and despair she had felt, of the savagery she had been subjected to, of the desire to kill that had followed. That night of brutality had initiated her in all those terrible emotions, and nothing in her life had prepared her to feel them. She no longer wanted revenge; fate had exacted that too horribly already. But the hate was still there, and it was still very real.

No, she would not tell Sander that she was expecting his child. Nor would she tell her father whose child she was expecting.

As to the child itself . . . what did she feel for that beginning life, growing hidden from the world? Could she bear to carry the child of a man she hated? She laid a hand on the still-smooth curve of her stomach and with a small sense of surprise felt the hatred begin to flow away and a great warmth steal through her to replace it. Still quick to follow her instincts, Domini knew in that moment that love was only as far away as the first kicking in her womb.

How extraordinary that she should conceive so easily, in the first encounter! Sander's virility, she supposed; even now Domini had to concede that it was a quality he didn't lack. And as for herself, Domini knew full well that the contact had taken place during a time favorable to conception. In her young life there had been no shortage of information about matters like that.

She felt no apprehension or shame at the prospect of telling her father, possibly because she herself had been born of an unsanctioned union. She was absolutely sure he would accept the idea of a grandchild; in fact, it never occurred to her to question that he would be anything but proud and delighted. It all seemed quite straightforward to Domini. With Sander soon to be off her conscience forever, she would cease to attend the

École des Beaux-Arts at once and leave for the Pyrenees long before the pregnancy began to show. When enough time had lapsed, she would phone Paris to assure herself that Sander's operation had been a success.

And he would never have to know that she had borne the seed of his anger.

Oh, how she longed to be home again, where life still followed a simple, beautiful pattern, where a child could be raised with love and warmth and laughter and the pure joy of living, where horrible emotions like rage and hatred had no part. . . .

She arrived home without warning, her face shining with eagerness to impart her news. In the very early morning she had caught a train to Pau, still in Béarn territory but at the gateway to the Pyrenees, with the majestic crown of the Pic d'Anie standing sentinel in the distance. As the little local train was not running on that particular day from Pau, she indulged in the extravagance of a taxi to take her the last thirty miles or so into the mountains, because to ask for Georges the chauffeur to meet her would be to ruin the element of surprise. Anticipation grew to excitement as she tasted once again the crisp wintry air of the Pyrenees and fed her soul on the clean snow-capped vistas she loved so well. How good it would be to live at home again!

The gates through the high stone walls were never locked, nor was the front door. Domini dismissed the taxi and entered with singing spirits, shedding her coat almost before she was through the great ironclad front door, secure in knowing that here, within these strong stone walls, was love.

Her arrival had been witnessed through the window, and Berenice materialized at once in the huge front hall, waving the servants away. Her dark, usually serene eyes were marked with an anxiety that did not at first pierce Domini's exhilaration. For half of Domini's life Berenice had been the mother she had not had, and she knocked her suitcase over in the rush to fling her arms impetuously around the older woman.

Her eyes danced as the hug came to an end. "Oh, Berenice! I have such wonderful news. But you'll have to wait until I've told Papa. Where is he? In his studio?"

Berenice's face was pale and she didn't answer the question at once. "He's been trying all day to reach you in Paris. What are you doing at home? Why didn't you phone to say you were coming? We didn't expect you."

"I didn't phone because I didn't want you to ask questions! I knew you'd wonder why I was coming home midterm, and this is the kind of news that ought to be told in person. Oh, Berenice, you'll be so thrilled! Where's Papa?"

"In his studio," Berenice said, her dark, expressive eyes troubled. The doubt in them at last penetrated Domini's consciousness, and she paused on the verge of dashing away to find her father.

"What is it, Berenice? Is something the matter?"

"Oh, my foolish little child," Berenice murmured, shaking her head sadly. "He already knows your news; he had a phone call from Paris this morning. Perhaps you will find him less pleased than you think."

Domini knew Berenice was genuinely fond of her and would not say such things lightly. Like a house of cards tumbling, her spirits collapsed. Papa not pleased! How could that be? He had taught her to be natural, had told her that lovemaking was natural. And he loved children. That she knew for a certainty, just as she knew he loved her. And if he loved her, would he not also love her child?

And how could Papa have heard? Had someone suspected? Was it those dashes from the breakfast table?

"How did he find out?" Domini asked, unnerved to think that if Papa had learned, Sander might also learn. The time in Paris had taught her that wagging tongues were one of the natural conditions of life in a pension.

Berenice laid light fingers on Domini's arm, a gesture of reassurance. "It's best if you talk about this with your father," she said quietly. "It's a serious matter, Didi, and I'm afraid you will find him very angry, far angrier than you've ever seen him. Now go to him at once; we heard the taxi arrive, so he already knows you're here."

Normally Domini would have run to her father and the news would have come out in a burst of uncontained ebullience. But the graveness of Berenice's tone slowed her as she walked through the rooms she loved so well, footsteps sounding on pegged wooden floors that were more than two centuries old. Her joy had been dampened, but her confidence had not. Papa might be angry about her pregnancy, but surely he would relent after giving her a stormy lecture!

Le Basque was in his studio but for once he was not painting. He was sitting at his easel, though, and on it was a finished portrait of Domini—a pensive study done in the courtyard some months before, prior to her departure for Paris. She sensed that it had been put there for a purpose, perhaps in the moments since her arrival had been noted. Her father's back was turned to the door and something in the rigidity of his posture warned Domini that Berenice had not been exaggerating about his frame of mind. She came to a standstill, entering the room no farther.

He turned to the door slowly, swiveling his stool without rising to greet her. On his face there was a great contempt. Unsteadied, Domini halted while his eyes moved over her as if he were inspecting a stranger he had strong reason to dislike.

"Papa," she whispered.

"Don't call me that." His voice shook with fury. "I acknowledge you no more. What you and D'Allard have done . . ."

A lack of instant comprehension prevented Domini from making the right connections in her mind. Completely engrossed by her pregnancy, she thought at first that her father believed she had been intimate with D'Allard. She shook her head, bewildered that he should even consider such an unlikely happenstance. "But he's not responsible," she said.

Her father's voice, once so warm, had changed to a hiss of hate. "Do you think it matters to me whose idea it was? I've already told him he'll handle my work no more. Yes, I consider him responsible—as responsible for showing the work as you are for signing it with my name!"

Partial comprehension dawned, but to some extent Domini was as bewildered as before. "But it's my name too," she said.

"Is it? *Is it?* I bled to earn that name! I starved for it! I painted for it! I struggled to print it when I was a young man, when I could not even read or write! I died a thousand deaths for that name! I suffered to make it great!"

There was no forgiveness in the strong seamed lines of his peasant face, no compassion for the way the color drained from Domini's cheeks. She had never seen her father like this before and it chilled her to the marrow.

"I allowed you to borrow my name because I loved you once," he said, trembling in the grip of his strong emotions. "But to borrow is not to own. My name has never belonged to you. Your name is the name of your mother. The name of a woman I never loved! If you must submit your bad paintings to be bought by bad collectors, use the only name you have a right to use! Your mother's name! Now get out of my sight and out of my life; I am sick with the disgust of speaking to you. But before you go . . ." He turned and picked up his palette and a large palette knife, placed at the ready on a small table beside his right hand. "Do you know what you are in my heart? Nothing and less than nothing!"

For shocked moments Domini stood rooted in the doorway as great slashes of black paint expunged her image from the canvas. And then, with her heart in a deep freeze, she turned and walked away without a word.

Berenice was in the front hall, her eyes sympathetic. She took both of Domini's hands in hers and said simply, "I told Georges he would be taking you back to the train. I knew, you see. Perhaps it is best if you return to Paris for a time."

Domini nodded, too numb to thank Berenice or discuss what Papa had done. It was only too clear that she had been written out of his heart and out of his life, and Domini was still in shock, her face fixed into a terrible rigidity and her feelings temporarily suspended.

Berenice saw and understood and didn't expect Domini to answer. "Try not to despair, little one," she murmured. "Try to remember that where there has been much love, there can also be much hate—for a time, at least. For your father this is a very serious thing. Perhaps if you knew of his youth you would understand."

There were more words, comforting words, but for Domini there was little comfort that could be offered. Nothing that Berenice said penetrated the glacier her heart had become until the very end, when Georges and the Mercedes limousine pulled up at the front door.

Berenice embraced her briefly. "Go back to Paris and wait, and if he starts to soften I will let you know. The pension is paid for the year, and if he will not pay your allowance I will pay it myself. And when summer comes again, who knows, perhaps there will be a melt. . . ."

It was not until the car was twisting downward on the road to Pau, putting the snow-gripped mountains behind, that Domini remembered the news she had come home to tell. Suddenly fearful, she buried her face in her hands. She ached for the release of tears, but they remained in her heart, unshed even for the child she would be bringing into a life that was too bitter to bear.

She could not stay in Paris, of course. In going home, a spur-of-the-moment decision, she had not informed the landlady of her intention to leave forever, although she had packed all of her considerable luggage and left it in her room for later pickup by a cartage company. She hadn't wanted to answer questions then, and she didn't want to answer them now. But her condition was far from being visible to the naked eye, and it was still safe to return to the pension while she decided what to do.

Her decisions were made calmly, with none of the impulsiveness that had characterized her actions until then. They were made easier, and perhaps inevitable, by the facts of her birth. Her birth certificate and her passport had both been issued in the name of Domini Greey; she had been born an American citizen, and she knew she would have no trouble getting into that country. Nor were there any language barriers: her education had seen to that. She was thoroughly fluent in the tongue of her mother country, and because her tutors had all been from the United States, even her accent and idiom would arouse no curiosity as to her background. And curiosity, anybody's curiosity, was something she didn't want. She had been forbidden to use her father's name, and use it she would not. And she would not beg; her wish to cry had long since given way to a cold, despairing pride.

She booked a flight, fortunately managing to take over someone's last-minute cancellation on a charter that was to leave almost immediately. Such funds as she had she withdrew from the bank, regretting the impulses that had led her to spend incautiously over the months. She repacked her luggage, weeding out all things that were too impractical or too youthful or too heavy. With dry eyes and icy resolve, she chucked her paintings in the garbage, refusing to let herself dwell on the childish confidence with which she had painted them. She spoke to the landlady briefly, long enough to discover that—much to that good woman's disgust—Nicole had found herself a protector, a wealthy American from Miami Beach, and left for the United States without so much as a word to Sander in the hospital.

"She came by to pick up a sculpture of herself," the landlady sniffed. "Can you believe, she pretends she loves him still? She says she stayed away only because she cannot bear to see him as he is. Pah! She loves only herself, that one."

The landlady also revealed that Sander was being moved to the clinic in Germany on the following day, affording some consolation to Domini that her dealings with D'Allard had had at least one beneficial result. As to her own plans, Domini said nothing of them during the conversation, although she left a note in her room saying that she had gone home. It was unlikely that anyone would discover otherwise for some time.

And then, with a set face that bore the stamp of a purely adult determination, she called a taxi to take herself and two large suitcases to Charles de Gaulle Airport, where she would wait until the time came for her flight. There, she simply pulled out her passport in the name of Domini Greey, and Didi Le Basque ceased to exist.

New York became inevitable, too, because she had insufficient funds to take her very far. She found a cheap room in the TriBeCa area just below SoHo, also an artists' colony, and took what work she could find: waitressing until her waist grew ungainly, and then preparing sandwiches and salads behind the scenes in a restaurant. With no job training and no skills to offer, she had few options, and a brief stab at illustrating children's books resulted in no takers. But somehow she managed, and somehow she put a little aside for her coming confinement.

About two months after her arrival in New York she placed a long-distance call to the pension, grateful that the new direct dialing system concealed the origin of the call. Using her rooming house phone by prior permission, she dialed the pension number, not Sander's. The person who picked up the phone was a new boarder, unknown to Domini, a circumstance that suited her perfectly well because she wanted to give no explanations to anyone. Reverting easily to French, she asked if Sander's operation had been a success.

"Sander Williams?" The person seemed unsure what Domini was talking about. She started to ask for the landlady, but before she could complete her sentence the new boarder interrupted, *"Un moment, s'il vous plaît,"* and vanished from the other end. Domini hung on, counting the tick of expensive minutes. And when Sander's distinctive voice came on the other end a short time later, her own shocked silence contributed another thirty seconds of delay.

He was about to hang up when Domini managed to croak a quick, "No, please don't. This is Didi Le Basque, Sander. I phoned to ask if . . . if your sight had been restored, that's all. I wanted to make sure you were all right. But I didn't want . . . I didn't expect I'd be speaking to you in person."

There was another long silence on the line, this time on Sander's end. "Where are you?" he said gruffly at last, answering none of her questions.

"I . . . I'm at home," she said, not lying because New York really was her home now. If Sander chose to think she was in France, the assumption was purely his.

"Ah, with Papa," he said dryly. "I take it you've decided you're safer there."

"Sort of," Domini prevaricated. "But I phoned to find out about you, Sander. I've been worried, and—"

"You should never have left your nest in the first place," Sander interrupted curtly.

"I want to know about your sight, Sander," she said urgently, thinking about the cost of all this.

"What on earth does it matter to you?" he retorted roughly.

"Because . . . well, I think I'm to blame. If you hadn't been upset about losing Nicole, you wouldn't have been driving so fast. I feel responsible."

"Then stop feeling responsible," he snapped. "My sight is fine; it has been ever since the bandages came off. The operation was a success. I'm back to sculpting too. And—" he paused, and a bitter mockery entered his tone—"to remove the last of your guilt, I'm reunited with Nicole. She came back from the States and we're happier than ever. In fact, I imagine we'll get married one of these days. So if you're thinking about coming back to Paris to see me, don't bother! One experience with a spoiled brat like you is enough to last me for the rest of my life!"

And there the conversation ended. Domini hung up without even answering his final unkind cut, accepting everything he said as gospel. His very rudeness seemed to give credence to his story, and in fact eventually helped Domini to start putting the bitter memory of Sander Williams behind her.

For the last few months of her pregnancy, due to the difficulty of standing all day long, Domini undertook a disappointingly unremunerative job selling subscriptions by telephone. But when Tasey was born and the expenses began to mount, she realized she would have to try to make her living in some other way, preferably at something that could be done with a small baby in tow.

As it happened, she invented a job for herself. While trudging the pavements in search of work after her arrival in New York, she had several times seen display people in the process of creating marvelously inventive windows on Fifth Avenue and in other exclusive areas of the city. SoHo, she noted, had lots of shops, but the windows were given to few flights of imagination; they relied heavily on merchandise display and very little on props. Casual conversations in several stores produced the information that Fifth Avenue displays were far too pricey for SoHo tastes. And so she started offering to take on the job for one merchant or another at cut-rate prices that would have made any established display firm blanch.

In time, the first few clients became a few dozen, and as the stored props increased in quantity, the rented room of necessity became a large sunny loft. Domini was not getting rich, but because she kept her prices to SoHo standards, her small one-person business was struggling along well enough to keep paying the rent.

In the beginning, when Tasey had been no more than a rosy bundle in a baby carriage, Domini had taken her daughter along on all assignments, and for a time she had taken her as a toddler too. But the difficulty of dressing windows with an active youngster on the sidelines had caused too many memorable moments, both tearful and hilarious. Some clients had not been amused. And so, when Tasey turned three, Domini had reluctantly arranged for day care, a considerable expense but a necessary one. Her next goal, still unrealized, was to upgrade her clientele to include some of the more exclusive boutiques she had been unable to approach while dragging a small child along.

During her stay in New York, Domini had made friends, met men, had dates, put much of the past behind her. Life had been a struggle but it had had its rewards: Tasey, for one. True, she still regretted the loss of her unrecapturable youth, still mourned in her heart for the joyful innocent she had been, still grieved at times for the fearless child who no longer conquered the unicorn and the universe except in paint. Because she loved her father deeply, there was inside her a great burden of unshed tears. In four years she had cried about other things, but never about that.

But life had not been totally unkind to her, as it had been unkind to Sander. That he had suffered in his blindness was engraved in every harsh, bitter line on his face. Domini tried to imagine what it must be like to live in a world where no colors existed, where no smiles could be seen, where no sunrises could be watched. What a terrible price for fate to exact from an artist!

Lying in his bed in the dim, unfamiliar room, choked by old guilt and new compassion, Domini thought about his eyes, those deep, embittered, sightless eyes. The eyes pulled her downward, downward, downward into their silvered depths.

Chapter Four

*D*omini sat bolt upright in the bed, alarm jolting her to full wakefulness at once. Oh, Lord. How could she have slept? The tranquilizer, of course. But why hadn't Miranda wakened her as promised? Through the gable window she could see that it was very nearly dark outside, the early darkness of December, and Tasey should be picked up about this time. In the half-light of the gloomy room she spotted no bedside lamp. She slid out from beneath the sheets, raced to the light switch at the door, and confirmed with a quick glance at her wristwatch, the last gift ever given to her by her father, that the day-care hours had ended two minutes before.

There was no pause to contemplate memories now or the circumstances that had brought her to this place. Domini's mind was fully in the present. She threw off Sander's shirt and snatched her own clothes, piled in orderly fashion on a straight-backed chair. The cream slacks and close-fitting brown turtleneck were pulled on in record time, and so were the fleece-lined boots, which had been standing neatly on the floor. Giving no thought to the disorder of her hair, Domini snatched her coat and handbag, and seconds later she was dashing along a very dim hall.

"Watch that floorboard!" snapped a voice.

The warning came too late; Domini was already pitching forward. Just in time a pair of muscular arms prevented her headlong plummet to disaster.

When reason reasserted itself, she found herself upright again, against the hard wall of a man's chest. It was Sander; she knew that with every quivering nerve she possessed. Badly shaken by the near fall, she started to gulp air, making no immediate attempt to extricate herself from his steadying embrace.

"Are you trying to add a sprained ankle to your other complaints?" he asked sarcastically. "In a strange house, my friend, it's wise to look where you're going."

Heart still palpitating erratically, Domini took a deep breath and tried to pull away. Two hands clamped over her upper arms, preventing escape. "I'm in a terrible hurry," she gasped. "My daughter . . ."

But Sander had no intention of letting her go, and his fingers only tightened on her arms. "Not so fast," he said. "Your daughter's been arranged for."

Gripped by anxiety, Domini only half heard what he had said. "I have to pick her up," she said, straining toward the stairs, barely visible now in the growing gloom. The door of the bedroom must have been hanging off plumb, because it had squeaked slowly closed, cutting off her one real source of light.

Sander didn't release his hold. "Miranda's already left to pick her up," he informed Domini dryly. "Your daughter will be quite safe, and there's no need to worry. Now if I let you go will you listen, instead of taking off like a bat out of hell?"

Domini nodded, relief flooding through her at the assurance that Tasey would not be left waiting. But with the mother in her relaxing, the woman took over, and at once she became piercingly aware of Sander's bigness and closeness, of the powerful hands that imprisoned her so effectively. A brief weakness invaded her legs, turning them wobbly as memories of their last physical encounter surged to the forefront of her mind. Barring the moments when she had been hysterical or unconscious earlier in the day, four years had passed since she had submitted to Sander's touch, and yet the memory of it was there in her bones and in her blood, giving the contact an impact that robbed her of reason. It was a moment before she had the wit to remember that he could not possibly have seen her nod of assent.

"I . . . yes," she said with a breathlessness that could no longer be blamed on her precipitate flight.

He took his hands away very slowly, as if not quite sure whether Domini could be trusted. "If you'd tried those stairs at the pace you were going, you'd most certainly have broken your neck," he remarked sardonically. "Are you always so impetuous?"

In the heavy gloom of the hall his eyes were no more than pools of darkness where no silver could be seen, his mouth no more than a grim shadow. Domini's nerve endings were still tingling, her pulses racing, her skin flushed with heat. Could he still affect her so deeply after all these years?

But she was a mother after all, and such thoughts were thrust aside as swiftly as they surfaced. "Miranda's gone to pick up Tasey? But she doesn't know where . . ."

"Oh, yes she does. You gave her your address, remember. She phoned the shopkeeper below your apartment and fortunately managed to find out where you take your daughter for day care. You were sleeping so soundly it seemed a shame to disturb you."

A new kind of alarm sounded somewhere in Domini's head. "Surely your sister's not . . . bringing Tasey . . . here?" she asked faintly, clutching at a dimly discerned wall for support. This was becoming a nightmare of the worst sort, and the fact that she could now see only looming black outlines added to the strong sense of unreality.

"As a matter of fact, yes. You're both staying for supper, and Miranda won't take no for an answer."

"Oh, Lord, no," whispered Domini, too aghast to obey ordinary caution in her reaction. And then she started to laugh shakily as the full impossibility of the situation hit her. In the last moments before darkness swallowed the hall altogether, she wondered wildly if she was imagining the whole crazy thing.

"Oh, Lord, yes," Sander contradicted, disapproval deepening his voice. "I'm not going to have to slap you again, am I?"

Domini forced down the returning hysteria. With an effort of will, her voice returned to some semblance of normality. "We can't possibly stay," she objected.

"Tell that to my sister," Sander said in a skeptical tone, his disembodied voice giving her some bearings in the dark. "Nothing can cure her of the Good Samaritan instinct. And this time I think she's right—you're in no condition to be going home with an active three-year-old who needs to be fed. We'll see you get home safely when it's the child's bedtime, and not before."

Rationality restored, Domini realized that she had no option now but to wait until Miranda arrived with Tasey. In fact the worst thing she could do was to go chasing off in hope of finding them; if she missed them it would only make matters worse. As to staying for a meal, however, that was quite out of the question, but there was no sense arguing the point with Sander. As long as she managed to get Tasey out of there before the two connected!

"Now come along, you can wait for your daughter down on the second floor."

She heard him begin to move along the hall in the direction of the stairs. "I can't see a thing," she said, expecting him to switch on a light.

"Dark already?" His short, harsh laugh was followed by the quiet ring of returning footsteps. "Sorry," he apologized as he reached her side. "It's easy for me to forget."

Domini froze as his palm stretched forward to determine her position and grazed against a breast. But the contact was fleeting, followed by a sure seizure of her elbow, as if that one swift touch had told him where to find it. With no choice, she allowed herself to be guided along the dark hall, her mind rebelling but her skin oddly sensitive where he touched her.

Near the stairs he halted and flicked a light switch that gave faint illumination to the landing below, leaving the third floor dark. "I'll lead the way," he instructed, at last releasing her elbow. "The stair carpet's torn, and it can be a little tricky."

Domini followed, picking her way carefully down the obstacle course of a stair runner so threadbare that it should have been replaced years before. Were Sander and his sister so pitifully poor? In his bedroom she had been aware of dingy walls and cheap furniture, but if she had given it thought—which she hadn't—she would have guessed it was only because a blind man would likely have little interest in brightening his surroundings. And on street level, which had to be kept presentable for business, the gallery had not suggested deprivation. But up here, hidden from the public eye . . .

With growing disturbance Domini noted the places where great chunks of plaster had fallen away, the tired wallpaper at least two decades old, the sagging bannister with paint so badly chipped that the wood was half denuded. As she reached the second-floor landing she felt a lump in her throat at the naked low-wattage light bulb suspended from the ceiling and the cracked glass in a curtainless hall window where someone's neon sign blinked monotonously through. For the first time the full horror of the various things she had seen began to penetrate. She herself lived in no particular luxury, but this . . . ?

There was no need now to wonder why Sander had

not switched on the light on the third floor; Domini knew. She remembered only too well the grumblings of the landlady in the pension. Were the pennies saved in electricity so desperately important to Sander and his sister?

All the old burdens of conscience returned with a choking force that clogged Domini's throat with compassion. Life offered so little for a man imprisoned by blindness. And for that blindness, although rationally she knew the brakes of a school bus in France were at fault, she still felt to blame.

"I can't take you to the living room because there isn't one," Sander said as he opened a door, flicked another switch, and stood back to allow Domini to precede him. On his face there was a proud, hard expression, as though he might have guessed at some of Domini's reactions to the surroundings. "As you'll no doubt see for yourself in a moment, some walls were ripped out in order to make one big working area. It's the only thing left on this floor—that and the kitchen. Won't you step in?"

Ahead lay a large room inadequately lit by another unadorned light bulb. Guiltily Domini remembered the one she had thoughtlessly left burning in the bedroom on the third floor, but the look of harsh pride on Sander's face prevented her from mentioning it. Unnaturally silent, she walked through the door and came to a halt.

The space Domini saw was Spartan in the extreme but by no means empty. As Sander had forewarned, the wall was scarred with raw plaster and open studs where partitions had at some point been ripped out to create one large room. There was no carpet. In the air was the smell of raw wood shavings, although the bare floor had been swept spotlessly clean. With different furnishings and better light, it might have qualified as a studio, but that name would have been far too pretentious for what Domini saw. Most of the room was taken up with the tools of carpentry and woodworking—two workbenches neatly fitted with a range of implements such as planes, chisels, screwdrivers, brace and bit, various clamps and vises, and neat rows of nails and screws in empty jam jars. There were no power tools that she could see. A collection of various kinds of saws hung on one wall in an orderly progression, largest to smallest, as if they always hung that way when not in use. On the shelves that lined another wall were assorted pieces of raw lumber, evidently stacked according to size and category. Domini had the strong impression that not a thing was out of place.

Had Sander taken to wood sculpture of some sort? For a blind man it would be somewhat easier than granite or marble, his former materials of choice. With the evidence of the unicorn, it seemed a likely guess.

"Won't you sit down?" Sander offered, indicating an area where four painted chairs in wretched condition were gathered around a large table covered in shabby old-fashioned oilcloth. Beyond the grouping lay a door that led to a darkened room, the kitchen Domini presumed, judging by the worn linoleum faintly visible in the angle of the doorway.

"Thank you," she accepted, chilled at the various evidences of extreme poverty. Depositing her coat and purse on one of the chairs and herself on another, she looked at Sander, expecting him to sit too. He remained standing, his head erect and his expression not particularly encouraging. Politeness demanded that she make some remark instead of sitting in total silence, and so Domini controlled her wayward feelings enough to say, "May I see some of your work? I love the unicorn so much."

"I agreed to your terms, by the way," he remarked abruptly. Then he gestured toward a wall behind Domini, not in her line of vision. "The rest of my output is over there."

Domini turned to some shelves she had not noted before. At once she saw that there was finished work on the shelves and that it was not work that should be done by a sculptor of power and potential, and because she could not bear to think of any gifted person being brought so low, the tears came stingingly to her eyes.

What she saw was toys. Simple toys. She remembered now that she had seen similar toys at the back of the gallery but had paid them no attention. Most of them were wooden building blocks of assorted sizes, but there were also tidy piles of other things: squat-legged pegboards fitted with big round pegs and toy hammers, balancing toys, several wooden weathervanes, a simple solid dollhouse. There were also the parts of what appeared to be a very plain wooden locomotive together with a pile of grooved wooden track. All were sanded and varnished in natural wood, with changes of color and grain afforded only by the choice of raw material.

They were the kind of handmade toys that had become relatively rare since the advent of plastic, mainly because few workers could be induced to produce such things for the pittance to be earned. Such toys cost the buyer a comparative fortune, but for the artisan they produced very little, probably not even the minimum wage, considering the time and care involved in the making.

With wet eyes and fingers pressed to her trembling mouth to hold back the words she wanted to say, she turned to look at Sander's shuttered face, at the bitter pride of it, the forbidding lines of denial and pain. Life had exacted a terrible price for him. How could one hate a man who had suffered so?

"Well, have you seen?" he asked, his voice edged with an acid self-mockery. "Do you approve?"

"They're . . . nice," Domini said jerkily.

"Your enthusiasm is overwhelming," he returned with heavy sarcasm.

Domini rallied, realizing that she could not allow herself any more emotional displays. There had been far too many already, and her feelings would simply have to be put into cold storage until later, when she was safely at home. If the years had taught her nothing else, they had taught her to curb her emotions and her tongue in public. She took a breath, closed her eyes briefly in a silent prayer for strength, and said in a perfectly level voice, "I like them very much indeed. It's just that I think you're capable of far more. I've seen the unicorn, remember."

"A copy," he said, his tone derogatory.

"That's so," Domini said slowly. "But when your sister was chatting about it earlier, she referred to you as an artist, not an artisan. Aren't you a sculptor?"

"I'm a carpenter."

"A man would have to be far more than a carpenter to make that copy, especially if he were blind. It's very good."

"I'm a carpenter," he repeated bluntly.

"Were you ever a sculptor?"

His long silence ended in a terse "Once."

"When was that?"

"Too long ago to remember," he said discouragingly.

Domini pressed on with questions to which she knew the answers, realizing she could not ask for details about Sander's past few years without establishing some basis of knowledge as a foundation for her interest. Gradually, and only by sheer doggedness, she managed to drag several grudgingly admitted facts into the open: that he had once been sighted, that he had worked in Paris, that he had worked in stone, that he had been in New York for only a few months less than Domini herself had been. And that he had never had any operation that might restore his vision.

Heart in her throat because of his dampening manner, Domini braved, "Why not?"

His lips drew back in exasperation, briefly baring clenched teeth. "Is that any of your concern?" he returned with outright rudeness.

Domini knew it sounded like idle prying, but she couldn't help continuing. "Isn't your condition operable?"

He remained silent, putting a wall around himself, his nostrils flaring with deep resentment.

"I mean, if there's anything that could be done to help you, it should be done," Domini went on, personal interest adding an urgent tone to her persuasions. "I wish there were some way to—"

"Help me? Do you think I want your help—yours or anyone's?"

Domini took a moment to answer. "I don't suppose you do," she said quietly. "But everyone needs help sometimes."

"I want none," he grated. His face had become a cruel mask, his mouth insolent, his eyes harsh with shadows caused by more than the uncertain lighting in the room. "And why such avid interest? Are you one of those women who feeds on freaks? To whom a handicap is an aphrodisiac? There are some like that." He paused partway through his sneering condemnation and added with brutal intent, "No, I think you have no particular interest in men. You were too prudishly nervous at finding yourself in my bed. Besides, your old-maid hairdo suggests as much. I felt it, you know, when I took your sweater off. Just as I felt your breasts."

He intended to shock her, of course, to hurt her in retaliation for her prying. Domini gazed at him, aching inside for the man Sander Williams had become. She knew to her own sorrow that that streak of cruelty had always been there, but it had not always been so marked. And there had been another side to him then—the man who had tried, at one point, to be kind while discouraging a lovesick teenager. Four years ago there had been good and bad in Sander Williams, and she had suffered at the hands of the bad and hated him for it. But she could not hate him now, no matter what deliberate unkindnesses he inflicted.

"Perhaps you judged me on the wrong evidence," she said levelly. "You're aware that your sister is picking up my daughter. Are you also aware that I've never been married?"

"No doubt your fiancé didn't like the sample," he cut back insultingly.

"Actually I wouldn't have married the man if he'd asked. Now are you so sure of your conclusions?"

That earned no particular easing of the unfriendly expression on his face, but it did put an end to that particular topic of conversation. "Is the day care center some distance away?" he asked curtly. "Miranda's been gone a long time."

Domini glanced at her wristwatch, marveling that she herself had not noticed how late it had become. Instantly worry creased her brow. "Well, they are taking quite a while," she agreed with alarm. "Oh, dear. I wonder if I should try to find out what's going on. May I please use your phone?"

There was perceptible hesitation before Sander said gruffly, "The gallery phone wasn't used much, so it was taken out last month. There's a pay phone in the restaurant across the street. You can make your call from there."

No telephone. Of course, she should have known. Domini stood at once and started to shrug her way into her fur-lined coat. "If Tasey turns up, tell her I'll be right back. And please, don't encourage her to think we're staying for supper. I have a stew at home, and—"

"Tell her that yourself," Sander interrupted. "Miranda just brought her in the door."

Domini's ears went instantly alert, but several seconds passed before she heard the sounds that Sander's sharper senses had detected. And then they came to her: Miranda's footsteps on the stairs, along with something else—the impatient clatter of a child's boots.

"Where is mummy? Where *is* she?"

Tasey erupted through the door, a small cyclone of energy undiminished by the planned activities of the excellent day care center she attended. Excitement lit her eyes, dark blue like Domini's, and snow dusted her flyaway hair, dark and vital like Sander's. A trail of powdery white, like a small blizzard, marked her passage across the room. She flung herself bodily into Domini's arms.

Domini picked her daughter up, lifting her high to administer the hug that always attended reunions, even daily ones. Normally, because Tasey's weight was growing too great for such displays, she would have put her back on the floor at once. But this time Domini hung on.

"Put me down, Mummy! I'm not a baby now!" Tasey sounded indignant. "I have to take off my coat!"

"Not now, poppet," Domini said. She adjusted the wriggling burden to rest on one hip and smiled at Miranda, who was standing in the doorway beaming, looking neither exhausted nor bemused as most people did after a bout with Tasey. "The lady has been very kind, and I want you to thank her nicely. But we have to get home now. We can't—"

"But we're staying for supper! She promised!"

Domini slung her purse over her free shoulder and aimed for the door at once, not wanting to linger so long that she would have to introduce Sander to his daughter. In fact, she thought she couldn't bear even one more minute with both of them in the same room. She could drop by tomorrow and thank Miranda properly, and perhaps speak more to Sander, too, after she'd had time to think. "Not this time, Tasey. We have to—"

"But she bought ice cream!" Tasey proclaimed, gyrating with such efficiency that Domini was hard pressed not to drop her altogether. It was like having an electric eel in her arms. "She asked me what I wanted and I told her! Fried chicken and cake and *ice cream!* And she bought chocolate sauce too!"

Too late Domini saw the parcels in Miranda's arms. Her headlong progress came to a sudden halt as she was struck by the awful realization that now there was no way to leave gracefully. Slowly she let her daughter slide down to the floor, keeping a firm grip on the small mittened fingers so that Tasey couldn't explode into action until she'd been given a few ground rules.

Domini's eyes went up to meet Miranda's. "It's very good of you," she said evenly. "Of course we'll stay."

How could she not, after the sacrifice that must have been made to put that ice cream on the table?

"Mummy, look!" came a small imperative voice as Tasey squirmed free, leaving only an empty mitten in Domini's hand. With the supper plans assured, her will-o'-the-wisp attention had turned to other things, and already she was dancing circles in a fever of excitement, deciding what she would make a dive for first.

"Look! Tools and saws and hammers and nails . . . and, and . . . lots of toys and—" She halted suddenly, her sturdy little legs coming to a rare standstill as she noticed Sander for the very first time. "Mummy, who's the man with the funny eyes?"

Chapter Five

"Oh, Lord, what am I going to *do* about him?"
Domini whispered to a flocked pink milliner's head she
was about to decorate with pink and white daisies. A
week had passed; Christmas had come and gone; the
unicorn had been given to Tasey. That, at least, had
been a success, making the occasion every bit as
magical as Domini had hoped, even though the only
other presents under the tree had been homemade, and
very simple ones at that.

Cross-legged on the built-in seat beside a big arched
window, and surrounded by the clutter of her work, she
was more preoccupied with thinking of Sander than
with the mannequin before her, which was intended for
a small display case showing spring fashion accessories.
Although the stores would start pushing spring almost
as soon as the holiday season was over, the head wasn't
really needed for a while. Most of the morning she had
been gazing out the window with troubled eyes, thanking her stars that most of her clients wanted no change

of window display until after the New Year. The few that had been requested had been done; the last of the large papier-mâché constructions required for January had been constructed. During the week she had refused all dates, partly to save baby-sitting money but mostly in order to devote the evenings to work. It had been hard slogging, but the next two days were free. She had freed the days because she knew she had to do something about Sander, although she still hadn't decided what.

The events of the previous week still troubled her greatly. The blindness, the poverty, the pride; all these things were seared into her consciousness. Before Christmas, Domini had dropped a small package off at the gallery by way of thanks for Miranda's good-heartedness, but she had not asked to see Sander because she could think of nothing to see him about. She could hardly tell him that she had made a resolution to help him, not only because he was sure to be angered by that, but because she didn't know what form her help was going to take.

"Why his *eyes?*" Domini muttered, taking one of the daisies from her lap. She stuck a long pin through it and jabbed it onto the faceless milliner's head, not as the first flower of a petaled wig as she had intended, but in the exact place where an eye would be. It stared back at her solemnly, the white petals like lashes around the soft pink center.

The supper a week before had been a disaster. As to Tasey's opener about Sander, Domini was still trying to remind herself that it had been a perfectly innocuous remark, not meant the way it sounded. At the time, Domini, in deep mortification, had turned toward Sander and seen the distinctive quicksilver sheen, particularly emphasized because at that moment he happened to be standing directly under the one source of light in the room. She had saved the situation as best she could. "That's Mr. Williams, Tasey. Don't you wish you had silver eyes too?" Oh, why was it that young children always managed to hit on the exact words that made you want to sink right through the floor?

It had not been an auspicious beginning, and the evening had gone rapidly downhill after that. Tasey had exploded in all directions. Normally it wasn't impossible to keep some kind of rein on her, but perhaps that night she had been infected by Domini's state of mind. Her inner turmoil had been adequately hidden from the adults, Domini was sure, but children had a way of sensing those things and taking advantage. Eventually, with a grim mouth, Sander had left the room.

And naturally, about that point, Tasey had begun to behave a little less like a human cannonball. In fact, a short time later she'd climbed into Domini's arms, yawned, transferred some remains of chocolate syrup from her mouth onto Domini's sweater, rubbed her eyes, and settled in for a sleepy cuddle. By then Domini could have gone home but she hadn't, wanting the opportunity to talk to Miranda without Sander present. And indeed she had managed to glean some information, an easy enough matter because the march of events had quickened the making of a new friendship. Domini asked if there were any photographs of the sculptures Sander had once done. A number were produced, and after that it was easy. Normally Miranda might have tried to put a good face on things, but Domini had seen the upstairs and there was little use pretending. Besides, Miranda was as anxious to share her concerns about her brother as Domini was to hear them.

She had been appalled to learn that Sander's condition was irreversible. Any hope that had been held out in France had been dashed in Germany years before. After countless X rays and consultations, the specialists had finally detected a telltale paling of the optic disc. It confirmed what they had privately suspected: that a fracture of the bone had severed both optic nerves.

Shortly after the grim diagnosis Miranda had traveled to Europe to escort her brother back to the United States. They had spent a number of days at the pension, sorting and settling his affairs in Paris. It was during this period, Domini concluded, that Sander had received her call and lulled her with his lies.

With careful questioning, she elicited the information that the Williams's family background was indeed one of extreme poverty. The father, a brilliant self-employed chemist, had died in a lab explosion while still quite young. He had left crushing debts, no insurance, and a widow whose fierce pride had led her to work herself to an early grave trying to settle old obligations, while raising two children as best she could. Following her example rather than losing themselves in the seedy neighborhood where they lived, Sander and Miranda had both earned the money for their own education, and both had graduated from college. Operation Bootstrap, Miranda called it. She spoke eagerly of her older brother's resolve during those early days.

Domini learned other things about their present life. Occasionally Sander did some picture framing when the task was not too complex; the more ornate frames required sight and had to be done elsewhere. Most of the tools had once belonged to Miranda's husband, who had done that work in addition to running the gallery prior to his death some years before. In palmier days, when the couple had lived in a suburb of New York, the upper part of the tiny gallery had been used for storage and picture framing only; business had been much brisker then.

"I guess the Santa's Workshop show was a bad idea," Miranda had sighed at one point. "Customers who want toys just don't walk into an art gallery, and when it comes to children most of my artists simply don't have a clue. I decided to give it a try because the toy shop Sander used to supply went bankrupt—too much prestige and not enough plastic. I had to show my regular artists, of course, but I managed to slide a few sales through for him as well. All the same, there are so many unsold things sitting on his shelves . . ."

It hardly brightened the horror picture growing in Domini's mind. At the time, she had refrained from remarking that Sander might have been better served if some effort had been made to place his output in a proper toy shop before Christmas and that Miranda might have been better served by putting on a decent show for herself.

"She was only trying to help," Domini told the milliner's head. Its one solemn eye looked unblinkingly back at her, offering no solutions. Helping other people, Domini had long since decided, must be one of Miranda's missions in life. A laudable aim; why did it so often backfire?

And after all, wasn't that what she herself was trying to do? Help Sander. On her limited budget she could not help him much financially, as she once had done. Things would be quite tight enough with payments still to be made on the unicorn. Domini spared a glance for it now. It occupied pride of place in the center of the room, the one spot that remained clear of the stored display props Tasey had been taught not to touch. Well, nearly taught.

Domini's living quarters were as cheery as Sander's were dismal. Piles of big puffy cushions served for the furniture she had not been able to afford. The walls were off-white, partly because Domini had decided there was more than enough color in the vivid, whimsical creations of her craft, but also because light bounced off white, and Domini liked light as well as needing it for her work. Gay colors were everywhere, even on the exposed water pipes, which had been painted like barber poles in bright pink and white stripes in order to take advantage of something that could not possibly be concealed. The whole loft was working space except the tiny kitchen, the bathroom, and one screened alcove big enough for two single beds. Domini had fixed it up herself, having had quite enough of dreary rooms during her early days in New York. It occurred to her briefly that given a free hand and some paint, she could do quite a lot to brighten up Sander's living quarters too. . . .

But what good would that do when he couldn't see? And anyway, what he needed was money. *Money*. Domini was certain that if she had the wherewithal, she would be able to find some way to get it into Sander's hands without his knowing, just as she had done once before. Unwillingly she spared a moment to think about the real unicorn, the original, and what she could have done with the money from its sale. Three hundred thousand dollars! The rocking horse had been *hers*, a gift, and the money should have been hers too!

But that thought only caused a bitter gall to rise in her throat, and she thrust it away determinedly. She'd never ask Papa for help now. "Learn to help yourself," he had said to her once, on the occasion when he had refused her request for a large amount of money. She'd been doing that ever since, and she intended to do it now.

"Learn to help yourself," she said sternly to the milliner's head with its one cockeyed daisy. The daisy looked grand, she decided with the professional part of her mind, much better than a floral wig would have done. Perhaps she'd place a few white petals like a lowered eyelash where the other eye should be. And from her sign painter she could order a showcard that read "Eye-openers for Spring" or some such thing.

Help yourself. . . .

The idea started to tingle through her, and suddenly she was on her feet, the lapful of daisies spilling everywhere. Domini laughed out loud. Of course! Why hadn't it occurred to her before? She could help Sander very little as far as money was concerned, but maybe she could help him to help himself. Maybe his pride would permit that much. It was certainly worth a try!

Before she raced for the telephone, which she kept

under a business listing, she spared a few more joyous words for the milliner's head on the window seat. "If you want another eye," she declared with a grandiloquent gesture at the haphazardly strewn daisies, "there it is. Help yourself!"

"What on earth . . . ?" Miranda asked in amazement a short time later as Domini trundled the first of two big round tubs through the doorway of the little gallery. As the tubs were extremely heavy, she had called a taxi for the short trip, a small expense but a necessary one.

"Some things for your brother," Domini explained. "Wait till I get them through the door and then I'll tell you all about it."

There was a man in the gallery with Miranda and he offered at once to help, going out to fetch the second tub, which had been left sitting on the sidewalk. Miranda stood at the door and watched, ready to hold it open for him.

Domini took off her coat as soon as she had deposited her load. Breathless and flushed from the exertion, with the sparkle of good health and excitement in her eyes, she looked younger today, an impression heightened by her plaster-smattered jeans and cotton shirt, working clothes worn except when on active duty dressing someone's window. Her hair, too, contributed to the appearance of youth. As she had dashed over directly from her loft, taking no time to change, it was merely swept back and secured at her nape with a big barette.

"Thanks for the Christmas present," Miranda said as she waited at the door. "Homemade carrot pudding! It was such a treat."

"A turkey might have been more appropriate," Domini smiled, "after the way you took Tasey and me under your wing."

She didn't mention that she had considered the idea of just such a gesture and discarded it as being too obvious. Turkey probably hadn't been on the menu in this house, but to present one would have been to point up matters best left to silence and pride.

The second tub came in, and when the man had placed it beside the first, Miranda introduced him as Joel Stevens. He had a warm smile, graying temples, and nice brown eyes.

"Joel owns the restaurant across the street," Miranda said. Domini noticed that Sander's sister was wearing the same black wool dress, carefully brushed and pressed, that she had been wearing a week before. And yet she looked different . . . why? Then Domini noted the faint traces of color in Miranda's cheeks, the tiny signs of animation in her face, the sidelong way she was looking at Joel. A budding romance perhaps?

"It's such a wonderful restaurant," Miranda enthused. "Great French cuisine. At least, it's been great since Joel bought the place a few months ago. He invited us there for Christmas dinner . . . now don't feel badly about your carrot pudding, Domini, because it was put to very good use. Instead of eating dessert in the restaurant, we all came over here." She angled a swift, grateful glance at her generous friend. Domini felt grateful to him too.

"All of us means Sander, me, Joel, and his two young sons," Miranda explained, giving Domini some more food for thought. Surely Joel must be divorced, or a widower? "So you see, your pudding fed five."

"Better than anything I had on the menu," claimed Joel, grinning. "I haven't tasted carrot pudding since I was a boy. When Miranda heard that, she insisted."

"What have you brought for Sander?" Miranda asked, turning curiously to the tubs.

"Clay," Domini said. "I was clearing out my loft and I happened to find it. I bought a supply the year I started in business, when I didn't know what I was doing. It's a rotten material for my kind of work. Too heavy."

Well, most of that was the truth, Domini reflected, although she had known exactly where to put her fingers on the clay, once the idea had hit her. A premixed clay, it had been in the two large plastic tubs where she had stored it in order to prevent its drying out.

"It occurred to me that your brother might be able to use it for sculpture," she went on, hoping Sander was going to be as receptive as Miranda appeared to be, judging by her expression. "He hasn't lost his sense of touch, after all. But working with a hammer and chisel, even with wood . . . well, it's very hard to feel your way with that. He would have to stop at every blow to discover what he's done. Do you mind if I take these up to him?"

"Why, I . . . what a wonderful idea!" Miranda's face was radiant.

"I'll take them up to him," Joel offered. "I can spare another few minutes away from the groaning board."

"Well, perhaps if you could carry one just to the top of the stairs," Domini agreed, bending down to hoist one of the weighty tubs into her arms. "I'd like to surprise him. Is he in his workshop?"

"Er . . . I'm not sure," Miranda said. "There's not much point in him making more toys, is there, until the ones he has are gone. That's why the clay is such a marvelous idea! But no matter where he is he'll hear you coming anyway, and he'll know it's not me on the stairs. He has the hearing of a jungle animal."

Sixty seconds later Domini was at the door of the workshop, the two heavy containers of clay at her feet. She rapped and received no answer and in the next few moments came to the conclusion that Sander must be resting in his bedroom. But then she heard the creak of stairs and saw bare feet and bare calves begin the descent from the third floor.

He came to a halt halfway down the stairs, where all of him was in view. He was wearing a well-worn navy bathrobe, and it took no leap of logic to determine that he had been in the shower or the bath upon interruption. His hair was still damp, gleaming darkly against the whiteness of the terry towel that was slung around his shoulders.

"Who's there?" he asked, his head inclined slightly as if listening for the sound of her breathing.

"Domini Greey."

His mouth tightened perceptibly, as though he didn't particularly like that piece of information. "I take it you must be looking for me."

"Yes, I am," said Domini.

"Then it must be bad news," Sander observed, his expression less than welcoming.

Domini's disbelieving little laugh held a faint tremor. "Why on earth do you say that?"

"Let me guess," he drawled in a derisive tone. "You want me to mend something. Has that holy terror daughter of yours broken the rocking horse so soon?"

"She's not that destructive," Domini retorted, an instinctive defense. She bit back the impulse to tell him that Tasey was his daughter too. "She didn't break anything the other night, did she? If so I'll be glad to pay."

"No, but she very nearly did," he came back tightly. "I'm still nursing the bruises from the fall I took. Haven't you ever taught your child to put things back in the right place?"

"Why, I . . . yes, I have," Domini said, dismayed. She tried to think what might have been left on the floor the other night. Most of the things had been returned to their niches with a little prompting—somewhat messily perhaps, but Domini was sure nothing had been left seriously out of place. Aware of the hazards such things held for a blind person, she had given the floor a quick visual check while saying good night to Miranda.

"I'm sorry," she said helplessly, knowing there must have been something. "I was sure all the toys had been put back in their pigeonholes."

Sander heaved a sigh and his expression eased marginally. "It wasn't a toy," he admitted wryly, using one edge of the towel to wipe some stubborn drops of water out of his ear. "It was a chair. I think your daughter must have used it to stand on while she was looking over the shelves. Actually Miranda should have noticed." He paused and then asked gruffly, "How does she like the unicorn?"

"She adores it, and so do I. I'm tempted to climb on myself!" Domini's light laugh was intended to break the indefinable tension that ran like a current between herself and Sander. Because he was standing at a higher level, directly above her on the sagging stairway, she remained very conscious of his bare calves, of the dusting of dark body hair over hard firm flesh. Knowing there was more of that bare flesh beneath the bathrobe, remembering how it looked and how it had felt against hers, did nothing for her peace of mind.

"Why are you here?"

"I've brought you something," Domini said and then repeated the lie about clearing out her loft. She didn't as yet tell him what she had brought, because she didn't want to be told to take the clay away. She had the strong impression that for Sander the very thought of sculpture was painful; if given the choice he would refuse to try his hand at it altogether. Certainly, in claiming to be a carpenter the other night, he had denied that creative part of himself. It had surfaced in the unicorn, but it was possible that he had permitted himself a lapse because that particular piece could be classified as a toy.

"I'm not telling you what it is," she said. "You'll have to come down and guess by the feel. Actually I'm curious to see if you can." She was sure he could because clay had a distinctive earthy smell, but she hoped the challenge would prick his pride. And once he had sunk his fingers into the medium, perhaps the sculptor in him would take over.

He hesitated for no more than an instant. "Whatever it is, take it on into my workshop, then. I'll be down in a moment."

He turned back up the stairs, to dress, Domini assumed. She opened the door to the workshop and rolled the first tub in, the task made easier because she didn't try to lift it. By daylight the room was brighter, and she soon spotted a good resting place against one wall, relatively removed from the natural flow of traffic.

She was still in the process of rolling the second tub through the door when, to her surprise, she heard someone behind her. She turned and saw that he had descended in the bathrobe and was standing dangerously close. He waited, hands thrust deep in his pockets and a sardonic amusement twisting his lips, until she had finished transporting the burden.

While she was still dusting off her hands, he closed the door and leaned against it. "Shall I guess now?" he asked dryly. "Or would you prefer me to do the feeling first?"

There was something unsettling in his voice, a strong undercurrent of mockery or sarcasm that Domini could not quite put her finger on. And the curl of his mouth was decidedly unnerving.

"I won't allow you to guess yet," she said hurriedly because she had the strange premonition that that was exactly what he was going to do. Impossible, of course —with the tubs closed the stuff couldn't even be smelled. And she didn't intend to open anything until his hand was poised to plunge in. "Would you mind coming over here?"

"Ah," he said sardonically. "So I'm to do the feeling first."

He sank to his haunches beside her, his closeness as disquieting as Domini had known it would be. But then, he had always affected her that way, and dealing with those wayward sensations was one of the conditions of helping him. And the bathrobe, though suggestive to her sensibilities, covered him perfectly well. Instead of drawing back, she gripped one of his wrists, held it above a tub, and said, "Keep your hand there and wait until I give you the word."

"And when you do, I dig in at once," he stated mockingly.

"Why . . . yes," Domini said, a trifle uncertainly because that streak of derisiveness had become even stronger. She left his hand poised in the air and hurriedly reached for the lid of the tub, intending to pry it open.

"Clay," he said.

Domini's fingers froze over the undone task. She looked at him and stared. "How did you . . . ?"

"Do you think I have no powers of reason? First, you told me it was something stored in your loft, something you had found impractical in your particular line of business. I'm well aware what you do for a living—it came up for discussion the other night. So what will it be? A bolt of tulle, a roll of chicken wire, a container of glitter dust? I think not. Then I hear you start to roll something through the door. Too heavy, then, for easy lifting, and it comes in a large circular container of some kind. A big can of paint? Hardly. A tub of dry plaster of Paris? Possible, but I don't think so, because you must use that all the time to make your papier-mâché constructions. And if I needed more clues, I need only remember your intense curiosity about my former . . . calling."

The scorn on his face had been joined by strong evidence of anger. His jaw was tightened, his mouth antagonistic, his dark eyes narrowed and trained on Domini, but with the marginal misdirection of a man who could not see. The effect was unsettling, giving the impression that he was looking right through her.

"You're too clever," she said unevenly.

"And no doubt you thought it was you being clever," he taunted. "You intended me to sink my fingers in, thinking the feel of the clay would fan some dead spark back to life. Did you think I wouldn't resent your ruse? As soon as I understood what you were about, I decided there was no point prolonging this charade.

That's why I came back down the stairs at once. Now take your gift and get out."

Domini remained kneeling on the floor but straightened, bringing her face nearly to a level with his. "No," she said evenly. "I won't go, and I certainly won't take the clay. It's a good medium for sculpture and a good medium for a blind man. Shall I do some guesswork too? You're afraid to feel it. Afraid to work with it. Afraid you might learn that you've lost your talent along with your sight!"

In his strong jaw the anger was evident briefly, only to be followed by a control that was almost frightening in its intensity. A cold pride had taken possession of his face, hooding the eyes and emphasizing the autocratic flare of his nostrils. His hand shot out and caught Domini by one shoulder, the fingers uncompromising in their hardness.

"Very well," he said with studied insolence. "You refuse to leave until I feel something? Then feel something I will. Stay still."

His tone warned her if nothing else did. As if he had told her his intent, she knew what he was going to do even before he lifted his free hand. His words on that previous occasion had given her evidence enough that he resented interference, that he would parry it by inflicting deliberate cruelties if he must. And she knew he would not feel her face because there was no real humiliation in that, nothing to make her cry out in shock, to rise and run.

All the same, when his hand began to take its liberties she was hard pressed not to leap to her feet. He cupped one breast deliberately, his palm and his long fingers covering it completely while his other hand compelled her to stay still. Domini froze, knowing full well that he was trying to drive her into fighting free and fleeing. And that she would not do.

When his effrontery brought no instant cry of outrage, he began to fondle the curves through the cotton of her shirt, an open derision growing on his face. Domini closed her eyes, bit her lip hard, and reminded herself that in the course she had chosen for herself, all was sufferable. Surely he would stop when he realized his presumption was not having the desired effect?

"Is it my turn to play the guessing game again?" he mocked when she failed to register an immediate protest. "Shall I go through what I detect about this . . . shall we say, mystery I'm feeling? First, she's wearing no brassiere. Nor was she wearing one the other day. I ask myself—is she proud of her breasts or is she simply brazen? Is she anxious to attract sexual attention?"

"I don't actually need a brassiere," Domini returned with as much control as possible. She hated the way he was trying to demean her, but she knew if she failed to outlast this difficult moment the clay was sure to go wasting. And so she submitted with what dignity she could muster. "I don't buy things I don't need," she added, knowing he would understand that particular kind of motivation. And perhaps he did, but it did nothing to stop his cold-blooded manipulation of her flesh.

"She doesn't shrink from a stranger's touch," he went on without pause, his use of the impersonal pronoun an intentional insult, an attempt to further degrade Domini. "She accepts it without question. In fact, I think she must like it."

Suddenly Domini was choked with remembrance of another time when he had felt her desire and then satisfied his own. "Please don't," she breathed.

"If she doesn't like it," he murmured cruelly, "I wonder why she submits? If she tried to run away, I certainly wouldn't stop her."

"I'm staying because I want you to try the clay," Domini reminded him in a low voice. The molding of a nipple was beginning to have an effect that must have been detectable through the cloth, and much as she tried to force her body into quiescence, it would not obey. "If I race off in indignation, you'll never try it at all, will you?"

He laughed harshly. "No," he conceded, releasing his grip on her shoulder. His other hand remained on her breast, temporarily stilled but by no means withdrawn. "I see you understand my purpose very well. Perhaps you have some wit in your head after all."

Freed from the fingers that had kept her pressed into stillness, Domini sank back on her heels, breaking contact only momentarily. Sander merely adjusted his position to come closer to her and restaked his claim with a small ruthless smile. He was leaning forward, and the lapels of the dark dressing gown fell away to reveal the muscular sculpture of his chest. It was as powerful as before, but paled by lack of exposure to sun, so that the mat of short black hairs appeared darker, each more crisply defined than in Domini's memory.

"I know perfectly well what you're trying to do," Domini said in a strained voice. "You're trying to humiliate me. Well, I refuse to be humiliated. Now will you please remove your hand from my breast?"

"Will you please remove yourself from my house?" he countered as his palm began its erotic movements once again, the fingers caressing the curve, the rough thumb stroking the nipple. "It must be clear to you that I have an intense dislike for your interference. If you insist on intruding, so shall I. If you don't like what I'm doing, I suggest you leave at once. The choice, my friend, is yours."

"I'll leave when you agree to try the clay," she said, maintaining control with difficulty. What did it really matter if he felt what had already been his?

"Is this the kind of woman you are?" he murmured. "A woman who can be aroused by any man? I wonder . . ."

And now his other hand moved. For a breathless moment Domini thought he intended to undo the buttons of her shirt and insinuate his fingers more intimately, to test the truth of what he must have discerned through the cloth. But the brief alarm passed as his hand rose higher to her face. He brushed her mouth lightly, the fingers roughened by carpentry passing fleetingly over the soft surfaces to read what was there. A strange emotion crossed his features, replacing scorn.

"Extraordinary," he breathed, just as he had breathed many years before.

Had he guessed? Domini's heart seemed to stop for several seconds as his other hand rose slowly from its intimate lodging place to join in the exploration of her face. But there was no recognition in his expression, only puzzlement.

While he read her features, she scarcely dared to breathe for fear he might hold some memory of the shape and substance of the girl he had known so briefly long ago. It was hard to believe he would. In his anger he had taken no time to discover the planes of her face, as a lover might have done. Moreover, since then her breasts had ripened to more womanly contours, and the length of her hair had changed. Those things would tend to mislead him.

His hands moved to her nose, to her cheeks, to her eyes. She closed her lids beneath the gentle probing, the soft stroking movements of the abrasive but sensitive fingerpads that must serve him instead of sight. He touched the lobes of her ears, the curve of her jaw, the soft hollows of her throat. No part of her face was spared; each was subjected to the feather-light exploration. For Domini, it was more difficult to bear than the insolent handling of her breast had been.

His hands at her temples discovered the unruly tendrils that so often defied capture, and then traveled to find the clip that held her long hair in place. He removed it and ran his fingers through the freed mass, sliding through the spilling tumble to test its texture, its weight, its length.

At last he removed his hands and said gruffly, "I think you must be a very beautiful woman."

Domini was still searching his face to see if some spark of the past had been ignited in his mind. But his features had become closed, enigmatic, telling her nothing at all. Almost at once he stood up and moved a small distance away. With his back turned to her he said tonelessly, "You astonish me. I didn't realize you were so upset until I felt your mouth."

So that was what had caused his surprise. Relief radiated through Domini, causing a relaxation of the tense lines that had formed on her face. She listened while he went on.

"Until then, I was going on other evidence—including what you said the other day about the father of your child. I thought you were beginning to . . . enjoy what I was doing. I didn't realize your nerves were tied up in knots."

Had he felt so much in her features? Domini touched a hand wonderingly to a cheek still sensitized from the passage of his fingers, unhappy to think that her face had given away so much of her inner distress.

"If you found it so very distasteful, you should have stopped me at the start. It would have been easy enough; all you had to do was get up and leave. If you'd started to struggle free, I'd most certainly have let you go. Why on earth would you allow a total stranger such liberties?"

Domini looked at her lap to see that her hands were still shaking in the aftermath of his touch. "It wasn't all that difficult," she lied. "There was a layer of cloth between us."

"Ah," he remarked dryly, "so that was to be your limit. Even so, it astounds me that you allowed yourself to be handled in that manner."

Domini shifted her jeans-clad legs to a new angle, no longer kneeling but sitting with her elbows propped on her knees. Relieved that she had survived two tests, one of mortification and one of recognition, she felt more confident now. "I told you," she said with some return of spirit, "I refuse to be frightened off until you agree to try the clay."

"Did Miranda put you up to this?" he asked tersely. "I can think of no other reason for you to take such abnormal interest in the affairs of someone you hardly know."

"Miranda had nothing to do with it, beyond mentioning that you were a very promising sculptor before you lost your sight, and showing me photographs of work you did some years ago. The clay is my own idea, and not a bad one, I think."

"A do-gooder," he said disparagingly. "Well, please take your good intentions and leave. I don't need your help."

"I'm not offering it," Domini said flatly. "If you have half the talent I think you have, there's no reason you need my help. I'm suggesting you help yourself. I think it's time you—"

"What in God's name do you think I've been doing for all these years?" he snarled, turning to face her with a furious lift of one arm toward the toy shelves. Domini glanced at them long enough to note that they had been restored to total order, each kind of toy in its own pigeonhole, the blocks impeccably piled once again. The habits of a blind man, Domini reflected passingly; such tasks must help to fill the empty spaces in his life.

"—time you used your talent again," Domini finished, keeping her voice temperate despite the towering wall of anger confronting her. "I know you must make toys; they're your livelihood. But you've got a good stock on your shelves, and until you find someone to handle them there's no point making more. Surely you could spare some hours each day to—"

"You're invading my privacy unforgivably," he cut in. He was shaking with fury, his whole stance tense with suppressed emotion, his hands clenched angrily at his sides.

Domini came to her feet and faced him squarely, knowing she must make a final bid before he threw her out bodily, which he seemed quite ready to do. "And you invaded mine, very nastily too," she returned bluntly. "As you yourself noted, I didn't like your wandering hands at all. In fact, I thought you were boorish, insolent, and sadistic. I think you owe me something in return."

"Do I?" he returned tightly with an arrogant flare to his nostrils. He moved threateningly closer, within inches of Domini. With apparent difficulty, he prevented himself from closing the gap; at the very last minute he jammed his hands into his pockets again, as if to prevent them from taking some measure he might regret.

"Do I . . . ?" he repeated. Perhaps she should have been warned by the brief sheen in his eyes, like silver swords catching some indeterminate source of light. But instead she listened to his words, the most moderate she had heard for some time.

"Perhaps I do owe you something," he agreed slowly. The passing brilliance had left his pupils and they were dark again, reflecting nothing. His voice was unrevealing too. "What you ask of me is a damn impertinence. However, I'm prepared to try the clay if . . ."

The space of silence was deliberate, leaving the "if" hanging in the air to punctuate the rest of his sentence. During the pause his lids drooped so studiedly that if Domini had not known of his blindness she would have sworn his gaze was caressing the length of her body.

"If you're prepared to model for me," he drawled. "I need a life model."

If Domini had any doubts that he meant in the nude, they were dispelled by the return of derision to his voice and of arrogance to his mouth. With her recent reactions to guide him, no doubt he was certain she would refuse, and that would put an end to the matter. And indeed, Domini's first reaction was emphatically negative. Her pulse began to pound at an alarming rate.

"I . . . couldn't," she protested through the obstacle of a heart lodged somewhere in her throat.

"Exactly," he said sardonically. "Neither could I. Now will you do me a favor and get out of my life?"

Domini forced her breathing back to normal. What Sander suggested would be very difficult for her, for reasons that had nothing to do with prudery. Sander's hands were his eyes, and the thought of giving his hands full freedom filled her with a distress beyond the telling. Moreover, there was the matter of her freelance work; finding time during the day would mean many late nights. But perhaps he had underestimated her after all.

She waited until her voice was ready and then said with a laudable lack of inflection, "Which would you prefer, mornings or afternoons?"

Chapter Six

Pot luck," Domini said into the telephone. "It's a penance for turning you down last week."

The man on the other end chuckled warmly. "And several other times too! I thought I was getting a permanent brush-off. Some payment for giving you a chance to try your hand at our displays! Of course I accept."

Domini hesitated. "I think I told you about my daughter, Tasey, the day we had lunch. I hope you like children."

"Love 'em," the man said good-naturedly. His voice lowered to a huskier, more intimate note. "Mind you, I'm a great believer in early bedtimes. My date, after all, is with you."

Moments later Domini rang off, pleased that the impromptu call had paid dividends. She liked Grant Manners, a potential client who owned a jewelry boutique, not in SoHo but on Fifth Avenue. While no competition for Van Cleef & Arpels—Grant's specialty was very "in" jewelry, rather than diamonds the size of oysters—it was an exclusive, expensive shop. Convincing Fifth Avenue that she had anything to offer was a difficult task, and Grant's boutique was the first tentative toe in the door in a planned crusade to upgrade her clientele, an impossibility prior to day-care days. In order to establish her credentials, she had offered to do the first of Grant's displays at cost, with no added fee. He had a problem window: although his merchandise was small, his display window was large. In the past the excess of space had been filled by mannequins dressed in clothes borrowed from neighboring boutiques. Domini had convinced Grant that there might be solutions that didn't call for promoting other people's merchandise.

She had not yet dressed a window for him but would be doing so in January. And part of the reason she liked Grant Manners was that he hadn't as yet changed the business end of the arrangement, although she had turned down several invitations to dinner, including two the previous week.

There was no need for Domini to examine her motives in issuing the invitation, a spur-of-the-moment action taken immediately upon returning home after her unsettling encounter with Sander. Grant Manners was an attractive man, well-to-do because of the family business he had inherited, quite as virile and good looking as Sander, and certainly far better tempered. She'd turned down the first few dates with him only because she'd wanted to establish from the first that her favors weren't dispensed as part of a package deal. Her instincts told her he wasn't the sort to use that kind of pressure; nevertheless she had intended to keep the relationship purely professional until after the first window had been done and the work assigned on a permanent basis. And at that time, she had decided, she would see.

But this was an emergency. She needed Grant Manners now; needed some form of immunity against the potent attraction exerted by the one man of all men she didn't want to be attracted to. Much as she hoped to help Sander, she was far from anxious to become involved with him in any serious way, a reservation that had nothing to do with his blindness. No longer totally blinkered by sexual attraction, as she had been in the past, she recognized his faults—the arrogance, the pride, the quickness to anger that had so blighted her youth. Those faults had been in him before and they were still in him now, multiplied a thousandfold by the embittered life he led. Why ask for trouble when he had such power to wound her?

And by agreeing to serve as his model, she was most certainly asking for trouble. Domini knew full well that if she didn't find another man, and fast, trouble was exactly what she was going to have. The afternoon's encounter with Sander had filled her with a great turmoil, a bodily restlessness she could not seem to control. She had become unbearably aware of the urges she had managed to suppress for so many years, at the very first because a small baby and lack of money for sitters had totally prevented dating, and lately because some men shunned women with small children, others became too importunate too quickly, and others were nice companions but she didn't feel any great love for them. Despite her unorthodox upbringing, Domini's experiences in Paris had long since cured her of the notion that sexual attraction alone was a sufficient basis for involvement.

The years had produced no man in whose keeping she wished to place her heart, let alone herself. But perhaps Grant Manners would be different.

As it turned out, he certainly seemed to be. Unlike most other dates Domini had invited to her loft, he was marvelous with Tasey. Throughout dinner he enchanted her by concocting a tale about a unicorn and a little princess, and after dinner he delighted her by fulfilling the function of a rocking horse with his own strong shoulders.

"Another piggyback!" Tasey squealed for the umpteenth time, her young fingers laced into Grant's light brown hair.

"Not on your life," he said firmly, slinging her off his back much to the detriment of his hair. He rose to his feet and scooped Tasey off the floor, holding her high and rubbing noses with her like an Eskimo. Tasey giggled. "Off you go to bed now, or next time I won't tell you the rest of my story. That's when the unicorn turns into a rich, handsome prince and sweeps your mummy away."

"And me too!" Tasey protested.

"Why would I sweep you away?" laughed Grant, tossing Tasey in the air much to her merriment. "*You* don't belong in a dustbin!"

Domini could quell a moment of unease only by reminding herself firmly that there was no real reason to associate Sander with the unicorn of an invented fairy tale. The rich, handsome prince was surely Grant himself. . . .

"You *will* tell me the rest?" Tasey insisted.

"Promise on my honor," Grant said, making a solemn face.

Domini took over the energetic bundle of her daughter, and within minutes Tasey had been scrubbed, brushed, and whipped out of her overalls into a flannelette nightgown. As she was being tucked into bed in the small alcove, she sighed, "I wish I had a daddy."

"I know, poppet." Domini kept her voice low because the bamboo screens didn't keep loud sounds from the main part of the room. "But you don't have one."

Tasey sighed again, more soulfully. "Then Marie told a lie," she said.

"What did Marie say?"

"She said babies can't be made without a daddy." Weariness had at last made Tasey's eyelids heavy, but even so she looked unusually pensive for this time of day. "Matthew says they just turn up under cabbage leaves. I guess Matthew's right. If I didn't come from a daddy, I must have come from a cabbage leaf. Ugh, I hate cabbage."

The day-care center, Domini decided, must be having its effect; Tasey had never broached such matters before. It was hardly a good time to be covering the facts of life, but Domini didn't want to lie. "You didn't come from cabbage at all. Marie's quite right," she said quietly.

"Then I do have a daddy?"

"Of course you did, once. I'll explain tomorrow."

"Will I ever have one again?"

"If I marry someone," said Domini.

"Are you going to marry someone?"

"I don't know, Tasey. Maybe I will someday, but I can't promise." Domini administered a final good night hug, turned off the light, and moved to the screened partition.

"Mummy," said a wistful voice, bringing her to a halt. "Do you think the unicorn will really turn into a handsome prince?"

"Why? Do you want him to?"

"No," said Tasey drowsily. "I couldn't ride him then."

"Go to sleep, darling. It's only a story. The unicorn won't change, not really," Domini assured her gently before she returned to Grant.

Three hours later, as she detached herself from Grant Manners's good night kiss, Domini was trying to tell herself that it had been the exact cure for her preoccupation with Sander Williams. If it hadn't quite recaptured the breathtaking dizziness of her very first experience, that couldn't be blamed on Grant, who had been considerate and skillful and ardent when he had gathered her into his arms. For Domini, Tasey's nearness had put a decided damper on the embrace, as it always did when she invited male admirers to her loft. Grant made it clear that he didn't consider the circumstances ideal either.

"Next time you'll need a baby sitter," he said firmly

after Domini had ushered him to the door. "I'm going to be away for two weeks on a skiing trip, but I'm taking you out the night I get back. I imagine you'll have my window done by then, and maybe we'll have reason to celebrate."

"I hope so." Domini smiled with considerable confidence. She had marvelous plans for Grant's window, plans she had not revealed; she was certain he could not fail to award her the job on a permanent basis.

"What's your favorite kind of restaurant?"

"Something with a view."

"Tourist traps," Grant scoffed.

"Maybe, but I haven't been to most of them. Besides, heights excite me."

"Then heights it will be," Grant agreed smokily as he bent for a last lingering kiss.

The magic was still elusive, despite the expertise with which he folded her into his arms. That long-ago delirium, Domini reflected ruefully as she wended her way to bed, must have had a very great deal to do with the circumstances of the moment. How could it possibly be recreated without the Eiffel Tower itself?

Sander had chosen afternoons, and the hour of two o'clock had been agreed upon, but it was only half past one when Domini arrived at the little art gallery. In her arms were more supplies taken from the stock she kept in a corner of her loft; this time a huge roll of chicken wire and some lengths of strong but bendable tubing. The materials were reasonably portable, and she hadn't needed a taxi for the trip—a small saving but an important one, because already Domini was planning for the day when she would buy Sander some additional clay. Her optimistic nature refused to contemplate the possibility that the whole venture might be a dismal failure.

"Something else for Sander?" asked Miranda as Domini came through the door and deposited her bulky burden.

"He'll need these to make an armature," Domini said. "If he's doing a large sculpture, he has to have something to build on. He can't make it out of solid clay. It would break too easily just from its own weight."

Miranda sighed and looked at the bundle askance. "I hate to tell you this, Domini, but I think you're wasting your time. Sander is dead set against trying this. In fact, he's been in a cold fury ever since yesterday. There's no way you're going to get him to do something he doesn't want to do."

"Doesn't he keep his promises?" asked Domini lightly as she removed her coat. Today her hair was carefully smoothed into its French knot, with only a few pale tendrils escaping to frame her face. She had donned navy slacks and a rib-knit gold sweater with the unsettling knowledge that she would only have to take them off. With thoughts of chilled skin as much as modesty, she had also stuffed a terrycloth bathrobe into her capacious shoulderbag. There was no point being naked more than necessary.

"Did he make a promise?" Miranda asked in surprise.

"Yes," Domini said. "In exchange for a promise from me." Miranda's confusion was evident, so Domini outlined her arrangement with Sander, keeping her tone light and her explanations simple.

Miranda's face turned increasingly dubious once she understood. "I should warn you, Domini," she mentioned without censure, "I don't think he has any plans of going through with it, no matter what he said. He told me you'd be coming, and he told me to send you up. But I heard him mutter something between his teeth. It was hard to make out, but I think it was something about making short work of the whole thing. Or maybe of *you*. He does keep his promises, I'll grant you that, so he must be intending to make you break yours."

That knowledge hardly helped still the butterflies in

Domini's stomach. "I'll face that when it comes," she said and shrugged with a light laugh. "Disaster is still half an hour away. Do you mind if I sit and visit with you?"

Miranda indicated a chair close to her sales desk. "By all means. Do you mind if I munch my lunch? I always bring a sandwich down because I don't like locking up shop more often than absolutely necessary." She circled the desk and sat down, then paused and eyed Domini anxiously. "Although I could do that for a few minutes this afternoon, if necessary. Do you think you'll need to be rescued?"

"I doubt it." Domini smiled, with more hope than conviction. "I'll scream if I'm in need."

"Have you eaten?" asked Miranda, extracting a sandwich from her drawer. "I'm not too hungry and I'll be happy to share. Not fancy, but if you like chopped egg . . ."

"I've eaten," Domini lied. Nerves had prevented her from getting a single morsel down her throat, even at breakfast time, when she usually ate the oatmeal porridge she made for Tasey. "Besides, Miranda, you could use it. You're all skin and bones. Very attractive, of course—but you could use a few pounds."

"Thanks," Miranda replied with a wry grin. Still in her carefully kept black dress, she presented a picture of chic respectability, but Domini wondered if she would not be far prettier in some lighter color—a soft dove gray, for instance, to enhance eyes that were many shades lighter than Sander's. But dove gray, Domini supposed, needed too many trips to the dry cleaner.

"You've hung a new show," Domini remarked, looking around the gallery. Gone were the indifferent art toys, and in their place was a collection of indifferent paintings. "You must have been working very hard to get them all up since yesterday."

"The picture rails help," Miranda said. "Joel came

over this morning to lend a hand. Sander keeps offering to do it, but I don't like to let him in case he falls. I get around it by not telling him when I'm going to rehang."

"Joel seems very nice. Is he divorced? Or widowed?"

Miranda was studying the sandwich in her hands. "Divorced," she said. "His wife went off to discover herself, or some such thing. Crazy, isn't it? Trading kids for a career! I'd give my eye teeth to have the choice, but I wouldn't make the same decision."

"I thought he looked decidedly eligible," Domini observed. "I gather you haven't known him for too long?"

"Just since he bought the restaurant." Miranda ducked her head and busied herself in brushing imaginary crumbs from her lap. Then she looked up and smiled brightly. "Now tell me about yourself. Do you know, in all the conversations we've had, you've hardly told me a thing? It's really unfair, the way I've dumped all my problems on you! Now start from the beginning. Where are you from? New Yorkers are never from New York."

"This one is," said Domini, smiling. The lie had become so much a part of her existence that she told it now without hesitation. But talking about herself was not the purpose of her early arrival. For the next few minutes she tried without success to turn away Miranda's questions. Today, however, Miranda would not be deterred, and so Domini went through an assortment of fanciful tales invented long ago: parents who had died in her youth, a kindly aunt and uncle who had reared her and then moved to Europe, a lover who had died in an airplane crash, leaving Tasey as his only legacy. The stories had served Domini well over the years, and by this time they came trippingly off the tongue.

It wasn't until shortly before two o'clock, after a browser had entered and left, that Domini managed to turn the conversation to the topic of Sander. "You know, there are stores that would be interested in the kind of thing he makes," she said. "Maybe not here in SoHo, but in the ritzier neighborhoods. Have you thought of approaching them?"

"Of course." Miranda laughed shakily. "I did try one or two, but I had to close the gallery while I trundled the stuff around. I have a suitcase full of his samples over there in the corner, but I simply can't spare the time to show it to any interested buyers. And as for Sander, he can hardly . . ." Her voice trailed off.

"Maybe I could try," Domini said thoughtfully, wondering if she could manage to squeeze in some calls when she was out looking for new clients.

"He'd probably resent that," Miranda said with a helpless shrug. "For some reason, he seems to resent *you*. I'm sorry that he does, because . . . well, frankly, you're the first new female he's met for some time, and, and . . . I was hoping . . ." Miranda covered her confusion by beginning to speak very rapidly in defense of her brother, giving Domini no chance to interrupt. "He is a very attractive man, even with his disability. He's a little reluctant to make advances nowadays, but women. . . . Well, it's not as though there's been nobody interested in him all this time. That nice nurse you met, she shares a big loft with several other girls. New apartment mates move in and out all the time—commercial artists, folk singers, dancers. There was one in particular, an airline stewardess who always used to want to see Sander whenever she was in town." She laughed half apologetically, torn between revealing confidences and establishing that her brother was not an undesirable man. "But you know, airline stewardesses come and go and they're not always, well, you know, serious. The girl was transferred a couple of months ago, so that was the end of that. And since then . . . well, I mean, blindness does scare some women off. And when you seemed so very interested . . ."

"My interest isn't like that," Domini said crisply, not wanting to give rise to Miranda's hopes. At least Miranda had answered one question in the back of her mind: she was relieved to hear that Sander was probably not in a state of dangerous frustration. "I have other male friends, and I'm not short of dates. Just because I agreed to model for him doesn't mean I'm looking for a husband—or an affair."

"Oh, well, of course not. I didn't mean—" Miranda broke the tension of embarrassment by glancing at her watch. "Two o'clock," she said. "Hadn't you better go up?"

Domini rose, smiling. "After what you told me, I expect I'll be lucky if I'm not thrown right back down the stairs."

"I'll catch," Miranda offered. "Good luck!"

Domini shouldered the tubing and chicken wire and started up the stairs with wry thoughts that perhaps all her efforts had been in vain. She couldn't deny that mingled with apprehension there was some sense of relief; the idea of modeling in the nude was not at all to her liking. Well, if there was any truth to Miranda's warning words, she wasn't very likely to have to go through with it.

"Very prompt," Sander said coolly as he met her in the hall at the top of the stairs. "I've been wondering if you'd show up. I confess I'm surprised and pleased."

Domini blinked with astonishment. After what Miranda had said, she had expected to be met with rudeness, insolence, or outright refusal to let her set foot through the door. But this? What on earth did Sander have in mind? She stared up at his face, but nothing in the carefully bland expression hinted that his polite greeting was anything less than genuine.

"I've brought you some tubing and chicken wire," she said. "I thought you might need it to make an armature."

He reached his hand forward slowly until it connected with her offering, and then with more sureness he took it into his own arms. "Very considerate, but it won't be necessary today. I need to get the feel of the material, so I've decided to start with a small model, a maquette. Come in, won't you?"

Domini walked through the open door to a rearranged room. The workbenches had been pushed to new positions, both against a wall, in order to free the main space for other use. Central in the room was a platform Sander had constructed of raw lumber. It was about the height of a bed, and the layer of blankets over the hard surface informed Domini that it was intended for posing. The big kitchen table had been pulled right up against the platform, with some clay, some modeling tools, some wet cloths, and a large pan of water resting at the ready on its oilcloth surface. Could Miranda have been mistaken about what she had overheard?

The door clicked closed behind her, and she turned in time to see Sander's enigmatic expression as he said, "I imagine you're unfamiliar with posing in the nude. No doubt you're nervous, but there's no need to be concerned. I'll be as impersonal, I assure you, as a doctor. You can undress whenever you're ready."

Wordlessly, and with feelings of total apprehension, Domini started to remove her clothes. Had she really once started to show herself to Sander in the innocent belief that that sort of thing should be done without reservation or modesty? She had been taught as much, of course. Her father's dislike of false prudery had been drummed into her from an early age, and she hadn't been in Paris long enough at that point to realize how truly unconventional her upbringing had been. On that day, when she had begun to strip, she had felt embarrassed and sickeningly ashamed of her embarrassment, thinking it some sort of lack in herself. Now, with more experience of the real world to guide her, she realized it had been natural enough in a young girl unused to displaying herself. She was more mature now and she thought it should bother her less, but it didn't, despite Sander's unemotional reassurance. Oh, how simple life would become if everyone were as open and uncomplicated as Papa would have them be!

"I'm ready," she said a few minutes later when the clothes were off and the terrycloth robe on.

Sander was idling with some clay, molding it into some indeterminate shape on the table. Absently, without turning to what he could not in any case see, he nodded toward the platform to indicate she should mount it. With trepidation, Domini climbed on only two feet away from him, still decently wrapped. "Are you ready? Shall I . . . take off my robe?"

"Please do," he said dryly. "Just lay it over the end of the platform. A moment, and I'll decide on the pose I want."

Domini discarded the last of her coverings, feeling very vulnerable and visible despite Sander's inability to see. For a time he continued to mold the clay as though getting the feel of it, a dark forelock falling over his brow as he bent his head and knotted his brow in sightless concentration. His frown suggested something less than pleasure with the new medium. During the wait Domini's apprehension mounted until she was shivering with nervousness as well as chill.

Finally he slapped the clay on the table in a decisive gesture and started to remove his shirt. "Old habit," he explained with a faint grin. "I always used to work stripped to the waist. Perhaps it will help."

It didn't help Domini. The uncovering of remembered muscles and matted textures had an awesome effect at this close range, multiplying every sensation a hundredfold. Alarm prickled over the naked surfaces of her skin. Her agony of suspense became almost unbearable, but she fought down the overpowering desire to flee.

"Will you be . . . long?" she said after he had wasted some more suspenseful minutes experimenting with the texture of the clay. By this time she was hard pressed to keep her teeth from chattering. "If so, I think I'll put my robe on. It's very—"

"No, stay just as you are," he said at once, grimacing as he put down the lump of soft clay and rubbed his hands together to remove the last of it as best he could. "I'm ready now. I'm afraid, Miss Greey, that you're bound to get some clay on you. You'll understand that I can't possibly wash my hands every time I come into contact with your skin."

"I . . . yes," Domini agreed as she warily watched him turn to the platform. He moved so close that she could smell the tang of him beneath the aroma of undried clay, an earthy male scent that further stimulated her wildly misbehaving imagination. His first tentative touch established contact with a knee. Her nerves leaped.

"Draw your feet up on the platform, please. I can hardly sculpt your legs hanging over the edge. Now adjust them so there's a bend to your knee. That's right . . ."

With his bearings established, he started exploring the shape of her feet, running his long, responsive fingers quickly over each particular toe and tendon as if to establish its shape and size. Then the ankles, the calves, the knees; and there he paused for some torturous moments, testing the soft sensitive hollow in the underpart of the bend. "Odd how one finds tiny pulses in such out-of-the-way places," he murmured thoughtfully.

Domini clenched one fist against her mouth as the fingers stayed in place for a full minute, counting a pulse rate that caused a fleeting smile to cross his features. But he made no particular comment, only moving the hand a few inches until it rested on the thigh directly above her knee.

"Very fine legs up to this point," he observed detachedly, as if commenting on the weather. "Good bones, good flesh, good surfaces and angles. If the upper thigh is as shapely, I think you may make an excellent model." He planted his second hand on her other thigh just beyond the knee bend, palms over the front surface, fingers lightly touching the inner flesh where her legs met.

"Now calm down; you're trembling like a leaf."

"I'm c-cold," said Domini, although by now there was a burning heat radiating all through her flesh, its source the very place where Sander's fingers were so intimately lodged. To the further disorder of her senses, she realized that the bend of his half-naked body as he leaned over her had brought his unclothed torso against her lower legs. At a slight withdrawal of her knees he only leaned further forward, reestablishing contact as his roughened chest brushed her smooth calves. Domini stiffened perceptibly.

"Would you like to stop?" came the dry offer. "I'm prepared to call it quits any time. If you want to back out of the arrangement . . ."

"No," Domini managed, trying to relax her legs. "I'll be all right."

Sander frowned as if he didn't like that news at all. For a few vital seconds his hands remained motionless just above her knees. Then, with alarming suddenness, they started a long swift slide to a new, more vulnerable goal. Involuntarily Domini clamped her knees together like closed scissors, heart palpitating at an insane tempo as she considered the exactitude of his aim.

Her reaction stopped him with an inch or so to go, but by no means did he withdraw his hands. His faint smile might have been pure reassurance, and his voice softened as though he were gentling an unbroken colt. "Now calm down. It's unsettling to have someone seize up like that. Are you all right? We can still stop, you know."

"I'm . . . fine," choked Domini.

"Oh?" he murmured pleasantly, without changing the dangerously suggestive placement of his fingers on her inner thighs. "I thought perhaps you didn't trust me. You must try to remember that my actions are totally impersonal. As I can't use my eyes, I'm only doing what I must. Otherwise there's no point continuing, is there? Well, what shall it be? Do you want to call it quits before I go further?"

Domini called upon every ounce of inner strength she possessed. So this was how Sander planned to chase her away. Of course; she might have known he would have some such wretched plan. And if she went the clay was sure to end up in the trashcan. Damn him! Well, she didn't like his intentions, which weren't impersonal no matter what he said, but by this time she was determined not to be browbeaten into leaving. It had become a battle of wills.

"Just watch where you're going," she said with a degree of annoyance that put a convincing tautness in her tone.

"If I could," he drawled, "I assure you I would."

After that one sardonic remark, Sander's expression became forbiddingly enigmatic. To Domini's intense relief his hands now quickly changed directions, sliding around to explore the curve of her hip, the precise flow of her bones, the slender hollows of her waist. But soon the relief changed to something else as the progress of his fingers began once more to waken sleeping fires, igniting each inch of skin subjected to his scrutiny.

He spared no part of her but lingered nowhere. His hands on her throat, her shoulders, her arms, her breasts, could not have been more objective in their swift, impartial search. This time there was no derisive smile, such as he had smiled on feeling her pulse, when he discovered the telling firmness of her nipples. If anything, he looked displeased and moved quickly onward to an area less sensitive to arousal. Domini, for her part, bit her lip to prevent gasping as his fingers roamed over her flesh, leaving a trail of exquisite but unwanted sensations in their wake.

At length he finished, with a swift repetition of the

tactile reading of her face that had been done so thoroughly on the previous day. He did not release her hair, as he had done before. At once he said crisply, "Fine. Now turn in the other direction, will you, and take a similar pose? Face the far wall. Under the circumstances, as I'm trying out a new medium, I'm not too anxious to have a stranger watch the experiment. And as for you, you may have an easier time holding your pose if you're not distracted by what I'm doing. If you wish, wrap your robe around your lower half to keep you warm. I'll be working on the upper only for today."

He spent some minutes adjusting her pose—the angle of her chin, the bend of her elbows, the eloquent twist of her fingers. With her head upstretched to extend the long, smooth curve of her throat, and her arms uplifted in the air, it was not an easy pose for Domini to hold. She suspected him of making it deliberately difficult, but at this point she knew better than to complain. Sander's attempts to thwart her had simply succeeded in stiffening her every stubborn resolve.

"Now whatever you do, don't move a single muscle," he instructed curtly before turning back to his sculpture table. "This is going to be hard enough for me without also having to remember the exact tilt of your head, should you alter it by a single degree."

Domini tried to obey, for she wanted him to find no excuse for calling an end to the sitting. The difficulty of holding her position was not diminished by the way his hands frequently came wandering around from behind to explore her shoulders or her breasts, damp clay still clinging to the fingers roughened by manual work. As the afternoon progressed some of the clay clung to Domini, too, each mote of it a reminder of where his hands had traveled and where they would travel again. Her neck began to hurt from stretching, and her arms began to tremble from being held in the air. If there was consolation at all to be found in the discomfort of her difficult pose, it was that it totally suppressed any other physical reactions she might have felt at such intimate recurring explorations of her flesh.

"What color are your eyes?" he asked at one point.

"Blue." It was a pallid description of their color, a rare bluish violet with the depth of wet wildflowers, but it would not have occurred to Domini to wax poetic about her own eyes. Her passport described them as blue.

"Hair?"

"Blonde." Domini paused and then thought it might be best to mislead him a little, in case at some point his fingertips produced the tactile memory of the young girl he had once known. "Actually, my real hair color is sort of light brown. I helped nature along a bit."

"Ah," he said, reaching around to make a thorough examination of the hollow between her breasts. He asked no more questions. Domini could hear the sounds of his work progressing—the faint noises as he pushed and stroked life into the clay, the picking up of small tools, the occasional dip of fingers into water, the muffled movements of his feet. At least he was working, and that gave her a satisfaction that helped ease some of the tensions that troubled her.

"Fine," he said at last, when about two hours had passed. "I think that's enough for today."

With an open sigh of relief Domini lowered her arms, abandoned the difficult elongation of her throat, and reached for her robe. Before turning, she pulled it quickly on without taking time to brush the clay from her breasts. Still trying to rub the crick out of the back of her neck, she slipped her ankles over the edge of the platform and rose to her feet. Anxious to see what Sander had accomplished, she hurriedly moved closer to the table where he had been working. He was still standing beside it stripped to the waist, his thumbs insolently hooked into the waistband of his jeans, facing Domini. The placement of his thighs interfered briefly with Domini's view of the maquette he had been working on.

"I'm so—"

But whatever Domini had been about to say, it remained unsaid and forgotten forever, for Sander moved aside a few inches and she saw.

She stared at the sculpture he had produced, anger washing through her in great waves that almost robbed her of reason when she considered the indignities she had been subjected to, and to no purpose at all. It was a sculpture of one hand. And not even Domini's hand at that.

"Well?" he asked mockingly. "Has it all been worth your while? Have I managed to capture the clench of my fist, do you think? The tight curl of my thumb? And how do you like the gesture? An angry one, I'm afraid, but that's the kind of mood I was in."

Domini didn't bother answering in words. With a tempestuousness she had not displayed in years, she raised one flattened hand and cracked him across the face—hard. Rage had doubled her strength, and his head jerked sideways from the impact. But other than that he didn't budge his position, and even the hook of his thumbs remained unchanged. Perhaps he had expressed all his fury in the form of his art, for the fleeting dangerous sheen that appeared in his dark eyes was the only sign that her anger was returned in any real way.

"Had enough?" he drawled. "As I told you before, I'm prepared to let you back out of our agreement altogether—any time you're ready."

Without answering, Domini raced across the room to where she had left her clothes. With a red rage affecting her reason, she was hardly conscious of getting dressed, beyond knowing that her shaking hands made it very difficult for her to do. When she finished she grabbed her purse and flung herself angrily toward the door.

"Good-bye—forever, I trust," came the mocking murmur, just in time to bring Domini to a dead halt at the door.

She turned to face him for one last moment, her face flushed and her eyes still blazing with bright blue sparks.

"Certainly not," she said, fury giving a vibrant edge to her voice. "Do you think I'd give you the satisfaction of backing out after *that?* I'll be back at two o'clock, first working day in the New Year. And next time I'm watching what you do!"

Chapter Seven

*T*wo weeks later Domini had grown almost accustomed to the task that filled the afternoons of each working day. Weariness from working late nights in order to free some hours during the day, and the continuing detachment Sander displayed in his tactile explorations, helped make the posing an impersonal rather than an erotic experience. Moreover, he insisted on poses that were every bit as awkward as that of the first day, a deliberate punishment for her stubbornness. There were moments of trepidation, to be sure, whenever she mounted the platform, removed her robe, and resumed the role of model. But the feeling soon passed as she became intent upon the difficulty of holding whatever position Sander chose to inflict upon her at that particular time.

He continued to work on maquettes, small pieces that did not require the substructure of an armature. He worked quickly, some days producing two or three, until one of the remote shelves formerly occupied by toys had to be emptied in order to receive the product of his new occupation. As the maquettes were covered by damp sheets and plastic in order to prevent premature drying, they were well hidden from view. To Domini, who understood such things, the moist coverings were an encouraging sign. Although Sander remained disparaging, she knew that only sculptures to be cast would be given such protection.

Sander's attitude toward Domini was marked by a grim silence that he seldom broke, except to instruct her curtly when he had had enough of some particular pose. In the working days of the New Year, their conversation had been minimal and anything but friendly. Perhaps in further retribution for her insistence upon their bargain, he never sculpted her face, leaving it blank and formless—an undignified lump of clay that left each work partially unfinished.

But at least he was working, and Domini's exultation grew as she watched. Four years ago he had been very good—but now he was even better. His work was simpler, more powerful, less clever, and even the unfinished face did not detract as much as he might have hoped. It was as though his lack of outer vision had given him an inner vision, a depth of feeling achieved in part because of the suffering he had undergone during these past years. Domini herself might not be a great artist, but she had been exposed to enough important art that she could recognize the quality of greatness when she saw it. And Sander's work had the quality of greatness.

"Do you mind if I leave half an hour early today?" she asked on the day of her date with Grant Manners, shortly after her arrival in the workshop. Only that morning she had dressed the window of the Fifth Avenue boutique, which had turned out to be quite as exciting as she had visualized. Domini could hardly wait to hear Grant's reaction. He was to return from his skiing holiday during the afternoon, and Domini was certain that when she got home, her telephone answering service would have some congratulatory message for her. The anticipation of good news had made her decide to beg off early. Besides, as she would be out for dinner, she needed extra time in order to prepare a meal for Tasey and the baby sitter, a motherly woman whom Domini used with enough frequency to be sure of her reliability.

"Leave at once if you wish," Sander replied curtly before Domini had even mounted her platform. Already standing beside his sculpture table, he was wearing a thin cotton shirt today, having abandoned some days before the pretext of needing to work stripped to the waist.

"I wouldn't dream of leaving without my sitting," Domini said haughtily, removing her robe and throwing it with carefree abandon on the floor before determinedly climbing into place. "Why, I'm actually beginning to enjoy this sort of thing."

He paid her off by forcing her into a pose of enormous difficulty, not unlike that of a runner crouched into sprint position at the beginning of a race, but with both hands upstretched in the air and head dramatically angled to one side. It might have been taken from the floor routine of an Olympic gymnast. Every muscle in Domini's body screamed in complaint. To add to that, fifteen minutes later her inner anguish became almost unbearable when a knock sounded at the workshop door and Sander called without missing a beat, "Come in!"

Alarmed, Domini dropped her hands in an instant scramble to cover herself. As if he had seen, Sander snapped, "Don't move! It's only one of Miranda's artists."

Indeed it was, a young man who had come to discuss some framing to be done. Although most artists were perfectly accustomed to seeing women in the nude, that didn't help Domini's painful frame of mind. She crouched with arms huddled over her breasts, agonizing at the distance between herself and the robe she had so lightly flung away. She was thoroughly mortified, her cheeks flaming and her skin hot, and the young artist's frank stare didn't help.

Sander spent some minutes discussing the pros and cons of various kinds of picture frames, drawing out the discussion as long as possible. Domini knew perfectly well that it was only another form of punishment on his part. Damn him, damn him, damn him!

"You moved," Sander accused after the young artist had finally drawn his reluctant eyes away from Domini and departed.

"You bastard," Domini sputtered.

"I imagine he's seen life models before," Sander mocked as he helped Domini to recapture her lost pose. The cruel amusement in his mouth was all at her expense. "I'll forgive you this time because he took you by surprise, but next time I won't. If you can't hold a pose through an interruption, you're not much use to me as a model. So next time someone arrives at the door, if I detect one altered muscle our agreement comes to an end."

"That's just what you want, isn't it!" she declared angrily.

"How did you guess?" he murmured as he went back to work. Domini fumed. With contorted muscles contributing to her agony, she was not in a good frame of mind when the day's work came to an end.

"That's enough for today," Sander directed at last, when only one hour had passed. The tiny maquette was finished, all but the formless face—a study in motion that captured in full the tension inherent in the pose. Sander's face was scornful as he added, "If you can cut our afternoon short by one half hour, I can cut it short by another."

Domini collapsed like a rag doll, throbbing in every limb, too enervated to object in any way. It took a few moments of deep breathing before she had the strength to reach for her terry robe, and even then her muscles were still trembling. She slid off the platform feeling somewhat like a marathon runner after a hard race, only to find that today her legs were just as wobbly as the rest of her.

From the expression on Sander's face she could tell that he was taking spiteful satisfaction in the small sounds that told him her job had been anything but enjoyable, despite her protestations. Out of sheer mulishness as much as anything, she forced herself to turn her shaky footsteps toward the shelf where he kept his maquettes, instead of immediately returning to her clothes as she usually did.

In several quick strides Sander had reached her side, and his arms barred her way. "You saw them when they were done," he reminded her roughly.

His apparent annoyance and the forcefulness with which he prevented her from moving farther only aroused Domini's curiosity, as well as her fighting instincts. It made her more determined than ever to look over the collection of maquettes whether he liked it or not.

"I want to see them again," Domini objected, trying to circumvent the immovable object he presented. "Is there something over there you don't want me to see? Perhaps a caricature of me—something you've done when I'm not around?"

For one instant she succeeded in circling his out-stretched arm. As she pushed past him his reaction was swift and furious. He seized both her shoulders with lightning fury, causing her to whirl around so that she was no longer aiming in the direction of the shelf. His fingers clamping on her soft flesh were like brands, even through the terry robe.

"What I do when you're not here is none of your damn business," he hissed through his teeth. "Even Miranda doesn't pry where she's not wanted. How dare you take such liberties in my home?"

"How dare you touch me like this? You're hurting!" she gasped in return, trying to struggle free. A part of her was beginning to react wildly as memories of the past infused her with an overpowering need to escape. She pushed at the wall of his chest, and when that had no effect she started to score his flesh through the shirt, using her fingernails as a weapon. When he remained immutable her feet, too, joined the fight.

Sander sucked in his breath and his brow creased with fury. And then, more swiftly than Domini could turn her head away, his face descended, the lightning glint of gray telling her too late that she had pushed him beyond the limits of his endurance. He pried her lips apart in a kiss that was pure punishment, repaying her intrusion with an invasion of his own, a brutal subjugation of her mouth to the male power of his.

That was how it started, and perhaps that was where it would have ended, had Domini's responses now obeyed some deeper instinct than that of flight or fight. All at once it happened, that crazy vertigo of the senses she had not felt for so long, and she was swept back in time to that moment of wild abandon when she had first felt Sander's lips on hers. Without volition, her fingers, which had been curled to scratch, were suddenly pressed against the light fabric of his shirt, roaming the surfaces to test the warmth and maleness of him. Her senses reeled with the intoxication of the kiss—the tastes, the smells, the marvelous potency of his closeness. They were man and woman, and the pain of the past had no part in the primal urges that swept through Domini now.

Another time she might have reasoned that she did not want his deep domination, but for Domini there was no reason in the moment at all. The woman in her gloried in his hot passion, his hard demanding lips; she exulted in his superior size and strength. He overpowered her easily, and yet oddly it was she who felt heady with a sense of her power over him. Brazenly she pressed close against the length of his body, knowing full well what ready response she would surely soon invoke. And with her lips and tongue she returned his probing ferocity with a like ardor that must have robbed Sander of self-control too.

Breaking contact except in the kiss, he pulled apart enough to give his hands the full freedom of her body. Roughly he pushed aside the lightly fastened robe to pass commanding hands over the softness that lay beneath, so familiar to the artist in him and yet so little known to the man. Perhaps control had kept his touch impersonal for too long; perhaps during these past days he had been coveting her flesh far more than he had wanted to admit. No longer the clinical observer he had been during the long daily sessions, he devoured her body impatiently in all its intimate detail, searching the valley of her breasts, the rise of each curve, the textured tautness of nipples corrugated with desire, the warmth of her thighs. Where he touched, she turned to flame.

"Oh, God," he muttered thickly when he lifted his mouth briefly from hers. There was an anguish in his voice that he did not try to hide. "You're so soft, so supple. Don't you know this is what you've been doing to me all along? Do you do it on purpose? I swear you've been trying to drive me mad, filling my dreams each night, torturing me each day with your softness, your fullness, the feel of your skin . . ."

But then with brutal suddenness, Sander thrust her away. With a muffled expletive he swiveled on his heel, turning his broad shoulders to her, firmly shutting her out. Burning with need for him, Domini had to fight the impulse to offer herself in the face of his stunning repulse. Shivering, she clutched her robe close and stared at him with a mixture of anger and hurt. Perhaps the past should have inured her to rejection by Sander, but it had not.

"Why did you stop?"

"I do have some scruples," he said in a rigid voice. "I imagine you forgot who you were kissing. Besides, I don't take advantage of nudes during or after life sessions."

"Don't tell me you've never had an affair with one of your models!" Domini burst out, thinking of Nicole.

"Yes, I have. By prior arrangement! If a woman wants to go to bed with a man, she ought to make a decision under circumstances a little more rational than this. Once you get your head together, you may reconsider."

After the way he had handled her body and the blazing kiss they had shared, his sangfroid enraged her. "How can you be so damn cold-blooded about it?" she cried. "Don't you feel a thing?"

He hunched his shoulders as if considering something and then slowly turned, his stance aggressive. "What do you think?" he said, his voice very controlled.

It was the only controlled thing about him. All the obvious signs of passion were there, emphasized by the close cut of his jeans and undiminished by the moments apart. Moisture bathed his brow and a dull red color suffused his cheekbones. Still angered, Domini said, "Good! It's about time! I've been wondering how long it would take you to react."

It wasn't intended as gloating, but it might have sounded that way. He sucked in his breath, clearly misinterpreting, and then his control burst, unleashing a torrent of retaliation. "Well, then, are you satisfied?" he lashed out in a voice clogged with anger and frustrated desire. "Now you know I've been wanting you, desiring you, aching for you every time I touch your hair or your throat or your breast. Don't you think it's time we called an end to this insanity? Now get dressed and get out of here, and don't come back if your only purpose is to arouse me. I'm damn tired of being pushed to the brink of hell every day!"

Reverberating with a conflicting mixture of emotions, Domini raced across the room to where she had laid her clothes. She dressed in silence, regretting her last thoughtless remark but too disturbed to apologize for it. As reason reasserted itself she became certain that Sander was right. She couldn't return now, know-

ing that beneath the impartial professionalism with
which he explored her body the primitive man in him
was being consumed by the dark, fierce fires of desire.
She reminded herself that she didn't love him, that she
would never love him again, that her reaction to him
was only due to the abysmal lack of sexual fulfilment in
her life. And surely the cure for that could be found
elsewhere!

At length, dressed, she turned to look at him again.
He was standing at the sculpture table, his palms
pressed against its surface, the droop of his head
denoting not tiredness but a continuing and powerful
tension.

Domini was calmer now and she managed to keep
her voice level. "I'm going now," she said. "As I doubt
that I'll be modeling for you again, do you mind if I do
take a look at your shelf after all? I assure you I won't
be angry if there's anything unflattering of me."

He took a while before answering, and then did so
without lifting his head. "I don't suppose it matters if
you do see now," he said in a forced, tight voice. "Go
ahead. Perhaps it will cure you of wanting to come here
once and for all."

Domini walked across to the shelf. Carefully she
peeled back the coverings. The shelf held a far greater
number of maquettes than she had expected. Those in
the front she recognized; they had all been done during
the daily sessions. But those in the back . . .

Domini's heart skipped a brief beat upon seeing the
largest of the small clay models, a sculpture of a naked
man and a naked woman entwined in the act of love.
Passion was in every line, every moving nuance of the
sculpture, and although the woman's face was buried
hungrily against the man's, removing the need for
facial features, Domini had no doubt that it was
intended to be herself. The woman's slender curves
were recognizably her own, and so was the hair captured in its French twist, and with so many small
models to work from, Sander would have no trouble

remembering those curves and that hair very well. As to the identity of the man, Domini was in no doubt.

So that was what Sander had not wanted her to see. Or was it the other maquettes at the back of the shelf? They were all of Sander's own face—strong, tortured models that captured his inner agony very well, each with a feature as distinctive in its own way as were the unfinished faces on the sculptures of Domini.

"They're very good," Domini said quietly, replacing the covers. "Which was it you didn't want me to see? The way you were making love to me—or the way you gouged out all the eyes in the sculptures of yourself?"

His voice was flat, unemotional. "Perhaps both. Or perhaps I simply didn't want you to know your ruse had met with success. Yes, it's true. I've been sculpting with frenzy for a good part of every day. I don't want to do it but I find myself doing it, driven by it, unable to stop. Are you satisfied? Isn't that what you wanted all along?"

"Yes," Domini replied, turning to face him and feeling terrible because of the purgatory expressed in those eyeless sculptures of himself. Had she only added to his inner torture by forcing him to face up to the unexpressed artist in himself?

"You'd better go now," he said without inflection.

"Who will you use for a model?"

He shrugged as if it were a matter of indifference. "Miranda, Joel, the shopgirl next door, some wino who'll pose in exchange for a meal. Does it matter? I won't stop now, and a clothed model is quite as valid as an unclothed one. You've made your point, Miss Greey, and really, I think for your own sake you're very wise not to come again."

"Domini," she corrected.

"Domini, then," he agreed with a bitter twist to his mouth. "Perhaps I should thank you but I won't. My new occupation doesn't add to my . . . peace of mind."

Domini walked slowly to the door, thinking her way

across each inch of floor. Before leaving, she stopped and turned. "I'm not sure I should stop modeling after all," she said. "I need to think about it. You do need a model, and I did agree. I could do it with my clothes on."

"I release you," he said tonelessly.

But Domini knew he could not really afford the models he would need if he were to continue with anything other than his bitterly unhappy and introspective self-sculptures. Miranda was busy, Joel was busy, and winos might be more trouble than they were worth. "I'll take a few days off and decide," she suggested. "I might come back."

Sander's strong jaw worked for a moment before he controlled the muscles of his face. "I wouldn't advise that," he said in a monotone. "You see, Miss—Domini, another time you won't be so safe with me."

"Is that a threat?" Domini asked, forcing a light, husky laugh.

Sander shifted and lifted his head so that his eyes caught a stray ray of light, illuminating their darkness for one illusory moment. Had Domini not known otherwise, she could have sworn he had seen the uncertain expression on her face.

"Yes, it is. If you arrive here to model for me again," he warned in deathly earnest, "I'll assume you've made some kind of choice. In which case I intend to take you up to my bedroom and make love to you very thoroughly and very lingeringly, not sparing any part of you at all. I don't need sight to do that, for any man who is a man can make love in the dark, and some prefer it. So please, don't come back unless that's exactly what you want."

Domini held her breath and then let it go. "I won't," she murmured, and at the time she thought she meant she wasn't coming back at all. She didn't realize until later that she had left her terry robe behind, perhaps a symbol of subconscious intent.

* * *

"You asked for a view," Grant reminded her as he placed his hand over hers on the tablecloth. "I couldn't think of a better one."

"It's dazzling," Domini agreed, her shining face turned toward the exciting skyline of New York. From this height, a quarter mile above street level at their prime table in Windows on the World, the city's skyscrapers were spread out in a sweeping pageantry of lights stretching upward toward the sky and northward to the far limits of vision. The Empire State Building and the famous Chrysler Building were recognizable in the panorama. Old skyscrapers were dwarfed by newer ones, and the newer buildings were in turn dwarfed by the one hundred and ten stories of the World Trade Center, atop which the restaurant sat. New York was never so impressive as when seen from a height, and never so magical as at night.

Grant had managed to secure a windowside table, a feat no doubt helped along by the discreetly folded banknote he had presented upon arrival. While Domini devoured the view, commenting excitedly as she recognized each landmark far below, a vintage champagne was uncorked. It frothed into two glasses, and Grant lifted one without releasing Domini's hand, where his thumb was tracing lightly over her palm.

"A toast to the future, now that I'm sure we have one," he said, his voice vibrant with meaning.

At last Domini dragged her eyes away from the breathtaking view and sought the stem of her champagne glass with her free hand. Flushed with optimism, she was sure that Grant was at last giving her the news she had been longing to hear. Although he had congratulated her on the window she had dressed, he hadn't exactly said whether he intended to award her the job on a permanent basis. But his words now tended to confirm that he did. Domini decided to probe a little, to assure herself that it was so.

"Oh, Grant, I'm so thrilled you like the display. That is the kind of future you're talking about, isn't it?"

He laughed lightly. "I wasn't actually referring to your window. But yes, I do like it immensely, and yes, you will get the job. It's very simple, very stunning, very effective. Several people have commented on it already. I can't think why you haven't been working on Fifth Avenue all along."

Domini had devised a simple but ingenious answer to Grant's window problem. Because of its size, the window needed mannequins, but dressed mannequins seriously detracted from the merchandise he sold. So she intended to leave them totally undressed, covering all the joints and the vital areas with one device or another. In the window just done, which was intended to promote pearls of all kinds, a long-haired siren of a mannequin was in the process of emerging from a gigantic oyster shell. Part of her was hidden by the huge hinged shell Domini had constructed, part by the hair, and part by the pearls that decked her body and spilled out ahead of her feet. On the sand-covered floor of the window, the showcard declared: "Bring on the Pearls!"

Grant's confirmation brought a sparkle of pleasure to Domini's eyes. "That's wonderful! Then I do have reason to celebrate tonight."

"You certainly do," he agreed, his lips describing a sensuous curve. "I can hardly wait to see what you have in mind for me next."

"I refuse to describe it, but I have something absolutely wonderful in mind," she said happily.

Grant's eyes smoldered. "So do I," he said, his tone so intimate that Domini could not possibly mistake his intentions for later in the evening. And if she had doubts, they were put to rest by the way his eyes swept meaningfully over the low neckline of her dress. A silky midnight blue with tiny shoestring straps, it was a youthfully flattering Paris gown saved from more fortunate days. That, and an embroidered cape that had never worn out over the years because it was too impractical for everyday use, allowed her to feel quite as well dressed as the worldly assemblage of people patronizing the expensive restaurant. If Grant's admiring expression could be believed, her appearance was second to no one's.

Domini was perfectly sure Grant intended to make advances before the evening was through, but she had no idea how she was going to respond. Once she would have responded with total naturalness, doing only what her heart told her to do; but life had tamped down some of Domini's instinctive responses. Her head told her that Grant Manners was a very eligible male—handsome, virile, wealthy, well-educated, potentially good husband or father material. For Domini, the heart had always ruled; long ago she had been taught that truth lay in the heart. But she no longer knew what her heart was telling her.

And so, if she had made any decision at all, it was that only time would tell—and yet she hoped her head would learn to rule. When the heart ruled, it was too easily hurt.

Several glasses of champagne later, after pâté and lobster Thermidor and little curlicues of an exotic vegetable known as fiddleheads, after conversation that ranged over Grant's real past and Domini's invented one, after anecdotes about Tasey and about Fifth Avenue and about Grant's recent holiday in Aspen, the chairs were at last pulled out by the unobtrusively attendant waiter. At Grant's suggestion, instead of leaving immediately, they moved for liqueurs to the bar at the south side of the tower, from which the view of the harbor replaced the view of the city in all its night splendor. From this vantage point the Statue of Liberty, so huge when seen at water level, looked like no more than a small toy doll.

Domini felt giddy, as much from the height as from the champagne with which she had been so freely plied. Her head, which had been trying to reach a decision about Grant Manners, was beginning to be incapable of any decision at all. Why did she have to keep thinking about Sander's recent passionate embrace, of the way his mouth had branded hers and the way his hands had blazed over her skin, instead of turning her mind to what was sure to be an equally dizzying experience with Grant?

"No liqueur?" Grant lifted his brows in surprise when the waiter came to take their order and Domini ordered a glass of plain soda water. "In that case let's not stay. I have better things in mind, more exciting things that can't be done in public. Those little straps of yours make a man's imagination work overtime."

Within minutes of the elevator's swift downward flight, Grant was giving directions to a taxi driver without consulting Domini. She made no demur, because the chill January air had cleared her head enough to remind her that this was what she ought to want. Besides, the baby sitter had been warned to expect a late night. How would her heart ever know how to feel about Grant if she didn't give it a chance to find out?

Grant's penthouse apartment was on Park Avenue, in a hushed, exclusive building with plush carpeting and a discreet doorman and a good deal of highly polished brass. Yet another elevator swept them upward, its roller-coaster effect this time felt in Domini's stomach and not just in the pressure of her ears.

"If it's heights that excite you . . ." Grant said softly as he opened the door of his apartment, and ushered her into an oyster-white space with a plate glass expanse that opened onto a view less lofty, but otherwise almost as stunning, as the view from Windows on the World.

He relieved Domini of her cape, and she walked across to admire the night scene while he busied himself at a sideboard that served as a bar. Moments later a brandy snifter was placed in Domini's hand despite her halfhearted protest. She set it down on a small table as soon as Grant once more left her side.

"Your view is fantastic," she breathed.

"It's even more so with the lights low," Grant promised softly as he adjusted several dimmer switches, leaving only a pale illumination that emanated from somewhere near an island of deep down-filled couches. He came to stand behind Domini at the window, so close that his warmth could be felt. Interior darkness had turned the outside to a fairyland of glittering diamonds blazing on black velvet. Surely this was a time to find magic with some man other than Sander Williams?

But even before Grant's arms came around her, hands seeking and stroking the soft swell of her cleavage, she knew that it was not. She twisted away without rancor, evading the intimacies of his embrace but making no move to escape when he closed in for the kiss he was most certainly expecting. A detached part of her mind told her that the skillful movements of his lips were pleasurable enough. But where was the exhilaration?

She pulled away as soon as it became possible to do so. "I'm sorry, Grant, it won't work," she said simply and directly. "I like you, but I'm not about to go to bed with you tonight or any night, and you may as well know it right now."

Grant rubbed a hand around the back of his neck in a gesture of extreme frustration. "You weren't exactly clear about that before," he reminded her in an explosion of irritation. "I don't think I made any particular secret of my intentions—in fact, I believe I stated them clearly several times. Why on earth did you even come up to my apartment if you didn't plan to make love to me?"

"Because I hadn't made up my mind," Domini said slowly. "I wasn't sure whether I'd say yes or no. I've been thinking about it all evening."

"And you're sure now, just like that, after a single

kiss? That's not exactly flattering." He finished with a heavy groan, and Domini realized he had been far more affected by the embrace than she.

Domini lifted her shoulders in a small apologetic shrug. "I'm sorry, Grant, that's the way it is. I thought it might work, but . . . you see, my heart has to be involved, and it's not involved with you."

He had controlled himself by now, the moment of anger swiftly over. "I didn't expect your heart would be involved, not yet," he said with sounds of strain. "On the other hand, I didn't expect your body to be so damn . . . *un*involved. You're an unmarried mother; it's not as though you're totally inexperienced."

"I've always thought it better to tell the truth about Tasey," Domini replied levelly. "Just because I never had a husband, that doesn't mean I'm prepared to fall into bed with any man, no matter how much I like him. I do like you very much, Grant. But I have to be in love, really in love."

He was silent for some difficult moments. "I wish to God you'd told me that before I started letting my imagination run riot," he said with a short, humorless laugh.

"I couldn't tell you because I didn't understand it myself," Domini said slowly as she turned to the window with its spangled view. As understanding dawned, her heart grew full with a great sadness and a great sweetness, and neither emotion had anything to do with the frustrated man at her side. Why had it not occurred to her before that what she felt for Sander wasn't purely sexual attraction? Why hadn't she known it was love?

Chapter Eight

"Sander told me you wouldn't be coming back," Miranda said, staring in surprise. Domini had just burst through the door of the small gallery, trailing wet slush from the thoroughly miserable day outside.

"Wishful thinking on his part," Domini said lightly, trying to make a joke of it. She began to brush the wet, heavy snow from her neatly anchored hair, but it was the kind of snow that melted quickly, and already the dampness had reached right through to her scalp, darkening the gold and plastering it closer to her head.

"But you haven't been here for several days," Miranda said. "I thought . . ."

"That I'd given up?" Domini forced a faked laugh as she shrugged off her coat with Miranda's help. She had worn neat navy slacks today, and a neat navy sweater over a neat printed shirt, all of them emotional armor against her next encounter with Sander, because she wasn't sure whether she intended to take them off or not. She thought she probably would. She turned to Miranda with a smile.

"The truth is, Sander's joy is in forcing me to adopt difficult poses, and my joy is in proving I have the stamina to do them. Why not? It's cheaper than going to yoga classes, and much better exercise too. Good for the soul."

Miranda grinned. "Sander showed me one or two of the maquettes," she admitted wryly. "I wondered how you had managed to suffer through the positions he made you hold."

"Easy," flipped Domini. "I'm a masochist." Her expression became more earnest. "They're good, Miranda, those things he's doing now. Why, I think they're even better than . . ."

She bit back the comparison between past and present, and instead said, "They're better than the things you're showing in your gallery. Why don't you think of handling some of Sander's sculptures down here? It wouldn't cost that much to have those small ones properly cast in bronze, in limited runs. A foundry would do them for a song. You could sell them for a decent price, and I'm sure you'd have no trouble finding customers."

"Sander won't let me get my hands on even one. He says they're not ready to show." Miranda eyed Domini dubiously. "Perhaps you can talk him into it?" she suggested, but with little hope in her voice. "I'm not sure how you go about it, Domini, but you seem to get your way with him a good deal of the time. And Sander's not an easy man to get around. Usually it's *he* who manages to get his way."

"You overestimate me," Domini said. She turned her back, ostensibly to study a tiresome contemporary canvas out of which the artist had ripped a big triangular hole as his particular contribution to modernism. It was the kind of meaningless painting Domini hated, but she pretended an intense interest. Miranda's words reminded her too forcibly of Sander's parting words the other day, and she needed a moment to readjust her facial muscles into unrevealing smoothness. Sander would most certainly want his way today; his warning could not have been more clearly worded. And much as Domini now recognized the pull of her heart and her body, she was not certain she wanted the kind of pain the future would surely hold in store should she become seriously entangled with a man who loved her no more now than he had loved her four years before.

And yet, despite several days of trying, she had not been able to stay away.

"Actually today I had other reasons for dropping in," she remarked lightly after a few moments, turning back to Miranda. She fished through her purse and secured her wallet. The necessary bills had already been counted into a neat fold, separate from such other funds as she had in her possession. She extracted them and handed them to the other woman. "I think that clears up what I owe you for the unicorn," she said.

"But—" Miranda held the bills without riffling through them, looking at Domini in surprise. "I thought you couldn't . . . well, that is . . ."

"No problem," Domini said. "A couple of my old clients paid me in advance, and I've found a new one as well." The new one, Domini realized, was still something of a pipe dream. Grant had verbally awarded her the work, but after the unsatisfactory encounter in his apartment, she had not liked to phone and press for an immediate confirmation. She knew she might yet lose the job. But that was a private business matter and one she had no intention of discussing with Miranda, who had enough problems of her own.

Miranda put the bills into her cash drawer without counting them at all, a sign of trust that Domini found touching, especially when a quick glimpse of the cash-box told her that the till looked to be quite empty, even of the distinctive paper-and-carbon slips that might denote a charge account sale.

"One other thing, Miranda. Tasey made a present for you." From her capacious shoulderbag Domini extracted a pencil holder made of an old tin can, pasted over with colored paper and lacquered into some semblance of smoothness. "It was her own idea. She's still talking about the nice lady who gave her ice cream and chocolate syrup."

"Isn't that wonderful," Miranda said admiringly as she accepted the prettily colored gift. She looked at Domini, her expression earnest. "I wish you'd bring her over to visit," she said wholeheartedly. "I absolutely adore children, you know, although I never had any. My husband and I were planning a family, but then he became ill." She sighed. "I'd love to have had babies. Joel says . . ."

She stopped, flushed, and busied herself with placing a miscellaneous collection of pens and pencils into the tin can.

"I imagine you'd make a wonderful mother," Domini remarked, guessing at what Joel might have said.

Miranda's hands stilled at her task, and she looked up with troubled eyes. "He's asked me to marry him. Oh, Domini, what am I going to do?" She bit her lip, hardly the expression of a woman who had recently received a proposal she must have wanted, judging by other signs. "Don't tell Sander," she finished in a low voice.

Domini needed no imagination to understand the dilemma. Although it had not been said in so many words, it must have been Miranda's sense of duty to her brother that had kept her from accepting. And where was the solution for that?

Domini reached a sudden decision, not a solution by any means but at least a step in the right direction. "What I really stopped for," she lied, "wasn't to see Sander at all. I came to ask if you'd like me to mind the shop for a while. You mentioned the problem of finding a new outlet for Sander's toys. Why don't you go off this afternoon and see what you can do?"

Miranda didn't answer at once. "You're too good to us," she said at last with difficulty.

Domini kept her voice breezy. "Not at all. When I think how you took me in that first day, took care of me and Tasey. . . . Go on, Miranda, you'll be doing Sander a big favor. He doesn't even have to know I'm down here. Besides, I have nothing to do. I freed up my afternoons for modeling, and frankly I'm not sure I want to go back to it again, at least not right away. Your brother is a hard taskmaster."

"Oh, Domini . . ." But the offer was too good to refuse, so after giving Domini a short initiation into the mysteries and machinery of writing up charge account bills, Miranda entrusted her with the key to the cash drawer and hastened off with the suitcase full of Sander's samples, a heavy burden but a necessary one. And so Domini found herself alone in the little gallery, with the rueful thought that should a customer come through the door she could not possibly even pretend to like the artistic offerings herself. Perhaps she was not doing Miranda such a very great favor after all!

The first hour wore on, producing no more than a few bored browsers who seemed to have absolutely no interest in buying, with Domini's persuasions or without. At last, to fill the time that was too occupied with distressing thoughts of Sander, and too little occupied with customers, Domini began to leaf through the neat stack of art magazines and reproductions on the top of the sales desk. Subconsciously she must have known what she would find, and find it she did. She pulled the picture of the unicorn out of the stack and held it in her hands, gazing with a great sadness upon the child she once had been.

Was that really herself, that golden little creature so ready to conquer life? And instead, life had conquered her. Or had it? There had been defeats and victories, pains and pleasures, sorrows and joys, good times and bad. In other words, human times. Sander's words came back again: "As unreal as you are . . ."

Domini remembered and wondered, and in that moment began to mourn a little less for the part of herself that had been so long ago destroyed. She had hated Sander for destroying that part, but what had he really destroyed? Perhaps the little girl had never been truly human at all; perhaps she could never have survived in the real world. But Domini Greey the adult had survived.

And there had been Tasey too. How could she ever have hated Sander for giving her Tasey?

With a sigh, because the reflections were too heavy to be continued for long, Domini started to return the picture to its stack. It was then, for the first time, that she noted it was not a reproduction taken from an art book, but a page neatly cut out of a magazine. An article, or rather part of an article, was on the reverse side. Turning the page over, Domini saw that it had been taken from *Time* magazine; the issue date was not far removed from the date of Tasey's birth.

The article was about Le Basque, who must have been the subject of that month's lead story on art. Much of the information Domini already knew, but a few small facts were new to her. The auction in which the unicorn had been sold had taken place in New York, about six months after her own arrival in the city, Domini judged. According to the story, the bidding had been spirited. A good deal of publicity had attended the sale, in part because the famous Louvre painting had been concurrently on loan for a tour of major American cities, attracting big lineups and a considerable amount of press.

No wonder the news had escaped her, Domini reflected wryly. At the time of Tasey's birth she had seldom had the price of a newspaper to spare, let alone the price of a magazine. She realized her father must have arranged to divest himself of the unicorn within a short time of disowning her; such sales could not be

arranged overnight. But the hurt to be found in that
was something Domini had already dealt with in learning that the unicorn had been disposed of at all, and so
she returned the clipping to its niche, carefully covering
it with other things so that she would not have to look
at it again.

Miranda was dispirited when she returned. "I went
to three stores but didn't make a single sale," she said
as she removed her coat. "With Christmas already
passed, it's not going to be easy. The people I talked to
were impressed, but they don't want to hold the
inventory. They said to come back later in the year."

"Where's the sample case?" asked Domini.

"I couldn't get to see the buyer at the third store, so I
finally left it there. Frankly, by then I didn't think I
could carry it another inch, and I knew I had to get
back to relieve you before day care hours were over. I
told them I'd return to pick it up tomorrow." She
looked at Domini, weariness and discouragement
stamped on her thin face. "I hate to ask this, but . . ."

"Yes, of course I can come back," Domini said
quickly. "Why, I'm just beginning to get the hang of
this. Do you know I actually made a sale? Not much,
just a small numbered lithograph. I think it was the
cheapest thing in the place. It was only forty dollars."

Miranda brightened considerably. "Really? I hope
you didn't have trouble filling out the charge slips."

"Not a bit," Domini came back glibly as she pulled
her nutria-lined coat over her shoulders and made
ready to leave. "The customer paid in cash."

"That's the very best kind!" Miranda exclaimed as
Domini gave a cheerful salute and hurried to the door.
Slung over her shoulder was a handbag that contained
one hastily folded numbered lithograph and almost no
money at all.

"Did the ice cream lady like my present?" Tasey
asked over a supper of baked beans and homemade
applesauce.

"She loved it," Domini said promptly with a small sense of guilt that she had forgotten to pass the news along to her daughter. "She put it on her desk and filled it up with pencils right away. It looked very nice, and she said to thank you very much."

"That's the last time I had ice cream," Tasey complained, curling a small fist around her dessert spoon and making a face at the bowl in front of her. "You don't buy ice cream anymore. Why?"

"Because I like this just as well," Domini said firmly.

"Ugh, I hate applesauce."

"Don't eat it then," Domini said cheerfully, knowing Tasey liked applesauce perfectly well. Unfortunately it had appeared on the menu a little too often recently.

Tasey dug in with a grimace that lasted only as long as the first spoonful, when her mercurial mind turned to other matters. "When is the man going to keep his promise?"

"What promise?" asked Domini, confused.

"About the story," said Tasey, downing another mouthful with gusto.

Of course. The story about the unicorn. Grant Manners was not much on Domini's mind, and the word "man" had triggered thoughts of Sander. Domini put down her spoon, her appetite waning at the thought of disappointing her daughter. For some nights after Grant's visit, now several weeks past, Tasey had been excited at the prospect of a return performance by the person she called "the piggyback man." At her young age she had not yet learned that promises were not always kept, and Domini hated to disillusion her.

"I'm afraid he's not going to come back, darling," she said gently. Whatever business transactions she might or might not effect with Grant Manners, she was absolutely positive that all personal dealings had come to an end.

"But he *said*."

Domini wondered how she could explain without making too harsh an impact on the trust that was such an important part of childhood. "It's sort of like Marie and Matthew, poppet. There are times you can believe people, and times you can't."

"Then he lied!"

"No, he didn't lie, any more than Matthew was lying when he told you about cabbage leaves. Matthew just didn't know the truth. The piggyback man—well, you see, he expected to come back. But he won't."

"Why?"

"Because I'm not going to invite him."

"Why?"

"Because . . . because he's not my handsome prince. I can't pretend he is, even to make you happy."

"Why not?"

Damn this "why" age! It was hard to find logic to satisfy a child of three. "Because if I pretended," Domini said, making a stab at a reason Tasey would understand, "then I'd be lying, wouldn't I? Would you want me to lie?"

"N-nooo," said Tasey unhappily, but the subject was still on her mind half an hour and a long splashy bathtime later. Domini had just finished telling a bedtime story in order to wind her daughter down for the night, when Tasey murmured sleepily, "I don't think I want him for a daddy after all. He *promised.*"

Domini deposited a last gentle kiss on her daughter's brow. "Go to sleep, darling," she said softly, but with a small sadness because she recognized that a part of Tasey's trust had been destroyed after all. Should she have encouraged Grant, simply for Tasey's sake? What Tasey wanted and needed was a father, something she might never have. Certainly never from Sander. In thinking about it, Domini decided it was a lucky thing fate had prevented her from taking an irretrievable step that afternoon. Had she spent some hours in Sander's arms, it might be that much harder in future to fall in love with someone else.

Unhappy reflections made it difficult for Domini to

produce her evening's work, a sketch of her intended plans for Grant's next window. Under the circumstances she didn't want to approach him again unless well fortified with ammunition to further her cause. It shouldn't have taken long to depict a mannequin gaily dancing behind a semitransparent bubble while hands from the footlights showered her with diamonds, but it was hard to portray a sparkling mood she didn't feel. It was nearly three in the morning before she was satisfied with her efforts.

Exhausted from her late night, and from a morning spent dressing the window of a travel agency and wrestling with a magic carpet that was too heavy for the invisible wires suspending it, Domini almost begged off her arrangement with Miranda. But she had promised. And so, after a hasty trip home to change into an outfit appropriate for an afternoon as shoplady, she arrived at the little gallery with no expectation of seeing Sander at all. Her neat printed shirt and pleated gray skirt had been put on with no thought of removing them under any circumstances.

Miranda's face was glowing when Domini entered. "Such marvelous news!" she burst out at once. "The toys are sold, Domini, *sold!*"

The story tumbled out, words spilling so quickly that it took Domini a few minutes to understand the sequence of events. Evidently Miranda had left the telephone number of Joel's restaurant along with the sample case. A call had come earlier in the morning, expressing interest. Too excited to wait for Domini's arrival, Miranda had closed the gallery and dashed off to follow through.

"Everything will be on consignment, actually, so the money won't come in overnight. But it will come as the toys sell. And they will sell; it's just the right kind of shop! Oh, Domini, isn't it wonderful?"

"Wonderful," Domini agreed delightedly. If there was some small reservation in her mind, it was because she would have been happier to see Sander pursuing sculpture, and having a ready market for his toys might call a halt to that. "Have you . . . told Sander?"

"Of course," Miranda said happily. "But do you know, I think he hardly heard me? He was busy building an armature."

"An armature . . ." Domini's hopes leaped. If Sander was building an armature, then he must be planning to make a larger sculpture. "Has he finished it yet?"

Miranda shook her head. "I don't think so. He was working like a fiend this morning, punching metal tubing into shape. He just grunted when I told him about the toys. It doesn't matter, though, there's nearly a year's supply up there."

The past few years had instilled some caution in Domini, but not enough to prevent impetuous decisions when they were made from the heart. "I think I'll go up and see if he needs help," she said without second thought and with no regard for the fact that her clothes were totally unsuitable for the task of building an armature. And as to Sander's threat . . .

Well, that was very much on her mind as she climbed the stairs to the workshop. The door into the work area was open, and she came to a halt. Sander was at work on the armature, wearing an unbuttoned denim shirt rolled up at the sleeves, arm-deep in a concoction of soft clay with which he had already covered much of the mesh surface of chicken wire shaped over bent tubing.

"You've come back," he stated without turning around, and Domini knew he must have recognized her footsteps. "I didn't think you would."

"Neither did I," Domini said quietly. "I didn't come to model, I came to see if I could help. I've had a lot of experience building armatures."

"I've had a little myself, like any sculptor. In any case it's nearly done." He smoothed some more of the clay casing over its chicken wire frame, muscles rippling with the fluid, effortless movement. Domini watched, her heart full of a nameless longing, too distracted by his powerful attraction to give more than cursory attention to the lifesize and still formless sculpture he was starting.

"What is it going to be?" she asked at last, her eyes turning to the crude preliminary outline that might conceivably turn into a reclining woman once the clay had been built up.

"You."

"But—"

"My hands have some memory of their own," he said. "It may not be quite the same thing my eyes would see, in fact I'm sure it's not. But it helps. I also thought that what I forgot, I could always call to mind by feeling the small maquettes. I spent some days regretting that I'd scared you away, because nothing really replaces having a live model. The flow of flesh changes when a person changes position. I shouldn't have told you so bluntly to get out."

"Is that an apology?"

"Of sorts." He ran his hands once more over the surfaces of his armature and then, satisfied, picked up an old wet towel to wipe the worst of the clay mixture from his hands. He turned to face Domini, his expression carefully guarded, the unseeing eyes darker today, the flesh around them scored with the cruel marks of sleeplessness. "Will you model for me again? I'm obsessed with the need to do this, and I do need a model very badly. Not just any model. I need you."

"You said something as I was leaving last time," Domini reminded him. "Are you telling me you take it back?"

The bitter lines in his face deepened. "Shall I tell lies in order to get what I want? Perhaps I should, but I won't. I take back no threats, and I make no promises. You understood what I said, and you made your decision by returning. Now take off your clothes and climb on the platform at once. I don't intend to start on the actual modeling of the clay right now, but I want to see if I have the rough dimensions right before I stop for the day."

It was a moment for decision, a split second when Domini's head should have been in control. But, as if her rational powers had been suspended by Sander's absolute and unquestioning expectation that she could not fail to consent, she walked automatically to the chair where she always left her clothes and started to remove them. As she unzipped her skirt, unbuttoned her blouse, unsheathed her silk-clad legs, it was as though she had no choice—as though Sander's harsh imperative ruled, and not her own common sense.

Today his impatience was marked; his scowl suggested that he thought Domini was taking too long to disrobe. The terry robe was where she had left it some days before. She threw it over her shoulders without putting it on and went to the platform immediately.

"You won't need this for now," he said roughly as his hands came into contact with the garment. He whisked the robe away before she eased onto her perch, feeling as vulnerable as she had on the very first day. But his hands remained those of a sculptor, not a lover, as they ranged over her body, quickly adjusting the curve of her thigh, the languid bend of her knee, the curl of a hand resting open-palmed beside her cheek, the head slightly turned to one side. For once there was nothing difficult about the pose: it was the sensuous posture of a reclining woman, as Domini had guessed.

Sander spent some moments moving back and forth between Domini and the armature, feeling measurements to ascertain that his proportions were indeed correct. Because today she was not occupied in holding some stressful position, she was more than ever aware of the rough texture of his fingers as they roamed lightly over this intimate part or that. And she knew that her body's quick responses must be detectable to Sander too.

At last he shrouded the sculpture with large damp cloths and a plastic sheet. Between sessions it would remain protected to prevent drying; the moistness in the clay would have to be maintained until the sculpture was cast. Then he relaxed and came to sit on the edge of the platform, once more using the damp towel to wipe the clay mixture from his hands. "Don't move yet," he said. "I want you to understand this pose you're doing, because mood is very important in sculpture, and what I feel in your face is what will go into the finished work. Have you any idea what your pose is supposed to express?"

"Not really," Domini said, although she thought she knew.

"You're not sleeping," he said, his voice low and murmurous, the quality of it more lulling than at any time in Domini's memory. "And no, you haven't just made love. If either of those were the conditions, I'd have loosened your hair. You're waiting for your lover, Domini. And that's what I want to feel in your face. The invitation in the lips, the tremulous expectancy. I'll want you to pretend you're watching him undress, waiting for him to come across the room. The feeling should be languorous, expectant, the ardor smoldering just below the surface . . . do I have to tell you more? You're not an innocent. You must know what it's like, that breathless moment just before the lovemaking begins."

Domini licked her lips. It was as if he was making love to her with his voice, wooing her in a way she was helpless to resist. Even had she wanted to, she could not have broken the magnetic tension in the air; he exerted his domination without touching her at all.

"Try for the mood," he commanded softly and reached his fingertips forward to Domini's face. Her moistened lips greeted his touch. Unsmilingly, with a sensual expression on his face, he ran a finger around the curve of them, spreading the moisture to each edge.

179

He tested the polished surface of her teeth, felt the soft indentation of her upper lip, ran a finger into the little valley above her chin.

"Part your lips a little more," he commanded in a voice so husky that its vibrations seemed to echo in Domini's core. Drugged with longing, she obeyed, believing it was only a prelude to the moment when his lips would descend. Waiting and wanting, she gazed at the hooded dark eyes, the sensuous, arrogant curve of his mouth, the bend of his head as he leaned over the place where she lay. On his strongly sculpted face the stamp of pride and bitterness had been replaced by a slumbrous passion, a dark burning of desire.

He touched her eyelids, her cheek, her jaw, to determine her expression. "I think you have it now," he said softly. "A woman who wants to be made love to . . . I'm sure I feel that in your face. I wonder if the rest of you is as ready for the moment of mating?"

Without lowering his head, he passed his hand downward to her breast, grazing the nipples to assure himself that what he wanted, she wanted too. And then he rose swiftly to his feet and turned his back, filling Domini with an aching emptiness because there had been no completion of the kiss she wanted and expected.

"Put on your robe now," he directed in a toneless voice. "That's enough modeling for today."

Sick with the longings he had awakened, Domini raised herself on one elbow. "Sander," she whispered in a low tortured plea that betrayed the need that now washed through her like a cresting wave, flooding her limbs, driving even pride before it.

There was tension in the broad set of his shoulders. "Yes, I intend to make love to you. But this isn't the right place—you know full well we might be interrupted. I'm taking you up to my bedroom, Domini Greey, because no one ever walks in on me there, not even Miranda. Now put on your robe and come, and be quick about it."

It was not a request but a command, a harsh and arrogant one at that. But it only echoed the command of Domini's own body, passionate by nature and too long deprived of passion. Without a word she rose, slipped on her robe, and followed Sander up the stairs.

Because it was still early afternoon, there was light enough in the bedroom. He closed the door and walked across to the bed, stripping the covers back in one fluid movement. Then he turned to face Domini, desire darkening his face and turning his breathing heavy. "Come here," he ordered in a rough voice that sent heat thrilling through Domini's lower limbs.

Again she obeyed the pull of her body and her heart. Moving across the room, she came to a halt inches from the man she now knew she loved, and looked up at him expectantly, her eyes feverish with wanting. His unbuttoned shirt revealed the firm flesh she longed to feel, the crispness of hair that disappeared beneath the beltline of his trousers. Something told her not to touch, not yet, although she could not have said why.

He raised his hands and pushed the robe from her shoulders, allowing it to slide unchecked to the floor. Not yet kissing her, he reached for the pins that fastened her hair and extracted them slowly, one by one. Then he ran his long strong artist's fingers through the freed mass, pulling it forward so that the gold of it spilled over her breasts, and through the curtain of hair his roughened fingertips sought the ripe swell of the breasts themselves, the caress expert, unhurried, supremely arousing against her nipples. If he was impatient, it showed in no way in the sensuous expression of his mouth.

And Domini knew that he intended to teach her to make love lingeringly and beautifully, as she had wanted to be taught so many years before. Instinctively she knew she was right to contain her own urgency, allowing Sander to do with her as he wished; a man of his particular mold and virility would not wish the advances to be made by her. Once, she had been too forward, and she would not make the same mistake again. This time she would leave the pace to him.

And so she stood, longing for his kiss and his mastery but willing to wait for the moment when it came. All the same, by the time he bent his mouth to hers, hands sunk into her hair to shape the curve of her ears, she was in a tremble of need that knew no bounds. Not breaking the kiss that started gently and deepened slowly, he lowered her to the bed and came down beside her, still fully clad but for the opening of his shirt, where the disturbing textures now abraded Domini's bare breasts. Against her thigh, she could feel the mounting male power of him, leashed only by the confines of heavy cloth. And now he twined one hand more urgently in her hair and his kiss became passionately probing, betraying his true hunger even as his other hand moved. It slid downward over the slender hollows of her waist, not halting until it reached a more intimate goal.

The contact was electric. Although she had sworn to herself that she would respond at the pace he set, Domini gasped and arched extravagantly against his hand because she could not do otherwise with shock waves invading her core. He lifted his head, ending the joining of their lips.

"So wild, so soon?" he murmured into her ear, the expelled breath against her lobe only serving to quicken her passion. He had not changed the placement of his hand. As if he knew what urges were possessing her, Sander laughed softly and triumphantly, the laugh of a conqueror who knows the conquest has been made and can afford to take the spoils at his leisure. He dragged his tongue temptingly across her lips, evading the parted eagerness of them with a forbearance that was a deliberate torture to her. Then with his hand he began a slow, expert stroking that caused Domini to moan and writhe, all thoughts of curbing her responses now flown completely out of her mind.

"There's a pleasure to be had in putting off pleasure," he murmured as his head slid downward and his mouth moved to her breast. He seized a taut crest gently between his teeth, slowly increased the pressure, then found it softly with his lazy tonguetip. Domini gasped again, a long, shuddering gasp that traveled the length of her naked body. It was the first time his lips had ever touched her in such a way, and as he began to caress her breasts in earnest, hungrily seeking the nipples even as the expert feathering of his hand continued to arouse, Domini reacted with a wildness and ardor she could not possibly conceal. Her fists clenched against his chest, ungentle in their urgency; her hips strained upward to invite the moment nature intended her to know. At once he withdrew his touch, again with the husky laugh of a victor.

"Do you think I'll let you escape so quickly?" he murmured in a low, husky voice. "You're too importunate, my lovely friend. Hasn't anyone ever taught you that half the pleasure lies in getting there?"

Alternately tormenting her and gratifying her, he led her to the brink again and again. As his parted mouth ranged her nakedness, plundering it, lingering and lifting, his tempting incendiary kisses sent a flash fire raging in her blood, until her weakness became wantonness. She began to clutch at his hair, dig her fingers into his shoulders, tear at the shirt that still covered his muscles too well. And at last, satisfied that she would reach no higher heights, he relented.

Still containing his own desire, he began to bring her to the breathtaking conclusion. She resisted nothing, invited everything with responses as uninhibited as the lips that seared over her vulnerable flesh. Where his torrid mouth traveled, her skin ignited, and when he moved onward to kindle new flames, the moist imprint he left behind left erotic fires burning in her flesh. His hands were like brands that roamed and aroused as masterfully as his lips, firing her blood, turning her restless thighs to molten gold.

And all too soon, brought to mindlessness by the

burning intimacies of his mouth and the expertness of his caresses, the fire in her exploded, consuming her in a final skyrocketing burst of ecstasy that sent her hips arching higher and caused her fingers to clench hurtfully in his hair.

She cried out in the moment of release, although by then she was so wild with wanting that she could not have said what words she cried. And then, limp and clinging, she shuddered helplessly as she floated back to earth.

At last, radiant with satifaction, she opened her eyes and turned her head to look at him, the well of her love deepened because he had reined his ardor to give full freedom to hers. So her instincts had been right years ago: Sander was indeed a man good at teaching a woman what it was to be a woman. She knew he had taught her skillfully and well, taking time to arouse every sensory response she possessed.

He had detached himself and lay a little apart with one loosely curled hand resting over closed eyes. His expression almost approximated pain, and Domini thought she knew why.

She reached out to touch him with light fingers. "Make love to me," she whispered, wanting to satisfy his deep need as he had satisfied hers.

His mouth turned callous, matching the sudden flare of his nostrils. He uncovered his eyes and opened them. Lighted by the daylight from the gable window, they seemed to glow as they turned unseeingly toward her. "Fair is fair," he said tersely. "I just made love to you. Isn't it your turn to make love to me?"

Domini stared, shocked at the sudden change in him. No more the considerate lover, he had become the arrogant man locked into a prison of bitterness and pride. She sat up, only to have hard fingers feel for and then curl around her wrist, preventing any attempt at departure.

"Can you leave me like this—unsatisfied?" He pulled her hand to his waist and below, forcing it against the cloth concealing the potent contours of his manhood. For a long moment he held her fingers in place with a grip of steel.

"I don't think you could be so heartless," he mocked as he finally released her wrist. "Now undress me."

He had read her well. Domini could not leave him now, and not only because she would be leaving him in a state of arousal. Already the touch of him had sent frissons of new excitement chasing over the surface of her skin. He might be trying to demean her by ordering her to remove his clothes, but that was exactly what the primitive part of Domini wanted to do.

Less disturbed than Sander might have hoped, Domini smiled a smile he could not see. Now that she understood that his intent was to hurt her for some twisted reason of his own, she thought she knew exactly how to deal with him. She simply returned her hand to its resting place of a moment before.

His reaction was sudden and violent. Expecting reticence, not forwardness, he practically jackknifed to a sitting position, sucking in his breath in a long unsteady rasp. Unable in his blindness to foresee her actions, he had been taken totally by surprise, and the surprise robbed him of whatever self-control remained to him.

His kiss exploded against her mouth, driving her back against the pillow. After that there was no pretense of waiting for Domini to undress him. He released her mouth long enough to tear off his clothes, baring the strong muscles, the virile thighs whose power she longed to feel. He came crushing down on her at once, knees intruding to push her legs into readiness, hands almost violent in their seizure of her exhilarated body, mouth already opening with desire as it descended to ravish hers. As his kiss took her he drove home with no waiting, his hard-muscled body claiming absolute and instant dominion over hers.

This time he seemed not to care for her response. Yet, wildly excited by his sensual savagery, she gave it.

She wound her arms around his shoulders, laced her fingers in his hair, clung to his mouth, arched to the pulsing age-old rhythms of love. And at the end she matched his final passion with her own, finding once more the culmination of desire.

Afterwards they lay silent, Sander's face so totally forbidding that Domini dared not speak. She spent the time with her eyes learning all the intimate shapes of him, storing them in memory just as he sometimes seemed to memorize her with his hands. In the wake of passion a great sadness seized her as she contemplated how little he cared for her. At last she became conscious that the slant of the sun decreed that she ought to leave. She eased over Sander's naked body, for he lay on the outer edge of the bed.

He caught her as she slid to her feet, gripping her hips to prevent immediate departure. He came to a sitting position himself. Domini didn't try to pull away; she merely twisted within his arms in order to take one more lingering look at the man who had aroused her so.

"I have to go," she said quietly.

"Will you be back tomorrow?"

In her unhappy reflections Domini had been wondering about that, but her voice made the decision for her. "Yes," she heard herself say. "I will."

For a moment he buried his face at her waist, and Domini thought she saw a small shudder travel over his shoulders. Then he released her, and she decided she must have been mistaken, for his expression was no warmer than before.

"Next time we have sex," he rasped with deliberate and unkind emphasis on the last part of the phrase, "remember that I can be much kinder if you don't cry out meaningless words at the end. As long as you avoid them from now on, I'll be more . . . considerate."

Domini paused midway through reaching for her robe. "I don't know what you mean," she said, honestly puzzled. And then she remembered that in one moment of rapture, she had given vent to some kind of feeling. "What did I say?" she asked in a very low voice.

"Surely you can imagine." His face was discouragingly enigmatic, his eyes brooding. "Please spare me any repetitions, for I assure you I have no intention of ever feeding you the same sort of lie that you fed me."

Domini retrieved the robe, slipped into it, and fastened the belt, taking time with her answer because she knew full well what she must have said. And she knew that to let Sander know she loved him was to put herself too much into his power.

"It wasn't a lie exactly," she said as casually as possible. "Just the sort of thing one says in the heat of passion. Haven't you ever heard a woman say 'I love you' before? It doesn't have to mean a single thing."

"It never does," Sander returned bitterly, and Domini knew he must be thinking of Nicole.

Chapter Nine

Winter slush had been replaced by weak spring sun, and weak spring sun had turned to cloying summer heat. Heavy coats had long since been shed, boots had been put in closets, and now bare-armed women complained about the abominable temperatures that sometimes scorched New York in June. Tubs of flowers appeared on the hot SoHo sidewalks, secondhand books were laid on outdoor tables for the delectation of passing browsers, and sales of air conditioners were brisk. The pavements were crowded, not with Christmas shoppers but with tourists. Architecturally minded visitors came cast-iron looking, taking pleasure in nineteenth-century lampposts and gargoyles and acanthus leaves and great arched windows; others came to sample the exotic extravagances in Dean & DeLuca's huge and fascinating food emporium. SoHo in summer was hot, alive, energetic, and colorful.

Domini had lost some weight. Her relationship with Sander occupied too much of her mind and too many of her afternoons, and because it was a relationship with no hope that she could see, it brought deep anguish, as well as moments of exquisite ecstasy when all the anguish seemed of no moment at all. Often she swore she would stay away from the small gallery, but just as often she found her heart and her body tugging her back.

Sander's small cruelties had ceased, to be replaced by a dark and brooding passion that meant as much time was spent in his bedroom as in his workshop during her visits. Miranda could not help but become aware of what was happening upstairs, and although Domini avoided discussing it with her, she knew Miranda approved. She had the idea that Miranda hoped it might end in marriage—possibly for her own sake as much as for her brother's. If Sander married she would no longer have the responsibility of caring for him and could follow her own heart.

Overtired by trying to do too much, Domini began in early spring to restrict her visits to two a week, even less if her willpower behaved, or if Tasey had to miss day care because of the inevitable childhood episodes of sniffles and croup.

When informed of the reduction in the number of sessions, Sander had made no comment beyond a brief tightening of the jaw, which Domini interpreted as annoyance that her private life should interfere with his wishes. Wanting her as a model, he had become more careful of her feelings. Although pride and male arrogance were a part of his nature, he was no longer so tempestuous in anger, although he remained satisfyingly so in bed. As long as she betrayed no compassion and no emotional involvement, Sander was considerate, ardent, at times dryly humorous or even engaging in his manner. When sudden arrivals knocked on the door of his workshop, he now draped a cover over Domini before answering, a change of attitude for which she was exceedingly grateful. On occasion, depending on who was at the door, he draped his damp sheets over the sculpture too. He never spoke of love, nor did Domini.

For a time she had dared to hope he would. There was sometimes a tenderness in him in the moving moments after they had made love, when he would hold her close and stroke her hair or simply lay his hand gently alongside her cheek as if to read what changing emotions might be patterned in her face. At such times his own expression would remain remote and unrevealing. But on occasion during the sculpting sessions, when he thought himself unobserved, she would see a fleeting anguish flicker across his face, an expression that closely approximated her own hopeless feelings about the affair.

At the beginning that passing pain, so seldom sighted and so swiftly masked, made her wonder if his feelings were becoming involved more than he cared to admit. But one day while modeling, she forced a conversation that sounded the death knell to such wishful thinking.

"Have you ever been in love?" she dared to ask.

He stiffened. "I hope that's not a leading question. I don't believe in love."

"Just idle curiosity." Domini paused. "All those years you spent in Paris . . . surely you weren't so cynical then? There must have been someone."

"There were quite a few," he said harshly. "Women come and go and they mean nothing to me, especially now. In the dark one female is much the same as another."

Domini thought he was lying. He had once loved Nicole, she knew that; and she was also fairly sure that Nicole's desertion must have soured Sander's attitude toward women. She waited until he was touching her again, stroking her side to determine the exact flare of hip bone in the indolent posture he had asked her to assume. "There must be some woman you remember from Paris," she prodded.

"And if there was, how should that be your concern?" he countered with little inflection, but his hand came to a halt. Domini wondered if she detected a tremble in his fingertips. Or was it mere imagination?

"Because I imagine she was one of your models, like me," Domini said. "I'm curious about the competition."

"Ah," he said unrevealingly, and his hand went back to its task.

"Was she your last model?"

"I've told you, life sessions don't always end up in bed," he retorted misleadingly.

Domini thought about squeaking bedsprings, and old jealousies came spilling back, surprising in their intensity. Her voice was a little stiff when she replied, "Maybe not, but don't tell me hers didn't!"

"And what makes you so sure?"

"I've seen pictures of the sculptures you did of her." Domini plunged compulsively on, uncaring whether the memories were painful to Sander or not; his evasiveness was a goad. "One or two of them looked like they had been done *after* lovemaking, not before." Sander's face was impassive as stone, neither confirming nor denying. Splintered with jealousy, Domini added, "What was her name?"

"Nicole," he said, frowning down at the hip he could not see. Domini saw a small pulse ticking in his temple.

"Did you love her?"

"Love is a word that's not in my vocabulary," he grated discouragingly. "It implies a certain depth of emotion."

"And you've never felt that deeply?"

"Women are too fickle to be worth the involvement."

Domini's reactions to that comment were very mixed. If he thought of Nicole as fickle that was well and good, but she resented being put in the same category. She made efforts to curb the tautness in her tone, without much success. "Well, then, did you . . . care for her?"

"Look after her—pay her way? Yes. Is that what you want? To be paid for your services, as she was?"

Usually Domini ignored barbed comments such as these, inflicted as they were out of Sander's embittered and eternal night. But this time she longed for him to dispose of Nicole forever with some damning verbal condemnation. "No, I mean, did you like her?" she pressed.

"Of course. If I didn't like a woman, I wouldn't take her to bed at all," he said in a clipped tone.

Domini's fingertips began to curl more than her pose called for. "Then you must like me."

"Well enough," he cut back, "for the purposes you serve."

Domini glared at him, her eyes hot. "Do you like me as well as you liked that . . . that woman Nicole?"

"As a model or as a mistress?"

"Both," Domini said, frustrated that he would speak no words betraying any emotional tie to her. Did he really cast her in the same mold as Nicole?

"If I dared to say she was better at either of those things, I'd have no model whatsoever for this sculpture." Sander's stance challenged Domini in some obscure way. "Choose the answer that pleases you best," he finished curtly.

That particular answer didn't please Domini in any way at all. If he cared so little about giving her the benefit of the comparison, perhaps he still carried some kind of torch for Nicole. How *could* he still feel anything for the selfish bitch after what she had done?

"Do you still think of her?" she pressed, her voice a little sharper.

"Clearly I'm doing that right now," he returned acidly, running his powerful fingers into the hollow beside Domini's hip and punishing her persistence with pressure a little too extreme for comfort. "But if I'm thinking of Nicole, it's only because you're forcing me to do it against my will. Once a woman is out of my life, I prefer to put her out of my mind altogether. I'd rather concentrate on the one at hand, which at the moment happens to be you. By the way, you're allowing yourself to get too bony for my liking."

"At the moment *happens* to be me!" Domini retorted, because she could not prevent some small outburst of jealousy. "You make me feel like temporary help! How long am *I* going to last?"

Sander's dark eyes glittered. With an arrogant and deliberate assertion of the rights she had ceded to him, he allowed his hand to slide downward to an openly intimate position. "You'll last as long as you continue to satisfy me," he retorted insolently as he took his liberties. "And I think I'd like to be satisfied right now."

"Damn you," Domini gasped, abandoning her pose and trying to twist away. But already the point of no return had been reached. Holding her in submission with a sweep of his muscular arm, Sander dropped his dark head to the pale flare of her hip, passionately kissing what he should have been sculpting, and before long they were clinging as they climbed the stairs to his bedroom, Domini as urgent as he and no longer asking for the words of endearment he chose not to say.

When she loved him so desperately, how could she deny him anything, even when his demands were issued in such peremptory and loveless fashion?

The sculpture of Domini progressed with agonizing slowness. This time the face was not left unfinished, and Domini saw—as Miranda must see, and as anyone but Sander could see when the sculpture was not shrouded—that it was the face of a woman deeply in love. There was sadness in it as well as sensuality. Sander spoke only of the sensuality, and if he detected the range of other emotions expressed in Domini's eyes and mouth and rendered faithfully by his talented hands, he failed to remark on them. Perhaps the subtler nuances were transmitted by his fingertips without actually registering their meaning on his brain.

In the passing months he had started and finished

other pieces equally large. Some of them were stored in corners of the workroom; some of them were stored in the basement of the gallery; some were stored in an empty room on the third floor. All other sculptures were of subjects other than Domini—Joel, Miranda, the attractive nurse who lived down the street, and others whom Sander had been able to cajole into sitting either clothed or unclothed. The nudes awakened no particular jealousy in Domini, as Nicole had, because with her heart she knew full well that for the time being Sander's only sexual obsession was herself. And with her heart she also knew that he was deliberately stalling the completion of the large clay model, declaring himself unsatisfied with this aspect or that, because he wanted her afternoon visits to continue and was too proud to suggest she come for the sole purpose of occupying his bed.

On several occasions and with no great sense of guilt, Domini had surreptitiously removed some of the tiny maquettes he had done in the early days. Sander was too obsessed by his larger sculptures to even note that they were missing. Domini had made the plaster of Paris molds herself and arranged for a foundry to cast them in bronze, twenty copies of each. Unknown to Sander, Miranda was handling the small bronzes in the gallery, and though unsigned they were selling very well, especially the figurine of a faceless man and woman entwined in the act of love. Domini had long since recovered her initial investment at the foundry, and as the sculptures sold for a modestly substantial amount, there was no need for Miranda to urge Sander back to the construction of toys.

With relief Domini noted the signs of easing finances during her visits. The toys, as well as the bronzes, were producing a decent revenue, and one of the younger artists handled by the gallery was beginning to enjoy some small success as well. A telephone appeared on the sales desk, and Miranda reluctantly admitted that prior to Christmas it had been taken out due to nonpayment of bills. A new table materialized to replace the one Sander had preempted for his sculptures. Miranda bought a couple of flattering new dresses, and upstairs the light bulbs became a brighter wattage. A few small repairs were done to fix the fallen plaster, and Domini noted with pleasure that a wallpaper sample book had joined the pile of old art magazines on top of the gallery's sales desk.

The workshop itself changed, tools of carpentry and workbenches giving way as the number of finished sculptures grew, until one day Domini decided it could no longer be called a workshop at all. It was a studio, a sculptor's studio, less sunny and pleasant than some but a studio all the same.

One chance conversation with Miranda produced for Domini a deeper understanding of the financial problems that had plagued Sander for four years, and also filled her with dismay. "It would have helped," Miranda sighed at one point, "if he had received payment for the sculptures he did while he was in Paris. But he didn't. There was some funny thing about his dealer advancing money by mistake because of a murky arrangement with a man named D'Allard. For some reason this D'Allard seemed incensed—made a fuss about putting money out of his own pocket. Sander didn't explain the whole thing, but he told me that because of the circumstances he had to reimburse the man. In lieu of cash, he had to sign everything over to D'Allard—all of the finished sculptures at his dealer's, and even some things in the workshed he used. I think they all sold, but Sander didn't get a penny."

Domini felt ill. So her trouble had all been in vain after all. Losing her father from his stable, D'Allard must have set out to recoup the money he had advanced for her own indifferent art. No doubt Sander knew what the foolish young Didi had tried to do too; it must have been explained to him at the time. Not vengeful by nature, Domini nevertheless remembered with spiteful pleasure that D'Allard must have suffered considerable losses when her father severed connections.

With her problems easing, Miranda's face began to look less pinched and thin, except when her mind turned to wistful thoughts of Joel. Domini thought they were probably having an affair but didn't feel it was her place to pry. One day Miranda did, however, admit that she was familiar with Joel's apartment. "It's not very grand," she said. "Only three bedrooms, all quite tiny. For now, he can't afford anything bigger. His restaurant does well, but he's still paying off the bank loan he got when he started up."

Domini gathered that two extra people could not possibly move in to share Joel's quarters on a permanent basis. Miranda, maybe; Sander never. All the same, if the financial picture continued to brighten, maybe a solution could be found. Domini knew Miranda was hoping.

As for Sander, Domini realized wryly that he was too possessed by his need to sculpt to even notice that money problems had become less pressing. In doing the sculptures, he had indeed been helping himself, although he might not yet know it. Along with the satisfaction Domini felt came the bitter realization that should he ever become truly successful, he might soon feel no more need of her at all. For sculptors of note, models were easy to come by—and so were mistresses.

Domini's finances were easier too. Her bankbook showed no great balance, but it did show a balance. Grant Manners had awarded her the job as hoped, reaffirming that her initial judgment of him had not been too far amiss. She had lunched with him several times, purely business luncheons during which he remained affable and charming, pressuring her in no way for a relationship she clearly did not want. She liked him and knew he liked her, and there the matter remained. Oh, why hadn't she been able to fall in love with someone nice and easy like that?

"Another of the bronzes sold!" Miranda declared

happily as Domini came through the gallery door one day at the end of June, when the heat wave had still not broken. In the humidity her cotton shift was clinging over damp skin, and even without nylons and wearing light sandals she felt uncomfortably hot. It was cooler in the gallery, thanks to a somewhat cranky air conditioning system, a relic of more prosperous days when Miranda's husband had been alive. The cooling system didn't extend to the upper floors; Domini knew to her sorrow that the third floor, due to poor insulation in the old Victorian roof, was like a blast furnace.

"That's wonderful, Miranda." Domini smiled. "It's about time I filched another maquette, don't you think? Or shall I just get some castings from the molds I've already made?"

"I think it's time I started looking after all that," Miranda decided, displaying some firmness. She looked at Domini, her gray eyes clear and friendly. "I can manage it now, you know. Believe it or not, this heat is good for business! People come in to get cool and sometimes stay to buy. All this year I've had good tourist traffic—and some decent things to sell. It makes a difference."

"In that case why don't you think about having one of Sander's big pieces cast?" Domini suggested eagerly. "The one of Joel sitting dejectedly on an old chair is a simply marvelous study."

Miranda shook her head and made a face. "I'd have something big cast if I thought for a moment I could sell it. But in some things I'm a realist, Domini. The customers who walk in here wouldn't pay the price I'd have to charge for a large piece like that. Truthfully, Sander needs a better dealer than me. Preferably a chic uptown gallery, one with a good reputation."

There was no way Domini could dispute that, because it echoed her own sentiments exactly. There were many reputable and important dealers in SoHo, but the best of them featured works more avant-garde in nature than Sander's. He was an individualist, not a

197

follower of fashions in art; Domini would have called his works contemporary classics. Some of the studies he had done were more experimental than the sculpture of herself, but they were still firmly rooted in realism. They would do well with dealers such as the one that handled Domini's own father, but they wouldn't mingle well with Campbell's soup labels and overblown comic strips and collapsed plumbing fixtures made of soft plastic.

But such tact as she had acquired over the years forbade Domini to agree with Miranda too strongly, thereby casting a slur on Miranda's little gallery. She murmured a vague "Maybe."

And then, obeying the internal compass that pulled her to its own personal magnetic pole, her eyes turned restively toward the stairs. A brief conversation with Miranda had become a ritual part of her visits whenever she had a few moments to spare, but today she didn't feel like prolonging it. Since the start of the heat wave she had not liked to think of Sander sweltering over his sculptures in the confinement of a poorly insulated house. He refused to sit in the cool of the gallery because of an in-built hatred of being on public view. Troubled by the confined life he led, early in the year Domini had pushed and prodded him to start walking outdoors, something he had not been given to doing on his own because he disliked carrying his white cane or accepting help from strangers. Miranda, anxious for his safety, had also had to be convinced. But now Sander did sometimes venture alone within the range of a few familiar blocks, usually at night when he felt more comfortable about his cane. During the day he still avoided such outings.

But in weather like this there was little relief to be had on the streets; they were like blast furnaces too. Ought she invite Sander to her loft, which was somewhat cooler due to its high ceilings and white paint? Or would that be a mistake? She decided it would. Sander never asked questions about Tasey, and Domini scrupulously avoided the topic herself. To take Sander to the loft would be to take him into a world where traces of Tasey were everywhere, and Domini didn't think she could bear a situation like that.

The bell at the door jangled, advertising the arrival of a customer. With a last murmured word to Miranda, Domini hastened up the stairs.

Sander was out of view in the kitchen. Domini could hear the clink of glass. "Start stripping," he called out at once. "Would you like a glass of ice water?"

"Yes, if it's big enough to jump into," Domini called in return. On a day like this there were distinct advantages to be found in removing one's clothes, and she did so in about two seconds flat. Sander entered the room while she was still removing her sandals, the last of the coverings to go. He was barefoot and naked to the waist, his only concession to decency a pair of cut-off jeans. His lean, hard torso was gleaming with perspiration, and in his hands were two glasses already dripping with condensation.

"What a good idea," he murmured smokily.

"What good idea are you talking about?" asked Domini, accepting the chilled glass and looking at him through her lashes while she touched her tonguetip to the ice and then quenched her thirst.

"A cool shower," he said, "or a bath. Something big enough for two to jump into. Something wet and very, very wanton."

Anticipation tingled through Domini's blood as his hand arrived to close over her wrist, locating it easily because of the clink of ice cubes. "Does this mean you've finished the sculpture of me?" she asked. Beneath its damp shroud the sculpture looked altogether complete to her, and she had been wondering when Sander was going to admit that it was done. On her last visit he had not touched it at all, claiming that it was too hot to work, and yet he had not found it too hot to vent his passion on the steamy third floor.

He bent his parted lips to bathe a wrist already damp

from the day's heat. His tongue was chilled from the ice, sending a sensuous thrill up Domini's arm. When he straightened, she tiptoed impulsively up to kiss him, too, and tasted the salt tang of his sweat-moist jaw on her tongue. "I'm not sure about the bath," she whispered happily. "You taste wonderful exactly the way you are."

"No more talk," he muttered, removing the glass from her hand and putting it down on a table. Then he drew her to the door.

"My robe," Domini reminded him, pulling back.

"A little risk only adds to the excitement. Besides, don't you think anyone with eyes to see my sculpture will soon be able to see exactly what you look like in the nude? Think about that, my beautiful friend . . ."

In the unrestored Victorian bathroom, the old-fashioned bathtub was huge on its massive clawed feet. Above it was the showerhead, with a light plastic curtain affording the only enclosure. Sander adjusted the spray of the nozzle, evidently having settled on a shower rather than a bath. Impatient for his sensual satisfaction, he lifted Domini into the tub and stepped in himself without taking time to remove his short frayed denims. As the shower stung them both, their mouths met urgently and with no hesitation, Domini reaching for his waistband with the abandon of a woman who knows her bold caresses are wanted.

Perhaps it was indeed the risk of having no robe that added to the excitement, or perhaps it was the sharp tingle of water on bare flesh, or perhaps the unleashing of Sander's turbulent and turgid passion, unquelled by the shock of cooling spray. Domini was by now well acquainted with all the secrets of his superb male physique, but the newness of the moment made the lovemaking itself seem new. Sander loosened her hair to let it stream free. Then he lifted her against his aroused body to command her with the kiss his greater height would otherwise not allow, his powerful muscles supporting her slender curves as easily and surely as if she were no more than a feather's weight. With one impatient hand imprisoning her waist and the other smoothing her willing hips into instant compliance, he sank his mouth greedily into the hollows of her arched throat. Domini gasped with pleasure as she felt him join her as if for the first time, and the wild savagery of his kisses against her wet skin told her that for him, too, the moment of joining was supreme.

With bodies bare and streaming and mouths hungrily exploring, with dark hair and gold soaked and mingling beneath the shower, with droplets beading on his chest and hers, they made impassioned love, although Sander might have chosen to call it sex.

"What an unbridled creature you are," his wet mouth muttered against her straggling hair a short time later when he had released her from his commanding grip. "You don't hold anything back, do you? And to think I once believed you had inhibitions."

"The shower washed them all away," Domini breathed, still quivering in the aftermath of his ungoverned and inventive ardor, which she had returned with wild shamelessness.

After that he soaped her and she soaped him with a slowness and sensuality that was pleasurable in itself, although both were too well sated for a renewal of the volcanic passion of before. When the shower had rinsed them, Sander closed the drain and allowed the tub to fill. And then, with the shower at last turned off, they sank together into the contained cool sea of the tub.

And there they remained for the next few minutes, Domini at first luxuriating in the coolness of her flesh, but soon turning reflective and unhappy as she lay enclosed in Sander's arms, in a tight embrace dictated by their close confinement in the bath. With lids lowered over the sightless silver eyes and a distant expression on his mouth, he ran his fingers over her body with the slow-motion indolence of a man whose passions have been fully slaked, lightly touching her breasts and the contours of her face, neither speaking nor asking Domini to speak. She accepted without question, because the lazy stroking of his now passionless fingers must needs serve him instead of eyes, and serve her instead of the words of love she wanted so desperately to hear.

To Domini there was no wrong in what she did. She loved and she expressed her love freely and fully and without reserve, as she had been taught to do in childhood. Although she was bound by neither vows nor inhibitions, she was bound by stronger bonds. Sander had fathered her child although he did not know it, she loved him although he did not know it, and Domini would have married him had he asked. She knew he would not ask, not only for reasons of pride or cynicism, disillusion or despair, but because his feelings for her did not include love. Were it not for her daughter, she would have moved in with him altogether and felt no shame, although she was certain that Sander would not have asked that of her either. He might want her physically, but he wanted her in no other way.

Domini's morbid reflections troubled her, and she decided she was only torturing herself by staying for the afternoon when no sculpting was to be done. Wordlessly she left Sander in the bath, wondering if the deep furrow in his brow was caused by thoughts as difficult as hers.

With passion no longer heating her flesh, she was more cautious on the downtrip, and so she commandeered Sander's dressing gown for the return to the studio. Moments later she was on the main floor, hair still damp and twisted into a quick ponytail.

Miranda was idling over a daily newspaper, one of several on her desk, but put it down as soon as Domini appeared. If she was surprised at the shortness of the visit, she didn't comment upon it.

"Sit down and take a break," she suggested with no

more than a faint smile at the sight of Domini's betrayingly wet hair, which had dripped down the back of her light dress, darkening the cotton. "I'm only catching up on last week's art columns, which I was too lazy to read at the time. And I'm still too lazy! I'd much rather visit. Besides, it's been ages since we've had a really good chat. You're always in such a hurry, first to get to Sander, then to get to Tasey. Or do you have to rush off to see some client?"

With the end of day care still some time away, Domini was for once able to take a breathing spell, and so she sank onto a padded bench near the sales desk, unwilling as yet to face the intense heat of the street. "No, thank God, my work's in good shape. I have no more windows to change until next week. Then I have a pile to do, but perhaps the heat will have broken. They say it's about to."

"How's Tasey these days?" The question was another small part of the ritual exchange indulged in during Domini's afternoon visits, one that had been neglected earlier because of the arrival of a customer. Ritual or no, Domini knew that Miranda's interest was genuine.

"She's fine, getting taller by the day. Do you know, her fourth birthday is only two months away?"

"I wish you'd bring her to visit." Miranda sighed.

Domini merely smiled and gave a small shrug. She was running out of excuses for her failure to bring her daughter back to the gallery, in view of the oft-repeated invitation. Tasey, too, sometimes asked when she was going to see the ice cream lady again.

"It might be a good idea if Sander got to know her," Miranda suggested too artlessly with another oblique look at Domini's dampened hair.

"And then again it might not," Domini said firmly. "Sander hasn't got marriage on his mind, Miranda."

"Maybe you could change it for him, if you let him know how you felt." Miranda leaned forward earnestly. "Actually I've been wanting to have a good long talk with you for some time, but you always race off before I can get my two cents in. I'm not half-witted, Domini. I know you're in love with Sander. Why, it sticks out all over you, and if he had eyes, he could see it for himself. The way you look at him, the way you say his name . . . good Lord, even the way you walk up the stairs so flushed and expectant. But when you come down, you always look . . . well, kind of sad. Hopeless."

"Is it that obvious?" Domini asked quietly.

"To everyone but Sander," Miranda replied. "Why, Joel noticed at once. Face it, Domini. Sander isn't going to suggest marriage because he wouldn't want to be a burden to you. He's too damn proud! But if you brought Tasey around once in a while, he might begin to understand that you need him as much as he needs you. You're always thinking about his problems—why don't you let him think about *yours?*"

"I don't have any," Domini said.

"Rubbish," Miranda returned, eyeing Domini skeptically. "Sharing troubles is a two-way street, and yet you keep all yours to yourself and try to solve ours. Don't think I haven't noticed how much you've helped us! You have a money shortage, too, I know it, but do you ever tell that to Sander? Do you discuss the difficulties you have with your clients? Do you talk about the nights you have to sit up when Tasey has croup? You never complain, and yet it can't be all that easy raising a child on your own, especially when you have to run a business too. If Sander could see that your daughter needs a father . . ."

Domini studied her fingers and tried to control their tremble. "I don't think he likes her," she said. "In fact, I'm sure of it. He cut me up for not keeping her under control the night she was here."

"Good grief, she wasn't that much trouble. Don't forget these past few years have been very difficult for Sander; it isn't easy for a man like him to adjust to blindness. He hates being helped and he hates feeling helpless. That's made him put a wall around himself and pour boiling oil on anyone who happens to get too close to the fortifications. But you know, Domini, he wasn't always such a bitter man. And he's not as bitter now as he was a few months ago, when you first appeared on the scene. You've helped draw him out of that terrible solitude he was in, you and the work he's doing now. I'll bet Tasey could help complete the job if you'd give her half a chance. Kids are so natural."

"I don't know," Domini said slowly. "I don't think it would work."

Miranda regarded her steadily and sternly. "If you just keep giving Sander more of what he wants, he's going to keep taking. It's time you asked him for something in return, and I mean something that doesn't happen in bed. As long as you allow yourself to be a sex object that's exactly what you'll be—a sex object and nothing more. Is that what you want?"

"No," Domini admitted unhappily.

"I didn't think so," Miranda said more kindly. After a moment's thought she suggested: "Why don't you bring Tasey here for the weekend? Ask us to look after her, make some pretext of going away for a few days. The spare bedroom's filled with sculptures, but there's a cot in there I can pull into my own room for her stay. You know I love children. And if you weren't around, Sander would get to know her better, simply because he wouldn't be angrily looking to you to keep her under control. He used to be quite good with children. If he had to help take charge of Tasey for a while, it could make him feel needed. I think he'd get a whole new view of you too. Why, it might be just the thing."

"I'll think about it," Domini temporized. Could there be something in what Miranda said? Or would it simply amplify the internal anguish of these past months if it didn't accomplish anything? If Sander and Tasey took a real dislike to each other, Domini didn't think she could bear it.

"Don't think, just do it," urged Miranda, and then as if Domini's extreme inward distress had registered in some way, she ceased to lecture. A moment later she tactfully changed the subject. "How's the unicorn? Still bearing up? Or is Tasey getting too old for it?"

"Oh, I don't imagine we'll be scrapping it for a while." Domini managed a brave smile. "There's a little mileage in it yet."

"I wouldn't scrap it at all," Miranda remarked, flicking a fingernail at the newspaper she had been reading. "Who knows, even though it's only a copy you soon may be able to sell it for a profit, because I imagine Le Basque's prices are about to jump to the moon. You know what happens when a great artist puts one foot in the grave—the collectors who've already bought are quite happy if he puts the other one in too! Even his laundry list will be fetching a fortune now that the news is out. Isn't it always the way?"

Premonitions of disaster clutched at Domini's stomach. "Isn't what always the way?" she asked, trying to keep her voice steady.

"Read for yourself," Miranda offered. She tossed the folded newspaper in Domini's direction. "He's had a massive heart attack."

Domini's face drained, and it was a lucky thing that two Japanese tourists chose that exact moment to walk into the shop, relieving her of the necessity of reacting to Miranda's revelation. Like an automaton, she turned her eyes to the art columns in the paper, finding at once the headline about Le Basque. While Miranda showed her customers a portfolio of large numbered lithographs, Domini quickly scanned the story, her numbness growing with every word she read. The columnist confirmed the worst. According to the story, Le Basque's three legal sons, Domini's American half-brothers, had been contacted by the newspapers and revealed that they were making plans to rush to his bedside.

And then, remembering something Miranda had said earlier, she looked and saw that the newspaper was a full week old.

She put the paper back on the desk but remained seated, trying to think through the swirl her thoughts had become. Papa dying! He was in his mid-seventies now, and it should not be a shock. But it was. He had always been so strong, so much a cornerstone of Domini's existence, that she had never thought of him in terms of death. And yet he was dying. He had been dying for a week, and she had not known. . . .

Her brain refused to work very well, but she knew what she must do, and she knew she would need Miranda's help. It didn't matter whether Papa loved her or not; she loved him. She couldn't take Tasey to France, and she couldn't afford a live-in sitter, let alone find one on such short notice. For months she'd been ignoring former friends, making excuses in order to free time for Sander, and having done that, it was hard to approach others for help.

At last Miranda finished with her customers. Whether two minutes had passed or twenty, Domini was not sure, but it was a period sufficient to help her get some grip on herself. Her face was calm and set, if a little white, when Miranda returned to the sales desk and sat down with a sigh because no sale had been made.

"I've been thinking about what you said," Domini started at once. "I'm going to take you up on your offer, Miranda, and I don't even have to invent an excuse. I had news a few weeks ago that my aunt is dying."

"No wonder you've been looking so drained," Miranda sympathized. "Is that the aunt who brought you up?"

"Yes, the one who lives in France." The lie needed little amplification because Miranda had been told of Domini's fictitious background several months before. "I had decided I couldn't fly over to see her because I couldn't afford a woman to look after Tasey. I simply don't have the money. But I'd really like to go because my uncle is very upset. The only thing is, it might mean leaving Tasey here for more than a weekend, but at least during the week she's in day care all day. If you could help me out, I'd be . . ."

The words choked to a halt as Domini bowed her head and pressed taut fingertips to her cheekbones. She ached for the release of tears, but they would not come. Had she really been making love to Sander while Papa was dying in France?

"You poor kid," Miranda said, coming to her side and putting an arm around her shoulder. "Didn't I tell you it's better to share your problems? Of course Tasey can stay with us. Bring her over any time."

There was just enough money in the bank, fortunately, to pay for a round-trip airline ticket. Domini drew it all out. As soon as she had wait-listed herself on half a dozen flights, pleading an emergency and earning a sympathetic but not entirely optimistic promise from the travel agency that was one of her own regular clients, Domini hurried back to her loft and placed a call to France.

The new servant who answered the phone was unfamiliar with the name Greey, and Domini had to assure the suspicious woman several times that she was not a member of the press, but a relative. Because her father had disowned her, she didn't wish to mention the exact nature of the relationship; nor was she sure of the reception her call would be given, except by Berenice herself.

The servant must have neglected to mention the name or had perhaps muddled it in the transmission, because when Berenice came on the line she was unprepared for the sound of Domini's voice.

"Berenice?"

"Didi," Berenice whispered, choked, recognizing Domini from the syllables of that one utterance, as if it had been only yesterday they had spoken. "Oh, Didi . . ."

"How is Papa?" Domini asked urgently, sliding easily back to the language of her childhood.

"Not at all well," Berenice said, and Domini could hear the tears and the worry in her voice. "You must come at once. You must hurry."

"I am coming, Berenice, as soon as I can. I only learned today. Where is he? In the hospital?"

"He refuses to go to the hospital. He wants to die at home."

"Then it's true," whispered Domini.

"Where are you? If you're in Europe, I'll send a car . . ."

Domini controlled her voice. "I'm in America, Berenice. New York. I'll be catching a flight as soon as I can. It's a little hard to get a seat because this is the tourist season, but I'm doing my best. Actually I'm planning to go to the airport on standby and take the first seat I can get. I'll call you from there as soon as I know when I'm coming."

Berenice paused for only a fraction of a minute. "No, no, leave it to me. Perhaps I can arrange something. Give me a phone number where I can reach you."

Domini did. "It's a business number," she added. "A little later I have to go out for half an hour, to . . ." But this was no time to explain about Tasey, who would soon have to be picked up from day care. ". . . to do something. But I have an answering service, so if someone picks up and says Displays Unlimited, don't be surprised. Leave a message."

"I'll be back to you soon," Berenice promised.

"And please, tell Papa I love him, and that I would be there right now if I could. Tell him I'm sorry about everything. At least, tell him all that if . . . if it won't upset him or make him worse in any way."

"I will tell him." Berenice's voice dropped to an anguished whisper. "He clings to life, Didi, for one thing only. He longs to see you."

So Papa had forgiven her at last. When she hung up, Domini dropped to the floor beside the yellow unicorn and wrapped her slim arms around its neck. She rested her dry cheek against its carved surface and wished she could shed some of the terrible tears the years had put into her heart.

Chapter Ten

Berenice used the kind of influence wielded only by the very great or the very rich. Domini was on a Concorde to Paris within hours, in a seat procured heaven knew how. No one asked for money to pay for the luxury flight, and Domini did not offer because she simply didn't have enough cash anyway; she presumed Berenice had looked after it. At Charles de Gaulle Airport a limousine was waiting to take her to a small airfield, where a light plane had been chartered to fly her to Pau. At Pau, Georges, the chauffeur of former years, was waiting to take her for the final lap of the trip, over the twisting route into rugged terrain where no airstrips existed. The loyal Georges reassured Domini that her father still clung to life. She asked few other questions during the trip, not wanting to interrupt his concentration; Georges was driving at top speed. Less than twenty-four hours after learning of her father's illness, Domini drew up at the great ironclad front door of his home.

There were a dozen cars parked outside the gates, and an ambulance stationed on the driveway close to the house itself. Domini hurried from the limousine to the front door, found it locked, and had to ring the bell. A servant—perhaps the same suspicious woman who had answered the telephone—arrived and went to fetch Berenice, leaving Domini waiting in a small reception room.

It opened onto the courtyard, and while she waited, pale in the wake of a long, sleepless night, Domini walked over to look out onto the flagged area, once an enclosure where farm animals had been kept. For some reason she wanted to see her father's stone, perhaps because to her it was a symbol of his strength. She saw at once that it had been moved to a new place, a raised platform constructed of large flat flagstones. The great stone sat squarely on top, high as a man's head, more important than ever in its new position. But the stone was not the only thing Domini saw. Disturbed, she realized why there were so many cars around. People whose purpose she could not imagine lounged outside in the noon sunshine of the courtyard. A maid was serving drinks, and a table of sandwiches had been laid out.

Domini guessed that some of the strangers were members of the press, and at least one woman was wearing the crisp uniform of a nurse. One was a famous French politician, come to pay his last respects. He was posing for someone's camera, smiling and looking like a puffed parrot, with one hand resting on Papa's special stone. Domini wanted to rip it off at the wrist, screaming at the indecency.

Domini saw D'Allard too. Perhaps her father had mended fences with his one-time dealer, or perhaps D'Allard was also looking for publicity. He appeared overly and insincerely lugubrious in his expensive black suit. Domini knew he had privately bought a number of Le Basque paintings and sketchbooks before the falling out; he had probably been waiting for Papa's death to put them on the market. Domini felt ill.

Two prosperous looking men, both in their late forties, were seated on a stone bench hunched in private conversation, with another slightly younger man standing behind them, listening intently. From photographs seen in her youth, Domini recognized them as her own half-brothers, who in all the time of her memory had never so much as sent her father a Christmas card, although he had settled enough money on their mother to make them all very wealthy men.

Domini turned away. Papa was dying, and the vultures had descended. And yet, would he feel that she was only one of them?

Berenice hurried into the room a moment later. They embraced wordlessly, too moved for immediate greetings. When Berenice pulled back, Domini saw that her father's long-time companion looked older than her forty-odd years, her fine dark eyes lined and deep with the strain of living in the shadow of death.

"Before I take you in to him, Didi, there are some things you must know about your father. Dying like this, with all these people around—" Berenice's voice broke and then calmed. "He would have preferred a simpler ending. But to bring you here, the whole world had to be told, and it was he who told me to tell them. If you doubt that he cares for you, think of that."

Domini's eyes stung, as if the tears she could not shed had already fallen. So she had been right in thinking that in his heart Papa did not change. Why had she ever doubted him?

"For a long time he tried very hard to find you," Berenice went on. "I'll explain later when we talk, because now there is no time to waste; you must go to him. One more thing. He has not been at peace with himself since . . . since that day. He cannot forget what he did. Can you tell him you forgive him?"

"Oh, Berenice," Domini said through a hurting

throat, "I did that long ago. I thought it was he who had not forgiven me."

"He doesn't know you're here yet. But I did tell him you had called, and every time he wakes he asks for you. Now come."

Domini controlled her emotions because she knew she must do so before going in to see her father. She followed Berenice through the familiar halls of her childhood, memories flooding over her at every turn, every time-indented stair. She knew it all by heart and loved every carved post, every mullioned window, every windowseat, every piece of paneling along the way. Her father's paintings crowded the walls, and many were of her; of those done during Domini's adolescent years, none had ever been sold. It moved Domini to see them still hanging. Remembering the destructive slashes of black paint that had destroyed one portrait, she had sometimes wondered if all of them had suffered a similar fate.

Inside the house it was relatively peaceful because all the visitors but Domini were for the moment outside. But there were nurses and two doctors in attendance in Le Basque's room, and equipment that must have been rushed from a hospital in Lourdes. Berenice told Domini to wait at the open door. "He will want to see you alone," she said, "and with no one to watch."

She hurried the nurses out easily enough, but Domini heard one of the doctors objecting in a low voice. Berenice literally pushed him through the door. "And what do you think you have been keeping him alive for?" she hissed, sotto voce.

Domini entered her father's room, closing the oaken door quietly behind her. This great sunny bedroom was loved and familiar too. In her very youngest years she had often come bouncing in to wake her father in early morning, certain of her welcome even when there was a mistress in his huge old four-poster bed. There had been romps and tickles and screams of laughter, the good-natured Basque women in their voluminous white nightdresses joining in as easily and naturally as Domini did herself.

The room was unchanged but for the I.V. stand and other medical equipment. Even the sun spilled in, and Domini knew it was because her father preferred it so; he had never liked sickrooms and darkened windows. She walked to her father's bedside. His eyes were closed, his face gray, his cheeks shrunken, his skin like parchment. He might have been dead already but for the faint, irregular breathing that lifted his once burly chest. Without hesitation Domini dropped to her knees on the carpet beside the bed and picked up a hand that looked far too limp and lifeless. She kissed it and then pressed it to her cheek.

"I've come home, Papa," she said.

His sunken eyes opened. Although his great heart had almost given out, the spark of life in his eyes was not yet dead. They were not focused on Domini though, and he muttered as if in pain, "Didi? I think I dreamed. Oh, God, I dreamed . . ."

"No, Papa, you're not dreaming. I've come home," she repeated and moved to sit on the edge of the bed where he could see her more easily. She kept his hand in both of hers. "I love you, Papa," she said simply and leaned over to rest her face against his time-weathered cheek. "I love you more than I can tell."

"Didi," he said, and Domini could feel the tremble in his mouth, the heave of his chest, the quiver of his hand. His voice was agitated. "There's so much to say, so little time to say it. I destroyed your picture, but—"

"Hush," she whispered to calm him. "It doesn't matter. I love you, Papa. The rest can wait."

For a time neither spoke nor moved. When Domini felt peace begin to steal through her father's body, she finally raised her head so she could see him. There were tears standing in his eyes, but he was calmer.

"Will you forgive me, Didi?" he whispered.

"Will you forgive me, Papa?"

"How could I not forgive, when I love?" he said, trembling. "I forgave you long ago."

"And so did I," Domini said gently. "I stayed away out of pride, only pride. I would have come before if I had known you needed me."

"Tell me about . . ." Effort had made his words weak, and although Domini could not hear the rest of his sentence, she guessed that he wanted to know where she had been, what she had been doing, how she had been surviving. And so she told him, in simple words and omitting all the more painful parts, including any mention of Sander.

"Anastasia," he muttered at one point, with a smile hovering at his lips. "Is she . . . like you?"

"She has my eyes, Papa. And . . . yes, I think she's a little like I was at that age. Very happy, very trusting, very . . . full of joy. I think you would love her."

"Yes," he said without question and did not ask who the father had been. His eyes closed tiredly, but he looked quite pleased. Serenity washed over his face while Domini talked on, telling quietly of happy times until she saw that he was growing too weary to listen more.

"Papa, you should rest now," she said. "I can come back in a short while."

At once he seemed to grow restless again, and his fingers found the strength to clutch at hers. "No," he mouthed, the word too weak to be heard. And so Domini sat, no longer speaking because she was afraid she had overtired him. Within moments he slid into a shallow sleep, not quite relaxed because every once in a while his mouth would twitch as though he were trying to say something.

When her father spoke again, his voice was so faint, so faraway, that Domini had to bend her head to hear it. "Something else . . . wanted to say . . ."

"You can tell me later, Papa."

"No . . ." Effort was rattling his chest, moving his

mouth in meaningless little mutters. ". . . sold the . . . sold the unicorn . . ."

"You don't have to explain, Papa. I don't mind at all. After all, I grew out of it years ago." Domini looked at her father ruefully, realizing from all she had learned that he must now deeply regret that time when he had tried to thrust her from his life. She wondered what she could say to put some peace in his soul.

"Do you know, just a few months ago I bought one almost like it for Tasey," she said gently. "It was only a copy, but I bought it because . . . because to me it meant love, your love. You gave me the most beautiful childhood in the world, Papa. If you sold the unicorn it doesn't matter, because it will always be there in my heart."

Le Basque's face lit into a dim smile, and he slept.

He died peacefully toward the very end of that same night, with Berenice and Domini beside him. The doctors had thought him improved. They and the nurses had been told by Berenice to stay out of the room, and because she could be very firm, they had finally withdrawn. She knew Le Basque's time had come, with the inner knowledge of someone who understood his true heart and not merely the erratic patterns on a screen. If she had been the great love of Le Basque's latter years, for her he had been the great love of her life.

The daily retinue of those who had come to see Le Basque die had left some time before. Some had returned to Paris, and some—Domini's half-brothers among them, and a few persistent journalists—were staying at a local hostelry.

Berenice had prepared a room for Domini, and because she alone of the visitors was asked to stay at the farmhouse, others remained for the time being unaware of her arrival. Only the doctors and nurses and a few of the servants knew. Berenice had suggested some discretion, thinking to spare Domini the agony of unnecessary publicity. Already there had been too many questions over the past few days about the whereabouts of Le Basque's famed illegitimate child. In the latter part of his life Le Basque had protected his privacy, and so it had not been generally known that Domini had vanished some years before; but one of the servants had let it slip, arousing immediate curiosity. Only the day before, a photographer had been caught trying to take a shot of one of the portraits of Domini in her late teens. The publicity could not be avoided forever, but at least it would not mar the time of deepest grief.

In the bedroom of her childhood Domini had slept the sleep of exhaustion after the afternoon visit with her father, and wakened for a late supper before joining Berenice for the long night's wait in her father's room. It was nearly dawn when he died, and even then Berenice did not call the doctors at once. Quietly she closed his eyelids, her final gesture of farewell. Then she said to Domini, "If they come now they will thump at his heart and do undignified things to try to make him live. Your father would not have liked that; he knew he was mortal. He will live, but not because of anything the doctors do."

And then Berenice bent her head and murmured, "He wanted no priests to be with him when he died. He said they would have him soon enough, and for all time." In the tongue of the Basque people she added so quietly that the words could hardly be heard: *"Orhait hilceaz."*

Remember Death. It was an inscription often seen in the Basque Pyrenees, where the end of life was accepted with peace—not as a penalty, but as a fair and natural price to be paid for the gift of living. Since that long-ago day when one dead lamb had been used to save the life of another, Domini had not been uneasy in the presence of death. *It is not death that matters, but life,* her father had said. Not long after the incident of the lambing, her father had taken her to a nearby country graveyard. There they had walked together hand-in-hand and looked at the tombstones of Basques who had died many centuries before. Most of the odd disc-shaped markers wore the patina of very great age, and they had seemed as timeless and enduring as the quiet mountains that guarded them. It was a place where peace seeped into the soul, and with her small hand in her father's the repose of that graveyard had held no fears for Domini. At the time Le Basque had told her it held no fears for him. And although she had not been able to imagine him ever dying, she had known he would tell her no lie.

Beneath the grass of that same serene and simple graveyard, soon he would rest. *Orhait hilceaz.*

And so they sat for a time, Domini's eyes hot and dry as desert sands, Berenice pale and tearless too. Half an hour later, when the sun rose, they retired to a small private sitting room, at last leaving the shell of the great man both of them had loved in the care of professionals. A servant brought coffee and croissants, which neither woman ate. It was the first time the two had been alone, and Berenice began to ask quiet questions, discovering some of the same things Domini had told her father. She listened with tired eyes, smiling faintly when she learned of Tasey, and stemming her own grief for some later and more private time.

"You made him content at the end," Berenice said, once Domini had revealed the simple facts of her existence during the past few years. "If you had not come, he would have died an unhappy man. And after what happened, I thought you might not, because he had been very . . . harsh. After you vanished, I regretted that I had sent you away so quickly that day, not taking time to help you understand why your father was so upset. It had a great deal to do with his own life. His youth, his first love, his marriage."

"I know very little about those things," Domini said.

"Yes," sighed Berenice. "Because he always hid

from you the hardness of his life. I think he told no one, until he told me. You see, my child, to your father his name meant a very great deal. Inside him there was a great pain for the life he had led to earn it. His strength and his sorrow came from that name, and when he saw it used so lightly . . . but how could you understand his anger without understanding his past?"

"Please tell me," Domini said quietly.

Berenice laid her head against the high back of the rocking chair where she sat, and closed her eyes. "Yes, I will tell. He asked me, in fact, to tell you the whole story, because he wanted you to know what caused him to send you away when he did. And I think he would want you to be told today, of all days. It may make many things clear. You are what you are because he was what he was. I can't start at the beginning, Didi, because to your father's story there is no real beginning, just as there will be no real end. His memory only started halfway through his childhood, and when it started he had no name at all."

"Amnesia?" asked Domini after Berenice had spent a reflective moment in silence.

Berenice nodded and opened her eyes. "Shock," she said. The word was spoken in the ancient tongue of the Basque people, so dissimilar to any other in the world. Except for the two familiar words spoken over her father's deathbed, Domini had not heard it used for four years, but it was as natural to her ear as French or English. And she knew that Berenice had used the archaic tongue because it was a language more suited than others to the telling of her father's history.

"He was found in a bloody trench at the Battle of the Somme, in the First World War," Berenice said. "No one knew how he came to be there. Everyone in the trench was dead but him, and because it was at the front lines, a trench that had been under heavy bombardment for several days, they had all been dead for some time. Perhaps he had been searching for some relative, perhaps trying to deliver a message when he was trapped by crossfire . . . no one will ever know. When they rescued him from the blood and the mud, he could not speak, not even to tell his own name. He told me he might have been about ten years of age at the time. He must have been in deep shock, and as people in deep shock sometimes do, he was behaving in an unaccountable way when they found him. He was playing a game with some small stones. And so they called him Pierre."

Pierre, the French word for "stone." Domini had always known her father's first name but she had not considered its significance. Was that why the great stone in the courtyard had meant so much to him? How little she knew about Papa, Domini realized with a heavy heart. And she had thought she knew him so well.

"They took him to an orphanage in Paris. Still, he did not speak, nor did he understand anything that was said to him, even the very simplest things. He thinks they may have talked to him in German, too, wondering if he had come from the opposing side. And he believes they tried other languages as well."

Berenice spoke of Le Basque in the present tense, as though he were still alive. Perhaps for her he was. "It was as if he did not hear. When given a pencil, he could not write, and he seemed not to recognize the letters of the alphabet. Still numb from his experience in the trenches, he failed other small tests of intelligence too. He vaguely remembers the tests, things with pegs and pictures. They wondered if he was deaf and dumb, but found he could hear sharp noises even if he could not understand soft words. When he heard the noises he turned violent, perhaps because of the days he had been under fire. When they tried to take his small stones away from him, he fought that too. Your father believes they decided, after a time, that he must be severely retarded or disturbed, or perhaps both. Because of the war the orphanage was very overcrowded, and they could not handle so difficult a child. And so

they moved him to another place, a place for simple-
tons and the insane. Now it would be called a mental
hospital, but more than half a century ago such places
had harsher names. He was not well treated."

Berenice went on softly while Domini listened and
learned true horror. Her eyes felt like burned coals, her
mouth like ashes. Papa, her papa, in a place like that?

Ignored except for the most basic of bodily needs, no
longer spoken to because it was believed he was too
retarded to speak, the boy Pierre had lived an almost
animal existence. He became unmanageable at times,
and so he was kept from the other inmates, most of
them in any case much older than he. He was given no
last name but a number, and he was taught nothing
except the hard lessons of survival. He hated the
asylum attendants, some of whom mistreated him, and
even if he had had words to speak by then, out of sheer
hatred he would not have spoken them. At times, when
he spoke with his fists or his feet, he was put under
restraint or in a padded cell. The rest of the time he
played a solitary game with the small stones, possibly
out of attachment to a past he could not remember.

"He lived there for four years, and the wonder is that
he retained any sanity at all. He escaped by hiding in a
load of dirty laundry. He had planned it for some time
and watched his chance. He was about fourteen, he
thinks. For a long time after that he lived on the Paris
streets, sleeping under bridges or in gutters, stealing
food, knowing no one, speaking nothing, despising the
world. He says that by then he understood everything
other people said, but his mouth was sealed in hatred.
For three years he was crafty enough to survive. If it
had not been for Élisabeth, he might have remained an
animal all the rest of his days."

"Élisabeth?" Domini pronounced the name as Berenice had done, in the French fashion, ending in a "t"
sound. She had never heard her father speak of a
woman named Élisabeth.

"The great love of his life," Berenice explained

simply and without envy. "She was the young mistress of an indifferent painter, a sidewalk artist who sold his views of Paris to passing tourists with bad taste. The two of them caught your father breaking into their larder. The artist wished to call the *gendarmes*, but Élisabeth said no. By then Pierre's only thought was escape, but because the artist stood by holding a stout stick in case of trouble, he did not at once try. Besides, he was hungry, and he understood that Élisabeth intended to feed him. She seated the dirty, unkempt lad at her kitchen table and watched while he wolfed down the cheese and bread and meat she gave him until he could eat no more. And then she took him to her bathroom and stripped the clothes from his back and scrubbed him until his skin was raw. It was the first bath he had had in three years, and the first time he became conscious of a woman as a woman. He was about seventeen then, with the sturdy build of a peasant, and she did not laugh at him when his naked body reacted with the reactions of a man. Instead, she muttered a few words that changed your father's life."

"What did she say?" asked Domini.

"What she said was not so important, although the words were: 'So much of a boy, and yet so much of a man.' What was important was the language she spoke. It was the tongue of the Basque people. Your father understood and he was electrified. He answered her in the same language, the first time he had spoken in seven years. He says his voice was rusty from not being used. What his first words were, he cannot recall, but he remembers well enough the way Élisabeth's face lighted to hear him. Perhaps in Paris she had been lonely for the sound of Basque. She gave him clothes and a mattress to sleep on, and the artist she lived with allowed it because he was not an unfeeling man.

"But Élisabeth . . . ah, Élisabeth. She was a simple, honest woman, virtuous not with the virtue of the body, but with the virtue of the heart. She was not well educated and she had little money, but she was generous with giving when she saw reason to give. She took the filthy street urchin into her heart as easily as if he had been her own flesh and blood. Soon Pierre was doing small tasks to earn his keep; he wanted to stay. The great hatred began to flow out of his soul. Élisabeth listened to him and talked to him and told him of the mountains he must have come from. Because he seemed to understand much about the pasturelands but little about the sea, she told him he must come from the high plateaux, and not from the Basque fisherfolk of the coast. She saw his small stones and said they must have come from the mountains, too, perhaps from some rocky pasture. She spoke to him of the Basque peasants, of their physical stamina, their customs, their costumes, their cleverness, their history. She told him of their fierce pride."

Domini understood, because those same things had been taught to her in her youth. The Basque people were the oldest racial group in Europe, a hardy warrior race that had withstood domination by the Visigoths and the Franks, that had produced men of iron will like St. Francis Xavier and St. Ignatius of Loyola, founder of the Jesuits. Even in the time of Roman conquest the Basques had resisted Romanization more than other races had done. Through the course of the centuries they had preserved their ancient ways as proudly as they had preserved their ancient and unique language.

"He listened eagerly when she told him that Basques had sailed with Magellan, that Basques had fought in the wars of the Crusades, that the Basque whalers of Saint-Jean-de-Luz had sailed to the New World near the time of Columbus. But it was when she spoke of the mountains that tears came to his eyes.

"Your father understood everything as if he had heard it all before, and in his mind he could see the mountains she described. Élisabeth told him he would not have survived his trials if he had not been a Basque. She guessed that his father might have been a herder of sheep, for such men learn to live with loneliness and hardship as few mortals do. It is possible that Pierre had been learning the trade himself, even at a very young age, if his father had gone to war. And it is a hard trade. A sheepherder will often sleep alone for days on end, with only the ground for bed and only the stars for roof. To guard his sheep, he must be strong, and wherever he stays he knows he must soon move on if his flock is not to starve. He learns to suffer and he learns to survive. If a Basque leaves nothing else to his sons, he leaves his ability to endure. Could it be otherwise, when the Basques have survived through so many centuries that no man knows their real beginnings?"

To Domini, some things Berenice said were not new. She was aware that people came from around the world to hire Basque sheepherders, who were prized for their stoicism and endurance under conditions that would drive lesser men mad. Men from the Pyrenees plied their trade as far afield as Nevada and California, leaving to their sons and their sons' sons the heritage of a strange language, a fierce abiding pride, and a strong talent for survival.

"And at last, as Élisabeth spoke of these things, your father began to learn some peace with himself for the sufferings he had undergone, because his own people had suffered, too, and survived.

"The artist died some months later, an accidental death. Your father thinks he was about eighteen when he moved into Élisabeth's bed. She was not so many years older than he and already he loved her. And because he knew he must put bread on Élisabeth's table, he picked up the dead artist's palette and his brushes and went out on the streets to paint, when he had hardly so much as learned to hold a pencil. He tried to copy the kind of thing he saw being done by other sidewalk artists and found he could not do it at all. He struggled to make his paintings copies of theirs, learning as he painted, but he was unable to copy other men's indifferent offerings too well. Sometimes he produced bent buildings and orange skies and hardly knew how he had done it until he saw his finished work on canvas. Very little sold. Tourists on the street didn't like his paintings because they were too different; they wanted their traditional views. One day someone asked him why he had no signature, and so he asked Élisabeth to teach him how to sign his name. She told him he needed a name to sign. And so she called him Le Basque, a name she said he had earned with his sufferings. She taught him to print it before he could even read."

Domini remembered the time her father had told her that, the same day he had cut her out of his life. It had not been a day to ask questions, but Domini had sometimes wondered about it since.

"For two years or so they survived. During those years Élisabeth taught your father how to read and write. He stole food sometimes, or money to pay the rent. He had promised Élisabeth he would not steal again, but he could not bear to see her go hungry. When she found out, she threatened to leave him, and so he stopped. Then one morning in a rainstorm he took shelter in the palace of the Louvre, the exterior of which he had been painting from the Place de la Concorde. In his desperation to learn of the art he thought he could not do, he took his last few sous and paid his admission. And what he saw changed his life again."

During her growing years Domini had often visited the Louvre with her father. He had always entered the part devoted to the impressionists and always followed the same course. Domini guessed it must have been the course he had followed that very first time. The Renoirs, the Cézannes, the Van Goghs, the Gauguins—she could imagine very well what he had viewed.

"For him, it was the second lightning clap, as riveting as the speaking of his own tongue had been. He had thought he could not paint because he had never seen great art, or indeed any pictures that could be dignified by the name of art at all. But in the Louvre he saw bent buildings and oblong apples and orange skies. He saw paintings of people, something he had never tried. The flesh tones especially moved him. A lesser man might have been humbled to see such works, but what he saw filled him with strength, for what he recognized in seeing these great paintings was the seed of his own greatness. After that, he knew he had much to learn, but he never doubted his own ability to learn it. He started to paint like a madman, no longer street scenes but canvases of Élisabeth. Your father said she was unhappy because pictures of people put no food in the larder. He didn't care; he was possessed by his need to paint. For the next few years he did little else. He no longer thought of food or rent and left such problems to Élisabeth. She was also shy of posing in the nude, but she did so without complaint. He says she grew thin as the stack of canvases grew large. None were sold. When he ran out of canvas, he painted her picture on the walls, and when the walls were filled he painted over his own paintings. When he ran out of paint, she produced some for him, and he did not ask how. He thought Élisabeth must have started stealing, too, against her own teachings; at the time he did not even care. Later he learned that she had taken to selling herself to keep them both alive. She loved him, too, you see."

Berenice bowed her head and paused in her story for a few moments, as if in silent homage. When she spoke again she switched to French, marking the end of one passage of Le Basque's life.

"She died in a fire, and with her all the canvases he had done and all the paintings on the walls. He even lost the small stones he had kept for so many years. Do you wonder that he found it hard to talk to anyone of these things?"

Domini shook her head, too moved to express her

feelings in words. And she had once asked her father what he had learned in Paris. Could she have guessed that he had learned such terrible pain?

Berenice talked on, perhaps relieving some of her own deep feelings in the telling. With the cruel irony often accorded by fate, Élisabeth's death had marked the beginning of Le Basque's success. After moving in with a kindly fellow artist who offered temporary shelter after the fire, he happened to learn of the manner in which Élisabeth had put food on the table during the previous few years. In rage and pain he had started a self-portrait as tortured and full of despair as the famous image Van Gogh had once painted of himself. Domini had seen it; it was hanging in the Louvre along with the painting of the unicorn. She had never liked the work, which troubled her deeply because it was not the Papa she knew.

The studio where Le Basque painted the self-portrait was next door to a small art gallery, and the dealer who ran that gallery had chanced by while it was being painted. He became interested. Soon there were more canvases, more important galleries, more sales, more successes. There were no more self-portraits, but the work remained unfailingly filled with despair. At last, unable to bear a Paris or even a France where no Élisabeth existed, Le Basque had left for America. There he learned a new language and continued to paint of his purgatory like a man possessed. Still young but already rocketing in reputation, lionized by critics and collectors alike, he met and after an overnight courtship married a woman who bore a strong resemblance, physically at least, to Élisabeth.

As it turned out, she was unlike Élisabeth in every other way. Greedy, grasping, and cold except in bed, she had married Le Basque for his already remarkable success. She was grudging with her body when she felt there was anything to be gained by withholding it. Out of bitterness and disillusion, Le Basque suffered through the marriage for some years, taking what little solace he could from the children she produced.

"He remained faithful to her, not because he loved her but because he had loved Élisabeth—and yes, she had the same dark eyes, the same dark hair, the same long throat. He never painted her, because he could not bear to paint with cynicism and dislike what he had once painted with love. Nor, after a time, did he care to share her bed very often. They had been married nearly twenty years when he learned of her infidelities, not done from necessity as Élisabeth's had been done, but out of wealth and boredom and too great a taste for pleasure. There was little left for him in the marriage. Already he hardly recognized his sons, who at his wife's insistence had been sent to private schools and fine country clubs and taught to turn up their noses at their father's uncouth ways. He walked out on her, taking no more than his paints, and leaving all else to her."

After that there had been a succession of models and mistresses, all painted with the brushstrokes of a bitter man. Anastasia Greey had been the last of these. As Domini already knew, her mother's death had deeply affected Le Basque; now she discovered why.

"While she was in labor with you, Didi, Anastasia told your father she had allowed herself to become pregnant only because she loved him. She said she had always known she could not hold all of him forever, and so she wanted a part of him to hold for a little time. He was cynical and didn't believe her; he thought her condition was due to miscalculation. But after she died in delivering you, your father learned that she had been strongly warned against the pregnancy, even before it started, and told that it might kill her to carry a child to full term. And yet, as they took her to the delivery room, she told him nothing of her fears, only of her love."

So her mother had loved her father, truly loved him. The knowledge gave Domini comfort and a vision of her mother that denied the shallowness depicted in Anastasia's portrait.

"He had almost come to believe that no woman but Élisabeth was capable of love and a generous heart. And yet, this mistress whom he had taken so cynically had wanted to carry his child. I think, perhaps, if he had been able to bring your mother back to life, he would have learned to love her after all. Instead he learned to love you. When you were born, it was as though he was reborn too. You gave him back the faith he had lost when Élisabeth died."

Domini knew the rest of the story because it was her own. Berenice's painful revelations had explained so much. Domini no longer needed to question the reason for the great stone in the courtyard, nor why her father had not sent her away to be educated as many men in his place would have done, nor why he had taught her to love with all her heart, without holding back. She understood his anger at the careless use of the name that had cost him such pain in the earning. She was grateful that Berenice had told the story, because now she could look back at her father's denial of her with a true and heartfelt understanding.

"Through you, Didi, I think he lived his own childhood, the childhood he could not remember. I wonder if you know how much you gave him?"

Domini thought of the father who had gone wading, done somersaults, lain on his stomach watching an ant with awe, danced the *jota* until sweat streamed over his broadly grinning face. She thought of the grown man who had deliberately squirted a *bota* at his chin at the cost of his dignity, who had chortled with delight to win at cards, who had watched *pelote* with the excitement of a boy. She thought of a hundred other memories and knew Berenice was right. Her childhood had been her father's childhood too. In a way, they had been children together, and Domini felt humble and grateful to realize that if her memories of childhood were beautiful, so must her father's have been.

"He loved you very much, Didi," Berenice finished gently, with tears at last springing to her eyes. "I was never jealous of the love he held for you or for Élisabeth, after I understood that without the two of you he would have had no capacity for love at all. He suffered when you vanished without a trace. He tried so hard to find you, but the most that could be learned was that someone in the name of Domini Greey had flown to the United States. So many private detectives he hired! Do you know, he even used influence—and it was not easy on short notice—to arrange for the famous portrait of you to be sent overseas on tour. He hoped that you might go to see it. In every city it was sent to, there were detectives watching the doors."

Domini stared, remembering what she had read not so very long ago. Realization came to her with a great instinctive sureness.

"And the unicorn," she said, her lips numb. "He sold the unicorn, too, for the same reason."

"Yes," Berenice confirmed. "He thought you might hear of the auction and get in touch to object. But you know, it nearly broke his heart to part with it."

Released at last, Domini put her face in her hands and wept until there were no more tears to shed.

Chapter Eleven

Le Basque's will was read on a Saturday, the day after a funeral that had called so great a number of important people to the Pyrenees that the small church and the rustic graveyard of his choice were incapable of holding them all. Most left immediately after the funeral, but those who had been advised to do so stayed for the reading of the will, filling the local inns to overflowing. Photographers had been strictly excluded from the funeral services, but on the following day they vied for position outside the gates to take pictures of those who entered or exited the farmhouse. Although reporters were now aware of Domini's presence, to her gratitude they were not being admitted to the house and therefore succeeded in taking no pictures of her.

It was bruited about that Le Basque's estate might be worth well in excess of three hundred million dollars, a figure to which Berenice scornfully retorted, "Pah!", pointing out that he had supported too many foundations of various kinds during his life for the figure to even approach accuracy. The wild estimate, she insisted, was based on what Picasso had left, not Le Basque. Nevertheless, the sums involved were considerable, and so was the attention of the press. When great or wealthy men died, the disposition of their estates was always news, and Le Basque had been both great and wealthy. Although he had not died intestate, as Picasso had done, the interest of the newshounds was considerable.

Among other stories, the disowning of Domini had become public knowledge, although the reasons remained murky; it was also reported that she had been allowed back into her father's house only when he lay on his deathbed.

For the reading of the will, rows of straight chairs had been arranged in the airy, carpetless room that had been Le Basque's studio, the largest and also the emptiest room in the stone farmhouse. At Berenice's instruction, windows were flung open to admit the warm July air. Sunlight streamed through the skylights that had been installed long ago. Large important canvases lined the walls, along with huge and elaborate floral arrangements, too many of which had been received for the small country church to hold.

As the interested persons called together by Le Basque's lawyers started to assemble, Berenice had a few hushed and private words to say to Domini. "Please," she said gravely, "don't be surprised by anything he may have done. Someday you will understand."

The will was dated several months after Domini's departure from the Pyrenees. Its reading took an interminable time. There were bequests to charities and foundations, bequests to servants past and present, bequests to good friends, bequests of particular paintings to particular art museums. The clauses were read in French and occasionally, at the request of a lawyer representing Domini's three half-brothers, translated into English. At first Domini listened with half an ear.

Insulated by her personal grief of the past few days, she cared very little about the details of disposition, although she was human enough that it had at some point crossed her mind that her own life and Tasey's might conceivably be easier from now on. And she might be in a better position to help Sander too. That was not an unwelcome thought.

And yet she didn't want to think of her father's death in terms of the money he might leave her. She hated the intent expression upon her half-brothers' faces and didn't wish to tar herself with the same brush. And so she deliberately allowed her mind to wander, thinking of other things. When the droning recitation reached the point of the bigger bequests, Domini had to drag herself back from painful memories of the last time she had been in this room with her father still alive.

The lawyer cleared his throat and took a drink of water to punctuate what he was about to read, and the succeeding clauses were read in both languages as a matter of course.

" 'To each of my three sons by my legal marriage,' " the will stated, naming each son by name and city of residence, " 'the price of one black mourning suit.' "

As the words were translated into English, shock waves reverberated through the air. Within moments Domini could feel several pairs of hostile eyes sidling in her direction and Berenice's. There was still a very great deal of wealth to be disposed of, and her three half-brothers now knew three people who were not going to get it. She sat stiff as a board, scarcely daring to breathe. Did this mean that Papa was going to leave a good deal of his estate to her? It was possible, she realized, because Berenice was a wealthy woman in her own right.

" 'To my beloved companion Berenice à Soule,' " the lawyer went on, " 'I leave the household furnishings of the farmhouse in the Pyrenees, which farmhouse was purchased by her at fair market value prior to the writing of this will.' " It was the first time Domini had heard that news; it surprised her that her father should have sold the house he loved so dearly. " 'To her I also leave whatever residue remains of my estate, after the bequest of my most valued possessions which are herinunder named.' "

There was a dramatic pause while those in the audience began to make mental calculations about the number of canvases hung in the farmhouse or stored in its cellars, the sketchbooks, the paintings still unsold at dealers both in France and abroad. It was known that the bulk of Le Basque's estate was in works of art, the prices of which were already skyrocketing due to his death. Now nearly all eyes were on Domini—the most important bequests were usually left to the last. The wording of Le Basque's will seemed to confirm her as his main heir. She sat motionless, her hands stilled on the lap of her navy pleated skirt, her hair pulled back into the golden twist that had made a few former acquaintances fail to recognize her at first when they had been gathering for the funeral the previous day. She felt frozen by the eyes upon her, at the moment too numb to think.

" 'To Domini, known as Didi, my own daughter born out of wedlock to Anastasia Greey, I leave my name should she choose to use it, and also my great stone. I wish the stone to remain in the peaceful place where it now rests, until such time as Berenice à Soule, owner of its resting place, requests its removal. In this I trust my daughter will respect my wishes.' "

That was the end. Nearly everyone knew of the stone and knew it was valueless. Domini knew it was not, and she had to fight to prevent her eyes from filling in front of so many spectators.

But she need not have feared. The spectators in the room had all turned their eyes, hostile or otherwise, away from Domini to fasten on the person the will had made wealthy. Berenice sat as calmly as though she had been aware of what was going to happen all along.

Berenice was not even a blood relative, and the

battle lines started to form almost before the beneficiaries had filed from the room. Domini saw her half-brothers, heads together with their lawyer, looking coldly furious. She wasn't yet sure how she felt about her father's will, but she knew she didn't feel anger. Thank God he had left it to Berenice and not to them!

It was a beautiful sunny day. Drinks and refreshments were being served in the courtyard because many people present—in particular those representing various museums and charitable institutions—had come from Paris or even farther afield and required some sustenance before starting the return trip. Within half an hour of the reading of the will, Domini's half-brothers cornered her privately and offered her a breathtaking sum if she would help them in contesting the will. "She must have exerted undue influence on a dying old man," argued one. "You lived with them for many years, you can testify. You must have seen what she was trying to do."

"He threw you out of his home only months before he wrote the will," prompted another. "There must have been signs of his mental deterioration even then."

"He left you nothing," claimed the third. "And then calling the stone his most valued possession! When he wrote that will, he must have been half mad."

Domini gave them a withering look and walked away, not even dignifying the proposal with an answer.

"Your father had to write his will like that, partly because he didn't know what had happened to you," Berenice told Domini some time later, when the others had finally departed. They were walking slowly in the large walled courtyard, alone with the sun and the stones and the trellised vines. "Your father had other reasons, too, although I won't go into them right now. But understand, Didi, that if he had left you any substantial sum in his will and you hadn't been located . . . well, in that case it would have been too easy for his true wishes to be disobeyed. Who knows what the courts would have done? I know what his true wishes were, and I intend to obey them. He wanted you to be looked after, for one thing. Come to France with your daughter and live here."

"Not right now, Berenice," Domini said slowly, thinking of Sander and the uncertainties of her future. "I have my own life in New York, a life I'm not ready to leave."

"The stone is yours, and the stone is the heart of this house. Who owns the stone really owns the house, no matter what it says on the deed, which is only paper after all."

"The house is yours," Domini reminded her. "You bought it from Papa."

"Ah, but that was because he wanted . . ." Berenice paused and started again, choosing her words carefully. "He wanted you to have it someday. To you, I can admit that he sold it to me, thinking to keep its succession safe in case you were never found. He didn't want your brothers to get hold of it. Are you afraid that two grown women can't be mistress of the same home? You needn't fear. I imagine I'll be returning to Paris to live within the next few months. I'm not an old woman and many of my friends are there. I must think of building myself a new life; even your father would have wanted me to do that. He will keep his place in my heart, of course, but he would want me to stop living no more than he stopped living when Élisabeth died. This home is yours because, in truth, that's what your father really wished. Reconsider, Didi. You belong here."

"Perhaps I do," Domini agreed, her eyes rising to the distant mountains beyond the stone wall. Her slow pacing came to a halt while she thought about what Berenice had suggested. The thought of raising Tasey in such surroundings had a very strong appeal. "Perhaps someday I'll return to this part of the world to stay, although I would have to find a place that was truly my own. A cottage, perhaps. But not yet. Not yet."

Berenice sighed. "If you must return to New York, you must. But I feel you need help, financial help. Do you think I have no eyes? That little navy dress you're wearing, Didi, is a very good one, but it's one we bought in Paris together nearly five years ago. Very few of your other clothes are new either; I've noticed that. And having a young child to support . . ."

Domini turned to look at the great crude stone she owned. The offer was tempting, but the stone said no. She faced Berenice again, feeling oddly lighthearted and happy for the first time since her father's death.

"If I need help, really need it, I promise I'll call on you. But do you know something? I think Papa's already given me all the help I need. He left me the two most important things he owned."

Berenice smiled as though she understood. "I think he's left you his pride too," she cautioned. "Sometimes pride can be a burden."

Domini was silent for a moment. "I'm not that proud," she denied finally. "There is one thing I'd like from you, Berenice, I'd like you to contact Papa's dealer in New York . . . Lazarus, isn't it?"

"You've met him, haven't you?"

"No, never. And I feel I can't approach him myself, because I want to protect my New York identity. There's a man—a sculptor whose work I'd like him to look at. That's all, just look at it. I don't want pressure applied for Lazarus to handle something he doesn't want. Sander wouldn't like it."

"About that, you need have no fear," Berenice said dryly. "Lazarus can be very rude, even to important artists and collectors. If I tried to apply too much pressure, he would hang up on me." She paused and then asked delicately, "This sculptor, this Sander . . . he is a good friend?"

"He's my lover," Domini acknowledged with the simple directness her father had taught her. "Come and sit down, Berenice, and I'll tell you all about him."

And so, sitting on a stone bench beneath the great stone she now owned, Domini at last told the story of

Sander, of Tasey's conception, of what had happened since then in their relationship. Some parts were glossed over, but others were not. Domini briefly explained her reasons for not wanting Sander to know her true identity and dwelled at greater length on the power of his work, a subject on which she spoke with convincing sincerity. Berenice agreed to use what influence she could with Le Basque's important Manhattan dealer, a man known for his integrity and taste, as well as for his occasional rudeness.

"I'll phone him at once," she promised as the two turned their footsteps into the now peaceful house. And then Berenice laughed, as she had not for many, many days. "No, no," she said. "I'll wait until Monday. By then the news of the will should have reached New York. I imagine he will have to listen to me then!"

"He'll have to pretend to happen into Miranda's gallery," Domini warned. "When he sees the small bronzes, he can ask if there's anything larger. She'll be glad to show him, especially if he says who he is. You'll be doing me a great favor, Berenice."

"Such a little favor for you to call it great." Berenice sighed. "Your father would expect you to accept much more. Is there nothing else I can do?"

"Nothing at the moment," Domini assured her. One side benefit of having no sudden inexplicable source of wealth, she mused with a touch of wryness, would be not having to explain it. It was a comfort, though, to know that Berenice could be called upon in moments of emergency, and Domini knew she would never really have to worry about money again.

"But you will stay for a while," Berenice said.

With the confusion of the past week, when the phone had been constantly ringing and people constantly filing through the door, there had been no repetition of the private hour spent together after Le Basque's death. Fond of Berenice as if she had been her own mother, Domini looked forward to a quiet visit without others around. She refused Berenice's invitation to stay for any length of time in France, but she did agree to postpone her departure for a couple of days.

A little later she accepted with pleasure when Berenice presented her with some small sketches her father had done during her youth. Some were of herself, some were of other people: former servants, former mistresses, peasants at work herding or doing simple, homely tasks. One Domini found particularly touching: a sketch of a sheepherder stretching the legs of an orphaned lamb to dress it in the small sheepskin coat that would save its life, while she as a child watched with huge, awestruck eyes.

"Sell them if you wish," Berenice said, and Domini knew she had taken this course instead of writing a very large check.

She also accepted when Berenice offered to look after the return travel arrangements to New York, knowing she would never be allowed to pay when the tickets were presented to her. But to accept less, under the circumstances, would have been ungracious, carrying pride a little too far.

A transatlantic telephone call assured Domini, not for the first time, that Tasey was getting along well and being no trouble whatsoever. When she placed the call, it was midmorning in New York, and on this occasion Tasey herself erupted onto the telephone. "The ice cream lady has ice cream every night," she said after the first excited moments. "Tomorrow she's taking me to the zoo."

"How nice of her! Are you having fun?"

"The clay man is letting me play with his clay today," Tasey answered somewhat obliquely. As it was a Saturday, with shop hours for Miranda but no day care at all, Domini guessed that Tasey was largely in Sander's care for the moment. Her fingers tensed over the telephone as she listened to the rest of Tasey's words. "He felt my face, too, to see what I looked like. He sees with his fingers, Mummy."

"I know," Domini said. "What else is he doing?"

"He makes me sit still. He says I'm like a wriggly snake. I miss you, Mummy. When are you coming back?"

"Not tomorrow, and not the day after that, but the day after that. Now you tell me when I'm coming back."

"Tuesday!" Tasey announced triumphantly after a few moments of counting on small fingers.

Domini wished she could ask directly whether Tasey had taken a dislike to Sander. Tasey certainly didn't like sitting still, and her wistful words about missing Domini suggested that the day might not be going too well. Miranda had assured Domini that the two were getting along, but that might be pure wishful thinking on Miranda's part. Her father's death had kept Domini from spending mental energy on speculations about what was happening in New York, but when she hung up after sending her hugs and kisses over the line, there was a small worry nagging at her brain.

The news of Le Basque's will reached the North American newspapers prior to Domini's return to New York. In all reports there was considerable guesswork about the size of the estate and particular mention of various legacies to American museums. Because Le Basque had spent so many years in the United States, years when he had reached his real preeminence, America almost considered him her own. There was some regret expressed that so few of his paintings would be coming to American museums. Paris papers told the story, too, with a slightly different point of view—they felt all bequests should have gone to the Louvre, keeping the great art of France in its mother country. On the inside pages of most papers on both sides of the Atlantic, there were stories about Berenice, pictures of Domini's half-brothers, pictures of Domini as a child taken from old newspaper files, eulogies from various public figures whose institutions had benefited from the estate. The personal biographies, devoid of early details, missed nearly all the important parts of Le Basque's extraordinary life, but only Domini and Berenice were aware of that.

There were no current photographs of Domini, and Le Basque's lovechild Didi was mentioned mainly as having been disinherited for unknown reasons some years before. There was some more speculation about this, all of it well off track. At least one reporter called Le Basque's last bequest to her a final slap in the face.

How could anyone but Berenice know that Domini's father had left her an independent and loving spirit, perhaps the most important legacy of all?

Domini arrived home Tuesday at midday New York time, suffering from jetlag and lack of sleep. Tasey was still in day care, and she had visions of dropping into bed for the afternoon after a quick phone call to Miranda. But her answering service had a list of messages so long it filled two sheets of foolscap. Many were from her regular clients, many from callers whose names she didn't recognize at all—suppliers, she supposed, trying to make sales. A listing in the yellow pages often brought calls like that.

The woman at the answering service told her that some of the callers had called half a dozen times and had grown increasingly distressed when Domini failed to return their messages. Uneasily she remembered that she had taken off ten days before with no explanation to her answering service or to those who expected window changes. With the required props and showcards locked in her loft, the merchants would not have been able to change the windows satisfactorily themselves. A few large signs had been for important sales events, and Domini realized she could expect some ruffled feathers. She would have to spend the afternoon soothing them; she couldn't afford to lose clients.

She called Miranda first. "I'm here," she announced and went on to say she would pick Tasey up from day care herself. "I'll drop by and get her clothes sometime this week," she finished.

Miranda asked the expectable question about Domini's fictitious aunt and received a fictitious answer in return. In case of a need to leave the country again, Domini had left the aunt fictitiously alive in her various long-distance conversations with Miranda.

"Can't you come over this afternoon?" Miranda asked excitedly once the politenesses had been attended to. "I have so many things to tell you. And a wonderful surprise!"

Domini thought she knew what the wonderful surprise might be—Berenice had fulfilled her promise the previous day and reported on its results to Domini. She had placed the call to Le Basque's Manhattan dealer in late morning New York time. As it turned out, his gallery like many others remained closed on Mondays, and so Berenice had had the call transferred to Lazarus's home number, unlisted and known to only a few select people. Unfortunately he had been sleeping and was in an accordingly grumpy mood when wakened, but at least he had already heard of the will and had not hung up. Berenice could be very persuasive, and as the chief inheritor of Le Basque's numerous remaining canvases, she had all the weapons of persuasion in her possession. Lazarus had agreed to her request, at the same time warning that he would use his own judgment about Sander's work. By now, if he had followed through first thing Tuesday morning, he might well have called on the little gallery.

"I'd love to come over and see you, Miranda," Domini assured her friend, "but I can't. In fact, it may be a few days before I get there at all. I'll do my very best, but I have a pile of work to catch up on and an angry client or two. Can't you tell me your good news on the telephone?"

"Absolutely not," Miranda returned promptly. "If you can't come during the day, you'll simply have to come for supper, and I mean tonight. Truthfully, I've been counting on it all along. How can you feed Tasey after being away for ten days? Even the milk in your fridge will be sour."

"I'll manage," Domini hedged. She longed to see Sander, but her body ached for an early night. "Besides, Miranda, I've got a bad case of jetlag."

"And I've got the cure!" Miranda laughed, refusing to take no for an answer. "Would you believe a bottle of bubbly? Domestic, mind you, but a very decent brand. Besides, I told Tasey you'd both be eating here, with ice cream for supper. She'd dying to show you what she's been making with Sander's clay."

And so Domini reluctantly accepted, knowing in advance that seeing Sander and Tasey together might mean a very trying evening indeed.

The afternoon was trying too. Some clients she placated easily enough, Grant Manners among them, who added with considerable thoughtfulness, "Don't bother changing my display this week either, Domini. You'll probably be going like hell to catch up, and you must be exhausted. I'm happy with what I've got now. My God, I've had more questions about that window."

Domini's last window for Grant had been great fun. It had been of a laughing mannequin having a bath in a giant golden tub, with a froth of glass bubbles covering all the vital parts. Glass bubbles floated in the air, as if kicked up by the mannequin's foot, and within each glass bubble was a piece of golden jewelry. Domini had used the services of a glassblower to achieve the effect, which showed off the jewelry to good advantage as well as attracting the eyes of passersby. "Get into gold!" the showcard had urged with effective directness. Domini hung up after arranging for a window change and a lunch the following week, wishing that all clients were as considerate as Grant.

She lost two. Both were so incensed they didn't even ask to hear Domini's explanations, and in both cases pride caused her to hang up without trying to give excuses at all. They hadn't been her favorite clients anyway, and she tried to tell herself they were no great loss. Nevertheless, her head was throbbing badly by the time she picked her daughter up from day care, due in good part to the worry about Sander and Tasey that hadn't been far from the surface of her mind for the past few days. Tasey's headlong dive at Domini didn't do anything to ease the pain in her temples.

With her purse full of unspent money withdrawn for the trip to France, Domini had decided to treat herself to a taxi. Tasey chattered like a magpie during the trip, but not about the happenings of the previous few days. Taxis were a novelty to her, and she loved novelties. She wanted to know everything: why the meter ticked, why they were sitting in the back seat, why the car didn't go faster, why there were so many other taxis on the street, why taxis were yellow, why there were lights on top, why they didn't take taxis all the time. By the time they reached their goal, Domini's head was pounding with so many "whys."

The gallery had already closed for the day, and so they had to ring the bell and wait. There were questions about that too; Tasey was accustomed to being admitted immediately when she was in Miranda's charge.

"Oh, Domini, what a morning this has been!" Miranda exclaimed at once when she answered the door. She waited only until her guests were inside. Then she picked Tasey up and swung her around the gallery floor in a dance of delight that sent Tasey into screams of giggles. Domini gathered that they had grown very attached to each other during these past days, and she smiled to see it. If only Tasey could have formed one tenth of that feeling for Sander . . .

"It's wonderful! It's marvelous!" Miranda sang out, looking happier and younger than Domini had ever seen her before.

"What's the occasion?" laughed Domini, despite her aching head.

Miranda let her wriggling burden slide to the ground.

"Run up and play with your clay for a few minutes, Tasey," she suggested. "I want to speak to your mummy."

Tasey bounded off with enthusiasm up the now familiar stairs. At last Miranda turned to Domini, her eyes shining. "I'd let Sander tell you the news himself, but I know he never will! In fact, once we get upstairs he probably won't let me speak of it either. There's another dealer interested in handling his work, Domini, and you'll never guess *who!*"

Faking all the appropriate responses was not too hard for Domini, because Lazarus's decision was in fact news to her, and the best possible kind of news at that. Miranda could continue to handle the small unsigned bronzes for the time being, but once cast, the larger pieces were to go uptown. The dealer had not gone so far, though, as to suggest giving an advance to help pay for the bronze castings that would have to be done. That had to be the artist's responsibility.

"Two of them are to be done right away," Miranda said. "I told him we could manage that. Fortunately I've been tucking a little aside for repairs, but they can wait. And by the time the other models have to be cast . . . well, I don't have to worry about that yet."

"I can lend you the money," Domini offered, thinking of the sketches Berenice had given her. Selling just one would do the trick, with money to spare.

"And exactly what are you going to do to get it?" Miranda asked. "Rob a bank, or just run yourself ragged by taking on a few more clients? Thanks but no thanks. You've done enough, and you work far too hard as it is. I'll find a way; I have time. There's no way Lazarus can think of mounting a show for Sander before December. He has other shows planned, and it's amazing he has a free slot even then, with all the important artists in his stable. In fact, even in December Sander won't actually be having a one-man show. Lazarus will be hanging some paintings too."

"Whose?" asked Domini automatically.

"He didn't mention," Miranda glowed, "except to say he'd arranged it only yesterday, and he expected he'd need sculpture because he wouldn't have quite enough paintings to do a really complete hanging. It was a stroke of good luck, he said, that he had managed to get enough paintings to put a show together at all. He sounded very pleased with himself. Do you know I think it may even be somebody *really* important?"

And Domini knew at once that it was.

"That ought to do wonders for Sander's traffic." She grinned, sending a silent thanks across four thousand miles. Wily Berenice; she hadn't said a word about that part of her plan! It was almost, but not quite, enough to cure a headache.

"Lazarus is planning to plant some publicity about Sander, to start building his name," Miranda mentioned with a wry grimace. "Frankly, that's why Sander won't want to talk about it. When Lazarus said the blindness made a very strong story, the two of them practically came to blows."

"Then I'll avoid the subject tonight," Domini agreed. Then her mind turned back to more immediate matters, the worrisome thing that had been nagging at her all through the hard afternoon. "Tell me the truth, Miranda. How have Sander and Tasey been getting along?"

"Go and see for yourself," Miranda suggested. "I'll give you three a few moments alone together. I have to go and buy some ice cream anyway."

Moments later Domini was standing in the doorway of the studio, staring with surprise. Tasey, wild child no longer, was sitting completely motionless, even to the young fingers resting as if at work over a small mess of clay. Sander was feeling her hands, and on a brand-new worktable there was a sculpture of Tasey, complete but for that one last detail. The model of her managed to convey some aura of perpetual motion, and Domini guessed that her daughter had not remained quite so still through the entire sitting.

She wriggled ecstatically at Domini's arrival. "See, Mummy? I'm making one of him and he's making one of me! We've been waiting just to show you! And my, my . . ."

"Sculpture," Sander filled in, straightening and giving up the pretense of work now that Domini had arrived. He turned toward the door, his face smoldering with an expression that told her he wanted very much to take her into his arms. Domini ached to go into them, too, but this was not the time to be demonstrative. "I'm not actually going to work at this tonight," Sander said, "but Tasey insisted we show you what we're up to. We posed when we heard you coming up the stairs. She wants you to see how I'm going to use the sculpture she did."

Tasey had slipped to the floor and was dancing with excitement, small fingers flailing the air. "My skullcher is going to be a part of *his!* He's not even going to make a copy of it! He's going to let me put it right in, the real skullcher of him! It's a secret so I didn't tell you on the phone! He said I could surprise you!"

"And you did! What a wonderful surprise!" Domini was half laughing and half crying with relief. She spent a suitably awestruck moment oohing at Tasey's unrecognizable work of art, which vaguely resembled a man's head if one took into account that a nose might sometimes poke in instead of out. The big round smile on its face made Domini wonder if Sander might not have actually been enjoying Tasey's company during the sittings.

Tasey picked up her pint-sized work of art, complete because it had been done on some previous day, and moved to where Sander stood at his worktable. "Now that Mummy's seen my skullcher, can I make it part of yours?" she asked, poking one small fist into Sander's strong grip with the confidence of a child who knows she won't be turned away.

"Go ahead," Sander said, and Tasey carefully placed

the sculpted head of her father into the right position. She didn't let go of Sander's hand.

Unable to resist some gesture, Domini moved a pace, or two and took his other hand, squeezing it privately to let him know how she felt.

"Do you really like it, Mummy? Do you?"

"I love it," said Domini happily, looking at Sander and Tasey together. For headaches, there was no better cure.

Chapter Twelve

Other than one snatched and sinful half hour that
was not spent in talk, Domini was unable to pursue her
relationship with Sander during the week that followed.
Window changes filled the balance of the working days,
and construction of required props as well as designs
for upcoming displays filled the evenings and the weekend. A lengthy transatlantic call to Berenice took more
long precious minutes, and for once Domini didn't even
think of the cost, either in time or in money.

On the weekend, at Sander's request, Domini
dropped Tasey off one afternoon so that he could finish
the final details of his sculpture. With glowing face, she
watched her daughter run up the stairs to the man who
was her father, almost as eagerly as if she knew the
secret of her birth. Domini longed to run up the stairs
herself. But the things she wanted to say to Sander
could not be said with Tasey around, nor in a snatched
half hour.

By the end of the working week the various phone

calls from unknown sources, probably suppliers, had still not been returned. At least two had called a second time. Domini resolved to attend to them first thing Monday morning, prior to the window change and lunch she had promised Grant Manners.

As it happened, she didn't. Over the weekend a burst pipe in the loft above one client, the travel agency, caused water damage to Domini's display. Remembering the help they had tried to give her, she raced over with a stored prop, symbolically enough a model she had once made of the Eiffel Tower in order to promote French perfumes. That and some travel posters and a roll of no-seam paper ought to have been enough to put the window back in quick working order, but the burst pipe had taken its toll, causing dye to run out of the crepe paper poppies used in the previous display. There was quite a mess to clean up. By the time it was done, Domini realized she was going to be late for her next appointment. She rushed home to change for the lunch, the navy dress again, and called a taxi while she was changing—she would need it in any case to transport Grant's props. Her cotton working slacks and shirt went into a bag because she knew she would need them during the afternoon. She was half an hour behind schedule and breathless by the time she reached Grant's exclusive boutique.

"Well, shall we drink a toast to the fact that you finally made it?" he asked with a tilted brow, when he and Domini were at last settled at a table in one of the discreet and expensive restaurants for which New York is justly famous. He lifted his martini glass as if to clink it against Domini's.

"Sarcasm will get you nowhere," Domini said lightly, without raising the spritzer she had requested in order to keep her head clear for the afternoon's work. "Surely you know by now I'm not in the habit of being late."

"Are you deliberately misunderstanding me, or are you just being modest? Good God, Domini, surely we're good enough friends by now that you don't need to keep that sort of thing secret from me. It isn't as though you've never spoken to me about your intentions."

"What are you talking about?" she asked, honestly puzzled.

Grant's hand was still raised in the unjoined toast. He lowered it slowly. "You mean you don't know?"

"Don't know what?"

He laughed, sounding surprised. "My God, you've had days to find out. I intended this lunch to be in the nature of a celebration. I didn't mean to ruin the surprise, but it seems I've let the cat out of the bag."

"You haven't done anything of the sort," Domini said, as confused as ever. "What is it I'm supposed to be celebrating?"

"Why, your success," Grant stated. "I thought you'd have doubled your prices by now! Last week I kept mum, but I knew you'd be hearing from several people. That last window of yours attracted a lot of interest, and I don't mean just from customers. I handed your name out freely because I remembered what you had said about intending to take Fifth Avenue by storm. A couple of merchants were so damn positive . . . my God, haven't they called yet? I could bite my tongue off."

Domini stared. "I haven't returned half my calls from last week," she said. "I've been far too busy."

Grant stared, too, and then started to laugh. He lifted his glass again. "Here's to returning your calls," he grinned.

Domini did, as soon as possible, and because that afternoon was spent changing Grant's window, as soon as possible meant the following morning. Some calls really were from suppliers; others weren't.

A few callers couldn't be reached, but by the way the telephone was answered Domini knew the calls had come from stores and boutiques, not from salesmen.

She left her name with a message that she'd call again, and when. Sitting cross-legged on the floor beside her telephone, she wrote herself reminders. Some callers were only cautiously interested and wanted quotations, no doubt to compare with the freelance display firms they were already using. Domini made appointments, most of them for the following week, fitting them in as best she could around the scheduled window changes for her regular SoHo clients. Two or three callers sounded really serious; they asked about Domini's current work load. She made more appointments. By the time her morning's calls were finished, her calendar for the next three weeks was jammed with good prospects. Or to be more exact, jammed all except for that very afternoon, which she intended to spend with Sander.

But if all went well, she'd be spending more time with him soon. Cut-rate clients meant long working hours, but with the halfway decent prices she could soon start to charge, that mightn't go on forever.

At noon, with most of her messages returned, she placed a quick call of thanks to Grant. "I find you've been singing my praises," she said. "I don't know how I can thank you."

"By agreeing to dinner instead of lunch," he returned without a flicker of hesitation.

Domini hesitated; she wanted no more soft lights and romantic settings. And yet, Grant had been a good friend. "If I thought you wouldn't get the wrong idea, I'd invite you here for a bite one night."

"Try me."

"Perhaps it's best if I don't. My attitude hasn't changed in the past six months, Grant."

"Ah, but mine has." He paused on that somewhat enigmatic statement. "I never did tell your daughter the rest of the story," he reminded her persuasively.

"Tasey would like that," Domini acknowledged slowly, thinking of the conversation about broken promises.

And surely Grant could get no mistaken notions with Tasey's presence as a deterrent. Coming to a quick decision, she suggested Sunday evening because it had fewer connotations of romance than other weekend nights.

Grant accepted and added, "I'll bring wine. We still haven't had a proper celebration in honor of your success."

"Sunday may be premature for that, because I may not have any new clients by then. I'm not seeing most of the prospects until next week."

"Then we'll simply have to find something else to celebrate, won't we?" he teased softly before he hung up.

The call made Domini vaguely uneasy, but not for long. Delight swiftly took over after she put down the phone. She danced across the room past the papier-mâché Shoe Tree she had been making, its bare, twisted branches soon to be garlanded with pretty autumn shoes. And then, hit by the irony of it all, she threw back her head and laughed. Wasn't it always the way, that fate sent its riches when one didn't really need them anymore?

"Fifth Avenue discovers Domini Greey!" she declared gleefully to her only listener, the yellow unicorn. "And do you know, I think it all started the day I went broke paying for *you?*"

Fifteen minutes later, and long before the usual hour of assignation, she was on her way to the SoHo gallery. There was a spring in her stride and the glint of determination in her clear amethyst eyes. The easy swinging confidence in her step caused a few eyes to turn, or perhaps it was the sunny yellow she had donned for the occasion because it matched her mood. If she had been certain of what she wanted to say to Sander before, she was doubly certain of it now. She intended to ask him to marry her. She knew he would never ask her; even Miranda had conceded that. But Domini had an idea she might be able to get him to accept, especially if she played on his pride. She intended to remind him that Miranda might like to live a life of her own, that in order to free his sister he should marry. That was her first weapon.

She thought she would leave love out of her proposal and do some of her persuasions with her second weapon: Tasey's need for a father. Sander was fond of Tasey, of that she was certain, having seen them together the other evening. Tasey seemed utterly at ease with him too.

As for Sander's feelings toward herself . . . was it possible that underneath that mask of cynicism and lovelessness, he might have developed some glimmer of affection for her? Enough to make a marriage work? Miranda seemed to think so. Domini was not quite so hopeful, because she had too often suffered emotional rejection at his hands. But he did want her physically, and that was a third weapon in her arsenal. She didn't for one minute imagine she could go so far as to withhold herself, a maneuver which in any case reminded her too much of what she had heard about her father's wife. But she did think she might be able to stiffen her willpower to resist Sander for a while, at least until he had listened to everything she had to say.

Perhaps, as possessor of her father's stone, she was feeling overly optimistic. Certainly she was buoyed up by the recent turn of events, no longer feeling hopeless as she had felt all spring. Sander's success in finding a dealer, for one thing, should help in her campaign. Providing his thorny pride didn't cause a falling out with the temperamental Lazarus before the show was even mounted. . . .

Not wanting to talk to Miranda right now, she was relieved that there were several customers in the gallery. She hastened up the stairs, thankful that the heat wave was long since over.

As she had come so early, Sander was not in his studio, but she went on in, knowing he would be down the stairs at the sound of her arrival. The sculpture of Tasey had been moved to one side of the room along with other stored works, while the sculpture of Domini, which last week had been in the corner, had resumed pride of place. It was still draped with its damp coverings, but she recognized it by its contours. Waiting for Sander to arrive, she moved closer and carefully peeled back a corner of the cloth and plastic, but that was all she had time to do.

The feel of hands fastening over her upper arms was her first notice that he had arrived in the room, silent as a predator. A wave of love and longing traveled the length of Domini's body. She turned to offer her mouth, eager as a young girl, allowing Sander the claim over her senses that was renewed each time she was in his presence. His hands sliding over her throat, her shoulders, her waist, proclaimed her his possession, just as she wanted to be. Could Sander kiss like that if he cared nothing for the woman in his arms?

"You're early," he muttered.

"I couldn't wait."

"Yet you haven't undressed," he said in a thrillingly husky voice. "Are you waiting for me to help you today?"

Domini reminded herself that today was not going to be a day like all other days. She shifted slightly, moving far enough apart to see his face, but unable to break altogether away from the magnetic influence of his nearness. His hands still gripped her shoulders.

"I'll undress later," Domini said. Her heart full of the thing she wanted to ask, she looked up at him, love and hope glowing in her eyes. "First there's something I want to say."

"Say it quickly then," he murmured. Although his voice smoked, there was a tenseness in his face; Domini hoped with all her heart it was because he had missed her. His next husky words seemed to confirm it. "This afternoon is already too short to make up for the past couple of weeks."

In her mind she had planned all kinds of persuasions and she forgot them, every one. She loved him far too much for reason to be applied, and so she said, as simply as she had once asked him to make love to her:

"Please marry me, Sander."

His face froze, the shadowed eyes totally dark for the moment, the strong mouth motionless. Slowly he released her upper arms and turned his back. "No," he said after a moment, the single word very clipped.

Domini stood still for what seemed an age, dying inside. She wished she had started with logic, but it was too late to use it now because it would sound like begging. And yet she had to make some overture. "Sander," she whispered at last, touching her fingertips to his muscled spine.

"What is it you want now?" There was violence in his voice, tension in the harsh set of his shoulders. "Love? I've told you no. I won't give it, and I want even less to receive it."

"I said nothing about love," Domini returned in a low voice, shedding some part of her pride. "I want a father for Tasey and a proper home life. I'm tired, Sander. Tired of racing around trying to find time to fit an affair into my days. I'd rather do it at night."

"I suppose it's a case of no wed, no bed," he said harshly. "If that's so, get out. If not, get upstairs and prove it. If you stay now, I never want to hear you talk of marriage again." He paused, letting his ultimatum sink in. "Well, what is it to be? Up the stairs or out the door?"

In Domini's heart there was no choice. But she had some pride left, so when she walked past him she didn't answer at all. When he heard the direction of her footsteps, he would know where to find her.

He took her masterfully that day, but with none of

the tenderness she wanted. There was a wonderful and terrible poignancy to the lovemaking, because natural though Domini's instincts were, she knew she ought not to have let the affair continue. But for the moment she gave with her heart, touching him in the ways he had taught her to touch, telling her love with her hands and her hips, and with eyes that he could not see. Sure of his power over her, he bathed her with burning kisses, ranged her flesh with his familiar hands, breathed erotic words into her ears, brought her to a wild forgetfulness that sent her soft, yielding thighs arching to meet the hardness of his. And soon, mindless with desire, she was swept to heights she had reached many times before, but which were new each time in the reaching.

In his own moment of release Sander threw back his head, his shoulders shuddering with passion, his body thrusting deeply in its final imperative demand. In the dark silver glow of his eyes, there was an emotion so intense it might have been pain. Or was it anger, passion, pride? And then he closed them, night returning to night, and the sudden silver was gone.

When his head bent to rest buried against her throat, Domini twisted her fingers into his dark disordered hair as if to memorize its texture for the first time, or the last. Spent but still quivering, she made no move to ease away from under the male body still welded to hers in the aftermath of release. In the passion there had been pain, and the pain was of her own choosing. Would she ever be strong enough to say no to her heart?

He rolled away at last and lay silent beside her, his head turned so she could not see his face. Before long Domini had become so unhappy with her thoughts that she knew she must not stay. She slipped off the bed intending to dress and leave in silence, as she had done on several previous occasions.

From behind, a hand closed over her upper leg. "Don't go," he said, but for once the cracking of his voice made it sound like a request, not a command. His tone stopped her because it conveyed some sense of a terrible personal hell. Domini's heart flew to him. Instinctively she knew he was afraid that after today she would not be coming back; perhaps he had read some of her thoughts. Loving him and wanting to give him reassurance, she said gently, "Do you want to work on the sculpture now?"

"Yes." The word was muffled, almost agonized.

"Then I'll wait for you down in the studio."

Because she had come upstairs in her street clothes, she dressed for the downward trip. Sander lay without moving, turned away from her, his length and nakedness familiar to her eyes and yet different because there was despair in the very lie of the muscles, the cording of the neck, the clench of the fingers over the pillow. As she slipped quickly into slacks, shirt, and sandals, Domini wondered about what she saw in his tense posture. She wondered, too, what meaning could be read into the unusual nuances she had heard in his voice. Could Sander sound so upset if he was as unattached to her as he pretended?

In the studio she walked over to look at the image of herself instead of disrobing at once. She peeled the damp cover carefully aside so as not to disturb the unset clay. Thoughtfully, mindful of the clues she had been considering upstairs, she studied it for the hundredth time and saw it with new eyes. It was a sensuous sculpture, the clay somehow creating an illusion of the flow of flesh, the glow of hair, even the texture of nipples and the softness of thighs. The face was tremulous with love. Could Sander create a sculpture so moving if he cared nothing for her at all?

When he arrived a few moments later, she was still unsure of her conclusions. She went to the chair where she usually left her clothes, watching Sander closely as he went over to his sculpture and touched it, readying himself for the sitting about to begin. Usually she watched his face or his long lithe body, but today she watched his hands. Was there something almost reverent in the way his fingers moved across his creation?

He had never admitted to any satisfaction with the work, and Domini wondered about that too. Powerful and touching in its simplicity, it was the best of all the sculptures he had done. During her last brief visit the matter of Sander's new dealer had been mentioned, so she thought it was safe to bring up Lazarus now. As she started to loosen the button of her cotton slacks, she asked with apparent lightness, "Which of the sculptures are you having cast right away?"

"None of them," he returned harshly, his hand coming to rest on the breast of the clay figure. Without removing his hand, he turned to face her.

Domini's fingers came to a halt, too, over her waistband. "But—"

"This morning Lazarus sent his publicity man over with a photographer. They read me a note from Lazarus saying he couldn't possibly put on a show without advance press to build my name. He was also clear about the kind of stories he intended to place." Sander's jaw was grim, as unyielding as granite. "I won't have my blindness traded upon. I told them to take their sob stories and tell Lazarus to go to hell."

"Oh, Sander," Domini whispered, immediately suffering for his sake. Did that account for his despairing mood today? And was that why he had been so callous in rejecting her proposal? A man like Sander would never marry if he thought he had nothing to offer a wife.

Domini knew she could no longer contain the burden of her own feelings. "Sander," she started, studying his shuttered features for reaction, "when you asked earlier, I replied that I hadn't spoken about love. Now I will. I love you. I've loved you for a very long time."

His mouth merely hardened. "Then you've wasted your affection on the wrong man. I have no affection to give in return."

Again Domini's eyes shifted to look at the languorous rendering of herself where Sander's hand rested, curved over the soft swell of a breast. The sculpture depicted a woman very much in love. Could it do that so well if it had been done by a man who had no feeling for the model at all? Was it she who had been blind all along?

"I don't think that's true," she said slowly. "I believe you do have feelings for me, and you've been hiding them because of your handicap and your pride, and maybe because of some bad experience with another woman. You lie when you tell me I mean nothing to you. You may not love me yet but you could, if you would allow yourself to love. Now that I understand how you feel, it's all quite clear."

His lips tightened, baring his teeth. "And what gives you such insight into my feelings?"

"The sculpture," she said. "Everything about it. The way you've curved it, shaped it, put so many emotions into it. Even the way you're touching it now, as if you care, really care."

And then she gasped. With no hesitation at all, Sander's hand lifted and smashed down in a fist, flattening the malleable mound of the clay breast.

"Shall I show you how I care?" he grated, eyes blazing with a silver that struck a terrible coldness into Domini's heart. "This is how I care!"

And with that he reached blindly for the sculpture, sweeping it off the table with one enraged movement of his arm. It crashed to the floor face-first, the head demolished in the moment of impact, large fragments of the soft clay body flattening, too, or tearing away so that the fretwork of the understructure could be seen poking through. For several horrified moments Domini stared at the armature where shapeless clay still clung, at the almost obscenely naked chicken wire of the devastated head.

She had lived through this scene before. Icy numb to the bone, brain frozen with shock as it had been years ago, her actions followed with the rigidity of a robot obeying remote control. She picked up her purse, went to the door, and walked down the stairs. In the gallery she was vaguely aware that Miranda was saying something to her. She walked past without acknowledgment, eyes unseeingly focused directly ahead of her, and left the little gallery with her heart in a deep freeze.

Chapter Thirteen

Domini managed to function despite the terrible iciness that gripped her. Even before she reached her loft, she knew what she had to do. Her first call was to France. Due to the time difference, it was the dinner hour for Berenice, but at Domini's insistence a servant finally went to fetch her from the table.

"I'm coming back," she said in French as soon as Berenice had come onto the line. Her voice was completely level, her emotions under tight rein, as they had been after her father's harsh dismissal. Numb in brain as well as in heart, Domini could not have said how she had reached her decision to leave, but she knew it was an absolute necessity for her own personal survival. To remain within range of Sander would be to die a death as sure as that inflicted on the sculpture.

Berenice began to express her delight, but Domini cut in. "I'm bringing Tasey, and I'm coming back permanently. I'd like to ask you another favor, Berenice. Something's happened, and I want to stay in New York no longer than necessary. You managed to get me on a flight immediately before. Can you do it again, this time for two?"

Berenice didn't hesitate at all. Typically she asked no foolish questions, although Domini's words must have aroused her curiosity. "Of course," she said. "I'll call you back as soon as possible. Will you be there?"

"Yes, but you won't be able to get through. My phone will be busy part of the time, and the rest of the time I don't want to answer it. I'll call you. How soon will you know?"

"Give me two hours," Berenice suggested. "Will you be ready to leave on short notice after that?"

"Yes."

Most of Domini's next hour was spent in calling her regular clients, advising them to look elsewhere for display services. When clients were out, she left the information in a message, with one exception. Grant Manners she knew she must speak to personally, much as she would have preferred not to. She cut questions short because there were other essential calls as well: the answering service, the landlord, Tasey's day-care center. When asked, she merely said she would be unavailable for some time and didn't mention that she was leaving the country. To her landlord, she gave verbal notice, informing him that he would be given a forwarding address, probably a box number, as soon as possible. Her possessions, she said, would be cleaned out sometime within the next month. She kept her arrangements simple, knowing that much could be done later by mail or by phone, possibly through intermediaries.

The second hour was spent in packing essentials for Tasey and herself, a mechanical function that allowed Domini to ignore the urgent and frequent ringing of the telephone. If that was Miranda or Sander, she didn't want to answer. When its strident ring became too hard to bear, she took it off the hook, hung up long enough to break the connection, and then took it off the hook for good.

At the end of two hours Berenice had done the impossible once more. "You're leaving by Air France in about three hours," she informed Domini, adding the necessary information about the flight number and the picking up of tickets. With a glance at her watch, Domini decided she and Tasey could leave directly from day care and wait at the airport. Thank God for Tasey's adaptability and trusting nature, which would make the sudden uprooting easier.

"You'll be met in Paris," Berenice said.

Domini made no demur; at the moment she needed all the help she could get. As soon as she was off the line, she arranged for an airport limousine. Her last call, made with one eye on her watch, was one more try at reaching Grant Manners. This time she got through without trouble because his secretary had advised him of her two earlier calls. "Mr. Manners told me to call him out of his meeting," she said.

"I'm sorry, I have to cancel our dinner," Domini told Grant. "I'm leaving for Europe at once."

"Your aunt died," he guessed wrongly, and Domini didn't deny it. "Look, that leaves you in a spot. How about all those appointments you've made?"

"They'll go wasting." Prospective clients were the last of Domini's worries now.

"Give me their numbers then," Grant offered. "I'll explain the emergency and tell them you'll call as soon as possible. Any idea when you'll be back?"

Domini hesitated, this time reluctant to admit that she wouldn't be returning at all. But it had to be done, for Grant as much as for other clients. "I won't be back, Grant," she said. "I'm moving to France, to . . . to stay with my uncle. It's only fair to tell you."

There was a stunned silence. "Then I'm coming over at once," he said.

"I won't be here. I've already called for a limousine."

Again there was a pregnant silence. "Domini, in that case I have something to ask you right away," he started urgently. "I intended to ask it Sunday night. It's not the kind of thing I should say over the telephone, but—"

"Grant," she interrupted gently, "please don't say it at all. I should hate to say no to you a second time, about anything at all. You've been a good friend, and I'll always think of you that way."

"Then give me your address, purely as a friend. I sometimes go to Europe on buying trips. If I knew where to contact you . . ."

"I'll be sending my landlord a box number. I don't know it yet. Now I've got to go, I think my limousine's here."

"Domini . . . !"

"Good-bye, Grant, and thanks for everything."

"But I won't be able to reach you!"

"No," she said, with sudden pain piercing through the numbness. "Nobody will."

Late autumn chilled the Pyrenees, sending cold gusts sweeping down the steep French mountainsides to warn of winter's coming. The first frosts touched each growing thing, robbing the vines in the courtyard of their luxuriant colors, sending trees to sleep and small mountain creatures scurrying to replenish their caches of stored food. Grasses browned, and sheepherders moved their flocks down the slopes to look for more protected pasture. In early morning little puddles could be found frozen solid. Only the great *gaves* or mountain torrents, still cascading wildly down their majestic courses, and the *cirques*, the huge natural amphitheaters of rock, seemed impervious to the changes of the season. Once, Domini had loved the bracing air, the skeletal feel of the land in autumn before the snows arrived, but this year her heart was not there.

For Tasey's sake Domini tried to mend. But it was hard, far harder than the mending process of some years before, and she had thought nothing could be harder than that. There was a constant dull heaviness inside her, much as if her chest had been weighted down by a stone as large and ponderous as the one her father had bequeathed her.

Tasey had adjusted well. A quick child, still at an age when language learning was easy, she already chattered quite fluently in French. Her lessons were not formal ones but those learned in the best possible way, from hearing those around her. Especially important to the learning process, as well as to Tasey's happiness, was the presence of another child, the five-year-old daughter of the household's cook. Tasey had posed innumberable questions, of course, at the time of the change. Somehow Domini had managed to field them all, even the difficult question about why they were using a different last name. At the time Domini had simply said that people in France had French surnames; the complexity of the true story was still a little beyond a four-year-old's ken. In time she would tell a part of it.

In the transition Tasey's genuine eagerness for new experiences had helped; so had the arrival of a familiar and beloved possession. With Berenice's help Domini had arranged for the rapid disposal of all the contents of her loft, except one thing. The yellow unicorn had been air-expressed to France. Domini herself might have preferred to abandon it because it reminded her too much of Sander, but because of Tasey's continuing attachment to the large toy, she had made the arrangement. All the same, whenever she was in Tasey's nursery, Domini tried to avoid looking at the creature. Now its secret smile seemed the cruelest form of mockery.

Domini had acquired a box number not in France but in New York. Arranged by Berenice's Paris solicitors through an American legal firm, the box was cleared regularly in order to pay the last of old bills. With little current outlay and some final checks still being forwarded from former clients, Domini had no trouble

meeting her obligations, once again through the good
offices of the legal firm, who sent her an accounting
each month while submitting no bill. Domini knew who
must be paying the bill. Other than that, she refused
Berenice's help, saying that she had accepted enough
by arriving on her doorstep. Berenice didn't insist.

Domini had asked that personal mail be held unfor-
warded for the time being. Her ex-landlord had been
told he could hand out the box number, which tended
to suggest Domini was still in New York. As yet, she
wanted to see no letters. She was certain that Miranda
would write, entreating her to stop by or at least get in
touch by phone. For now, Domini wanted to see no
such entreaties, and yet she didn't want letters thrown
out. Once time had eased the pain a little, she thought
she would be able to face reading them for what news
she could glean of Sander.

She owed Berenice the full story, and so she had told
it soon after arrival. "Perhaps he was disturbed about
the fight with Lazarus," Berenice had suggested sympa-
thetically.

"He was," Domini had agreed, but it did nothing to
ease the great burden in her heart. "All the same, I
want no more to do with him. I can't maintain a
relationship with a man who cares so little for me."

At the time, Berenice listened with the uncritical
sympathy of the good listener and didn't insist on
psychoanalyzing Sander's motives or Domini's reactions. Perhaps she thought time would heal the wounds
more effectively than words.

Several weeks after Domini's arrival in the Pyrenees,
word arrived that Lazarus intended to mount the show
for Sander after all. Domini concluded that they must
have resolved their differences. When Berenice told
her late one evening, Domini didn't even smile; her
face felt as if it had forgotten how.

"In that case, Berenice, I'm going to ask you one
more favor. Do you think you could arrange for

Lazarus to give some kind of advance? The bronze castings have to be paid for, and it will cost more than Sander has. If necessary, I'll supply the advance myself by selling one of the sketches you gave me."

Berenice agreed to contact Lazarus and picked up the phone at that very moment, as it was a good hour to call New York. "Would you like me to ask for news of your friend?" she queried with the receiver already in hand.

"No," Domini said, averting her face.

After Berenice had completed the call, she told Domini that no advance would be necessary. Lazarus had already sold one of Sander's sculptures at a magnificent sum.

"He said it would cover all of Sander's expenses, with money to spare," Berenice told her. But she was not about to let the subject drop. "I'm intrigued that you still want to help the man. Are you sure, Didi, that—"

"I don't want to talk about him, Berenice."

The Basque woman looked at her thoughtfully but said no more. When a large packet of advance publicity was received from the Manhattan gallery in early November, a month before the joint show, she didn't bring up the subject again. Instead she left the material strewn over a coffee table where Domini couldn't fail to notice it, tactfully letting her make the decision to read or not to read.

After a few days Domini read. She wanted not to, but she thirsted for news of Sander. The press release and some glossy photographs suitable for reproduction had been included in the press kit; so had some clippings from publicity already received. The photographs were mostly of works of art, both Sander's and her father's. In all the material there were no pictures of Sander himself and no mention of his handicap. Domini concluded that it was Lazarus, not Sander, who had backed off in his demands.

There was some reference, however, to the interruption of Sander's career. The press release revealed that a motor accident some years before had interfered with what had been "a rapidly rising career in the Paris art scene. Several important collectors were starting to acquire his works about the time of the accident that caused a serious lull in the powerful creative output of a man who may someday become almost as influential as Le Basque himself . . ."

The release mentioned some of the important collectors by name, giving Domini pause. The list was not long but the names on it were very impressive; they represented some of the world's finest private collections. So D'Allard must have done very well out of the sculptures he had taken from Sander! But this time she was not quite so angry with her father's former dealer, for she recognized that being already represented in such important collections would greatly enhance Sander's prestige for the coming show. Collectors and even museums felt more comfortable when their judgment was seconded by others of their ilk. Past sales helped future ones; they also served to justify Lazarus's astronomical prices.

There was little more to be learned. With a sense of dull gratitude that she had at least accomplished her initial purpose of rekindling a great sculptor's creative fires despite his blindness, she placed the material back in the manila envelope that also lay on the coffee table, so that Berenice would know she could put it away.

Later in November news arrived that Domini's half-brothers were joining in an action to contest Le Basque's will. After breakfast one morning, when Domini and Berenice were sitting over second cups of coffee, a special delivery communication arrived from Paris. Tasey had already been bundled up for a morning of outside play with her new friend. The two women were alone. Berenice read the lengthy missive from her Paris solicitors, the same highly respected firm in which her estranged husband was still a partner. In silence she handed the papers to Domini.

"I've been waiting for this," Berenice said quietly after Domini had had a chance to skim through. "Your father knew it would happen too. Now I must leave you and go to Paris. There are battles to be fought, and I must work with the legal minds who have to fight them."

"Mentally incompetent," whispered Domini, her thoughts winging from Sander to her father. "How can they say such things? How do they think they can prove them?"

"He was an unconventional man." Berenice sighed. "I suppose they have found some people to testify as much. Dismissed servants, rivals, jealous men. As long as they find no trace of his early life—" Berenice halted abruptly and started again. "I agree, he was not mentally incompetent. All the same, it may drag on for years."

"I'll come to Paris too," Domini said. "You can't fight this alone."

Berenice said gravely, "No. It's time, Didi, for you to become mistress of this home. I've already had the deed prepared. I'm putting it in your name on condition you don't move the stone without my permission. The house is yours; it was your father's wish that you have it."

Domini's face was very pale. "I can't accept, Berenice, even if it was my father's wish. It's your home now, not his, and if I owned it I couldn't afford to run it anyway. As it is, I've imposed on you far too much. Perhaps it's time I started working again. If I could do window displays in New York, surely I can do them in other cities too."

"With the house goes an allowance to run it. Believe me, Didi, I discussed such things with your father."

"And yet," Domini said slowly, "you bought the farmhouse from him. You paid for it with your own money. It's not his money you're talking about, Berenice, it's yours. With a court case his estate may be tied up for years, and you won't have the benefit of it at all. I won't accept."

Berenice began to look exasperated. She tapped the glass-topped breakfast table with a fingertip, as if considering something. At last she burst out, sounding annoyed, "I really do believe you're proud enough and foolish enough to make things difficult for yourself. You are a true Basque at heart! Am I going to have to tell you the whole story now?"

Domini looked at her steadily. "Yes, you are," she said, "if there's anything to tell. I've been accepting your hospitality, but at the moment I see no reason to accept your charity."

Berenice regarded Domini through half-lidded eyes, a glint of amusement appearing to vie with the annoyance of a moment before. At last she murmured, "There's another characteristic the Basque people have, and your father, he was a Basque in all things. He was a wily man. Do you think he could not foretell what might happen after his death? He started making plans long ago, in order that his true wishes might eventually be done. After you vanished, the situation changed a little. And so he did three things. First he sold the house and property to me. Oh, it was a perfectly legal sale, at a good market price. But he gave me something to auction, something that would more than cover its cost. The something really belonged to you, and he had other reasons for auctioning it as well. Yes, Didi, the unicorn."

"The unicorn," Domini repeated in a stupefied whisper.

Berenice was watching Domini closely. "Your brothers can't even dispute the source of the money for the sale," she said, "because the unicorn was yours to give, not your father's. Oh, he knew how they might start prying around in his affairs and mine! If he had given me one sou for the farmhouse they might have quarreled with the sale. But how can they do so under the circumstances?"

"I see," said Domini thoughtfully. And her half-brothers were trying to say her father was mentally incompetent!

"The allowance I talk about—that, too, comes from the same source. After the purchase of the farmhouse and the land that goes with it, the rest was invested in sketches your father did, a perfectly legal sale your brothers can't dispute. There are many of them, not only those I gave you earlier this year. If you were to sell them all now, they would provide you with a decent income for life. Not overly generous, but enough to run this house quite comfortably."

Domini was still struggling to assimilate the news. "Why didn't you tell me this before?"

Berenice eyed Domini warily, as if uncertain of her coming reactions. "I could tell you were upset about the unicorn, for one thing. Do you remember how you wept when it was spoken of after your father died? I might have told you about the farmhouse then, but for that. And I think you still mourn for the unicorn's loss—I've seen how your eyes evade the copy your daughter owns. I was afraid some stubborn streak in you might refuse to take profit from its sale."

Domini pondered that. Berenice was right; a few months ago she might have felt that way. She remembered that she had been almost relieved to receive no money, not wanting her grief obscured by acquisitive thoughts. "I won't refuse now," she acknowledged. After a moment she added curiously, "What was the second part of Papa's plan?"

Berenice relaxed visibly, evidently relieved that Domini intended to accept her good fortune without question. "His second action, you already know. He wrote the will leaving most of his estate to me. He did so in part because, as I told you before, he knew what might happen if you failed to reappear."

"You mentioned his plan had a third part too,"

Domini said when Berenice spent some moments in silent contemplation, as if wondering how to phrase her next words.

"That . . . ah, that. First let me tell you what your father's thoughts were. He had other reasons for leaving his fortune to me. He believed his will would be in the courts for some time, and he thought the best person to fight your brothers would be myself. I have resources for one thing, and important friends who understand the law. Not knowing what life you were leading, but being a man of imagination, he imagined you would have neither of those things. He also knew you might never be found, and if you were, such legal tangles might disrupt your life for years. He knew I had the resources and the strength and the will, and perhaps even the wit if all goes well, to fight his battles in the years to come. And so he chose to leave the fighting to me."

Domini nodded. "I understand that," she said.

Berenice toyed with the legal document she had received, a small·smile playing across her lips. "When his will was contested, as your father was sure it would be, he knew that clever men would start questioning his sanity. He lived a private life, but servants do have ears. Several knew of how he destroyed the portrait of you. His voice was loud, and they saw the ruined painting later with their own eyes. It's likely your brothers have already discovered the story of how he threw you out, and intend to make use of it. Is this sane, a man destroying a work of great value? Disowning his daughter for using the name she has used all her life? Your father knew D'Allard would be only too happy to testify against him, too, should the matter come to court. His fury with D'Allard was unreasonable also, if one has no reason to understand. Truly, your father was like a madman at that time."

Domini felt anger rising inside. "I'll testify to the opposite," she said spiritedly.

"Will you? Can you? Yes, they will call you and put

274

you under oath, and you'll have to tell the truth. Will you also be able to tell a court exactly why your father's name was so important to him?"

"No," Domini realized, sinking back in her chair.

"Your father thought they would make much of the incident, for there are no other truly important incidents they can use. Oh, they will discover small eccentricities, and they will talk of them too." Thinking of somersaults, Domini could imagine. Berenice went on: "When he moved his great stone to the new pedestal, for instance, he insisted on doing all the work himself, although he was over seventy at the time, and to work with a block and tackle was not easy, nor was the moving of heavy flagstones. But little eccentricities do not mean a man has altogether lost his reason, so no doubt they will also say I influenced him too much. If they wish to win their case, your brothers will have to make you out a victim, and me a villain. They will produce witness after witness to prove those two things."

"Of course," Domini said, worry creasing her brow. She knew that was exactly what they planned: she remembered their approach to her. Out of hope, not conviction, she asserted, "They can't possibly win!"

"Ah, but they can. They have a very good case. In fact, your father was sure they couldn't possibly lose. It's unreasonable that a man with such a huge estate should leave so very much money to his mistress, and leave his three sons and his daughter totally unprovided for. Besides, he gave me a good number of paintings during his life and although many of them were of me, and given only on the giving occasions of each year, your brothers can easily prove I did indeed profit greatly from his generosity. For a time I will be made to look like a very avaricious, scheming woman. If your father left everything to me, as well as what he gave in his life, he must have been mentally deluded. After what he showered on a mere mistress, to leave his own sons the price of a mourning suit—it seems madness indeed! And to leave you nothing but a worthless stone which you cannot even move, without my permission . . . what could be more unreasonable than that?"

Berenice's eyes were twinkling so distinctly, her mouth curved in a smile so reminiscent of the unicorn's, that Domini knew she had not yet heard the whole story. "And that must lead up to the third part of Papa's plan," she said aloud, although she could make only sketchy guesses as to what the third part would be.

"When they have produced all their witnesses, there will be a little wait before the judgment is handed down. And then, during that time, I shall ask you to move the stone, and publicly announce why. Your father wished the stone, in any case, to be placed upon his grave. Beneath it, in a metal box laid into the pedestal, lies another will."

"His real will," whispered Domini, staring.

"Yes. In it, I receive nothing, because while he lived your father gave me exactly what he wished me to have. Believe me, there is no cause for you to think I will suffer in any way. The second will was written a day after the first, and it covers his true wishes, including a statement that he directed me to leave it unfound until any court case was about to be decided. He leaves most of his fortune for the foundation of a number of places where retarded or severely troubled young people, girls and boys such as he was once considered to be, can receive the help and special care they need."

"I'm glad he did that," Domini said after a moment, emotion creeping into her voice as her thoughts turned to her father's early life. "The amount's really too large to be owned by any one individual. But why on earth didn't he look after this during his life, instead of waiting for his will? It would have caused much less trouble, especially for you."

Berenice's small smile was evocative of the Mona Lisa. "Because your father was a clever man, and he wanted to leave enough money not for a few places but for many, in many cities and countries of the world. He knew his paintings would be much more valuable after his death. When a great artist dies, he produces no more, and so what he has already produced increases greatly in its worth. It has been some years, Didi, since your father sold anything of consequence at all. Hadn't you noticed?"

"Yes, I had," she said, thinking of the portraits of herself, and others that filled the walls and the storage rooms of the farmhouse to overflowing.

"Some time ago he realized his own works were the best form of investment. They doubled and tripled even while he was alive, and now that he's dead . . . ah, I imagine the original guesses as to his worth may have been grievously wrong after all, just as I told the press. But truthfully, they were too low. For one thing, there are far more paintings and sketches than anyone knows. For another, your father's prices have already leaped since then, by staggering amounts. Why, next month Lazarus will be selling only a few pictures that belong to me, and the sums he talks about are in multiples of millions. Who knows what your father's work will fetch in a few years once the court case is through?"

Domini no longer needed to question why her father had left the fight to Berenice. And yet it would be a long and difficult fight. Domini was humbled to think that Berenice was prepared to undertake a legal war that might rage for many, many years, during which aspersions of all kinds would be cast on her character and motives.

Berenice went on. "In the second will the rest of the estate is disposed of much as in the first, with a few exceptions. There's one large new bequest for a person he dearly loved: you, Didi. Someday, perhaps many years from now, you will inherit a good deal, as much as your father settled on me while he lived."

"But my half-brothers will fight the second will too," Domini pointed out, unconvinced, still struggling to understand all the reasons for her father's deviousness.

"Of course," Berenice agreed placidly. "They will not want the money to go to confused and troubled children any more than they want it to go to me. But how can they win? They have proved me a villain, and yet I have produced a second will that cuts me out of the inheritance altogether. They have proved you a victim in order to establish your father's mental incompetence. Yet in the second will you are not a victim— unless you say you are, and I think you will not say that or feel it. Are you then a villain for being given money your half-brothers want in their own pockets? One cannot be victim and villain at one and the same time! If they have succeeded in proving their first suit, they will have trouble proving their second. They will still try to call him incompetent, but where is their case? That he moved a large stone to protect his real will? That his head was befuddled by a mistress, when in fact he was clever enough to leave her nothing at all? That he gave his money to a worthy cause instead of giving it to a woman who was already wealthy—or to *men* who were already wealthy? That he left his daughter provided for, instead of destitute? That he put off his actions during his life, as he states in his will, in order to double or even triple the good he could do?"

"All the same—"

"Even your half-brothers benefit a little from the second will, not a great sum but enough, it states clearly, to cover any legal costs they may have by then incurred, provided they undertake no more actions to dispute your father's wishes. Your father didn't hate them, you see; he only thought them greedy and grasping like their mother. He knew they had money to pay for lawyers and investigators, and so he was afraid they might succeed in overturning a will, especially one which involves so very much money, Didi, that even your brothers would gasp. Should they try to contest the second will, their own logic and some of their own evidence can be used against them. I think any judge would soon see your father was a very clear-headed man, in full possession of all his faculties."

Domini started to laugh for the first time in months. Wily, wonderful Papa!

Berenice regarded her affectionately, waiting until the brief laughter died. "You must realize he trusted you greatly to ask me to tell you of his early life. If it were ever known he had once been in a place for the insane . . ."

Sobered, Domini gazed at her father's companion of many years. Within her a sure knowledge dawned, in which jealousy had no part. Gratefully she realized that Berenice must have brought her father a deep happiness during his final years, even in the midst of his sorrows over herself.

"He trusted you even more, and for very good reason," she said softly. "You didn't have to tell a soul about the second will."

"I had hoped not to tell you yet, because I know you have problems of your own, and this might only add to them." With a sigh Berenice put the legal papers aside. "But perhaps it is as well you forced the issue. I always knew I had to tell someone, because if anything should happen to me . . . well, someone has to know, to carry on the fight."

"Yes," Domini said simply, making the promise with that one word. After a reflective moment she added, "You told me once that Papa loved Élisabeth and me, and I believe that's true. But you know, Berenice, I think he must have loved you most of all, to leave you with such a great trust."

Berenice bowed her head, and tears came to the thick lashes lowered over her fine dark eyes. She made no comment on Domini's observation. Instead she murmured, "He said when he felt the great stone come to its final resting place, he would know his true wishes had been done. And then, he told me, his heart would be at peace for everything he had suffered in his life. And do you know, Didi, I think it truly will."

Chapter Fourteen

Don't quote Milton to me!" Sander snapped at the man he would never see. Lazarus was a voice in the void, a thorn in the flesh, a goad, a prod, another affliction in this black tomb that was his living death. Lazarus was a faceless foe who came in the guise of a friend. Sander knew that his dealer's motives might be good, but they were probably self-seeking too. Already, with the show not even open, Lazarus talked of excitement in the art community and was urging Sander to return to work. Would the wretched man never stop these attempts to flog him into creating what he no longer wanted to create?

Grimly the granular voice repeated itself, starting once more at the beginning of the interrupted quote. "'When I consider how my life is spent, ere half my days, in this dark world and wide . . .'"

Sander slammed his palm on the oilcloth of the old table that had once served for sculpture. His mouth was twisted with inner pain. "Damn you, Lazarus! Don't you think I know Milton was blind? Don't you think I understand a dark world well enough without his help?"

"'And that one talent which is death to hide,'" the relentless words went on, "'lodg'd with me useless . . .'"

Sander knew his Milton, too, that poem especially. Angrily he quoted back to Lazarus: "'Doth God exact day-labour, light deny'd . . . ?'"

"Yes!"

Sander rose to his feet, shaking with a cold fury. "Go to hell," he rasped toward his unseen adversary.

"What?" came the rude retort. "You want company down there?"

"Get out!"

"I'll go," the disembodied voice agreed, "but I leave you with a question. Was Milton's talent useless? Good-bye for now, my friend. I'll be back."

Lazarus always came back. Sander could hear the soft fall of footsteps retreating toward the door. There they came to a brief halt, and the next words were said implacably, in a tone devoid of pity:

"About the blindness, you have no choice. But you can die in the dark, or you can live in the dark. Which will it be for you, my friend?"

The squeak of floorboards along the hall diminished down the stairs and told Sander he was at last alone. He sagged visibly, his proud posture changing to one of defeat. He went to the door, eleven slow strides taken without the care he ought to exercise when a stranger had been in the room to displace possessions. He thrust it closed because he wanted no one to intrude, not even Miranda. Then he returned to the table, his dragging tread still painfully slow under the great weight life had become. He felt for a chair, fumbling a little because he had not left it exactly in place. He slumped into it. Soon his head drooped, and he covered it with his hands in abject surrender to the black demons that possessed him.

The darkness was dense with despair. For months it had been a despair so great that it engulfed all hope and sapped him of what small strength of will he had retained after Germany. Then, he had tried; God knew he had tried. Until he had learned his craft of carpentry, the simple toys had been made at the cost of banged thumbs, bleeding fingers, and stepped-on nails. Often the long efforts had been ruined at the last by a badly angled screw or a misdirected sawblade. It had not been easy but it had served his pride better than making brooms.

With the sculpture, too, he had tried. For a time it had consumed him, that need to create. During that time he had almost begun to feel like a whole man again. He had started to walk in the world, not as a sighted man walks, but at least with less sense that the world would never be for him.

But then, in that time, he had had Domini for light. And now there was no Domini.

She had reached down into his dark heart and twisted herself into the very fiber of it until she had become as necessary to life as the air he breathed, the food he ate, the very blood that pumped in his veins.

He no longer wanted to try. What had once been a darkness only on his eyes and on his soul was now a darkness that destroyed everything: his life force, his courage, his will to survive. If the blood stopped pumping or the world stopped turning, he would not care. There was no Domini.

No Domini. He knew now that Miranda had tried hard to reach her, at first without his knowledge. She had phoned only to receive no answer; she had gone to the loft only to find it empty; she had written several times to a box number only to get no letter in reply. She had talked to Domini's landlord and to the day-care center, and she had ranged SoHo in search of Domini's former clients. With all her efforts Miranda had found no trace.

To Sander, Domini's disappearance was proof of how

deeply his behavior had hurt her—as if he had needed proof. He had known for a long time that she loved him. Early in the relationship, almost from the beginning, he had sensed it in her face. Why she loved him he was not sure, but he had known it was true, not because of her few unguarded words, but because his fingers told him so. For months he had not been strong enough to send her away, and so instead he had resorted to verbal cruelties whenever the moments became too tender. He had always known he had no right to encourage her hopes in even the smallest way.

On that last day he had known it must end. The knowledge had filled him with a great rage at fate, at what the future could never hold for him. Had he been rational, he would not have allowed his frustrations to erupt so violently. But perhaps it was as well: his violence had performed drastic surgery to uproot Domini's misplaced affections.

He knew of Miranda's search because she had finally told him when she reached her last resort. Then she had begged him to dictate a letter himself. She had offered to write it if he would only sign—yet another reminder of his wretched disability. He had dictated nothing. How could he beg Domini to return and share his night? How could he pull her down into his black world, his pit of despair, his perpetual damnation? How could he be certain his darkness would not in time extinguish her light?

No Domini. Never to hear the music of her voice. Never to feel the silk of her hair. Never to reach out and find her soft hand. Never to drink the morning fragrance of her skin. Never to listen to the quiet tick of her heart, in the silence of a room that no longer seemed so dark. . . .

He thought of her entrance into his life, of his initial resentment, of the first wisps of feeling he had had no right to feel, of the way she had fought to make him express his creative urges again. Domini would have echoed Lazarus's exhortations, of that he was sure. She

had never been overprotective, as Miranda had sometimes been. She had slapped him, been stubborn with
him, encouraged him to go walking by himself, been
angry as often as she had been gentle with him, had
faith in him when he had had no faith in himself. She
had even been unaccountably, humanly, crazily jealous, and that over a man no woman would want. She
had accepted his blindness, but not his despair.

Suddenly, with a shock of realization, he lifted his
head. *She had accepted his blindness.*

It was so simple, so self-evident, so much a truth that
he could hardly credit his own stupidity. Of course she
had accepted it, because she had had no choice. Why
had it never struck him before? Domini was a warm,
strong, loving, courageous woman, neither a seeker of
freaks nor a bleeding heart to base a relationship on
suffocating pity. She hadn't loved him because of his
blindness, or in spite of it; she had simply loved *him*.
The blindness hadn't entered in. And he had been ten
times a fool not to see it, a kind of seeing that required
no sight at all.

With a great wonder growing, he examined this
simple truth. She had accepted his blindness as she
accepted his other faults: his quick temper, his harsh
tongue, his mask of pride. He had railed against the
future, but Domini had trusted in it. And yet in that
regard no eyes, not even hers, could see what lay
ahead. She had been ready to step fearlessly into an
unseen future, and she had hoped he would learn to do
the same.

Gradually, as understanding dawned, it came to him
that Domini had wanted one thing above all: she had
wanted him to live. To *live* in his darkness, not to die.
She had wanted that even more than she wanted his
love, which she had not demanded from him ever, not
even at the end. Had she really cared for him so very
much? Even in her unspeakable unhappiness on that
last day, she had sensed his despairing mood and
suggested a return to sculpture—knowing, perhaps,

that despair could be sublimated in creativity. From the first she had known that a part of him would perish without his chosen work.

That one talent which is death to hide . . . it was indeed death of a sort not to sculpt, less of a death than the loss of the woman he loved more deeply than his soul, but a death all the same. Was there still reason to fight for life in the darkness even though the darkness contained no Domini for now?

"About the blindness, you have no choice. But you can die in the dark, or you can live in the dark . . ."

The words whispered again through his mind, and in one of those strange exchanges the mind is capable of, in memory it was Domini's voice he heard. Like an echo in his endless night, she whispered, "You can live . . . live . . . live."

With a sense of awe and humility, because he had done nothing in this life to deserve the love of a woman like Domini, he rose slowly to his feet. If she had trust in what could not be seen, so should he. The darkness was there; it would always be there—but he still had a choice. The decision he made was a conscious one, an acceptance of the man he was, the man Domini had accepted long ago.

With a courage he had not felt for months, he moved to the corner of the room where the tubs of clay were kept. He had no model but he didn't need one; he held the memory of Domini in his hands.

Chapter Fifteen

*D*ecember brought winter's full force to the mountains and it was a year of early snows. Normally the Pyrenees were much milder than the Alps because of their southern latitude, but such could not be said this year. To Domini, the deep freeze seemed symbolic of her inner state.

One evening at the beginning of the month, shortly before the opening of Sander's show, she received a call from Paris. After the first greetings Berenice brushed aside Domini's various questions about lawsuits and living accommodations. "I've phoned about something else," she said, "something I thought you should know. I've just been talking to Lazarus in New York. By chance he mentioned your friend Sander. Evidently he went for some months into a state of black despair. He didn't sculpt, and he hardly ate. Lazarus was very worried about him. He was afraid Sander had lost the will to live, although of course he had no idea why it might be so. Can you still think you mean nothing to him?"

Domini's long silence was filled with such a turmoil of concern that she was unable to speak. At last Berenice began to fill in the empty spaces over the telephone wire.

"Actually, before you start worrying needlessly, I'll tell you that Lazarus was jubilant on the phone because Sander finally set to work again last week, with double the vigor. Lazarus says it's a good thing too—already, in advance of the show, two museums have indicated an interest in making acquisitions. Your friend is going to be a great success, Didi. Don't you think that may change his attitude toward everything?"

Domini's initial alarm had dissipated with the news that Sander was working again. "I don't know," she said slowly.

"And he's consented to the mention of his blindness. Doesn't that tell you something? Lazarus believes he's learning to accept his condition, to live with it. I knew I should tell you at once, because if there's been a change in your friend's attitude, it may alter how you feel about things. If you were to go to him now . . ."

Domini took a moment to think. It was good news that Sander might be coming to terms with his handicap, news for which she would give long thanks in her heart for many years to come. But in what regard was the situation really changed for herself? If he had been upset at her departure, it was clear he was now mending, certainly better than she. Already, despite Berenice's optimism, the personal heart-heaviness was beginning to return.

"No," she said, struggling to understand her own confused reactions. "I won't go to him. He has no feelings for me, Berenice, except destructive ones. I don't want to lay myself open for that kind of pain again."

"Pride." Berenice sighed. Then she added, with a

note of slyness, "Perhaps if he knew who you really are, where you were to be found . . . then the choice would be up to him. It could be done very casually, through Lazarus."

Domini took a hard grip on her emotions. "No," she said in a low voice. "And remember, Berenice, you promised long ago you'd reveal nothing. I don't want Sander to know where I am or who I am. If you tell, I won't forgive you."

"How do you know he doesn't love you? When a man is blind and bitter, he does destructive things."

"And perhaps he always will," Domini answered with the despondency that had become a condition of her existence.

Berenice clucked her tongue in annoyance at Domini's unnatural pessimism. "If you want to find out how he really feels, you'll have to swallow your pride. And it is pride, Didi—just as it was pride that kept you from your father."

Domini could not deny that. Nevertheless, despite Berenice's urgings, she refused to give permission for any revelation of her whereabouts. "I'll have to do some serious thinking about it," she said. "Maybe someday I'll decide to approach him, but I want to make the decision myself. I have to think what's best for Tasey too. There's a lot of pride to be swallowed, Berenice, and I'm not ready to do it yet."

"When will you be?" Berenice asked heatedly. "When you hear your lover is on his deathbed?"

It was a low blow, but when Domini hung up she had to acknowledge to herself that there was some truth to it, just as there was truth to Berenice's contention that she didn't really know Sander's true feelings at all. But in Domini, the capacity for love went hand-in-hand with the capacity for hurt, and Sander had hurt her very badly indeed. Her pride was not ready to be shelved, if indeed it ever would be. In the Basque blood she had inherited from her father, the ability to endure ran very deep.

All the same, Berenice's arguments occupied much of Domini's thoughts for the next two weeks. At first she toyed with daydreams. With its large empty studio, the farmhouse in the Pyrenees would be a perfect place for a sculptor. If Sander moved to France, it would be good for Miranda too—his blindness was the only thing that had ever prevented his sister from living her own life. Miranda might even be able to sell the little gallery, which she hadn't been very good at running, in order to devote herself to mothering Joel's children, a task for which she had a good deal more talent.

If Sander had been in a state of depression for some months, Domini reflected, surely he had more feelings for her than he had ever betrayed. At such times she almost relented. But then she would remember the destructive crashing of clay, the terrible deep-freeze of emotions, and the wishful dreams would disappear like smoke. How could she ever approach him after what he had done?

Moreover, Sander's revitalized interest in life might simply mean that he had become involved with someone new. . . .

When that thought first occurred, Domini thrust it aside as best she could. Models didn't always become mistresses, and just because Sander had never lived long without a woman in his bed, that didn't mean he had one there right now. All the same, with jealous imaginings beginning to eat at her, she managed to convince herself that some other woman must by now be ensconced in the role she had once fulfilled. And if not yet, then soon. With the success his talent was sure to bring, a prospect about which Domini had no doubts, there would be ready candidates for the position. Even if Sander had once loved her, he was unlikely to be faithful to a vanished mistress forever, any more than he had been faithful to Nicole.

If anything caused a final stiffening of Domini's pride, it was the return of Nicole to her thoughts. Would Sander have been so hurtful to *her?*

No, Domini would not let Sander know where she was, at least not yet. And maybe, just maybe, never.

Mid-December brought unseasonably heavy snows. Great sweeps of clean white powdered the outlines of the land, softening the granite jut of the high inclines and gathering in huge, slow drifts in the lower valleys, where the winters were normally less harsh. For a time Domini and Tasey and the household staff were deeply snowed in. But then the laden skies gave way to crisp, clean days when sun sparkled on unsullied snow. Christmas was coming to the Pyrenees.

Three days before it did, when the smaller side roads were at last clear, a large parcel arrived from Berenice. From Paris she wrote news of the impending lawsuit, about which she remained optimistic although the press was already starting to vilify her in a campaign that must have been cleverly orchestrated by Domini's half-brothers. Berenice was guarded in her letter, but she did write: "Do not be angered by what they are saying, my dear. This stage is necessary if the next stage is to work. It will only be for a little time, and then I, too, will be at peace."

She also wrote that she was not coming back to the mountains for Christmas, as Domini had expected. Her holiday season was to be spent with old friends. "For me the farmhouse holds too many memories. At this time I will do better to be elsewhere, although my thoughts will be with the small family in the place where I spent so many happy years. But what is Christmas for a child if someone is being glum?"

Domini agreed. With the approach of the festive season she had tried extra hard to shed her own pall of gloom, with at least surface success. Underneath, her frame of mind was not at all good, because in her memories of the previous Christmas were mingled too many thoughts of Sander, and in her recent reflections were too many painful imaginings of him finding solace in some other woman's arms.

The parcel was filled with brightly wrapped presents. With Christmas only three days away, Domini realized her own present for Berenice, and Tasey's, would never reach Paris on time. But then she noticed that Berenice's parcel had been shipped by a special air freight service to Biarritz and delivered from there by van. It had started its journey only the previous day. Perhaps there was hope after all? That afternoon Domini had planned to shop for a few last-minute things, not in the nearest hamlet but in the picturesque village of Saint-Jean-Pied-de-Port, which was within easy driving distance. But errands could just as easily be done farther afield, and Domini resolved to have Georges and the limousine take her instead to the resort city of Biarritz, a twisting two-hour drive to the Atlantic seaboard, where the craggy Basque coast melted into the marshy forests of the Landes.

Then she noticed a manila envelope tucked in with the wrapped gifts and lifted it out. Without comment Berenice had enclosed various materials sent by Lazarus immediately after the opening of the show in New York. It had opened to stunning reviews in the art columns. Domini read them, although she would have preferred to forego such masochism. The Le Basque paintings had been snapped up within hours, at any price; many important collectors had been on hand. Although they had been a little more cautious about the first major show of a little-known sculptor, it seemed that Sander's pieces had been in demand too. At Lazarus's skyhigh prices, that must have been rewarding news for him.

The clippings mentioned Sander's disability with little of the sob-story slant he would have abhorred, but as an obstacle that he had overcome. For his sake Domini was grateful that his handicap had been treated so matter-of-factly, with far more attention devoted to the merit of the sculptures themselves.

In one paper there was a news photo of him standing beside the bronze sculpture of Joel. He looked thinner, and he had not smiled for the camera. Because a number of elegantly dressed people were also visible in the background of the shot, Domini knew it must have been taken at the opening of the show. It was a fairly clear reproduction, and she started to study it closely to see what she might glean from the picture. With a small sense of shock she recognized one person in the background grouping, talking and laughing with the others. Nicole.

Nicole!

It was so clearly she that Domini knew she was not mistaken. She well remembered that Nicole had vanished some years before with a wealthy American. With all the advance publicity that Lazarus had managed to place, Nicole would have had no trouble reconnecting with Sander if she wanted. And she had obviously wanted. Nicole had always had a sharp eye on the main chance, and with Sander's new success . . .

And Sander must have wanted, too, or he would not have invited Nicole to his opening. Domini knew about openings like that; one couldn't simply walk in off the street.

Feeling sick and angry, she read no more. She threw the clippings in the wastebasket, saving only one. That she put aside to show to Tasey, who was outdoors in a lather of ecstasy over a snowman she and her friend were making in the courtyard. Through the window Domini watched them for a while, gradually calming as she reminded herself that nothing must be allowed to mar the magic of a four-year-old's Christmas. If Sander was fool enough to take up with Nicole again, she didn't want him anyway. Ever!

By noon Domini had fought her way back to normal. The parcel for Berenice was ready for the trip to Biarritz and so was she, practically clad in narrow ski pants and a thick alpine sweater she had owned in her youth. She had found it in mothballs on her return to the farmhouse, along with a cupboardful of other carefully stored clothes. With roads the way they had been, it was best to dress warmly for the trip; one never knew if the car might get stuck somewhere along the way. Domini intended to wear her old winter coat too. Although she had money now, she had had little heart for buying new clothes, and with its nutria lining the old coat was still the warmest thing she owned.

"I put this aside for you to see, Tasey," Domini announced at lunch, handing the picture over.

"My skullcher!" squealed Tasey, one buttery finger homing in on the exact spot where her small work of art had become part of Sander's. "My skullcher of the clay man!"

"Sculpture," said Domini.

"Sculpture," said Tasey.

Domini laughed and tousled Tasey's hair. "You are growing up," she said. "What a difference a year makes! Soon I'll have to start calling you Stasy."

"Or Anna . . . Anna Stasy." The way Tasey said it, it was not immediately recognizable as Anastasia.

"That's too big a name! You'll have to do some growing before anyone calls you that."

"The clay man called me Anna Stasy once, when he got cross."

Domini's smile died; she hadn't realized Tasey had taken to handing out her full first name. Not that it mattered anymore, but in New York Domini had always had the thought that some particularly knowledgeable person might recognize the name of Anastasia Greey. It had never been a great fear, because the name would be known only to art historians who dealt in esoteric information; the portrait of Domini's mother in the Museum of Modern Art was called simply "Woman with Apple." There were no other pictures of Anastasia on view to the public. The name would have meant nothing to Sander.

To cover the moment, Domini returned to the clipping from the art review. "Your sculpture looks very nice," she said.

"I wish I had some clay," Tasey sighed. "Snow is fun, but it goes away."

"Then we'd better add clay to Santa's list," Domini replied, making mental note of the request. "I won't be home for supper tonight, Tasey. I have to go shopping in Biarritz, and Biarritz is a long way from here. It takes two hours to get there and two hours to get back, so I won't be home until about your bedtime. Maybe even later."

"Won't you tuck me in?" came the somewhat wistful request. Tasey liked the housekeeper, Hélène, a loyal retainer who had been at the farmhouse for many years, but bedtimes were special. Now that she had turned four, she expected a story, and Hélène was not too good at telling them.

"I'll do my best, but I won't promise," Domini said, conscious that the leaden heaviness of the sky held the threat of a new snowfall.

It came, too, but fortunately not until Domini was well on the way home from her long afternoon's expedition. For the last few miles of the return trip, the headlights of the limousine barely pierced the blinding wall of white flakes, slowing progress on the precipitous road to a careful crawl. Domini reflected that the farmhouse might very well be snowed in again for the holiday season. Thank heaven the larder was fully restocked and the last of the Christmas errands done!

The lights of the farmhouse, glimmering through the haze of swirling snow, were a welcome sight indeed. Dismissing Georges's offer of help so that he could take the car directly to the garage, Domini filled her arms with her purchases and stepped out at the entrance to her home. With hands occupied in carrying and eyes half-blinded by the soft fat flakes, Domini struggled to turn the knob of the ironclad front door. She pushed it open with one booted foot.

"Mummy!" cried a glad young voice. "Look who's here!"

Domini stood stock-still in the open doorway, shock

rooting her to the spot, robbing her of the wit to think of the snow driving into the house from behind her. "Sander," she whispered. For a fraction of time her heart seemed to stop.

He was standing across the hall, cradling Tasey high in his arms, facing Domini. He was not smiling, and yet on his face there was an expression of such depth and such meaning, an expression so profound and so personal, that her heart flopped and then started thudding wildly again. She understood nothing except one thing, and to her that one thing was everything. Sander had come to find her.

"He was going to tuck me in and we heard the car! Now you can tuck me in too!"

The delighted exclamation broke the spell. For a moment Domini had almost forgotten her surroundings, locked as she was by the invisible chains that linked her to the tall figure of Tasey's father. Without taking her gaze from Sander, Domini pushed the door closed behind her and put her parcels on an old oaken breakfront. She could think of absolutely nothing to say except what she was saying with her eyes, and although he could not see, it was a message he seemed to return with his. In his dark pupils there was a silvered warmth, an intensity of emotion too deep for simple smiles.

"He brought some ice cream, Mummy! He gave me a piggyback! He told Hélène he would put me to bed!" The words tumbled out, a measure of Tasey's excitement. "I told him a story! And when I'm in bed he's going to tell me one too!"

Domini's expression must have been confusing to Tasey, because she added, "Aren't you *surprised,* Mummy?"

"Yes," Domini managed jerkily. She felt moisture gathering on her lashes and tried to fight it back. They were tears of pure joy, and if she had been alone with Sander she would have allowed herself to shed them. But she knew she couldn't explain her emotional state to Tasey, to whom tears meant hurt and unhappiness.

"Oh, Sander, I'm so . . ." Choked into silence, she could not finish the rest of her sentence. But perhaps he understood.

"So am I," he said quietly. And she knew he did.

"What's the matter, Mummy? Aren't you *happy?*"

"Very," Domini whispered, her chin trembling.

"Then don't cry!"

"It's only snow, melting on my face," Domini said. But she needed a moment alone to get her emotions under control. And so, before saying more, she lowered her head and dropped to her knees, ostensibly to remove her boots. Somehow, for Tasey's benefit, she succeeded in keeping her voice in a natural range.

"Why don't you take Mr. Williams to your bedroom, Tasey? I'll be up as soon as I've hung my coat."

"You don't need to come. I'll look after her tonight."

Immediately Tasey started bouncing in Sander's arms. Domini could see the flounce of a candy-striped nightgown and two small dangling feet. "Will you tell the other half of the story?"

"Only if you'll promise to go to sleep the moment I finish," Sander returned, his voice ringing with a stern note Domini recognized and concurred with. This was a time for grownups to be alone.

"Mummy has to tell me a story and tuck me in too," Tasey replied, showing youthful signs of artfulness.

"No, she does not, Miss Anastasia Greey! This is your mother's night off! She's not going to tuck you in at all!"

He let Tasey slide to the floor. "You'll have to show me the way," he reminded her gravely, and Tasey's small hand reached out to lead him through the unfamiliar halls.

Almost immediately, while Domini was still wiping away happy tears that prevented the immediate removal of her fleece boots, the housekeeper, Hélène, arrived to ask how soon she wished her supper served. On her haunches with head ducked, Domini managed the appropriate responses. Earlier she had suggested ragoût to the cook, thinking a stew the simplest solution because it was easily reheated. Now she didn't care about food at all, but it did occur to her that Sander might not have eaten, and that was confirmed when Hélène informed Domini that he had arrived by taxi only an hour before, after Tasey's suppertime. There was ample ragoût, the housekeeper said, for two.

Domini asked that the stewpot be left on the stove. "We'll help ourselves when we're hungry. You can dismiss the staff for the evening," she added, knowing she wanted no servants up late tonight. If Sander's smoking and somber expression was to be believed, this was a night to be alone.

"Will the gentleman be staying?" asked Hélène.

"Yes," Domini said.

"Then I'll prepare a bed—"

"No," Domini answered. "That won't be necessary." In this household, of all households, there was no need for pretense.

"Of course," Hélène said tactfully and left.

How had Sander found her? He wouldn't be here if he didn't know her true identity. And how had he discovered that? Surely not through Berenice, who was not one to break promises. Surely not from the small clue Tasey had provided in letting the name of Anastasia slip—if that had triggered any question in Sander's mind, he would have pursued it at the time. So how had Sander found out?

But the question chased through Domini's mind without her feeling any real need to seek the answer. There was only one thing of true importance: Sander had come to find her.

The white cane leaning against the oaken breakfront was reminder enough that the trip could not have been easy for him. And yet he had braved it, not trusting to the telephone or the mail. Did he really love her so much? To Domini's overflowing heart it was the final proof.

By the time she ascended the stairs in stockinged

feet, her face was reasonably well schooled. Tasey now inhabited the room that had once been Domini's own, a bright room well suited for a nursery because it had a large play area with roomy built-in shelves just the right size for toys. The shelves were still quite empty, but Christmas would soon see to their filling.

Domini came to a halt in the darkened hall, not entering because of what Sander had said. From this position she could see without being easily seen by Tasey.

Tasey was already snug beneath her blankets, her eyelids growing heavy as they always did almost as soon as her dark head came to rest on the pillow. Sander was sitting on the edge of the bed, and he didn't look up when Domini came to the door, although his shoulders tensed enough that she knew he had detected the silent pad of her feet. His face was bent in Tasey's direction. Unruly dark hair fell over his forehead, leaving his eyes in pools of shadow. Domini's heart twanged to see the two of them together, as she had thought she might never do again.

"Of course the unicorn doesn't turn into a handsome prince, unless you want him to," Sander said, and Domini realized that Tasey must have told her father the invented story once related to her by Grant. She must have asked Sander to finish it. "Do you want him to be a prince?"

"No," Tasey murmured, snuggling in against the strong hand that stroked her hair. "I like my unicorn the way he is."

"Then I won't bother finishing the first story, except to say that the little princess kept her unicorn forever and a day, just the way he was. I'll tell you a different story, a true one that has no prince in it at all, although it does have a unicorn, one very much like yours. Did you know that some people think unicorns mean love?"

Tasey's eyes traveled to her beloved yellow unicorn, which stood in a corner of her room, smiling its eternal and inscrutable smile. Her mouth had already taken possession of a thumb, so she answered with a sleepy shake of her head, forgetting that Sander could not see.

He waited for no answer but went on, his voice low and vibrant and meant for Domini's ears as well. "One day the man in my story saw a golden-haired girl riding an enchanted unicorn. She was a very special, magical person, and also the loveliest thing he had ever seen. She was young and innocent, as pure as the driven snow. When she saw him, she asked him to kiss her. But the man was in love with . . . with a beautiful black-haired sorceress who had put him under her spell."

In Sander's slight hesitation Domini detected a reluctance, as if that was one part of the story he preferred not to tell. Perhaps it was as well he was unable to see the changing expression on her face.

"Because he was under a spell, he knew he mustn't kiss the golden-haired girl, or something very wrong indeed would happen. She would fall off the unicorn's back, for one thing, and change into . . . into an ordinary mortal instead of a magical person. The man didn't want to hurt her, and so he refused to do as she asked. In fact, he got very angry with her."

"Why?" Tasey got the word past the obstacle of her thumb.

"He was angry she had asked, because it was very hard for him to refuse. He was an ordinary mortal man, you see, and he wanted to kiss her very badly. Mostly, though, he was angry with himself. He started to get sick inside just from thinking about how much he wanted to kiss her. He tried to remember he was in love with the sorceress, and for a time he fooled himself with that. But still, he thought a lot about the lovely golden-haired girl and the kiss she had asked for.

"She asked three times. The first time she asked, he told her no, he didn't like her; and that was a lie. The second time she asked, he told her no, he didn't want her; and that was also a lie. The third time she asked he told her no, he didn't love her, and that was true enough—or so he thought at the time, because of the spell he was under. But the golden-haired girl answered by saying she loved *him*. So that third time . . . well, you know what always happens the third time in fairy tales. He was still angry but he kissed her after all."

Tasey's thumb came out of her mouth. "Did she fall off the unicorn?"

"I'm afraid so," Sander said ruefully, head still turned to his daughter. "She fell a long, long way off, such a long way that no one knew where she was at all. The man thought he must have hurt her, just as he had been warned, but he couldn't tell because he hadn't seen her fall. He lost his eyes, you see, in punishment for what he had done. He was blind."

"Like you," Tasey murmured before her mouth occupied itself again. Her dark blue eyes were glazed with sleep, her expression contented in expectation of a happy ending.

"Exactly," Sander agreed soberly and then went on with his story. "The man felt terrible to think of what he might have done. Maybe he even deserved to lose his eyes. Because everything was black, he grabbed for the unicorn and hung on for dear life. For a long time it was the only thing he had to hang on to at all. After many adventures it led him to a strange land very far away. After a time he even lost hold of the unicorn, and then life was very black indeed, for the new land was filled with monsters he couldn't see. They were hard to fight, because without his eyes he felt like only half a man.

"But then one day he met someone who wasn't a monster at all. In fact, when she was around his monsters went away. He couldn't see her face, but he began to like hearing her voice. He liked the feel of her hands. He liked the way she laughed and the smell of the soap she used. He liked the sound of her footsteps. Little by little he liked more things about the lady he couldn't see, until one day . . ."

Tasey's eyes were closed. Slowly Sander's head lifted to the doorway, his sightless eyes wearing a tortured expression that tore at Domini's heart.

"One day she asked him for three kisses, just as the golden-haired girl had done. He desperately wanted to say yes, but he thought his kisses would surely destroy her, just as they had destroyed once before. He would rather have destroyed himself. And so, very angrily and very rudely, he told her to go away."

Although Sander's voice remained low and level, it had taken on a hoarseness that conveyed deep emotion, to Domini's ears at least. Tasey's drowsy smile suggested that she understood only the fairy tale narrative, but Domini knew that with his simple words he was trying to express the very real anguish that had ruled his actions for so long.

"When she went, his monsters came back. He fought a great battle with them, and because there was now true love in his heart, he finally won. And so his bad spell was broken."

Tasey sighed pleasurably and her lashes fluttered. Through her thumb she mumbled, "Could he see?"

Sander bowed his head, and for a long moment Domini could see the muscles working in his throat. Then he said gruffly, "Yes, he could see."

It was the lie Tasey expected, but perhaps there was truth in it too. The silence extended before he continued. "And so he went searching for his lady-love. Although he had never seen her face, he knew he would know it with his heart. He searched the four corners of the winds, and in the lonely lands to the west of the sun. Then one night in the mountains of the moon, he found a lady, and because he saw with his heart, he knew at once she was the lady he loved. It was the golden-haired girl and she hadn't changed a bit, although the spell had come absolutely true. She was still special for him, but she was an ordinary mortal, with ordinary human feelings and a wonderful human heart. He loved her more than ever that way. And so he said yes, as he should have said at first. Yes, yes, yes."

Sander's head was still lowered, penitent, asking a question rather than giving an answer. There was no mistaking what he had said yes to, and Domini's heart soared with love, the leaden unhappiness of these past months forgotten in the fullness of the moment.

Seeing Tasey almost asleep, Domini inserted some quiet words from the doorway. "She always was human," she said.

"Yes," Sander agreed softly. "She had never been magical at all, although he hadn't known it. The magic was all in the unicorn, and the unicorn was love. But if he had seen that right at the start, there would have been no story to tell."

Tasey's last sigh of contentment ended with a final flutter of eyelids, leaving her thick dark lashes curling over her young cheeks. Sander sat with bent head and waited for the sounds of regular breathing. With Tasey finally asleep, he kept his voice low but made no effort to hide the deep emotion that was evident in his expression. "I'm sorry there is a story to tell," he said, his regretful eyes lifting blindly to the door.

"So am I," Domini whispered, forgiving him all the same, for everything. Sander's simple story had revealed a great deal about his varying emotional states through the years. It was hard for a proud man to give excuses for his actions, to tell of the hell he had undergone and the remorse he had felt. Domini knew he had tried to tell her in the best way he knew. The story was a kind of penance for all his actions.

He dropped his head to Tasey once more, his hand still resting against the dark hair so like his own. "Will she wake?" he asked.

"No. She wears herself out during the day."

"Whose child is she?"

"Does it matter?"

"No," he said, although his voice jerked a little in the saying. "I won't ask again, either you or Tasey. I have to admit I put some offhand questions to her, but she could only tell me about some former man friend of yours. It seems she wanted a father, and for a while hoped it might be him. He sounded nice. Was he?"

"Yes."

By the clench of his jaw and the tautness of skin over his knuckles, she could see that Sander was struggling with jealousy. She might have paid him then for whatever had happened recently with Nicole, but that wasn't like Domini. She gave forgiveness when it was asked, and she knew that Sander had asked it, for everything, with his story to Tasey.

"She's your child, Sander. There's been no man but you. Tasey doesn't know the truth yet, but I've never lied to her either. I told her I would tell her someday who her father was. And someday I will."

That he was deeply moved showed in the tug of muscles around his mouth, in the way one hand rose to his bowed head. With thumb and forefinger pressed to the bridge of his nose, he struggled for control. When he spoke a moment later, his voice was choked. "Do you mind if I sit with her for a little while? I knew it was possible, of course, because I knew her age. All the same, it's a big thing to hear in so many words. When a man discovers he's a father . . ."

Domini understood. He needed to be alone, just as she had needed to be alone a short time ago. Strong men had weaknesses, too, but to display them would go against the grain of someone so proud.

"My room's right across the hall," she said without offering to return and guide him. In strange surroundings she knew he could not be sure of his route, but she was confident he would be able to make his way alone. Hadn't he found his way across four thousand miles of ocean?

Unready so soon after her father's death and Berenice's departure to take over either of their rooms, Domini was using what had been a guest bedroom. A pleasant space, it had simple solid furniture and large rag rugs, but it was somewhat chilly at the moment. She turned on one low lamp. In the fireplace, one of many in the farmhouse, fresh logs had been laid, and while she waited Domini busied herself in lighting it, watching while the flames caught at the kindling, their brightness reflecting the moisture glistening in her eyes. When Sander arrived, feeling the doorframe as he came, she was crouched in front of the fire, poker in hand, coaxing warmth from the newly crackling fire.

She turned her head without rising, tears of happiness shimmering unconcealed on her lashes.

"Domini," he breathed, a hoarse breath during which his face was turned so surely in the direction of the fire that she knew he had heard her movements. Slowly he entered and closed the door behind him, his tall figure moving for the moment no farther into the room. Between them a bond extended, making the distance unimportant.

"Sander," she whispered. "Oh, Sander . . ."

He came across the room, moving cautiously but not faltering, testing for obstacles en route to his goal. Domini watched with a full heart, knowing that time would give him a familiarity and confidence he did not yet have. When he had come far enough, she reached out to touch him, telling him where she was. He dropped to the rag rug beside her, where the leaping flames cast changing shadows into his dark, regretful eyes. He put his arm around her and stroked her hair, a gentle caress devoid for the moment of any message but comfort and love.

"How did you find me?" she asked in a low voice. "How did you know?"

"I knew, or I came to know, because I love you," he murmured huskily, touching his lips to her hair. "You're engraved on my heart, Domini Greey."

Domini asked for no more immediate explanations. For a time they sat by the flickering fire, still but for the slow movements of Sander's hand, sharing emotions too deep for words. Both seemed to know intuitively that to kiss would be to go far beyond a kiss, and the time for that had not yet come. They had shared beds and they had shared caresses, but this was a moment to share feelings and hearts.

Contentment seeped into the very core of Domini's soul, until she grew ready for talk. "There are so many things I need to know," she whispered at last. She shifted until she could see his face. He had lost a great deal of weight, she realized with a wrench; his features had grown quite gaunt. And yet there was about him a repose that had not been there before.

"Please tell me, Sander. Tell me everything. Was it true for you, the story you told Tasey?"

"In essence," he murmured, stilling her questions with a finger placed gently against her mouth, caressing the soft surface so intimately that it might have been a kiss. In his dark eyes, illuminated to a new warmth by the golden flames of the firelight, there was a glow of love that replaced all the bitterness of before. "Perhaps later I'll talk of my past, but not now. Now is a time to think of you. I love you, Domini. Desperately. So very desperately."

He loosened her hair, letting the dark gold spill over her shoulders, tumbling to catch the light of the fire. Then gently his mouth closed over hers, hard lips brushing across soft, with a patient and aching tenderness that told her of his feelings more surely than any urgency would have done. There was no haste in his hands as they touched her ears, her hair, her throat, rediscovering the soft hiding places where tiny pulses ticked. Domini forgot the things she had wanted to know, forgot the past, forgot the future, forgot everything but the moment and the happiness in her heart. She laced her arms around his neck, telling him of the need that rose in her, as surely as in him.

And soon, when neither wanted to wait, she led him to the bed. Love and the expression of it were as natural to Domini as life itself, and for the first time Sander was ready to return her love with the warmth she had always wanted. As he undressed she reveled in what the room's soft glow revealed of the man she loved: the firm flat stomach, the virile shoulders, the hard male flanks. To her he was a whole man and always had been.

Out of habit while she watched, she had started to strip herself, starting with the heavy alpine sweater. She was working at the buttons of the light silk shirt she had worn underneath when he came down beside her and stilled her with his hand. "No," he said huskily. "I want to undress you tonight, and I want to do it slowly. For once we have all the time in the world. Be patient, love."

"Yes," she said and trembled back to stillness.

Each part of her clothing came off with exquisite slowness, and as each part of her body was bared in turn, his hands and his mouth roamed in slow praise over the curves they already knew so intimately. As he touched and trailed and rediscovered, he whispered the words she had always wanted to hear, little words, tender words, beautiful words.

At last she lay naked, flesh quivering not from the coolness of the room, but from the racing of heated blood not far beneath the surface of her skin. His unhurried kisses, sparing no part of her, had awakened fires in every secret inch of skin. She was weak with wanting, and yet she wanted even more to let this be a night of lovemaking to remember.

And then he waited no more. With a groan of deep desire, he parted her legs and his long lithe body shifted to cover hers. Murmuring love words in her hair, he united his hardness with her softness, his maleness with her quivering, willing womanhood. He moved gently at first, worshiping her breasts and her hips with his hands. Domini arched to meet him, inviting his fuller possession. With a helpless moan of need she pulled his head down to hers, openly offering all the sweetness to the mastery of his tongue.

And gradually, as the poised male power of his limbs

followed nature's course, the tempo grew more urgent until at the end, with one long last kiss that united their mouths in a message of deep abiding love, he brought her to a final blaze of pure unequaled passion.

Later they lay entwined, Domini still warm in the afterglow of his ardent possession. Had any woman ever been more skillfully, more beautifully loved?

The high-burning logs had by now warmed the room, and so they lay without covers, sharing the intimacy that comes when lovers know themselves well loved and well sated. Occasionally one or the other expressed the feelings of the moment with a slow, undemanding caress. At last Domini touched a gentle fingertip to the furrow between Sander's brows, where the years of darkness and bitterness had put little lines of pain that would never be fully erased.

She murmured, "Was it very hard to find me?"

Sander's arm tightened its grip around her. "Not half as hard as not finding you would have been," he murmured in a somewhat elliptical answer to her question. But he didn't want to talk about himself. With one hand stroking the tendrils at her temples, he said somberly, "Yesterday I heard most of your story, Domini. I know about what happened to you years ago, and I know you haven't had an easy time."

Domini knew that no newspaper had ever unearthed her true story. There was only one way Sander could have heard. "Berenice," she guessed. "You've been talking to Berenice."

He nodded, confirming it. "Lazarus gave me her address, and I spent a day with her in Paris before coming on here."

"Then it was she who told you the truth," guessed Domini. But at the moment she was unutterably glad that Berenice had broken her promise.

"No, it wasn't. She told me a great deal, but as to your identity, I already knew it. However, she was very pleased that the one small clue she provided had helped trigger the search."

"Clue? I don't understand—"

"Just before the start of the show, she air-expressed one last small painting to Lazarus. She knew about my sister and knew she was sure to be seeing the show. She hoped Miranda might notice the painting and draw it to my attention. And Miranda did—but unfortunately not at once. As you can imagine, opening night was quite busy with one thing and another."

Indeed, Domini could imagine what one thing and another had been, for Sander at least. Jealousy snaked inside, but she curbed her tongue, biting back the acid questions about Nicole. It hadn't escaped her that in his story to Tasey, Sander had never fully disposed of the black-haired sorceress, and it seemed he wasn't going to mention her now.

"The painting's very small, so it was hanging in an obscure corner. As a result, Miranda didn't spot it until she went back some days later for a more leisurely look at the show. Berenice says she was only able to send items out of her own personal collection because the will is still being probated. Otherwise she would have sent a more dramatic example. It was a portrait of you, Domini, at about twelve years of age. Although Miranda at once recognized it as an older version of the famous Didi, she also noticed a striking similarity to you—enough to catch her eye. Even so, she would probably have put it down to a farfetched coincidence if she hadn't seen the title."

"Title?"

"*Daughter of Anastasia Greey.* Berenice says she named it herself, because the portrait had been untitled. Miranda was riveted at once; it's not a common spelling for that surname. Naturally she rushed home to tell me. And when I remembered Tasey's first name . . ."

So the name had had some bearing after all! Jealousy flew from Domini's thoughts as she found herself thinking: clever, clever Berenice. Without breaking any promises she had sent a very clear message to New

York. "So you started to think," she said with a delighted little laugh.

"Started to think!" Sander's harsher laugh held no amusement at all. "My God, I'd been doing nothing else. I suffered the tortures of the damned, thinking I might never find you."

Domini looked at him with love in her heart. "Yet a few months ago you wouldn't have admitted to feeling anything for me at all."

He lowered his head, an almost humble gesture. "True," he admitted. "All the same, that's how I felt." He took a ragged breath and went on. "I was dumbfounded when I heard the name Anastasia Greey. Miranda said the portrait *could* be you, the eyes and the smile especially. And when she heard that I had once known Didi Le Basque . . . well, a lot of little things started to fall into place. It was clear that Anastasia was the mother of the famous Didi, but was she also your mother, and Tasey's grandmother? Was Domini Greey the same girl I'd known so many years ago? If she was, a unicorn in a little art gallery would certainly have caught her eye. And if she was, mightn't that also account for her persistent and extraordinary interest in a blind man's well-being, when she stumbled into his life? Why she put up with his rudeness and resentment? Why she fought to make him feel his creative fires again? It all seemed logical enough. And yet I had grave doubts. If you were the same person, why were you living in New York, speaking English with no French accent, not using your father's name? Remember, I knew nothing about your part of the story then. Had you lied to me about your true hair color and a hundred other details? I had to know.

"So who could help solve the mystery? Lazarus was the only person I could think of. It was after hours by then and he wasn't at his gallery, but I called him at home. He came over at once. He . . . he's been a good friend."

"And he phoned Berenice for the answer?"

"He didn't need to." Sander placed a hand alongside her cheek in a gentle curve. "I showed Lazarus a sculpture I had done a few weeks before. It was of your face, Domini, the face that's carved in my memory."

Domini gave a surprised little laugh. "But I've never met Lazarus," she said. "He wouldn't know my face."

"Ah, but he does. For one thing, he was familiar with various portraits done in your later teens. He saw them during a long visit to the Pyrenees, when he came a few years ago to help estimate the value of your father's paintings—a futile exercise, I gather, for none were put on the market."

Domini smiled a small smile to herself as Sander added, "Lazarus also knows what Didi Le Basque looks like today. He saw you at your father's funeral."

"I didn't even know he was there," Domini murmured, wondering which in the sea of faces that day might have belonged to the New York dealer. "I don't think Berenice knew, either."

"Knowing Lazarus, he probably sat in a back row and left as soon as it was over. Anyway, thank God he was there. He took one look at my sculpture and told me it was the face of Le Basque's daughter. As soon as possible I was on my way to France."

"I'm glad," she whispered, silently thanking Berenice and Lazarus and Sander's sensitive hands, and all the other chances of fate that had brought him across the sea.

Sander's fingers caressed her throat. There was a catch in his voice as he murmured, "You're beautiful, Domini, so very beautiful. I knew it with my hands, and now I know it in my mind's eye. But I'll never sculpt you again, at least not in the nude. In some ways I'm sorry I ever did."

Domini had grown impudent with knowing herself much desired. "Why?" she teased, lacing her fingers in his hair.

"Can't you guess?" he muttered fiercely. "I want no other man's eyes to possess you in any way."

"And what about you!" she cried, jealousy at last bursting out. She pulled away from him and sat up. "You and your s-s-sorceress! I know Nicole was at your opening! No wonder that night was busy with one thing and another! And you didn't even mention she was there!"

Sander's expression became immediately unreadable, his mouth mocking. He murmured, "Oh, didn't I? An oversight. She's married now, you know. She was there with her husband, an American. He's a very important person, director of a large corporation and a well-known art collector too."

"Oh," said Domini, subsiding and feeling foolish.

"I agree, I should have told you at once," Sander drawled. "Thanks to Nicole, I've been offered a very handsome commission. She wants a gift for her husband, something to add to his private collection."

"That's . . . nice," Domini said, although the words were definitely grudging. A commission might mean that Sander would be seeing more of Nicole in the future.

"I imagine Nicole doesn't have a very easy life," he went on with a sigh that sounded far from sincere. "Her husband is quite an old man, and very crotchety. Why, on the night of the opening I hear she practically had to prop him up so he could get around to see the show—until he left with his chauffeur, that is. Fortunately he allows Nicole some small amount of freedom. She stayed on because she wanted to make her proposal to me."

"I see," Domini said, her tone decidedly chilly.

"Jealous?"

"Not a bit," Domini lied haughtily.

"Ah. When I was telling my small story to Tasey, I wondered if you might feel a fleeting resentment when I mentioned the beautiful black-haired sorceress."

"It was the description," Domini said coldly. "I wouldn't have minded if you had said witch."

"Witch?" Sander's brows lifted. "I don't think that

describes Nicole too well. She does have some merits, you know. There's a will-o'-the-wisp quality to her, the kind of thing that can captivate a man. She's very flighty, very charming, very amusing. Oh, a little hot-tempered, too, but that only adds to the spice—or sorcery, if you prefer. I'd be lying if I pretended I'd never been under her spell."

"Really, you needn't justify your actions to me. I don't give a damn what you felt for Nicole. Or *did* with her on the night of the opening."

His eyes glinted silver, perhaps paying Domini back for her ready suspicions. "Good," he said coolly, "because what Nicole asked for was a nude sculpture. She was intrigued to learn I now work with my hands and she intends to model for it herself."

Enraged, Domini started to fly off the bed altogether. Sander caught her and flung her back against the pillow, pinning her very effectively in place, laughing down at her with an easy male arrogance. Breath knocked from her body, Domini glared at him, panting, unwilling this time to forgive.

"You might ask me what I told the . . . er, sorceress when she made her suggestion."

"I won't!"

"Stubborn woman," he murmured, still shackling her. "Do you really think I can still care, even in the smallest way, for some woman who left me to my damnation as she did? I thrust Nicole from my mind years ago. She loves too easily, and only in fair weather. Nicole may still be a sorceress, but her spells will never again work on me."

Gradually Domini subsided. After a moment she asked unwillingly, "What did you tell her then?"

"Something not very polite. To put it euphemistically, I told her to—ah, vanish in a puff of smoke."

Domini laughed and instantly forgave him all over again. If Sander had done that three weeks ago, not knowing her whereabouts or whether he would ever find her again, then he must indeed have put his former love out of mind. Perhaps, after all, the specter of Nicole could be laid forever to rest.

He released his hold and smiled down at her, so warmly and tenderly it almost seemed he could see the lovelight in her face. "Do you think I don't know how you've stood by me, Domini? I didn't lie when I told Tasey I hung on to thoughts of the unicorn after I lost my sight. Because I couldn't bear to think of Nicole, I used to think of you, a device to blot out the despair and bitterness I felt. You became my lifeline, a sort of icon against the dark. I can't pretend I truly loved you then; that would be an oversimplification. But you did help me through some hard times. I didn't expect anything from you, because I knew I'd treated you unkindly, with a great deal of anger. At one time, when I hoped the clinic in Germany might be able to restore my sight, I intended to make amends as best I could. But then . . ."

For a moment painful memories crossed his face.

Softly Domini said, "That time I phoned to ask about your operation . . . why did you lie?"

"What part of the truth should I have told? That I lived in a world of perpetual night? I didn't want your pity. That I was alone? I didn't want you leaving the safety of your father's house, where I believed you were at the time. That there were creditors banging at my door? I didn't want your money. By then, Domini, I had learned of the way you tried to help me through my dealer. I was touched, but I didn't want you doing anything so foolish again. I wanted you to stop thinking about me."

Domini was deeply moved. She sensed that it must have been very difficult for him to lie at that time, spurning the very thing that had become a lifeline for him in his darkness. And more recently it must have been equally difficult for him to spurn her proposal, judging by the emotional truths revealed in his simple story to Tasey. How lucky she was to be loved by a man of Sander's caliber and courage, a man who stood tall among men.

"And yet you hadn't stopped thinking about me," Domini murmured proudly, wrapping her arms around his neck, putting all of herself into his keeping, for all time.

"No," he said huskily, "and I never, never will. I suppose I should thank fate for giving me a visual image of you. I have a golden memory of you, Domini."

"I'll grow gray someday," Domini whispered against his descending mouth, "along with you."

"Not to me," he breathed as he moved his lips gently across the temples of gold he saw with the eyes of his heart. The words that stirred her hair were hushed, almost reverent. "Never to me."

FREE!!
BOOKS BY MAIL
CATALOGUE

BOOKS BY MAIL will share with you our current bestselling books as well as hard to find specialty titles in areas that will match your interests. You will be updated on what's new from Pocket Books at no cost to you. Just fill in the coupon below and discover the convenience of having books delivered to your home.

BOOKS BY MAIL
P.O. Box 901, 517 Lorne Avenue
Stratford, Ontario N5A 6W3

Please send Books By Mail catalogue to:

Name_____
　　　　　　　　(please print)
Address_____

City_____

Prov._____ Postal Code _____
　　　　　　　　　　　　　　　　　(BBM2)